## PRAISE FO[illegible]



"Kept my interest from beginning to end . . . Really looking forward to reading more in Ms. Harper's Grim world, and I definitely recommend *Storm Warned* if you're in the mood for some Fae."

—*Literary Addiction*

"Wonder touches Spokane Valley, Wash., and the life of veterinarian Morgan Edwards in Harper's beautifully narrated foray into Celtic myth and legend . . . Harper provides excellent texture and depth with a touch of sincere empathy for animals, rounding out an already excellent novel."

—*Publishers Weekly*

"Harper skillfully builds characters and situations that evoke empathy for the good citizens of both the human and shapeshifter species . . ."

—*RT Book Reviews*

"*Storm Warned* is captivating! The characters are great and the world the author has built is strongly reminiscent of the original dark faery tales."

—*Bibliophilic*

"A delicious and elegant read, filled with humor, beauty, friendship, hotness, and a little horror (as things with the fae often are). I think Dani Harper is a MUST READ!"

—*Fangs, Wands, and Fairy Dust*

"Harper has created touching stories about love and loyalty with an added bonus of humor."

—*I Smell Sheep*

“Not your everyday werewolf story line. *Changeling Dawn* has romance, kidnapping, and murder . . . along with some mystery and intrigue.”

—*Dee’s Musings*

“Dani Harper’s *Changeling Moon* is one of those rare stories that literally catches you with the first paragraph and never lets go.”

—Kate Douglas, author

“Harper’s changelings are among the best in the genre.”

—*RT Book Reviews*

“Dani Harper breathes life into her characters.”

—*Coffee Time Romance*

# STORM CROSSED

# ALSO BY DANI HARPER

## The Grim Series Novels

*Storm Warrior*

*Storm Bound*

*Storm Warned*

*Storm Crossed*

## The Changeling Shapeshifter Series

*Changeling Moon*

*Changeling Dream*

*Changeling Dawn*

## A Dark Wolf Novel

*First Bite*

## The Haunted Holiday Series

*The Holiday Spirit (All She Wants for Christmas Is a Ghost)*

# STORM CROSSED

DANI HARPER

This is a work of fiction. Names, characters, organizations, places, events, and incidents are either products of the author's imagination or are used fictitiously. Any resemblance to actual persons, living or dead, or actual events is purely coincidental.



Published by Montlake Romance, Seattle

www.apub.com



ISBN-13: 9781503948945
ISBN-10: 1503948943

Cover design by Jason Blackburn

Printed in the United States of America

*In memory of Dianne MacDonald. Thanks for being a loving mom to my daughter when I couldn't be there. Thanks for raising such a wonderful young woman to be my daughter's best friend, too! And thanks for being my friend. I always appreciated your smile, your ready laugh, and your encouragement. No writer could ask for a truer or kinder fan. I hope you're reading this book over my shoulder!*

*When the student is ready, the teacher appears.*

—Unknown

# PROLOGUE

Darkness held no terrors for the boy. Shadows were soft, colors veiled, sounds muted. A relief from the overbright and noisome day that jangled his senses and hurt his head. And when the moon rode the indigo sky, everything was brushed with silver: his rock collection, his coloring markers in their lumpy clay cup, his bookshelves, and even the rows of crazy copper-wire creatures on his desk had paled to a gentle pearl gray. The moon's light created a magical and comfortable world just for him.

Tonight, the moon was round and fat. The boy lay on his side in bed, where he could watch through the tall window. Once, his teacher had read a story about a man who lived in the moon. But although the boy always looked, he didn't see the man.

The moon *was* his friend, though. And sometimes, the moon's light showed him things: hazy images of new places or new people. The boy understood that it was sort of like a television show—they weren't *really* in his room with him. But he knew they would come into his life soon. A few days, maybe a week or two, but they would come. It was nice of the moon to tell him ahead of time, as if it understood that new things made him uncomfortable.

The light of the night was soft and silent as it inched over the floor and crept across his bed. Just as it brushed his Squishy Bear, the silvery glow rose like gentle smoke and shimmered to form a picture. *A man and a dog.* The man was tall, with long white hair and strange eyes, but there was something else different about him . . . Try as he might, the boy couldn't see what it was. Besides, what he really wanted to look at was the dog. It was crazy big, bigger than any dog he'd ever seen, maybe even the size of a lion. The boy liked dogs, even big ones. Animals were always easier to understand than people. Easier to be around, too.

Gradually the picture faded and sank into the sheet of moonlight atop his blanket. But the man and the dog were fixed in his mind. *They're coming. Soon.*

And they were going to need his help.

# ONE

*Royal Court, Palace of Queen Gwenhidw*
*Heart of the Fae Realms, Wales*
*A Thousand Mortal Years Ago . . .*

There is no such thing as love!" Trahern shoved at his twin. "Your foolish ideas will get you banished, and for what? Nothing in the Nine Realms will change. *Nothing!* Eirianwen will rule the House of Oak for yet another millennium, while you live out your days in exile. What will you have proven?"

Braith shoved back and followed it with a punch of magic that sent Trahern sailing backward across the royal garden until he slammed high into the trunk of a tree in a flurry of golden leaves. It was as if they were children again, testing each other like young stags. But that was centuries ago, and this was no game. The palace loomed large over them as they argued in its sprawling gardens. Braith had been called to appear before the Royal Court.

"I will have Saffir, and her alone. I will not bend to Eirianwen's wishes. I will not consent to this pairing with Idelle."

Trahern landed lightly on his feet and brushed oak leaves from his tunic. The fact that he would bear a bruise or two was not without irony. The amber and claret crest of the House of Oak bore the creed *Our enemies break upon us.* Briefly he considered retaliating, but it would be no contest. His brother's blow had been pure luck magnified by anger. Almost all fae beings possessed magic to some degree, but Trahern had been gifted with the rare, full measure of a sorcerer's power. Despite his years of study to hone his talent, however, he didn't know of any magic that would alleviate his twin's stubbornness or persuade him to see reason.

Even Braith's own talent was of no help. He had been born with the most coveted of all abilities: he was a *farseer*, able to view the future. It was a cruel paradox, however, that the nature of that gift prevented it from being applied to the seer's own life. Braith was as blind to his future as anyone else—although a lifetime of dealing with the matriarch of the House of Oak surely should have taught him that resistance to her will was purest folly.

"Why Saffir?" Trahern finally asked. "She belongs to no noble house and has no wealth or connections to speak of. Idelle is the daughter of one of the three princes of the House of Rowan, and they would be valuable allies. What does Saffir have to offer us?"

"Listen to yourself. You sound like Eirianwen—everything must add to the power and standing of the family." Braith spat on the blue-flowered grass. "And you know full well that she doesn't want allies, she only wants pawns and resources. Rowan's leadership is weak, and Eirianwen will have them all supplanted before long."

Trahern knew that *supplanted* likely meant systematically slain. *Which is precisely why Braith should not defy her.* He sighed then, knowing that Braith would be of the opposite opinion. Despite being twins, they differed as greatly in personality as they did in appearance. Trahern's long hair was white from birth, a color much preferred by the Tylwyth Teg elite, while Braith's mane was the blue-gray of a storm cloud. Braith's temperament was that of a storm as well. Trahern had assumed the role of the quiet and studious one, the one who stood in the background observing. The favored one, perhaps, if any offspring of the House could be called a favorite. If not totally obedient, then at least the one wise enough to never give offense . . . or clever enough not to get caught. As children, if they were called to task by anyone other than Heddwen, their guardian and tutor who knew the brothers better than their own kin, it was the recklessly impulsive Braith who was blamed and punished. While there was nothing strange about his current rebellion, the consequences this time would be far worse than losing favored toys.

Trahern tried another tactic. “Idelle is fair to look upon. And well accustomed to the Royal Court.” He left unsaid that Saffir, though lovely, would be considered quite plain by the Court’s standards. And surviving that den of whispering vipers required carefully veiled intent and masked diplomacy. Perhaps because she wasn’t of the nobility herself, or perhaps because she was a healer and therefore more practical, Saffir spoke her mind without regard for the station or office of those she addressed. *The Court would eat her alive and spit out her bones.*

“The love that I share with Saffir is the most beautiful thing I know,” Braith said simply. “We are *Pâr Enaid*.”

*Twinned souls?* Surely his brother did not believe Heddwen’s nighttime stories. “A pleasant myth and no more, but if it pleases you, then keep it. Agree to an official pairing with Idelle, then spend your time with Saffir.” Most members of the Court publicly dallied with whoever they pleased—and often as not with their partners present. “Eirianwen will have gotten what she wants, Idelle will have a much-coveted bond with the House of Oak, and you will have this *love* that you speak so highly of.”

Braith shook his head. “You do not understand. To do as you have suggested would make me no better than a betrayer. My feelings for Saffir are sure.”

“I *understand* that your so-called feelings will bring down Eirianwen’s wrath. She will banish you.”

“Then so be it.”

“This is madness! If you care not for yourself, then think of Saffir. Eirianwen has eyes everywhere. If she learns that this woman is at the root of your defiance, she will have her slain or worse.”

"Eirianwen doesn't know. Besides, fae law supports our cause."

Trahern put little faith in ancient fae law. It had slowly eroded over the ages, until it was strangely silent on many acts—even murder—yet adamant about far lesser infractions. One of its few remaining statutes, however, was devoted to the subject of pairings. No citizen of the Nine Realms could be forced, threatened, or otherwise coerced into a binding partnership, and Queen Gwenhidw and King Arthfael had reinforced this in a royal decree soon after their own pairing. Come to think of it, theirs was said to be a love match. Some stories claimed that the royal couple were *Pâr Enaid* and that Gwenhidw yet mourned her husband's death after all these centuries.

*Stories and myths, surely.* Trahern was too young to have seen the rulers together, and he had certainly never witnessed anything that could be construed as love among the Tylwyth Teg nobility. In fact, he doubted them capable of such an emotion, if it did exist. Still, many whispered proverbs and old half-forgotten songs claimed the unthinkable: that the Fair Ones envied mortals their fabled passions. Especially love.

*Proverbs will not help my brother, and neither will the law.* Aloud he said, "You cannot hope to keep Saffir a secret. She will be discovered sooner or later."

"After I have answered this summons, I will take her to the human world."

Trahern could not believe what he heard. "Leave the Nine Realms? You might be expelled from the Court, perhaps even from our territories, but you need not leave our world entirely. And surely you would not choose to dwell among *mortals*?"

"If I cannot have the life and love I wish here, then yes, and gladly." Braith smiled. "And if you visited their world for more than simple plants for your potions, brother, you would not appear so shocked. Though their lives are short—or perhaps *because* their lives are short—humans possess many worthwhile attributes that the Tylwyth Teg have all but forgotten."

"How can that be? Do mortals not call us the *Fair Ones*?"

"Truly, most have forgotten us entirely," said Braith. "And those who yet remember do not give us pleasing names out of admiration—"

The sudden deep resonance of a stone bell forestalled any further discussion. Though the self-absorbed courtiers observed little by way of ceremony, no one would fail to heed the uncommon call to convene. Trahern and Braith turned as one and strode into the palace.

Trahern was no stranger to the Royal Court, his lineage assuring him a permanent position in it. As usual, the spectacular costumes, towering headdresses, and shimmering adornments of those who frequented the grand hall failed to impress him. Features visible behind the vivid trappings were flawless, but he was well aware that the exquisitely beautiful faces were masks as well. A radiant smile could conceal the most devious of intentions—but today there were no smiles at all. Many glittering eyes turned to appraise him and his brother as they walked. Normally there would be a few jovial greetings, some flirtatious comments or bawdy invitations at the very least. Instead, there were only hushed whisperings, and the crowd shrank away as if he and his brother were diseased. Among them, however, Trahern glimpsed a hooded figure in a sapphire tunic. Something about the figure seemed familiar, and he paused—

*"Eirianwen of the House of Oak!"*

The announcement caused the courtiers to scatter like a flock of bright and chattering birds, and the stranger who had caught his attention disappeared from his view. The colorful crowd clustered around the massive crystal columns that lined the walls, still whispering among themselves despite their genuine dread of the grand matriarch. And with finer emotions rare among the Tylwyth Teg, Trahern had no doubt that the trepidation throbbing in their blue-blooded veins was as delicious to them as the spectacle.

In his own heart, however, beat true fear for his twin. And despite the novelty of the sensation, there was nothing pleasant about it.

His brother stood alone in the very center of the gleaming tiled floor, the sudden absence of the crowd revealing an intricate mosaic dotted with precious stones at his feet. It had been a long time since Trahern had been able to fully see its depiction of a formal faery procession through the ancient Silver Maples forest. The detailed figures were breathtaking, particularly the likeness of their leader, Queen Gwenhidw. He had met her face-to-face only once, when he was yet a child, but she was impossible to forget. He'd lost a filigreed ball in the palace garden and was sick with dread he would be punished when suddenly the most beautiful woman he'd ever seen, before or since, found it for him. Her gown was the deep blue and silver of the night sky, and therefore she must belong to the House of Thorn. *The Royal House.* He'd braced for a reprimand, maybe even worse, for trespassing in the garden. Instead, she gently dried his eyes and wiped his dirty face and hands with her exquisitely embroidered sleeve, then played a game with him until Heddwen arrived to take him away.

Among the vast jeweled trees on the floor loomed darker figures in the design, mounted on glowing-eyed steeds and accompanied by pure-white hounds: *The Wild Hunt.* Their role was complex in the fae world, even more so in the human world above. While they protected Gwenhidw certainly, it was also said that they kept the Balance, acting as both protectors and judges, defenders and executioners. Although the queen ruled all else, the mysterious Hunt was an entity unto itself, as was its dark lord, Lurien.

Right now, however, the exquisite mosaic seemed only to mock Trahern. *Both Gwenhidw and Lurien are said to be just. Surely one of them will intervene in this matter!* But the queen's banners did not fly over the palace at present, signifying that she was in residence elsewhere in the Realms. And in truth, she rarely graced the prattling

Court with her presence, preferring the formality—and perhaps the quiet—of the great room that housed the Glass Throne when her people required her. And as for the Hunt, who knew where they might be found?

And so, his twin stood without a champion. Braith was lean like all the Tylwyth Teg, but few of them could boast the hard muscle of his bare arms. As tall and strong as he was, however, he seemed strangely small, lost in the immensity of the cavernous room, the vaulted crystal ceiling so high above him that even echoes could not find their way back.

At that precise moment, the grand matriarch glided over the threshold of the imposing entrance. Older than even Gwenhidw, Eirianwen's appearance alone was yet sufficient to turn every head. *She never seems to age*, thought Trahern, and wondered anew what kind of powerful glamour she used to stave off the paintbrush of numberless centuries. Her exotic beauty required no enhancement—but enhance it she had, to devastating effect. She was dressed to emphasize her station this day, her autumn-colored robes woven with oak leaves of amber and claret, and her snowy hair piled high on one side with gilded branches and jeweled acorns, left to fall like silken water over the other. Each delicate finger sported a long golden talon. Gold dust tipped her long eyelashes and emphasized her high cheekbones. Even her wine-colored lips were brushed with gold.

As she stepped forward, a camarilla of her most powerful kindred instantly appeared and fanned out behind her, each formally attired in her colors. The Court held its collective breath, and the matriarch's melodic voice poured into a vessel of utter silence. She didn't bother with preamble. "Braith, you are guilty of treason against the House of Oak."

"I am guilty of nothing," he retorted. If he was afraid, he did not show it.

Trahern didn't show it, either, but he was suddenly very much afraid. *Treason?* It was the most heinous of all crimes. What game was this, that Eirianwen would accuse his brother of such a thing?

"Your rebellion is an act of betrayal," she continued.

"I betray no one. I merely seek a life of my own. The law states that I have the right—"

She cut him off with a wave of her delicate hand, its gold talons glinting in the light. "We are not here to debate your foolish ideas or your imaginative interpretation of fae law."

"I will be heard!"

"You will not. We have already concurred that your life is forfeit, and we are merely here to carry out that sentence."

*Forfeit.* The word stole the breath from Trahern as surely as if he'd fallen into an icy lake. *She cannot mean that. She must be trying to frighten him into submission.* His brother, however, would never submit. Sudden fear for Braith sharpened his focus beyond what he could normally call upon—

*Tân mawr!* He shouted it in his mind. *Tân du!*

Instantly, a tall curtain of oily black flames spread into a wall around his brother, barricading him from harm. As it sucked light from the room, the fire cast a dull purplish glow like a kraken's dying ink. Eirianwen arched a brow as her camarilla consulted among themselves as to how they might attempt to countermand the spell, and Trahern instinctively wished he had not chosen black flame. It was the most difficult to master and beyond the abilities of most sorcerers. So much for concealing the level of his skills . . .

"I see you have improved upon your talents," she said.

He walked boldly across the open floor, his fine boots making the only sound in the entire room, until he stood by the fiery barrier surrounding his brother. "I fear my talents lie more with building the wealth of the House of Oak through simple commerce. This is merely an illusion I picked up on my last trading expedition to the outer realms." He thrust a hand into the flaming wall. Anyone else would have lost a limb, but he had to make it appear harmless. *Yn diffodd!* The flames extinguished, leaving only a circle of amethyst-colored birds upon the floor. They took to flight immediately. A heartbeat later, they drifted down to the steps of the dais as scented purple flowers. A type he knew Eirianwen favored.

The crowd clapped delightedly, then seemed to remember whose presence they were in and fell back to apprehensive silence.

Braith's voice was far from silent inside Trahern's head. *Have you taken leave of your wits? Her wrath will engulf you as well!*

*Be silent*, he shot back. *You've dug a big enough pit for yourself already.* As twins, they had shared mind speech since birth. They would not share much more if he didn't think of some way to ease the situation fast. *And arguing will only make things worse*, he added quickly. In such a public venue, the matriarch's dignity and station must be acknowledged and preserved—and that meant his only useful weapons were appeal and appeasement. Trahern knelt, his carefully composed gaze never wavering from Eirianwen's perfect face.

Stony silence greeted him, then stretched interminably, but he waited. To speak first could ruin everything—and there was no guarantee that Braith would remain quiet for long. Thick tension permeated the very air as if a tempest gathered strength. Just as his taut nerves seemed ready to snap like a bowstring, a slight flex of the matriarch's index finger permitted Trahern the opening he sought.

"Fair and Shining One, you have led the House of Oak to unimaginable heights," he began. "You have expanded its holdings and its territories, and many Houses rightly fear your boldness even as they are undone by your cleverness." Spoken to anyone else, such flattery would have been summarily dismissed. In Eirianwen's case, it was simply the truth—though only part of it. She was *most* famous for utter ruthlessness.

"First you display a foolish entertainment; now you intend to introduce further tedium by begging for your brother's life?" The faintest of smiles played around those golden lips, but Trahern knew it was not inspired by mirth. "You'd do better to bore me with a full report on your latest acquisitions."

"I intend neither," he said aloud, his expression as bland and detached as he could make it. "Many of your triumphs have been won by your formidable talent for planning." That was an understatement. The woman had recently gained a large stretch of Alder territory with a strategy that had taken fifteen mortal centuries to play out. "By example, you have taught me that all things have their usefulness in the right time and the right place. This has served me well in bargaining on your behalf. I merely suggest that my brother may be of use to the House of Oak in a time yet to come."

Her eyes glittered. Yet she laughed prettily as she turned to the assembly. "He would be of some use *now* if he would accept the pairing we have so carefully negotiated, would he not?" The Court tittered their assent nervously, fearful to join in but too afraid not to.

"True words. I simply submit that Braith's talents may yet be required. Should they not be ready at hand to serve you, as an arrow is kept in a quiver, as a dagger in a hidden sheath?" His words would be a complete mystery to the assembled courtiers but not to Eirianwen. She'd made good use of his brother's capacity as a farseer, consulting with him on numerous occasions before assembling her tactics against other Houses. *Surely she would not discard such a valuable tool!* Trahern waited in agony as she made a show of considering his words. She didn't confer with her camarilla, or anyone else, of course. Her followers would do whatever she said, agree to anything she commanded. The entire Court was still, hushed and waiting for her decision, but he knew full well that their shallow hopes were for further entertainment, not for his brother's life. Nothing would delight them more than to see Braith's blood stain the elaborate mosaic he stood upon.

Eirianwen's golden lips parted, and it seemed that every being in the vast room leaned forward as one. "We would not want it said that the House of Oak wasted a potential asset." She smiled then, her teeth gleaming white and feral. "Nevertheless, the family has already made its decision. Braith, I pronounce upon you the *Sancsiwn Teulu*."

Trahern rose to his feet in spite of himself. A *family sanction* was not only extremely rare, but its ancient penalty was immutable, even by the Throne itself. But Eirianwen had not finished speaking to his twin.

"It is most fortuitous for you that your brother has made such a convincing argument for your continued existence. If the sentence is not to be satisfied by your death, then perhaps it can be fulfilled by your transformation." Still smiling, she waited a beat and was not disappointed.

"What kind of transformation?" asked Braith warily. Though his face had paled somewhat, he still stood firm and unmoving, his hands fisted at his sides.

"Why, into something much more serviceable to us, of course! Something loyal. Faithful. And most of all, *obedient*. Consider your new form a kind of mold, something we hope will permanently shape, and therefore alter, your rebellious nature." She motioned to those behind her. Immediately, several of the highest-ranking members of the House of Oak crossed the floor, every one of them a full-fledged sorcerer. Trahern had known them all his life, followed them, learned from them, eaten and drunk with them, but their eyes were expressionless as they formed a circle around him and his brother. Instantly he braced his feet and drew energy through the very floor, gathering it to his palms unseen. His powers were potent enough, disciplined enough, to take down at least two of the camarilla at once, then strike again with the rebound of the energy.

But the remaining would have the advantage before he could deliver a third blow. If he coordinated with Braith, however, his brother's limited magic might help shield him—

*Stop!* Braith's voice was loud inside his head.

*I will not let them do this to you!*

*My brother, you cannot save me. Even if we destroy the entire circle and every member of her retinue, we cannot prevail against Eirianwen herself. And I will suffer far more if they take you, too. Get out of here now!* Braith even put a mental punch behind his words, as if he could compel his brother by sheer force of will.

Trahern refused to move. By the stars, there had to be something he could do, something he could say—and that's when he saw the space in the circle. Eight of the most powerful fae in the whole of the Nine Realms stood waiting. But everyone knew it took nine to enact a *Sancsiwn Teulu.*

Nine. He shook his head slowly, horrified beyond words.

Eirianwen's triumphant laughter was as delicate as a cascade of crystal bells. Her exquisite face was animated, her eyes vibrant. "If you truly wish him to live, my dear, then you will take your place," she said.

He should have remembered that his mother was at her most beautiful just as she sprang a trap.

# TWO

Viewed from the very bottom, the cave was long and narrow, as sinuous as a dragon, until it faded into distant darkness. Countless stone chambers lined one wall, carved into the rock itself. Glittering things hung on the opposite wall. At Trahern's approach, they coalesced into countless woven silver collars and thick chest plates that resembled heavy chain-mail. His sorcerer's sight revealed the green aura of binding magic around them.

No magic was needed to sense the aura of misery and despair here.

He was close to despairing himself.

Nine suns and twelve moons had passed since Eirianwen ordered what was left of his brother to be taken away to the kennels. Nine suns and twelve moons that Trahern had counted breath by painful breath, before the smug matriarch finally tired of her prolonged games at Court and left, taking her camarilla with her. Nine suns and twelve moons before he was finally free to search for his twin.

*To the kennels.* He'd assumed she meant where the Wild Hunt housed its horses and hounds far beneath the castle at the base of the mountain itself. But the *lleolwr* spell he'd cast to locate Braith had led him in another direction entirely, to this deep and dismal place where shadows moved like living things in the weak gray light.

Trahern conjured a bright, glowing sphere in his palm and used it to peer into each den as he passed. All were empty. Just as he wondered if anything dwelled here at all, a huge, shaggy black shape burst from a kennel immediately ahead of him. The immense dog looked neither left nor right, its glowing red eyes trained on the jagged break in the ceiling high above. In a single leap, it was airborne, its menacing shape dissolving into a mass of fine particles that swept upward like a giant flock of dark birds, intelligently moving as one. Between the space of one breath and the next, it had shot through the rocky orifice into the world beyond and was gone.

*A grim.* Trahern recognized the creature for what it was, though he'd never seen one transform before. A grim had many names—*gwyllgi, ci du, barghest*—but only one purpose: to travel to the mortal world above the fae realms and foretell the demise of humans. He shone his light into the black dog's lair.

No bedding here, only a bare stone floor worn smooth over millennia. No silver bowl of water as Lurien's hounds enjoyed; in fact, there was no sign of food or drink at all. It was said that grims felt neither cold nor heat, did not hunger or thirst. They were a fae contrivance rather than a natural animal. Yet the absence of comforts seemed wrong somehow.

The only similarity between these kennels and those of the Hunt's well-tended hounds was the ornately carved archways, devoid of doors or bars. Trahern was about to turn away when his light revealed something more: a finely chiseled inscription in the stone of the threshold. He looked more intently, perceiving now that the engraving bore the same greenish aura of binding magic as the silver collars he had passed. In fact, all the kennels were marked with the very same words—**CENNAD O FARWOLAETH.**

Messenger of Death.

*My brother should not be in this place. He is but a common hound.* But what better trick to throw Trahern off the trail? *Perhaps Eirianwen hoped I would not search here.*

He looked up just in time to see a flicker of movement in one of the last kennels. Could it be Braith? Trahern took a single step forward—until the sight of writhing flesh and impossibly contorted limbs blazed afresh across the inside of his eyelids. His ears rang again with the horrific crunch and pop of bones changing shape and the agonized screams that suddenly transmuted to ululating howls.

Long moments passed before the horrifying memory released him. When he came to himself, more emotions than Trahern had ever experienced in his lifetime battered him from within. Most were strange and nameless, but all were painful, and guilt loomed large among them. Whatever these feelings, however, he couldn't permit them to hold him back. *Whether Braith forgives me or not, he needs my help now.*

Taking a deep breath, he walked to the stone lair and stooped to enter. There, his worst apprehensions were confirmed, and he simply sank to his knees. The bright sphere in his hand tumbled to the floor, revealing the prone form of the largest dog Trahern had ever seen. This was not the same dark-furred canine he had witnessed in the circle. No mere hunting hound, this. Thick folds of skin draped a monstrous muzzle, while pendulous lips and flews curtained bone-crushing jaws. Heavy-boned legs ended in leonine paws.

*My brother is a grim . . .*

Out of nowhere, a woman in an Oaken cloak lunged at Trahern like a maddened warth and succeeded in knocking him backward. "How could you?" she screamed, pummeling him with hard, sharp blows that found their intended targets, clawing him with silver-tipped fingers. The great dog was on its feet at once, its bark a deafening roar in the small space, adding to Trahern's confusion. Instinctively, he tried to seize her wrists, only to have her head-butt him, then sink her teeth into the base of his thumb. The pain focused his wits, and he shouted a word that sent her flying backward into the beast. The impact knocked the wind from her, and she gradually slid down to sit at the dog's feet, where she glowered at Trahern . . . and he recognized her.

"Saffir." The great dog sat stolidly at her back and nuzzled her as if to check that she was all right. The cloak had fallen aside, and her pearl-colored hair spilled over her shoulders like tumbling water. Dark-blue blood welled from her mouth and nose, accusing Trahern, but it was the rich sapphire of her hooded tunic that struck his senses like a slap to the face.

*She was in the Court!* She'd witnessed what he'd been forced to do to his own brother.

"How could you do such a monstrous thing to him?" she demanded, as if he'd spoken aloud. "He loves you!"

"How could you?" he shot back. "Were you not at the root of this? Was it not your imaginary love, your so-called *Pâr Enaid*, that condemned him? If you sought to improve your status by pairing with my brother, you have surely miscalculated."

She stilled then, even as the dog began growling in Trahern's direction. Blood still trickled freely from her bruised mouth and nose, but it didn't detract from her sudden quiet dignity. "Is that what you think? That what Braith and I share is not real? That I wear the appearance of feelings as an enticing garment to serve selfish ends? You are no better than your coldhearted dam."

"I am nothing like her! Nothing!"

"Then you have been her foolish puppet. Has she sent you now to see how her plan progresses?"

"A puppet truly." Bitterness mixed with bile. "But not entirely foolish. If I had not done her vicious bidding, my brother would now be dead, and I would be unable to help him."

Her eyebrows rose. “If you wished to help, why did you not come at once? Braith said you would not abandon him, but I have not shared his certainty.”

“Our mother’s spies are not easily discouraged, and Eirianwen herself only left the palace this very day.” Saffir’s interrogation poked at his anger with a sword point. “And how do I know that you were not hired by her to entrap Braith from the very beginning? You wear her colors!”

“As you are doing now, or do you not dress yourself? As a healer, it is my privilege to come and go wherever I wish, and I have long been tending one of the Hunt’s horses whose belly was torn by a basilisk. I took this cloak from one of your mother’s guards. The stupid *dihiryn* blocked my way, thinking he could gain some pleasure for the great favor of letting me pass.” She partially drew an opal dagger from a sheath on her shapely calf. “His body lies in the abyss behind the south tower. The guards have been too timid to come down here since he vanished.”

“You’ve been here all this time?”

“When they took Braith away, I followed at once.” Her voice quieted. “I did not think they would bring him to *this* place.”

“Nor did I.” It was obvious now that Eirianwen had planned Braith’s fate from the very beginning. *My speech must have amused her greatly.* Would he have done anything different had he known his brother’s true fate? *It doesn’t matter. It can’t matter. I am here to help him now.* Slowly he rose and approached the massive dog, noting that Saffir kept one hand on her dagger as he did so. He touched the animal’s heavily muscled shoulder but could not find his voice. *Braith?* he ventured in mind speech.

The majestic head lifted from Saffir’s shoulder, and a large pair of deep-set eyes regarded him solemnly. Was it the light that made them glow? Not only were they not his brother’s eyes, they were not the eyes of any Tylwyth Teg, and Trahern's heart sank even lower. *I have destroyed you.*

*I yet live, my brother. My form is not your fault. You had no choice.*

It was hard to know which steadied him more, Braith's familiar voice in his mind or the words that held no condemnation. *We will argue over that another day*, Trahern said. Aloud, he asked: "Are you injured?"

*No.*

"No," said Saffir. "But the change is violent, and very hard on the body. It will take time for him to gain his full strength. As you can see, Braith's appearance has changed much since you saw him last." Her voice caught. "I have tried to slow it down, but my magic is primarily for healing, not sorcery."

"I don't understand. Eirianwen wanted him transformed to a hound, and that was bad enough. But why this?"

"Why would a mother do any harm to her own child?"

A lifetime of defending Eirianwen automatically brought an excuse to his lips. "Braith defied her wishes, and she was determined to teach him a lesson." He didn't believe it for an instant, however. And Saffir's derisive snort informed him that she didn't, either.

"Being taught a lesson implies that he would be restored once he had learned it," she said. "Eirianwen didn't care about the pairing with Idelle—and yes, Braith told me of that. I felt sure that something else was at the root of it, and I begged him not to go to Court." She paused for a long moment before continuing. "Perhaps what your mother truly sought was an excuse to make an example of him, so that others would fear her all the more."

It rang true. "Of course," he murmured. "Who would dare to cross a woman who would punish her own son so severely? But surely being made a hound was enough to accomplish that twisted purpose." He left unsaid that such would have been easily reversible.

*She is afraid of me.* Braith's voice in his mind held absolute certainty. *Of us.*

Trahern stared at his brother, though he still couldn't catch a glimpse of the man he knew in the creature's fierce eyes. "Eirianwen fears nothing but losing her power," he replied. "It is all that matters to her."

*True, and what she fears most is that we will take her place.*

The notion seemed ridiculous, but he dropped back to mind speech just the same. *Has she not always spoken of leaving the House of Oak in our hands? In my earliest memories I hear her voice, saying that we must pay close attention to everything she does, that we might be fit to follow her.*

*Perhaps that was her intention at the time,* said Braith. *But that was long ago. We are grown men now, with minds of our own. Though neither of us desires her position in the least, she sees only threat. Have a care, brother. My hand has been dealt, and yours will be next. I have seen it. Flee while you may yet change your destiny.*

Trahern could not suppress a shiver as the truth of his twin's words settled on him like frost. He did not fear for himself, though sense said he should. No, it was the image of the eternally beautiful Eirianwen coldly calculating the betrayal of her own children that interlaced his spine with fingers of ice. He had never once expected her affection, but he had blindly trusted in her loyalty.

Aloud he simply said, "It is long past time we left this place."

"He cannot, or I would have taken him far from here by now." Saffir's voice was unexpectedly bitter. "Do you not know how grims come to be?"

"I know they are not born but made." Trahern knew little more about the actual process involved. Until now, he'd never had a reason to study it.

"Most often a death dog begins its existence as a human, transformed instantly as a punishment for the wrongs he or she has committed. But Braith is not mortal. For a full-blooded fae, your spell was only the first step." She waved a hand at their surroundings. "The grim kennels are enchanted, and it is their magic that completes the transformation for those whose blood runs blue. You see how much bigger he has become, how much stronger he is? His body has nearly completed the change.

"If he remains here, his mind will change as well. His coat is yet gray because he is not wholly grim, but it darkens by the hour. Once his fur turns black, he will suffer the same compulsion as all other grims. He will be drawn to the human world by impending death, and he will be unable to resist." She paused and swallowed twice, as though the words were painful. "He will be lost to us forever once that happens," she whispered. The great dog leaned his head on her shoulder and licked a stray tear from her face.

"All the more reason to leave. Why have you not taken him out of here?"

Braith's own voice entered his mind then. *I cannot cross the threshold. Something blocks my way.*

Trahern had been so shocked by his brother's appearance that he hadn't paid attention to anything else. Now, as he stretched out his senses, the invisible curtain of magic that covered the doorway was obvious. Thinner than the skin of a water bubble and stronger than the stone foundation of the palace, it had no effect at all on him or Saffir. It was linked only to Braith, sealing him in to his terrible fate.

Renewed fury at Eirianwen's cruelty churned in Trahern's gut, but once more he forced it down. *Now is not the time . . . but by the stars of the Seven Sisters, there will* be *a time!* Instead, he felt carefully around the archway, judging the type of magic used, the flavor and color of it, the style. It was masterfully done—but he knew he could undo it. "Both of you turn your faces away," he ordered, and pulled his sleeves back to reveal a few of the *ledrith*, the words and sigils of power that covered his entire body. Two of them glowed as he began a low incantation, almost a song. He repeated it, a halftone higher each time until suddenly a flash of blue light half blinded him.

The curtain of magic was gone, leaving behind only the faint scent of burnt oak leaves.

"It is done," he said aloud, rubbing one eye and blinking to clear his sight. Saffir turned her head and nodded, then drew her cloak away from Braith's face. The great dog struggled to rise.

Trahern frowned. He could shift them all away from here with a spell—but the Royal Palace had been deliberately built upon stone that prevented that type of magic, lest enemies appear within the walls. "Brother, can you walk?"

*I will crawl if I must, to escape this place.* He proved it by taking slow, halting steps until he was well outside the kennel, where he shook himself with gusto.

Saffir quickly followed and placed a gentle kiss on his broad, velvety forehead. A tear fell upon his muzzle and glistened there.

Trahern knew better than most that appearances were usually deceiving. Nevertheless, he found himself believing that this woman genuinely cared about his brother. *Pâr Enaid* might be imaginary, but there was something between Braith and Saffir that he could not define. Was this what his brother had called love? *Whatever it is, it cannot be worth the terrible price he's paid for it.* Aloud, Trahern chose his words carefully, not wanting to rob his twin of hope. "I came prepared to counter the spell from the *Sancsiwn Teulu.* But there are more complicated magics at work here than I first suspected, my brother. Much time and study will be required before I attempt to restore you."

Saffir was much blunter. "There are several potions that will effect a change from two legs to four and back again. None that I know of will return a grim to his true form if he has once been fae."

He hated that she was right. While on rare occasion a human-turned-grim might be restored, the transformation of fae to grim was considered permanent. It wouldn't stop him from trying, however. *You know that I will never give up*, he said to Braith.

*Just let all of us be gone from here, and it will be enough.*

All of us. Trahern found himself with a new problem. While he could use Saffir's help to get Braith out of the palace, what would he do with *her* then? If he took her with them, would she slow them down? *Worse, if I leave her behind, will she betray us?* He sighed inwardly and turned to her. "I must tell you that I had not planned for another. There are but two horses, and one is fitted with a pannier to carry a hound. I had not imagined Braith's very size would change. You are welcome to ride with me, but we must travel fast, and the way will be difficult—"

Without warning, a massive dark face filled his entire vision, and enormous teeth snapped shut a scant finger's width from his nose. *SHE COMES!* His brother's voice thundered within his head to the point of pain. Quickly Saffir soothed and patted the snarling beast into backing up a few steps. Keeping a tight hold of one pricked ear, she placed her body squarely between Braith and Trahern.

"Your plans will have to change," she said. "Eirianwen has placed no less than eighty mercenaries by the main road. I do not know what they are, but I am certain they are not of our realm. The camp appears as a market, and they themselves are disguised as merchant kobolds, but they have not bothered to conceal the warths they hunt with."

"Warths? Are you certain?"

"There is no mistaking them, and there are many. The mercenaries have used them to patrol both the palace grounds and the forest beyond since Eirianwen left. Whatever mounts you left out there are surely in their hands now, if the warths have not gotten to them first."

Trahern cursed his mother's lethal thoroughness. If the arrangement he'd made with the Bwbachod had been honored—and he had no doubt they had been true to their word—there were swift, strong horses waiting for him outside in a distant stand of rowan trees. Thus mounted, Trahern would have pitted his sorcery against Eirianwen's hired thugs without hesitation. *But against warths?* As large as Braith, the striped predators were lithe and powerful, with long, serrated teeth. He'd never heard of anyone successfully taming them as hunting beasts, but they would make formidable hounds. Few creatures could outrun a determined pack of them, but most to be feared was the warthen sense of smell.

No magic could disguise a scent from them for very long.

While gods surely existed, Trahern had never paid homage to one. Still, he found himself praying silently to any that might be listening for their aid, vowing allegiance to whichever one would help his brother escape. In his own experience, however, the gods favored those who helped themselves. "What is to be done, then? I will not leave Braith in our mother's hands."

"Her men do not dare guard the Wild Hunt's entrance. It is fortunate for us all that Lord Lurien values his animals, for there are several horses yet pastured in the Black Marsh at this moment that will come to me when I call them."

"You suggest we steal horses from the Hunt? They are no ordinary mounts!"

"Exactly," said Saffir. "And they are your best hope to outpace your enemies. Give them their heads, and they will take you where the Hunt rides nightly, to the only place that Eirianwen will not follow you."

"The human world."

"Braith was going to take me there." She slid her arms around the dog's massive neck. "For now, it will be up to you to help him escape, and I will follow when I can."

*You cannot stay behind!* Braith's anguished words were intended for Saffir, but only Trahern could hear them. The message was clear, however, when the great dog lifted his muzzle and began to howl.

Bluish tears appeared on Saffir's fine features, and she buried her face in his fur as he poured out his pain.

"If you die, my heart will die with you," she said when at last he fell silent. "Do not ask me to give up both our lives when there is yet a chance we may be together. There is work to be done here that may make a difference to our future."

At last Braith fell silent, leaning his lowered head against her as they made their way to the legendary lair of the Hunt. Saffir led them through the sprawling array of spacious stables with the ease of long practice, until they finally came to the entrance. It was wide and low, a grinning mouth at the base of the mountain that could easily accommodate thirty riders abreast, and overhung with tangled trees and thorny vines. She put up her hand. "Stay here," she said. "I will get your mounts."

Trahern couldn't help but think it would also be a perfect opportunity to alert the mercenaries to their presence, but he quickly put aside that notion. To get his brother out of here now, he had to trust someone, and Saffir was all he had.

Through the trees, he could see her step out into an open area with tall tussocks of serpent's grass surrounded by dark water. She made no sound that he could hear, yet two horses quickly appeared in the distance, standing shoulder-deep in the marsh as if they were deadly kelpies waiting for doomed riders. The pair swam to the fae healer at once and climbed onto the bank, shaking onyx droplets from their coats. Waterweeds fell away from their long legs as they followed Saffir to the cave. Trahern kept a number of blooded fae horses, the very best he could find, at his own stable. But nothing prepared him for these.

The golden one was dappled, with tail and mane the color of fine flax. Its broad forehead denoted intelligence—but what the backswept horns and clawed hooves signified, Trahern could not say. The other was as gray as fog, with strange white eyes. Tusks protruded from its dark lips. Both horses were exceptionally large and heavily muscled, and he noticed with a start that they floated a scant finger's width above the ground.

"This is Cyflym the Swift," said Saffir, with a wave at the gold beast. "The other is Cryf the Strong. They are steady and fearless, and among the best of Lurien's herd."

"And Lord Lurien will have both our heads for this," he muttered.

She shrugged. "He will not be overly pleased, but he despises injustice more than the loss of good horses. Upon his return, I will ensure that he hears of what has been wrought in his absence."

With a word, Trahern raised Braith to the back of the gray Cryf. The beast was as steady as Saffir had claimed, unmoving despite the inelegant process of organizing the great dog's position until all four legs were awkwardly straddling the horse's broad body. Trahern then uttered a fixative spell. "It will be uncomfortable for you as we ride," he told Braith.

*It is uncomfortable for me* now. *Surely I can run beside you!*

"You cannot run fast enough yet."

Saffir agreed. "Speed is everything, with warths on your trail." Braith nosed her shoulder, and she pressed her face to his massive muzzle. "Be strong, dear one. I promise I will join you when I can. There is nowhere you can go that my heart cannot find you."

Trahern reached over to pat the great dog's shoulder. "The spell is strong, my brother. You can dismount whenever you wish, but I swear by all the stars that you will not fall." He mounted the dappled gold horse with ease, despite the lack of a saddle, and wound his hands into its long mane. He looked down at the woman beside them just as the howl of a warth could be heard to the east of the mountain.

"Come with us," he said.

She shook her head. "I cannot. For the sake of your brother, there are tasks I must perform."

Nothing Trahern said would persuade her to elaborate further. It made him uneasy—was Saffir planning something? Was this all an elaborate ruse to ensure that they were pursued and slain by the Wild Hunt? *Eirianwen would emerge blameless, of course.* Yet he found he could not entirely discount the relationship he'd witnessed between Saffir and Braith, even if he didn't understand it.

"It cannot be safe for you here," he said at last.

"It is safe enough. None dare enter the den of the Hunt." She put a hand on her dagger. "And I am not without my talents. Now *go*. Let the horses carry you where they will."

He bowed from the waist, as if she were a woman of high standing. "Be well. Meet us when you can."

When she could no longer see them, Saffir pulled a tiny crystal bottle from an inner pocket. With a silent prayer for Braith's safety, she pulled the stopper and pressed the bottle to her lips . . .

# THREE

No sooner had he brushed Cyflym's side with his heel than both horses erupted from the cave entrance like bats escaping into the night. For a brief, frantic moment, Trahern wished he'd glued his own body to his mount with magic. A few rapid heartbeats later, he adjusted to the frenzied rhythm. These were like no animals he'd ever ridden. Their speed was incredible—and deathly silent, save for the wind rushing by his ears. No hooves touched the ground as they dashed beyond the marsh and into the deep forest beyond. Veering as one, the horses left the main trail almost at once and galloped single file along a narrow stag path. Trahern ducked over the horse's neck to avoid the branches and saplings that slapped at him, glad that Braith was already as low as possible on his own steed.

Leaping over riverbeds of amethyst water, dodging impossibly tall trees that sported monstrous glowing shelves of fungus, the fleet horses didn't slow for an instant. Trahern had traveled much, yet this part of the realm was strange to him—but then he'd never followed the Hunt, nor used their gateway to the human world above. The landscape became ever more alien, filled with plants and terrains he had not imagined—

The warth came out of nowhere, knocking him cleanly from his horse and into a thicket of red-leafed bushes. Trahern recovered faster than he had when Saffir had attacked him, driving his dagger deep into the big animal's chest and binding the still-snapping jaws with a wordless spell. Another warth quickly appeared, however, crouched to spring.

And another.

Braith appeared and tore into one of the warths with a terrible gurgle of rage, shaking it by its long, striped neck until the light faded from its yellow eyes. It gave Trahern the chance to yank his tunic over his head, baring his upper body. Though he could draw energy from the earth through his clothing, direct contact with his skin allowed him to pull it from the air as well. Immediately, the *ledrith* that marked his body began to glow as if his flesh had cracked to reveal a molten core. The intense magic was a shiver to the skin, a burn in the blood, a fire in the bones. He pressed his back against an outcrop of rough stone, joining its strength to his.

Red flame spun from Trahern's fingers, and violet needles of light arrowed from his palms, taking down a dozen more warths in rapid succession. Yet more swarmed to replace them. Many of the spells embedded in his skin were weapons, needing only his unspoken intent to release them. What he truly needed, however, was another impenetrable circle of fire, and no *ledrith* existed for such a thing. Though he was a master, the spell required highly focused thought and word each and every time. Right now, the predators were too fast and too relentless in their attacks.

Braith, too, was relentless. He had always been a superb swordsman, anticipating his opponent's every move and countering them fiercely. As a grim, those same abilities made him a consummate war dog, terrifying in his killing efficiency. The pile of dead warths grew as Trahern and his brother fought side by side, their backs against the rocky outcropping.

Above the chaos, a sudden drumbeat of sound signaled a cavalcade of horses fast approaching. *Eirianwen's mercenaries.* Just as Trahern glanced above to find a better position to which he could levitate himself and his brother, a warth leapt down from the rock behind him, scoring his neck with a long, hooked claw.

Trahern grabbed at the wound with one hand, feeling hot blood squish between his fingers. His other hand gripped the throat of the warth, its serrated teeth scissoring mere inches from his face and its fetid breath stinging his eyes. A deafening battle roar diverted the warth's attention, and Braith slammed into the creature with his full body weight, knocking it away from Trahern. The great blue-gray grim savaged the predator at once, but as soon as he lifted his bloodied muzzle, a fresh pack of warths encircled them. These were a little warier than their predecessors, hanging back just long enough to finally give Trahern the opportunity he needed.

Calling Braith to his side, he used almost all his remaining strength to summon a standing circle of black fire around them, the same lethal blaze he'd called upon at Court. The warths within the ring abruptly withered to ash. Those outside threw themselves against the magical barrier. Most died instantly, but one very nearly got through—until Braith tore off its head. Belatedly, Trahern realized his wound weakened him. Quickly, he wrapped magic around his injured throat like silver gauze and silently cursed himself that he hadn't thought to do it sooner. If his strength waned, his magic would dwindle with it. How long could he keep the wall up? The flames had already shifted from oily black to purple, and even as he watched, it blushed with crimson. The fire would continue to fade as he did.

*You've lost a lot of blood*, said Braith.

*You can't bleed at all. You can still escape. Leave me and go—they will not kill me, only drag me back to our mother for judgment.*

*Can you not translate us?*

He shook his head and wished he hadn't as a trickle of fresh blood escaped his wound. The rock that surrounded them was the same that formed the palace foundations, rendering ineffective any spell that could whisk them away.

"Hold!" an imperious voice shouted, and the warths left off their attack, reluctantly crouching in place. Trahern narrowed his eyes, straining to focus—and saw a large band of mounted soldiers in ragtag armor. Gray skin was visible behind their strange helms, and their eyes shone green. He didn't recognize them at all, but his sorcerer's sight could not mistake the crimson aura that surrounded their swords and spears. *Iron weapons.* Very few in the Nine Realms could approach such things, and the cut of an iron blade was a slow but sure poison to any Tylwyth Teg. Faint and dizzy, he held on to Braith with one hand to steady himself and pressed himself harder against the rock to bolster his remaining power. Last, he eased off his boots. The ground was cool beneath his bare feet, and he drew in energy like drawing fresh breath, pulling it up from the very bedrock, renewing him, aiding him for one last—

A deep shadow abruptly fell across the forest, and thunder rolled from a formerly clear sky. The soldiers glanced around uneasily as their horses twitched and danced beneath them. The warths slunk silently away, and Trahern felt the hair on his head prickle and rise. *Braith, get down!*

The entire world erupted into white light and noise beyond hearing as a bolt of lightning crashed to earth before him.

Trahern wasn't certain if he had lost consciousness or not, but it was an abysmally long time before he could see and hear again. Braith was on top of him, apparently trying to shield him. *Move*, he said in his mind.

*Are you well?*

*I would be better if I could breathe. Move!*

The great dog slid his bulk from Trahern's chest, and he rolled over with a grunt, gratefully filling his lungs. His vision blurred and cleared, blurred and cleared, but he could make out that only a handful of the mercenaries remained, and most looked like they wanted to leave. He had to give the leader credit for nerve—but the man no longer looked at him at all.

"In the name of Eirianwen of the House of Oak, we have come to arrest the fugitive Trahern," the man shouted.

"Her name means nothing here." The new voice came from high above, and Trahern struggled to see. A burly stallion, as glossy and black as obsidian, stood upon the rocky outcrop behind him, and its tall rider was dressed in dark leathers. His hair was as black as his mount, falling to his waist in hundreds of braids and stirred by an unseen wind. Save for the dangerous glitter in his jet-colored eyes and the glow of the light whip resting on his thigh, it was like staring at Death itself.

"He—he is a traitor, My Lord, sir. We have a right—"

"As trespassers in the Nine Realms, you have no rights." The great horse stepped down from the steep rocky outcropping as easily as if walking across a meadow. The mercenary captain paled visibly as Lurien, Lord of the Wild Hunt, placed himself squarely between the soldiers and their intended quarry. "Our laws state that betrayers and traitors are the rightful prey of the Wild Hunt," said Lurien, then leaned forward in the saddle, his next words measured and menacing. "If he lives, he is mine. If he dies, he is also mine. Stay if you wish to join him."

The captain wheeled his horse and fled. What was left of his company followed hard behind until the forest was again silent and empty. Before Lurien could pivot his own mount, however, Trahern summoned the strength to make a last desperate effort. *He must not find us weak, my brother!*

When the dark fae's gaze fell upon them, Trahern was on his feet. Though he had to lean against a snarling Braith for support, he held a tightly contained vortex of power in his hand. Both the *ledrith* embedded in his skin and the whirling magic in his palm glowed with amber light that grew brighter with every heartbeat, readying for an outward blast of his own life force. In an impossible situation, such was the ultimate weapon of every trueborn sorcerer.

"I will die before you can return us to the Court," said Trahern calmly. "And I will take you with me if need be."

To his surprise, Lurien merely laughed and dismounted. In an eyeblink, he was in front of Trahern, with a gloved hand restraining Braith's enormous muzzle. The great dog growled deep in his throat but appeared unable to move. Trahern's lips moved to form the single word that would release the fatal power—and abruptly found himself on the ground with Lurien's boot pressing his wrist into the dirt and his magic completely extinguished. "You are brave, sorcerer," said the Lord of the Hunt. "But you are also wounded and weak. Perhaps we will discuss my death again when you are well."

"I will not let you take us back—" gasped Trahern.

"We are not the Court's dogs, to act upon their petty whims. Hast thou broken any laws?"

"Nay. My brother and I"—he struggled for breath now—"keep the ways of Gwenhidw."

Lurien eyed Braith with a raised brow, releasing his hold on him. The dog immediately stretched himself full-length beside Trahern's prone body as if to guard him. "This fledgling grim is your brother?"

Trahern could only nod.

"Then whatever offense you gave the House of Oak appears to have been amply paid for. As for the Hunt, you will find that the squabbles of the Houses are of no interest to us." Lurien tossed him a silver flask. "This will help. Drink all of it."

Hands shaking, Trahern clumsily uncorked the narrow-necked container and took a careful swallow. He'd expected absinthe or other *wirodydd.* Instead of burning his throat, however, the liquid was as a slurry of spring ice, cooling and enlivening. He drained its contents gladly, and his vision cleared in time to see Lurien raise his hand—

A host of riders appeared among the trees like shadows sprung to life. Pale clouds swirling at their feet resolved into a large pack of pure-white hounds.

"Bring their horses back," he instructed, and a rider broke away from the rest at once. Lurien glanced down at Trahern with what looked like amusement. "Or should I say, *my* horses?"

"Necessity . . . required that we . . . *borrow* them, My Lord," he managed.

"Indeed. I have declared that you belong to the Hunt, so you may borrow them a bit longer if you wish. I have need of riders." He glanced at Braith. "And a grim might make an interesting field hound. If you give us your allegiance freely, Eirianwen will have no further power over either of you."

"She will not . . . be satisfied . . . until we are dead."

"Then she will have to remain unsatisfied, will she not? Not even the queen herself has power to take you from us—although you are free to withdraw at any time." Trahern's surprise must have shown on his face. "Despite the stories told to frighten children, only the guilty are bound to follow us forever," explained Lurien. "I will warn you, however, that leaving the Hunt divests you of the power and protection of my name."

Braith nosed Trahern's face. *We cannot travel to the human world until you are well and I am stronger. Our mother would never expect us to run with the Wild Hunt—and it may prove to be an adventure!*

Even as a dog, his brother retained his impulsive nature. *I'm sure you've also thought that Saffir will be able to find you that much more easily.*

*I admit that such a thought entered my mind. It is a good plan, is it not?*

*It appears to be our* only *plan.* "We accept your terms with thanks," said Trahern, wondering at the words even as they left his lips. *May I not regret this decision!*

"A wise choice. Particularly since you already vowed allegiance to whomever might help you save your brother."

Trahern could only gape as he recalled his own desperate prayers in the cave of the grims. *I said nothing aloud!*

Lurien only winked at him, then signaled one of his Hunters, a woman whose tousled white hair was barely the length of a finger. Trahern had never seen any Tylwyth Teg, male or female, with hair so shorn. "Hyleath, it seems that the matron of the House of Oak has taken great liberties in a palace that is not hers to command. More, she has purchased the loyalty of *daemons* who are arrogant enough to defy the peace of the queen's own forest and defile it with iron weapons. See that Eirianwen is presented with a suitable offering that will send a clear message to both parties."

A feral grin crossed Hyleath's sharp features. "Eighty heads, Lord Lurien?"

"Your taste in gifts is impeccable as always."

"And the bodies?"

"Toss them into the dry swamps of Corsydd, to sink below the grasses there. There they will remain until I have occasion to call the dead to join the Hunt."

Hyleath reared her mount and waved a light whip over her head. Vividly colored lightning leapt from it, and thunder crashed overhead loud enough that Trahern could feel it in his very bones. He watched in awe as most of the company raced away, horses and dogs alike climbing into the air as if it were solid ground until they galloped high over the tops of the trees.

The few remaining riders automatically moved in behind their lord. One led Cryf and Cyflym. "You need a place to heal," Lurien said to Trahern. "But I think the queen's palace would be a poor choice at present, even in the den of the Hunt. Wren and Nodin will take you to a safer place, one that is not known to your mother and her network of spies. For now, it will be unknown to you as well."

Trahern didn't see the Lord of the Wild Hunt move or hear any incantation fall from his lips. Nevertheless, he felt the impact of powerful magic like a stunning blow to his entire body. Before he could form a single word of protest, a tide of dizziness swept him away into a darkness that glittered with stars.

# FOUR

*Walla Walla, Eastern Washington, USA*
*Present Day*

The ear-piercing screams would have done a pterodactyl proud as nine-year-old Fox entered total meltdown mode in the produce department of Naturally Yours Organics. As usual, the din won either disapproving glares or pained expressions of sympathy from other shoppers. Today the glares were in the majority. In a last-ditch effort to defuse the situation, Lissy sat down on the hardwood floor next to her son's flailing body. "Just breathe, bud. Breathe in and out." She kept her voice calm and matter-of-fact, even as she slid his beloved Squishy Bear close to him. Sometimes the soft toy was a life preserver in a storm of stimulation that he couldn't process fast enough.

Not today.

"It's okay, we're going now." She got to her feet and hefted Fox, all fifty-one struggling pounds of him, onto her hip. He was small for his age—what on earth would she do when he got bigger? *Either rent a hand truck or get a hip replacement.* Especially when he continued to thrash like a netted tuna all the way to the front of the store. Once she'd taken a few steps outside, however, he went completely limp, his shrill screams subsiding into strange, silent sobbing, punctuated only by the occasional hiccup. Lissy remembered plenty of occasions those first few years when she'd sobbed all the way to the car, too.

She settled his rag-doll body into his booster seat, placed his bear and his favorite video game within reach, then half sat, half collapsed into the driver's seat. The closing of the car door shut the world out with a satisfying *clunch*, and Lissy imagined a baseball umpire yelling, *Safe!* Taking a couple of deep breaths in the blissful quiet, she turned the key and switched on the air-conditioning. The car was parked in the shade, but temperatures climbed early at this time of year. Besides, cool air often relaxed Fox, no matter what time of year it was. She checked on her son in the rearview mirror. He lay unmoving, his blond head turned away from the window, face pale and his ever-serious blue eyes staring. He looked exhausted. Although he lost control much less often now, an episode still took a toll on him.

Truth be told, it took a helluva toll on her, too. But Melissa Santiago-Callahan would never give up. The word *quit* just wasn't in her vocabulary. Sometimes, though, she couldn't help but wish that things were different—

*She had been close to finishing her doctorate in geophysics when she met Chief Warrant Officer Matt Lovell, on leave from Fort Carson.*

*Funny, thoughtful, intelligent, and every bit as driven to succeed as she was, the tall helicopter pilot fell hard for her—and she for him. On the six-month anniversary of their first date, they were engaged. Two months after she said yes, he was deployed to Iraq. And one month later he was gone. Death came for him not in the skies that he loved so much but on the ground in an IED explosion.*

*The shock to her heart was enormous. To go from such a high-intensity relationship to nothing in the space of a heartbeat was hard enough. But even as she swung between soul-searing pain and frozen numbness, Lissy discovered she was pregnant.*

*And seven months later, Fox was born by emergency C-section.*

*Despite his abrupt introduction to the world, her son was healthy and strong. Lissy was determined to be the very best parent possible, and if the universe was fair, it should have worked. She should have been able to shower Fox with love and have everything turn out fine. But by the time his third birthday rolled around, she realized that her beautiful son was different from other children—*

A light tapping at the window made her jump. An old man with a torn sweater and no teeth waved at her. She hesitated until she spotted the authentic army insignia on his worn ball cap, then opened the window an inch.

"Can I help you, sir?"

"Sorry if I scared ya. Didn't mean to scare ya. Just wondered if ya had any change. Pension just don't pay fer much these days." His creased face lit up as she pressed a five-dollar bill through the opening in the window. "Thank ya, honey. Thank ya, thanks a lot. Bless ya!"

"You're welcome. Good luck!"

As he shuffled away, Lissy turned to look at Fox. He wasn't asleep, but he hadn't moved a hair. If he'd heard the exchange between his mom and the old man, he didn't show it. Mentally she scolded herself for wandering down Memory Lane. Focusing on anything but the present drained her energy, distracted her. And right now, she had a meltdown to analyze.

*Okay, okay, let's go through the checklist.* Surprises and spontaneity were not happy things for her son. Because of that, she scheduled their shopping like she did everything else in Fox's life, and Saturday-morning trips to buy groceries were part of a dependable routine. There were fewer people to contend with at 8:00 a.m., and Fox was usually fresh from a night's sleep plus his favorite breakfast of scrambled eggs and toast, with exactly four ounces of orange juice in the blue glass. He probably wasn't concerned with the amount as much as he desperately needed the orange juice to line up with the design of the glass . . .

Of necessity, Lissy patronized very few businesses, and Naturally Yours Organics was by far her favorite. The store never played music or made startling loudspeaker announcements, nor did it have the overbright lighting of most stores. The aisles were spacious and uncluttered, with freestanding displays. There was less metal and plastic, too: the walls and shelves were wooden like the worn oak floor. Many foods were in bulk barrels or glass jars. All was friendly, old-fashioned, warm, and welcoming, and Fox had been here countless times before.

*So what was different today?*

She frowned. Brent Peters had been cleaning up almond milk in the dairy aisle. Lissy hadn't smelled any cleanser, but Fox had bionic senses. He was aware of nuances she could barely detect. Many things that she found pleasant—like the soothing scent of lavender—were downright excruciating for him. *But he didn't react badly when he saw Brent with the mop.* In fact, he had stopped to ask the man why he used a string mop instead of a spray 'n' wipe model like the one they had at home. Brent, one of the owners, had kindly explained how much more absorbent it was for large messes, and Fox had walked away satisfied. Well, except for telling Lissy: "You really ought to get a mop like that, dude!"

*I give up.* Whatever today's trigger was, she couldn't begin to guess. It was very possible that there wasn't a single cause but a string of tiny irritations accumulated over the course of hours or even days. She would talk with Fox later, of course, but despite being exceptionally bright, he could seldom articulate exactly what had bothered him. In fact, he probably had no more idea than she did.

*Nothing to do but go home and try again some other time.* Nothing Lissy could do about the groceries she'd left behind in the cart, either, except hope that a clerk—or more likely, the ever-patient Brent—would put them away before the grass-fed butter melted. She'd talked to the owners and staff on more than one occasion, explaining about Fox's challenges as best she could. Though they didn't totally understand, they were blessedly supportive. They all knew that once she left the store with her son, she probably wouldn't be back that day.

*Damn. I really needed the bread. And the orange juice, too.* Briefly, Lissy thought about asking her mother to pick up a couple of things for her—but only briefly. The most obvious reason was that Olivia Santiago-Callahan was probably in a packing frenzy prior to flying out Sunday to visit relatives in Veracruz. But even if she wasn't busy, Lissy wouldn't risk the now-familiar lecture: *You need a life, too,* mija. *When was the last time you went anywhere? You know that Fox will be fine with me.*

While it was true that the boy enjoyed being with his grandmother, he already spent his after-school time with her while Lissy taught geology and physics at the local college. And as tough as it was, Lissy knew she had to keep trying to help Fox learn skills that would enable him to deal with the world instead of protecting him from it. His diagnosis at five years old had been a blow: Asperger's Syndrome, one of the autism spectrum disorders. No known cause and no cure, but three things could make a vital difference in Fox's life. *Routine. Management. The development of coping strategies.* She repeated them to herself often, like a mantra.

A small voice suddenly spoke up from the back seat. "He has a dog."

Lissy craned her neck to scan the parking lot but saw nothing. The old man was gone—had a pet been with him? "Who has a dog, bud?"

"Dude, *he* does. The really tall man with the long white hair. I like dogs."

That was an understatement. Fox adored all animals, and the feeling was usually mutual. "I like dogs, too," she said, but still saw nothing. The old man who had asked for money had gray hair—and not much of it. And he wasn't very tall. Maybe Fox was talking about someone he'd seen earlier, perhaps even the day before. In fact, it wasn't unusual for him to start talking excitedly about an event from months ago as if it had happened that morning. A man with long white hair could be Santa Claus, for all she knew. *Oh, sweetie, I wish I understood you better . . .*

She might have left it at that, but at breakfast her son had talked about seeing such a man in his dreams. It hadn't sounded like a nightmare, but was it bothering him somehow?

*A tall white-haired man.*

Was this the source of the meltdown? She tried again to engage Fox. "I must have missed him. And I didn't see a dog."

"It's a really big dog. You'll see them for sure when they get here."

*Them?* The back of her neck prickled. "When *who* gets here?"

There was no reply. A glance in the rearview showed that Fox had finally stirred enough to pick up his game. And whatever he'd been talking about was probably already forgotten as his thumbs rapidly worked the controls. She wished she could forget a few things that easily . . . Meanwhile, this *man with the white hair* thing was worrisome. *You'll see them when they get here*, Fox had said. He'd always told her about his dreams, amazing her with his ability to remember them in such vivid detail.

Lately, though, Lissy had realized there was something more going on. A lot more. Like a few days ago, when Fox had announced over breakfast that he had dreamed of blue chairs.

*"What blue chairs?"*

*"Dude! The ones we're going to see today," he said, as if that explained everything. "They've got little red-and-yellow squares on them. And circles. Green circles. There oughta be triangles on them, too, but they must've forgot."*

*"We're going to the dentist after school, bud. Remember, we've been talking about it? You go every six months on the first Tuesday at four p.m."*

To be honest, she had no idea if he could grasp a routine that spanned such a length of time, but just in case, she scheduled those things as religiously as she scheduled his daily routine. She pictured the waiting room in her mind, the drab and dated neutrals relieved only by a few bright posters.

*"Dr. Janey's chairs are brown, remember?"*

*His voice rose. "We're going to see the blue chairs!"*

*"Okay, well, we'll definitely look for some blue chairs afterward."*

*"Won't have to, dude," he said confidently, and turned his attention back to his breakfast without further comment. Lissy had let it go—after all, she needed to get him to school and herself to work. But after school, he'd presented her with a picture, painstakingly drawn and colored. Bright-blue chairs. Teeny yellow and red squares. Tiny green circles.*

*"He went right to work on it as soon as he got here," said her mother, beaming with pride. "Our Fox is such an artist!"*

*Lissy had admired it thoroughly, of course, tucking it into her briefcase to keep it safe. She planned to give it a place of honor on the fridge later—*

*That is, until she saw the dentist's office.*

Shaking her head did little to free her mind of troubling thoughts, but Lissy attempted to focus on the here and now just the same. Should she drive home or should she wait and see if Fox recovered enough to attempt the grocery store again? *He's older now. I should really give him a few more minutes, just in case. I could treat this like a time-out, like they do at school.* There, a time-out wasn't a punishment but a chance for Fox to breathe and pull himself together. The veteran teacher, Alaina Fletcher, allowed him to determine when he felt ready to rejoin the class. Sometimes it was ten or fifteen minutes. Sometimes it was two hours. Whatever it was, Alaina was smart enough not to remark on it or ask him questions, simply allowing him to slip back into his desk. Maybe if Lissy waited long enough, they could *slip back* into the grocery store—

A loud and much-too-cheerful chime from her phone interrupted her reverie. She had a text from her best friend, Brooke:

Come 2 Palouse Falls w us later. 6 p.m. Campfire supper.

A second text included a bevy of dancing marshmallows, a smiling hot dog in a bun, a tent, and what looked like a brown sheet of plywood—no, wait, make that a graham cracker. It would be tremendous fun for her, but Fox hadn't exactly been crazy about the outdoor sleepover experience last time . . . *That was when he was five. Six! But it could be different now, right?* She needed to give him a chance to try it again.

Just then a third message popped up with four familiar images. Brooke always used very specific icons for everyone she knew. The symbol for Fox was obvious, of course. And with a passion for geology, what else would Lissy be but a smiling pet rock?

On-screen right now were a superhero (*Sharon*), a vampire (*Katie*), a horse (*Morgan*), and a tiger (*Tina*). Her best friends since their high school days, every one of them was an official "auntie" to her son. They hadn't all gotten together since Sharon's wedding two years before. Lissy's hands shook with anticipation as she texted back: 4 sure?

A burst of music startled her into almost dropping the phone. "Black Magic" by Little Mix signaled that Brooke was on the line. "It's a spur-of-the-moment thing," her friend blurted excitedly. "I just got off the phone with Sharon. Our little gang will be all together again!"

*Omigod, this is awesome!* It was all she could do not to jump out of the car, squeal, and dance. Morgan lived just three hours away and was able to visit now and then. Katie and Tina were in different states, however, and Sharon was all the way on the other side of the country. To have them together in one place was rare and wonderful. Mindful of her son in the back seat, however, Lissy somehow managed to keep her voice even. "That's really great to hear." Her "mom mind" was racing, though. Would there be enough time between this morning's spectacular fail and tonight's outing? *They're hours apart . . .* She was probably safe from accidentally rewarding undesirable behavior. Besides, this counted as a special occasion! Which reminded her, she needed to check if Fox was even invited. "Say, Brooke—will that activity be adults only or family-rated?"

"You should *definitely* bring Fox. Everyone wants to see him," assured Brooke. "And hey, we all know the drill on how to behave around him—easy on the stimulation, right? No mass huggings and kissings, no endless questions. I'll pick up that little pup tent from your mom's yard that he likes so he'll have a place to retreat to that's familiar. And you don't have to say a word, because I know he's probably nearby."

If there was anything better than a friend who understood you, it was a friend who understood your kid, too. "We'll definitely try it," Lissy said aloud. *If he's really uncomfortable, I can always take him home.* But maybe, just maybe, she wouldn't have to . . .

"By the way, we already agreed on a dry party, since Morgan and I are both preggers. We're going with a chocolate theme instead."

"Sounds wonderfully decadent. What should I bring?"

"Yourselves. Tina's got an extra-big tent to share with you and a couple of sleeping bags, so just bring what you think you might like—maybe your own pillow if you have a favorite. I know *I* can't sleep without my body pillow these days," said Brooke. "Oh, and definitely bring whatever you think Fox will need to be comfortable. I've already got a few things packed that are sure to occupy him. Like a brand-new box of gemstones and rocks that just came in for the store."

Lissy wasn't a crier by nature, but her eyes moistened at her friend's thoughtfulness. "You're the one who *rocks*, you know that? So when are we meeting up?"

"Rhys and Morgan are already there. Aidan's going to drive up with me later. You know how the guys are—they want to check the place out and make sure it's safe, but they *promised* they would camp down the road a ways. That lets them feel like they're close enough to protect us, but we still get to have a girls' night!"

Lissy laughed. "That'll work!"

"I know, right? And you know what's even better? There's only a handful of campsites, and Katie and Sharon booked them all, so we'll have the *whole place* to ourselves after sunset! It's gonna be great—*Rory!* Rory, dammit, stop rolling on that soapwort! I just planted that! Gotta go—"

The abrupt silence told Lissy that her friend had gone to deal with the most outrageous of her three felines. In fact, Brooke's last phone call had ended similarly when the small black cat decided to drop a dead mouse on a carefully laid spread of tarot cards—right in front of a client. *I wonder how she's going to manage with both Rory* and *a baby . . .*

A glance in the mirror showed Fox still absorbed in his video game, and that was a good sign. He would play until he felt normal again—whatever normal felt like to him—and then he'd nap. As for her, the grocery shopping might have been a total *fail*, but the anticipation of seeing her dearest friends picked up her spirits like nothing else could.

# FIVE

The morning star glittered near the sinking moon, and the Wild Hunt wheeled as one. Trahern didn't have to order the dozen riders to return to Tir Hardd. The night had belonged to the fae since the beginning of the world, but the overbright day was usually abandoned to mortals. If he closed his eyes now, he would feel the pull of the faery realm as surely as metal was drawn to a lodestone. The lathered horses felt it. All of them, including Trahern's own horned mount, Cyflym, sprang into a gallop with renewed energy. Hard on the horses' heels, a pack of grinning white hounds, the tireless Cŵn Annwn of legend, lengthened their pace as well.

He glanced down. As always, a much larger and more powerfully built dog ran effortlessly beside him, broad head level with Trahern's silver stirrup and large leonine paws striking the ground in eerie silence. With his enormous jaws, he could easily have dismembered any or all of the white hounds. Instead, while Braith didn't deign to run with the pack, he was swift to defend them from danger.

*As he once defended me . . .*

The immense dog slowed his pace as Trahern reined in his mount to allow the rest of the riders to pass. A few of the younger ones touched their fingers to their foreheads as they went by—and by all the stars, he wished they wouldn't. It wasn't an acknowledgment of his current position of Huntmaster in Lord Lurien's absence. Rather, it was an automatic gesture of respect for his noble lineage from one of the leading Houses of the Tylwyth Teg.

As soon as they'd passed, he spat into the grass as if he could rid himself of the reminders of that long-ago life. One of the things that defined the Hunt was the purposeful lack of station. Ability was the only thing that counted here. Even Lurien himself claimed no royal blood and was no respecter of it.

*I belong to the Hunt,* Trahern thought fiercely. *And none else.*

He wondered if he could belong to this new land as well. A strange thought for him, birthed by an even stranger yearning... The vast, open grasslands and rolling hills formed a restless ocean of dappled silver beneath the moon. Here and there this land-sea broke against outcroppings and bluffs of tall columnar rocks and fell away into steep ravines and canyons. What was it about this land that struck a chord in him, called to him, promising freedom from all limits? He almost believed it, too. Added to that was the sheer novelty of the vista, unlike anything he had ever seen in his long, long life. Barring outright violence or a malicious spell, all fae creatures were virtually immortal. For many of the Tylwyth Teg, however, the price of their longevity was tedium. *Surely no one could ever be without wonder in this wild place.*

At least he didn't think so. The only time he'd experienced boredom himself was in his former life among the shallow and frivolous members of the Royal Court. Thankfully, he no longer needed to concern himself with their petty games and subtle intrigues; he was dead to the Court since Lurien had claimed him for the Wild Hunt. In fact, the only time he'd set foot in the queen's palace as a hunter was at a recent costume ball where he'd been part of a team trusted to guard Gwenhidw herself. Fortunately, most of the courtiers avoided the event entirely rather than associate with the multitude of other clans and creatures the queen had invited. Not that any of the Tylwyth

Teg nobility would have recognized him . . . Trahern had taken his cue from the long scar on his throat and costumed himself as a prowling warth!

The scent of sagebrush drifted on the night air. No warths lived in this place. No hungry bwganod, either. But if they did? *If the land were blasted and barren and infested with poisonous* dragons, *I would yet embrace it for its distance from the Nine Realms!* There was a generous ocean and most of a mortal nation between the new fae territory of Tir Hardd that flourished below eastern Washington and the ancient fae lands that sprawled beneath the country of Wales. No courtier, least of all one of Oaken lineage, would ever consider traveling here to what they mockingly called the *Queen's Folly*.

Trahern flatly disagreed with their assessment. Despite its size—and every fae realm was immense in relation to whatever tiny human domain lay above it—the Nine Realms had become untenably crowded over the eons. And though the other residents of the faery world vastly outnumbered its ruling class, the Tylwyth Teg were thoughtless or downright cruel in their treatment of them. *Sometimes even killing them* . . . He quickly banished those ill memories and spat again for good measure.

No, there was no folly here. With vision and determination, Queen Gwenhidw had thrown open the doors to a much better life for many of her subjects. Not only had she opened a portal to this new territory, she had broken with all tradition in its governance. She had shocked everyone by setting representatives from *all* the tribes and clans to rule by common consent. It was even said that while she advised, *she did not interfere in their decisions*! No wonder the Royal Court espoused such a low opinion of the place—they were probably terrified of its precedent. Gwenhidw had gone even further, refraining from building an opulent palace for herself. Instead, she maintained a modest chateau in the very center of Tir Hardd, and her bright banners flew over her home whenever she was in residence.

As she was now.

*And as long as the queen is here, Lurien will make certain he is elsewhere.* Trahern was puzzled by this new strain between the two people he admired most. He'd followed the enigmatic Lord of the Wild Hunt for a very long time, and if Lurien had a weakness, it was that he appeared to harbor deep feelings for the long-widowed queen.

*The belief in love leads only to ruin.* Was the evidence not with him in the majestic dog beside him? And what of the object of Braith's love? Saffir had promised to follow Braith as soon as she could, but as of yet she had failed to appear. To break one's word was nearly unknown, even among the Tylwyth Teg. Trahern feared at first that Eirianwen had discovered her identity and exacted some hideous vengeance, but Lurien's spies failed to find any evidence of such a thing. Besides, his ever-efficient mother would have found a way to utilize the woman. It would have been a simple enough matter to hold the healer hostage until Trahern and his brother voluntarily renounced the Hunt and returned to the House of Oak. Yet no such thing had happened, indicating that Braith's beloved was not only still alive but free.

*Free to choose to abandon her lover.*

The fact that Saffir had not been seen by anyone, anywhere, meant little. Changing one's appearance was simple. If one did not possess sufficient magic, such glamours could be purchased. Perhaps Saffir had adopted not only a new facade but a whole new life, because she understood the true hopelessness of Braith's condition . . .

*No.* Trahern had resisted that verdict from the beginning, and he still did. Had he not promised his brother that he would never stop trying? When he wasn't riding with the Hunt, he worked constantly on one spell or another. Hundreds of spells. Thousands of variations. And so far, every single one of them had come to naught.

Worse, Braith himself had changed. Whether it was the result of mourning Saffir or some natural progression of the enchantment that bound him, Trahern didn't know. Once, his brother had been able to hear Trahern's every thought and respond in kind. Gradually, however, Braith's voice in his mind had faded until it ceased altogether. His brother's mannerisms had altered, too, descending into purely animal traits. Now, though he remained utterly devoted to Trahern, Braith had finally become as other dogs. He was not a true grim. But neither was he a man.

"Your wish to know love has brought you to this sorry state," said Trahern aloud. "But I am the one who has failed to find anything that can save you."

The noble creature looked up at once, his eyes questioning but recognizing only that the object of his fierce loyalty was troubled. He chuffed once, then turned his intent gaze to the Hunt as they vanished in the distance.

Trahern shook his head. "We will follow later, perhaps tonight. I would linger in this land a little longer and see these hills by the light of day." Dawn reddened the sky as he veered his horse to race along a high rocky ridge, with the great dog at his side. No matter how hard or fast Trahern rode, however, some memories could never be left behind.

Nor could guilt.

The prospect of the campfire get-together didn't excite Fox. In fact, he didn't want to go at all. "Dude, it's Saturday," he stated simply. "There're three episodes of *Tiger Ninja* tonight, and you have to make popcorn."

Lissy sighed inwardly. She'd been in this position many times, walking a tightrope between piquing her son's interest in an activity and causing him to stress out and reject it. If she didn't maintain a perfect balance, she wouldn't be going anywhere. As parties went, it was pretty small—six adults hardly counted as a crowd. But to Fox, it could mean far more interaction than he could handle. *He goes to school now, in a whole* room *full of kids. And he hardly ever needs a classroom aide anymore.* Sometimes Fox still used noise-canceling headphones when he had an in-class assignment and concentrating got too hard. The sound of other kids breathing, wriggling in their seats, rustling papers, and dropping pencils could be too much to bear for her sensitive son. But this wasn't work, and focus wasn't required. *He can handle this; I know he can.*

Finally, she lucked upon the magic words that changed his mind. "Brooke has new stones and crystals for you to look at. She wants to know if you think they're good enough for the shop."

He hesitated for almost a whole minute. She could all but see the wheels of interest starting to turn in his mind. "But what about *Tiger Ninja*?" he asked at last. "And popcorn?"

"I'll record all three episodes so you can watch them tomorrow as many times as you want. And we'll make lots and *lots* of popcorn before we go, then take it with us to share with your aunties. Deal?"

After another long pause, in which she feared she'd lost the battle, Fox finally nodded. "But Squishy Bear comes, too. And my light. And my magnifying glass. And my book."

"We'll take everything you want to take," she said, then mentally kicked herself for not phrasing it better. Fox just might fill the car with everything he owned because he couldn't make a decision on what to leave behind. "Everything you need for rocks and for bedtime," she qualified, hoping that would keep the number of items down somewhat. *I'm not going to worry about it. If he packs his entire room, I'm not saying a—*

The phone rang, and Lissy picked it up as Fox ran to his room to start packing.

*"Mi precioso!"*

"Hi, Mama. Did I forget something?" Lissy went down her mental list, then slapped her palm to her forehead. Her mother was getting on a plane tomorrow! "Did *you* forget something? Do you need help?"

"I am fine, *mija*. You have a key if you want a change of scenery, your oldest sister has all the information on where I'm staying, and I already collected *mucho* hugs from you and Fox when you picked him up after work last night. But I wanted to tell *you* something. I just saw that young man, Guillermo's son, Vincente, on my way to the mailbox. He is a pharmacist now, you know, and he owns that drugstore just off Fourth. Anyway, he said he would love to meet you for coffee one day soon."

"Mama! I can get my own dates!"

"If that is so, why do I not see you doing it? You have been alone a long time, *mija*, and it is only one date. It is not good for you to . . ."

Lissy rolled her eyes and softly banged her head on the wall as her mother launched into one of her more frequent speeches. To be fair, her mother hadn't said the *D* word for the first few years of Fox's life. But lately, the subject just wouldn't die. "We've been over this, Mama. I have enough to do between my job and my son. I don't have time for a relationship right now."

"You know what I think, *mija*? I think that you are hiding behind these things. You think that no one can be like Matt, so you do not want to try."

It shocked her. "What kind of a thing is that to say?"

"It is the thing a mother says who has also avoided meeting new men because no one could ever be like my dear Jack. I loved your father."

"I know you did," said Lissy, softening a little. Her parents had had the kind of marriage that inspired everyone who knew them. Until a heart attack claimed Jack Callahan much too soon. It had been many years now—Lissy and George had still been in middle school—but Olivia had steadfastly refused to reenter the dating world.

"I am thinking my example has not been a good one for my children. That's why I've promised Guillermo that I will go to dinner with him as soon as I come back. We have even picked a restaurant, that little place over on Ninth Avenue I told you about."

If they had picked a ring and a date, the news couldn't have been more astonishing. "Mama—that's incredible! I'm so happy for you."

"Thank you, *mija*. Just promise me you'll think about it, too. Ask yourself why you don't go out more."

"I *am* going out! I'm camping with my girlfriends tonight."

"Wonderful! I am very happy to hear it."

In Lissy's mind, it would have been a perfect conversation if only it had ended at that point. But a mother was a mother, and Olivia couldn't seem to help herself. "But you know, it is only coffee you are having with Vincente," she persisted. "Surely I can tell him you will think about it?"

*"No!"*

Several minutes later when Lissy hung up, she felt that she needed a drink. *Too bad it's a dry party.* But there would be chocolate and good friends—

*Crap, I've got a ton of popcorn to make!* She rushed to the kitchen to get out her biggest pot.

~

Palouse Falls State Park was an amazing place by day. Jutting basalt formations framed a deep canyon that had been carved out by Ice Age floods. The river that now ran along its bottom resembled a blue ribbon from this height, reflecting the sky as it wound its way toward the larger Snake River in the distance. Most amazing of all, however, was the waterfall itself. An angel-white torrent plunged nearly two hundred feet into a perfectly round bowl of glassy green-blue water.

At Fox's insistence, the two of them toured the canyon trails, stopping to read every interpretive placard. His aunties were already on-site, setting up tents and tables, but he'd barely even said hello to them yet—he was much too keen to see all that the park had to offer. Fox had an intense passion for rocks of all kinds, and not just the pretty ones. It was one of the very few things that Lissy had in common with her son that permitted them some rare moments of bonding. His pockets were already bulging with chips of volcanic basalt, quartz, and feldspar, and he'd half filled Lissy's pockets as well. Fox would insist on keeping every last one of them, of course—and who knew how many more he'd have collected by the time they left. *I sure hope I can find room in his bedroom for another box of "specimens."*

The sinking sun brushed the canyon with gold when they circled their way back to the main viewing area closest to the campground. It was Lissy's favorite spot. Near the lip of the falls stood a strange formation that some called The Castle. It stretched more than halfway across the spillway like a pocketed rampart of oddly shaped stalagmites, now gilded in the lengthening light. Even her background in geology couldn't fully answer how the structure managed to remain intact with swollen spring waters pounding relentlessly around it. It stood high and dry in the hot, arid summer, however, and the shrunken river flowed politely beside it like a companion just before it tumbled off the cliff.

Suddenly, a faint rainbow rose from the mist to crown The Castle, adding to its magic.

"I think it's a faery house," said Fox.

"You do?"

"Yeah, dude, like in the story Grandmamma gave me when I was a little kid. You know, the one about the Nodkins. They built a big apartment building out of flat stones for all their brownie and sprite friends to live in so they could be safe from the bad mice."

Lissy could well imagine *real* faeries frequenting a place like this. Not the dainty fictional beings from childhood books, who sipped dewdrops from flowers and granted wishes, but the full-scale badass variety that so many of her friends and family had encountered in real life. Morgan and Rhys had fought more than one battle with the dangerous creatures. So had Tina's cousin Liam. He'd had to free his wife, Caris, who had been kidnapped by the fae. And it wasn't that many years ago that a faery woman would have succeeded in *killing* George if it hadn't been for Brooke's quick thinking and quicker magic. In fact, Brooke's own husband, Aidan, had once been called to ride with the Wild Hunt, the only human to do so freely. And the only one ever permitted to leave . . .

But the Hunters had used Steptoe Butte, eighty miles away, as their entry to the human world. *My world.* Lissy shivered a little, though it wasn't cold, and was thankful she'd never run into the otherworldly beings. *Well, except Ranyon, of course.* But he didn't really count—the strange little ellyll had left his world behind in favor of living among humans, and he was family to all of them now.

"Can I have some popcorn? And some juice. And a hot dog with no mustard."

"You can have juice and popcorn right away, and we'll check and see if the fire's ready for your hot dog."

"I want to cook it myself!"

"Of course you can—you're a pretty big guy now." Fox was forgetting his *please*s, but she let it slide. His demanding tone indicated that he was tired and hungry now, and he needed to refuel ASAP before he could cope with social niceties. She passed him a juice box from her pocket.

"It's not cold! I need it cold!"

"I know you do. Do you want to take this and trade it for one from the cooler, or do you want to drink this one *and* a cold one?" *Choices.* The same child who needed structure and routine like he needed air also needed options. Not too many because that would be overwhelming, but *some* choices, *some* control, to stave off the frustration of a world that didn't quite match up with his needs. As always, Lissy felt her feet on the tightrope, trying to maintain the delicate balance that made sense only to her son. A moment later he drank the juice, and she felt herself exhale.

The glow of the fire faded long before it reached Fox's little "camp," but the bright moon more than made up for it. He'd chosen the site himself, the farthest one from the group, a grassy knoll among a scattering of trees. And with his official Nat Geo headlamp switched on full, it was easy enough for Lissy to keep an eye on his whereabouts. As expected, however, Fox hadn't moved from his spot. He sat cross-legged in front of his Scooby-Doo pup tent with a huge magnifying glass and his favorite Smithsonian book about rocks, totally absorbed in inspecting the contents of a large box: the latest shipment of crystals and gemstones for Handcastings.

*Brooke always saves her new specimens for him to see* first, *bless her heart.* And every time they visited the shop, she couldn't help but feel a renewed sense of connection with him (and not a little pride) as he appraised each sample on the shelves. Yet there were only certain stones he would actually touch or bring to her with questions. Lissy's mother, Olivia, wasn't surprised by this behavior at all. "He has good instincts, that boy, just like you do, *mija*. He already knows which crystals have positive energy for him and which do not. Our little Fox has gifts, you know. Very strong gifts."

The night was warm, but ice seemed to skitter down her spine. *Gifts.* That was really what scared the hell out of her lately. Lissy had heard tales of the so-called Santiago "gift" all her life. Her grandmamma had been a powerful and much-respected *bruja*, a practitioner of Magic with a capital *M*. Her mother, however, had inherited only a handful of the skills. The full measure of power had passed Olivia by, and—much to Lissy's personal relief—had also passed by her children.

Still, there was a tiny whisper of magic in Lissy's blood. While sometimes that magic manifested in the form of dreams, more often she picked up vibes, *feelings*, about things that didn't make sense until later. She had a feeling now, and she didn't like it one bit.

*Damn those blue chairs—*

Leaving her friends, she walked over to join her son. As she approached, she saw something heave and shift underneath the big open book next to Fox. A whip of a tail protruded, identifying the culprit as Tina's dachshund, Jake, changing position before settling back into sleep. *I didn't even know he was there!* The last time she'd seen the dog, his pointy little head was inside an open bag of marshmallows . . .

Though sweet and affectionate with his owner, Jake had long reigned supreme as the terror of Morgan's veterinary clinic. In fact, Lissy didn't know of anyone in their circle who hadn't experienced the wrath of the bad-tempered dachshund at one time or another. Her twin brother, George, called him "El Diablo." Her friends often joked about it being a rite of passage—*you can't officially be part of the gang until you've been crocodile chomped by Jake.* And although the dog was getting up in years, he still showed no signs of mellowing out.

Unless Fox was present.

Her son's first encounter with Jake had been purely by accident, when Fox was a toddler. Lissy had taken him with her to visit her girlfriends at Morgan's house. Since Fox was having a rare good day, she'd set him on the living room floor with his Squishy Bear before walking into the kitchen to see if she could help . . .

*She heard the front door open and Tina gleefully announcing she'd brought her infamous "Sex in a Pan" squares. She'd brought something else, too. Without warning, the little dog had thundered into the living room like an avenging alligator, fangs bared, drool flying. Lissy had turned just in time to see her Fox, her* baby, *sitting calmly, his plush bear extended to the advancing animal in one vulnerable chubby hand. Time slowed, as it often did at the beginning of irreversible tragedy. She was much too far away, yet she instinctively gathered herself just the same, prepared to somehow make the impossible leap to place her own body between the demonic dachshund and her child—*

*But Jake stopped abruptly.*

*All growling ceased as his lips curtained his needle-sharp teeth. The dog trembled and whined. Suddenly, he dropped to his belly and crawled slowly across the rug to the smiling Fox. The dachshund lifted his head just enough to rest his narrow chin on the child's knee as if in supplication. And went immediately to sleep!*

*Everyone bunched up in the doorway, staring, and none of them, not even Lissy, dared to move or speak in case the spell broke. It was Tina, white-faced and shaking, who made her way over to sit ever so carefully next to Fox. Even she was hesitant to try to remove the dog—he was just too dangerously close to the child.*

*Jake paid no attention to his owner, however, not even waking until Fox himself finally stood up and wandered off. The dachshund immediately trotted along beside the little blond-haired boy as if attached by a string, while Fox babbled to him in some semblance of conversation. He never left the child's side until it was time to go home.*

In the years since, the dog's reputation for canine terrorism remained intact, but he also retained his total adoration of Fox.

Lissy sidled over and sat down on the opposite side of her son, hugging her knees—though she'd much rather be hugging *him*. "So, how's Jake tonight?" she asked.

"He's okay. He's tired because he's old, but he likes it here."

That was a lot more information than she expected. Fox hadn't taken his eyes off the mineral he studied, a fibrous blue crystal of kyanite. She took a chance and asked a question. "So, um, I notice you don't ever *pet* Jake."

The boy's response was matter-of-fact. "He doesn't like being touched."

"Really? Why do you think that is?"

"Duh! It makes his skin itchy—no, *prickly*, kind of."

"That wouldn't feel very good. Is it like that for you, too, if I hug you?"

He just shrugged.

She sighed inwardly. *No real information there.* "So, Jake's comfortable if he just lies next to you, huh."

"Yeah. He says he feels good there."

"He says so?"

Another shrug. "We're friends, so he tells me." Fox turned back to the box, his hand hovering over the wrapped stones as if debating over a box of chocolates. Finally, he chose a polished golden sphere of citrine that was nearly as large as his fist and pulled the book off the sleeping Jake and onto his lap.

Lissy recognized the signs. Whatever door had briefly opened was closed again. He was done talking for the moment. But she had some new things to think about as she stood and moved a couple of steps away to give him his space. Morgan had told her once about a senior cat who had abruptly started scratching his owner when she stroked him. *Sometimes pets become really sensitive when they're older, and it's too stimulating for them. It feels differently to them than to us. It has nothing to do with whether or not they like us.*

*It feels differently to them . . .* Even as a baby, Fox frequently resisted being picked up or cuddled. He still hated hugs. Sometimes he would approach her or her mother and lean against them, but that was all the contact he ever seemed to want. Just like the dachshund was content to lie next to Fox.

*Jake says he feels good there.*

*Jake* says. *Says?*

*Fox doesn't actually* communicate *with Jake, does he?* Lissy frowned. Her son was so literal that she was almost certain he wasn't pretending. *He's just really good with animals, that's all. Lots of people are good with animals!* Maybe Fox simply sensed what they were feeling. Heaven knew, they certainly sensed Fox and came to him immediately. *The dogs we meet in the park, that trooper's horse in the parade, the chickens in the Easter display . . . even Brooke's cats.* Rory, Bouncer, and Jade never left Fox's side for a second whenever he visited the shop.

Another gift, perhaps, just like her mother said. Maybe magic, maybe not.

At least this gift wasn't as scary as the incident with the blue chairs—*dammit, I've got to talk to Brooke about that before I go crazy. Maybe Wednesday or, better yet, Thursday, I'll take Fox to Handcastings.* He could be ready for another outing by then. And while he played with his feline buddies, she could confide her fears to her friend. Brooke would undoubtedly tell her not to worry, and that would be that. Still, Lissy shivered again, and goose bumps ran up and down her arms and legs. *Nerves. Just nerves.* Maybe if she sat close to the campfire for a while, she could dispel the sudden chill.

Of course, it was a lot more than a mere campfire at the moment. Sharon and Katie had worked for more than an hour to construct a towering bonfire. Aidan had brought by an unbelievable amount of wood earlier in the day just for that purpose, and Brooke had whispered a spell of diversion on the enormous pile so no one would see it or run into it. Park rules forbade open fires, providing tiny iron grills for charcoal instead. The rules were there for good reason considering the tinder-dry conditions of the surrounding land, but again, Brooke's magical talents contained the tall blaze and every spark it cast. When the park opened for visitors in the morning, there wouldn't be so much as a scorch mark left upon the ground.

A fresh burst of laughter erupted from the fireside, and Lissy sighed, then smacked a palm to her head. *Some of the people I love most in the world are right here, right* now, *and here I am wasting this precious time worrying about something that's probably nothing. I'm going to sit by that fire, have a good time with my friends, and forget I ever heard about magic!*

Just as she was about to reclaim her camp chair, however, a movement in the distance caught her eye. Something huge and dark emerged from the shadowy canyon—

There was no time to shout a warning, no time to even draw breath before it was among them. Lissy was dimly aware of her friends screaming and scattering. Instead of pursuing them, the nightmarish beast leapt impossibly high above the roaring bonfire, where the tall flames appeared to hold it aloft like so many supplicating hands, outlining its immense proportions with vivid orange light and glowing red sparks. Her startled mind registered massive jaws, long pointed teeth, and a heavily muscled body as the gargoyle / creature / animal / *Jesus, is that a dog?* landed soundlessly in front of her on four paws that would dwarf a lion's.

Lissy braced for the attack. But the massive canine ignored her completely. Instead, it almost knocked her down as it bounded past, heading straight toward her son.

Every protective instinct she had took over. "*Fox!*" she screamed as she ran. The big animal was fast, but she was desperate, throwing herself on his hindquarters just as he reached the little boy. "Get away from him, get away!" Grabbing great handfuls of the dog's hide, Lissy hauled backward with all her might. Fury and fear gave her strength, but the velvety pelt was loose, hanging in great folds like the skin of a bloodhound. The dog himself remained completely unmoved. He hadn't attacked Fox—yet—but his great wrinkled muzzle hovered over him, sniffing him as an immense tiger might sniff a tiny mouse, considering whether it was worth eating. Lissy seized its shoulder, next grabbed an ear, then the pendulous creases of its face, pulling herself along as if traversing a cliff face, until she could shove her own body between the enormous mouth and her child. Wisely or not, she turned her back on the beast to curl herself around Fox, caging him in her arms, uncaring what might happen to her as long as he was protected. Her friends were attacking the dog now, yelling at it, hitting it, trying to drive him off. Sharon had a black belt in karate. A fiery shower of violet sparks struck the ground nearby—Brooke was using her magic. Even Jake had leapt to Fox's defense and now hung by his sharp little teeth from the giant dog's thick lip. A whittled hot-dog stick clattered to the ground beside her, and Lissy snatched it up—

"Mom! *Mom!*" Her son struggled in the tight confines of her arms.

"It's okay, baby, it's okay. I won't let anything—"

"*No*, Mom, stop it, the dog won't hurt us. *He won't hurt us!* Make them stop hitting him! *Make them stop!*"

Something in the tone of his voice got through to her. Fox should have been terrified, yet he wasn't afraid. Not for himself, not for her. *He's afraid for the dog!* Because of it, he was teetering on a high-wire, about to lose all control. The last thing they needed was for him to have a kicking-screaming-crying fit in this situation—who knew what the big animal would do? Lissy turned her head ever so carefully and glanced upward. The dog's face looked as broad as a grizzly's and was mere inches from her own. Nostrils the width of her fist flared, taking in her scent. And without any warning at all, a wet tongue the size of a *towel* blanketed her face.

Fox took advantage of her surprise to wriggle free.

She scooted backward, spitting and wiping her face on her sleeve. Her vision cleared to take in a surreal sight. Her friends had all stepped back, unsure of what to do—save for Jake, who still swung like a furry earring from the monster dog's slobbery flews. But nine-year-old Fox stood with his arms as far around the dog's tree-trunk neck as he could reach, though his headlamp barely shone over the animal's broad back. Incredibly, his great tail wagged slowly but enthusiastically.

*A gift . . .*

Heart hammering, her legs felt shaky as Lissy made it to her feet. "Fox," she called softly. "Fox, honey, we don't know anything about this dog. Maybe you should come away from—"

He rolled his eyes in exasperation. "I *told* you he was coming, dude. I *told* you and you *didn't listen*." As if she were an idiot. As if there wasn't a goddamn hellhound standing in their midst, looking for all the world like a drawing from her brother's comic-book series, Devina of Hades. The implications suddenly struck her like a blow. A hellhound. George's award-winning artwork hadn't sprung entirely from his imagination . . .

*Omigod.*

"Brooke? Morgan?" She hated that her voice trembled, but she forced the question out just the same. "This isn't a grim, is it? *Is it?*" A grim was a herald of Death, according to the old fae legends. "You've seen them before. You can tell, can't you?" She glared at the dog. *Not my son. Not my child, not Fox. You can't have him!*

Big yellow-gold eyes stared calmly back at her, and she was again forced to fend off the giant tongue with her hands. "Yuck, *no*!"

Her question broke the paralysis of uncertainty that had gripped everyone but Fox. Morgan stepped up and ran her hands along the heavily muscled frame as if examining a prize steer. Sharon was right at her elbow, still in a karate stance, guarding the veterinarian.

Strangely, the animal took no notice of them.

"I admit, it does resemble a grim," Morgan said at last. "But it looks a lot *more* like a Neapolitan mastiff, both in conformation and color. Although it's sure a lot bigger than my Fred." That was saying a lot—the veterinarian had adopted a rescued mastiff the size of a small pony, and *its* shoulders were level with Lissy's waist. "Frankly, I've never seen *any* canine this tall."

Tina was still brandishing a tree branch like a club. "The color's wrong," she declared. "Grims are supposed to be black."

"I'm with you guys on this. Not a grim." Brooke walked slowly around the great dog. "For one thing, he's not giving off any bad vibes. Plus, the strongest spells I have are for protection, specifically for defense against evil intent. They just fizzled out as soon as they touched this big guy. But I sure don't know what he *is* or why he's here."

"This whole situation is *nuts*! Will you look at us, just standing around talking about a dog big enough to ride? It's like one of those giant pet pictures on Facebook." Katie had already lowered the camp shovel she'd been wielding and took snapshots with her phone. "But everyone knows those memes are *Photoshopped*, and this is so frickin' *real*."

"Yeah, but define *real*," said Sharon. "I used some of my best kicks, but I couldn't even get Mr. Wrinkles's attention. I'm pretty sure a flesh-and-blood animal would react. Even an elephant would react a little. So what does that make this thing but an escapee from the fae realm?"

*Not a grim.* That was some relief at least. Lissy had eased her way around the creature's huge head to stand by her son. *But what do I do now? Who lets their kid maul a strange dog—or a fantasy creature—capable of swallowing him whole?* It was like being trapped in the tiger cage at the zoo.

Sure, she could forcibly pick up Fox and carry him away, but her son would almost certainly have a meltdown of truly epic proportions. Lissy was prepared to deal with that, but how would Fox's giant new pal react? What if it upset the dog? What if the dog thought the boy needed protecting or, worse, that his screams made him sound like prey?

Right now, the oversize canine simply stood there in their midst like a big goofy pet, its long tail still wagging and an affable expression on its enormous wrinkly face. And despite her friends' determined attempts to defend her and Fox, the dog didn't seem to hold it against any of them in the least. *Yet.*

"What are you doing here?" demanded a new voice, a rich, masculine voice, and every one of her friends fell silent.

*Oh, great, we've attracted a park ranger*, thought Lissy as she turned to face this new issue. *How are we going to explain—*

It was no ranger. The first thing her eyes took in was a heavy black cloak, thrown back to reveal strange leather clothing. Ornately tooled and trimmed with silver, it hugged a lean frame.

*No*, some instinct decided, not lean but *lithe.* Lithe like a big cat, all coiled agility and snake-strike muscle in a deceptively relaxed package. She was forced to tilt her head to see the strong jaw that underscored the man's angular face—and beneath it, the silvery scar that ran diagonally across his throat from beneath his left ear until it disappeared into the right side of his collar. Far from being a blemish, however, the scar only added interest to otherwise perfect features. Less obvious was a strange *otherness* to his appearance that she felt rather than saw. Human, yet decidedly *not.* And no human she knew boasted hair like that. Pulled into a thick braid that fell halfway down his back, it was white in the way that snow was white—not a single shade but many.

She had to remind herself to breathe. This was no lost cosplay enthusiast or a *Lord of the Rings* extra but an actual living, breathing member of the faery race. Somewhere in the back of her mind, a faint thought protested that such a thing was completely impossible. It wasn't very convincing, however, with a flesh-and-blood dog the size of a goddamn Volkswagen already in front of her.

The man's pale hair glowed in the fire's light. A fistful of loose strands fell across his face, and beneath them his eyes were watchful, alert. A panther scanning for prey.

And he had found *her.*

# SIX

The stranger's unnerving gaze lingered for only a moment before apparently dismissing her. "What are you doing here?" he asked again, and Lissy realized he spoke to the enormous canine behind her.

"Wait a sec. This is your dog? Yours?" All the shock and fear of the past few minutes transmuted into anger. She'd been prepared to die defending her child, and *this* man, this *being*, was responsible! It was as if a switch inside had been thrown, and she stepped into his line of sight. "What the hell were you thinking, letting this animal run around loose like that?" she demanded.

He merely looked around her, as if she were a tree or a bush or a goddamn *rock*, and that just ramped up her fury. "You! I'm talking to you!" Without thought but backed by a considerable amount of adrenaline, she shoved him with all her strength. The element of surprise gave her an extra advantage, and the tall man stumbled back a step.

*Now* she had his full attention.

Most nature documentaries she'd watched advised against locking stares with wild animals, yet Lissy stood her ground and met the stranger's riveting gaze boldly—despite her resentment at having to look up to do it. She all but bared her teeth as she stated her case: "You. Endangered. My. Son."

"There was no danger to your offspring. The hound does not devour mortals."

Was he mocking her with that imperious tone? "Yeah, well, *us mortals* had no way of knowing that your monster dog doesn't snack on humans. You have no right to frighten people like that!"

"I require no rights from you. I ride with the Hunt."

Her gaze flicked to a faint ripple of movement at his side. The heavy cloak drew aside as if by its own volition, and the fae's hand casually rested on the handle of a large coil of plaited leather at his hip. Ghostly tongues of bluish light flickered continually over the heavy whip, here then gone in an instant only to reappear in a different spot, as if they were living things.

Lissy could hear some gasps from her cluster of friends and some hurried words between Morgan and Brooke. Though she'd never encountered the Wild Hunt herself, she knew that had to be what the stranger referred to. As a mere human, she should be utterly terrified.

Instead, she couldn't care less if he were a unicorn. "Well, I require a goddamn apology from you, mister," she heard herself say, and folded her arms to wait.

Brooke was at her elbow immediately, whispering urgently in her ear. "Come on, let's go. We should just let this *fae*"—obviously she emphasized the word in case Lissy hadn't clued in to the stranger's species—"take his pet and leave."

"He's not a pet!" The indignant voice came from Fox, who still clung to the dog like a limpet, although Sharon and Katie were working hard to coax him away without triggering a nuclear incident. "He's his *brother*."

The bizarre statement was enough to make Lissy decide in favor of Brooke's advice then and there. Before she could even take a step, however, the tall fae loomed over her son. His otherworldly features were still as emotionless as a mask, but his tone was clearly that of someone accustomed to being obeyed. "Tell me why you say that!"

"Hey, you don't get to question him!" she shouted, trying to break the combined death grip of Morgan, Sharon, and Brooke. Her friends had hold of her arms as if she were about to leap into an active volcano. "He's a *minor*! He's just a little boy!"

Her son showed no fear, however. The fae and the child regarded each other, oblivious to her or anyone else. "Because Braith told me," Fox said with a shrug, then paused. "He says to tell you that he hasn't forgotten who you are." He eyed the tall being curiously from head to toe. "If he's really your brother, dude, why would he forget you? And how come he's a dog? Can I have a dog for a brother? I like dogs. Do *you* like dogs?"

The towering faery was silent. Although his expression betrayed nothing, Lissy got the impression that he honestly didn't know *how* to respond. And she'd bet money that he'd never been called *dude* in his entire life! *Welcome to my world*, she thought wryly. Since Fox had first latched on to the word, she'd seldom been called *Mom* since. The lack of response from the fae didn't discourage her son one bit, however. Fox only talked when he felt like it, but once he got started, there was no stopping him.

"Braith is a way cool name. I like the way it feels when I say it. Braith. *Braith.* Do you have a cool name, too? What is it?" he asked. Without waiting for an answer, he added, "My name is—"

"Time for bedtime snacks!" Brooke shouted, startling everyone into looking at her. Her attention was solely on Lissy's son, however. "I have peanut butter cookies in my backpack just for you, bud." Ignoring the tall stranger completely, Brooke walked over to the child with her hand outstretched. "Do you want to eat them in your tent or go home and eat them at your house? You tell me which idea you like better."

"With milk in a blue glass?"

"Absolutely."

Fox addressed the giant dog. "You can be my friend, Braith. I gotta go now." He looked up at Brooke. "Can my friend have some cookies, too?"

"He doesn't eat . . . *cuhk-eez*," the fae said stiffly, but the child no longer listened to him.

"Sharing is a kind thing to do," Brooke said to Fox. "But human treats aren't very good for dogs. My cats can't eat them, either. Do you know it gives them a stomachache? Rory got into a bag of Oreos once, and I had to rush him to Morgan's clinic." As she continued talking about her cats, Fox allowed himself to be led away in the direction of the main parking lot. Lissy's friends immediately closed ranks around him like an armed escort. Tina walked backward behind them, still clasping the tree limb in both hands, as watchful as if they were in a combat zone. Even Jake finally released his bulldog hold on the giant dog to race after the group—but not before trotting over to dribble a few drops of urine on the tall fae's boot. Luckily the man didn't look down . . .

Silently blessing her friends for protecting her child, Lissy knew she should follow. But the longer she could keep the guy's attention firmly on her, the longer the others would have to escape. Besides, she had unfinished business with this being. As he turned the full force of his awareness to her, however, she suddenly couldn't remember what she wanted from him. Instead, her thoughts tumbled into a wild flood of questions. Like why couldn't she figure out the color of his eyes? One moment they seemed green, the next, gold, and the next, a hue she had no words for. Maybe the firelight distorted her perceptions. But she couldn't even decide how old the guy was. His ethereal face was as young as her own, but there was an aura of years about him. It was like looking at a mountain, unable to fathom the eons that had shaped it.

"Your friend was wise to guard your son's name," he said. "Such a young adept must be protected. What *ddewin* is charged with his training?"

*What?* Her brain snapped back into the here and now. "He goes to school just like any other kid. And you still owe me an apology, mister."

"The child is untrained?"

"For your information, he's perfectly well behaved most of the time!"

The fae shook his head, and his white hair now curtained one eye. It didn't reduce the intensity of his gaze, however. A lesser woman might have withered under such scrutiny, but Lissy returned the look in kind, with a healthy dose of *fuck you* for good measure.

It probably wasn't a smart thing to do. After all, faeries were dangerous, not to be trusted. Her brother's words came back to her: *They don't think like we do,* hermanita. *They don't perceive right and wrong like we do.*

*So why am I still standing here?* Like a bird before a snake, she might have been paralyzed by some strange hypnosis. Yet she remained completely free to look away or walk away. Of one thing she was certain: the fae had no power over her only because he chose not to exert it. *I shouldn't be taking chances like this. I don't really give a damn if he apologizes or not, as long as Fox is safe.* Some strange impulse urged her to persist, however. A feeling. A vibe.

Like a wave building, building, then suddenly breaking on the shoreline, *there it was*: a recognition—no, a *connection*, as if some rarefied energy now flowed between them. She dared not take her eyes off the stranger in case he disappeared. And the longer Lissy looked, the more she wanted to see. The more she *could* see.

She saw surprise.

There was no hint in his face, not a single tell that even a consummate poker player would discern. And yet she perceived a spark of disbelief in his alien eyes.

The moment ended as abruptly as if he'd slammed a door in her face. Whatever she'd witnessed in his gaze vanished beneath a frown.

Nope, that was definitely a scowl. *Are you trying to intimidate me?* she wondered.

*I would not presume to try.*

*Hey!* While she was still trying to process that he had just spoken to her in her head—had, in fact, heard her thoughts and responded in kind—he reached out to place a hand on the dog. Both vanished from her sight.

Lissy sat down abruptly. All the strength was gone from her body, and spots bounced before her eyes as if she'd stared directly into a camera flash. *So much for close encounters of the fae kind. Ugh!* She'd probably never see him again (and good riddance) but she was left with the most ridiculous sense of loss over a perfect stranger. *Emphasis on the perfect.* If she hadn't been so damn mad, she would have enjoyed the view. Maybe it was the sudden withdrawal of that strange momentary connection, but she found herself wishing she'd at least gotten his name . . . even though she felt lucky to remember her own.

*Trahern.* It was the same voice in her mind, *his* voice. Quiet with an undercurrent of power, as if it was being deliberately reined in or toned down for her benefit. *My name is Trahern.*

Her lips tried to form the strange name but couldn't—

"Lissy!" Another voice suddenly shouted way too close for comfort. "Earth to Lissy!" Sharon and Katie were hovering over her. As soon as they got her attention, each took an arm and hauled her to her feet, then half hurried, half dragged her in the direction Brooke had taken Fox.

"Are you okay?" asked Sharon, without slowing for a moment.

"Just tired," was all she could force out. Her entire body felt like a wet noodle, and she only managed one step for every three or four of theirs.

"Adrenaline dump, I'll bet."

"Could be magic, too," said Katie. "Do you think he put a spell on her?"

"Brooke will know—*hey!*"

Far across the park, an eerie ball of green light blazed to life at the base of The Castle, illuminating it with an undulating glow as if the Northern Lights had fallen into the canyon and tangled around the rocky spires. Strange shapes moved in the heart of the emerald sphere, as it moved quickly toward the glittering falls. Lissy squinted to identify them from this distance.

"Holy crap, is that a *horse*?" asked Sharon.

Not only a horse but a rider—*and a hound*. "It's that damn fae and his big-ass dog," said Lissy. "What the hell are they doing up there?"

She yelled in surprise as the vivid light abruptly hurled itself over the falls like a falling star to plunge silently into the depths of the immense pool two hundred feet below. *No splash and no sound. Like watching a ghost performing a high dive.* She sank to the grass again, and this time her friends sat down with her, just as Brooke ran up to them, with her husband not far behind.

"Did you see that? Did you *see* that? I'll bet the water is another portal to the faery realm!"

Lissy didn't give a damn about portals. Exhausted, she only wanted to know one thing. "Where's Fox?"

"Sitting beside Rhys, full of cookies and milk, and wanting to know when he can see the giant dog again," Aidan said, then grinned. "Plus the lad insists you owe two dollars to the swear jar."

Yeah, she did. She'd have to pay up, too. Once he accepted a rule, Fox was fanatical about it—the fact that his mother had been scared out of her mind over his safety notwithstanding.

"Anyone have change for a five?"

~

Trahern emerged in Tir Hardd with Cyflym at full gallop. Though he reined the horse to a walk, there was no slowing of his own thoughts. He stole a glance at Braith, trotting along in his usual position, to the right and just behind Trahern's stirrup. He seemed relaxed enough. *Certainly more so than I am at this moment.* The mortal boy's revelation had been staggering. Braith's essence, that which made him who he was, still lingered in his canine shell. *I should be happy for this.* Instead, Trahern was nearly overcome at the horror of it, the idea of not only being a captive in the body of a beast but incapable of expression, of words. *A prisoner now more than ever.*

Worse, Trahern had assumed his brother was lost to him, that he had become fully *dog*. A loyal enough companion but constrained and bound by its nature. Now he knew differently. Braith still thought, still remembered, still—what? *Does he despair of an end to his imprisonment? Does he miss Saffir?*

No doubt he missed real conversation and needed to hear of Trahern's thoughts, since he could no longer touch them . . .

He slid from the saddle and knelt before the great grim, pulling the massive blue-gray head against him and rubbing the soft velvety ears. "Forgive me, my brother. I knew not that you yet suffered. I have said so little to you, addressed you so seldom. I have treated you as a true hound, unaware that you were still . . ." Words failed him. Braith's condition was as a dagger in his heart, and the weight on his shoulders threatened to crush him. The dog wagged its tail, however, and rolled playfully to look up at him, its thick lips falling back to expose enormous teeth grinning foolishly.

"I will yet find a way to free you," Trahern whispered. "I swear it." He sat for a very long time with his arms around the dog's neck. *Just as the boy did*, he thought at last, and allowed himself to consider the strength of the child's gift—and the strength of his mother.

She *shone*, her aura bright as flame. Different in every way from the females of the Tylwyth Teg. They were far taller than she, slender and pale like winter saplings, with silken hair the color of ice and eyes that glittered with many secrets. The human woman had long hair, too, but it was richly colored, the dark curls cascading over her shoulders. There was a golden cast to her skin, as if the sun had warmed it, and her eyes were the deepest brown, nearly black—

Those sable eyes had all but sparked with fury, too. She'd been as fierce as a female kelpie protecting her young as she challenged him. Had he ever witnessed the Tylwyth Teg personally safeguard *their* offspring, in word or deed? *Eirianwen would never have bothered . . .* Trahern rubbed a hand across his chest, recalling the feel of the mortal woman's palms when she'd dared to push him. Ordinarily, he would have thought the act foolish, certainly insulting, but found himself unable to do so. She'd been utterly committed to defending her son despite the odds, and for that Trahern could only admire her courage.

It was a new feeling. He'd never observed any mortal worthy of admiration before. Of course, the Wild Hunt only rode down the guilty. Betrayers and offenders all, they usually succumbed easily to fear, their pleadings cut off quickly by the crack of a light whip as they were condemned to join the host that trailed after the Hunt. Even in Lurien's absence, Trahern only pronounced judgment on them—he certainly didn't converse with them! The jarring mix of colors in their aura told him all he needed to know about them. In fact, he had never deigned to make the acquaintance of any mortal, though he rode through their realm almost nightly.

Braith's long-ago words suddenly replayed in his mind: *Though their lives are short—or perhaps* because *their lives are short—humans possess many worthwhile attributes that the Tylwyth Teg have all but forgotten.* His brother couldn't have meant the pathetic beings who the Hunt stole away. Was it possible there were others like the boy and his brave mother?

*I gave her my true name.* Trahern had no idea why he'd done so, except it seemed appropriate. *Names possess power.* In the traditions of his kind, to volunteer one's name to a stranger was a gift. But the human female likely had no concept of the honor he'd paid her.

Dismounting, he led his horse inside the newly created stone stables—the first of their kind in Tir Hardd and lighter and airier than the ones in the old palace—with Braith following amiably behind. Trahern waved away the pyskies who offered their help. He usually preferred to see to his horse's needs with his own hands. And if he was honest with himself, he wanted to be alone so he could think more about the woman he'd met.

*I don't have* her *name.*

It shouldn't matter to him. After all, he would probably never encounter her again . . . but he found that he didn't like that idea at all. Something else bothered him just as much. *The boy is not trained.* The mother's aura had truly shone with fire, but the child's aura was an entire universe of swirling magics. Power had come to rest upon him, had chosen him, as it had once chosen Trahern. Ancient stories spoke of some mortals who could wield magic as ably as any fae. A few were said to still walk the earth. But he'd never met any until now.

There had been other women with the boy's mother. Three had been openly admiring of Trahern, and all of them had whispered to each other about his physical attributes without realizing he could hear them easily—though there were a few things he didn't understand. *What exactly is a hunk? And who is Legolas?*

Of them all, however, only the clever woman with the short black hair, the one who had led the child away, was a practitioner of magics. Her clear-blue aura pronounced her a healer much like Saffir, and much skilled, but she was not powerful enough to train the boy. Of that, Trahern was certain. And the child's fierce mother? She was astonishingly perceptive as well as brave. No one, not even his twin, had ever stared into Trahern's eyes and truly seen him when he did not wish to be seen. It had shocked him to the core that a *human* could look past his defenses as if they didn't exist! Still, although her aura was vivid, it showed only a modest amount of magic. And without enough magic herself, she might be unaware of the dangerous potential her son possessed.

*Something must be done.* Trahern had trained the occasional student, but never a mortal one, of course—

The silver pail dropped from his hands, scattering moon-gathered marsh grain across the stone floor, as he realized just what it was he considered. *I am of the Hunt! My loyalty and my responsibility lie with them alone*, he told himself sternly. Humans were of no concern to him, and it was best to put such foolish thoughts aside. A quick incantation caused the spilled grain to float upward in a lazy vortex and deposit itself neatly into the horse's feed bin. Cyflym nosed it curiously, then settled in to eat.

Annoyed with himself, Trahern turned on his heel and stalked out of the stable. His usual habit was to spend his time experimenting with spells for Braith's sake, but the evening's events called for a visit to a coblyn tavern. The noise and the brew would be equally potent there, and with luck, he might be able to drive all thoughts of the woman and her gifted son from his brain for a time.

The gardens outside the stable were half-wild, filled with scarlet flowers on towering stems. Brilliant butterflies hovered among them, glinting like jewels. The air was redolent with sweet nectars, and a cool breeze carried the scent of distant petrichor. Perhaps the tavern could wait. *Braith might well prefer a companionable walk to an earful of coblyn chatter.* Trahern turned to speak to his brother—

But the great dog was nowhere to be seen.

# SEVEN

Although there'd been some talk of driving home last night after the unexpected visit from the fae and his canine companion, it was short-lived. Brooke had phoned Aidan and Rhys at their camp down the road, and the guys had come on the run. Both were big, heavily muscled men who looked like they could tear a fae in two like a phone book. They'd be glad to do it, too. Furious that their wives and friends had been frightened, they volunteered to keep watch for the rest of the night. In the end, everyone, even Lissy, felt solid about staying.

As for Fox, he wasn't frightened at all. Instead, he'd fallen asleep in his pup tent with his little fingers crossed that the giant dog would come back. Lissy wished she could fit in there to cuddle him for the rest of the night, but he never seemed to enjoy sleeping with her. *You know I have to sleep* straight. *You take up too much room, and then I have to curl up like a snail*, he'd once told her.

"I'll be sitting right outside the boy's door till morning," Rhys assured her. "And by all the gods, no one and nothing will come near him. You get some sleep yourself now. Sharon and Katie will be cooking their special pancakes in the morning, and you won't want to be missing that."

*Trust a man to know what's really important.* She laughed and went to Tina's tent, where Jake was already snoring loudly on Tina's cot.

"You all right?" her friend asked over the buzz-saw noise.

"Yeah. It was just a surprise, that's all. I never expected to bump into a real live fae, never mind a dog the size of an elephant."

"You handled yourself really well—and so did Fox. He's not even upset!"

"You're right," agreed Lissy. "Out of all of us, it should have been scariest for him. But he *did* handle it." *Like a champ, too.* She fell asleep on that hopeful note and wakened refreshed to a bright, sunny morning.

Fox was in rare form, far more outgoing than he'd been the night before. He sought out Rhys and insisted on showing him all the trails, then played a string game with Aidan. He showed Morgan and Tina the beautiful crystals from Brooke's box, naming each one for them. Sharon and Katie had indeed made their famous mile-high pancakes topped with fresh strawberries, whipped cream, and chocolate curls, and Fox declared them *pretty okay*. High praise indeed from a child whose world could crumble if his toast wasn't cut into perfect triangles!

With her son busy and happy, Lissy decided she couldn't wait any longer. Quickly, she pulled Brooke aside and told her about the blue chairs incident. "The whole waiting room had been completely redesigned. New paint, new artwork, and new furniture—and every chair was just as Fox said it would be, just the way he'd drawn them."

"Wow, big change. How did he react to it?"

Lissy wasn't surprised by Brooke's total acceptance of Fox's apparent clairvoyance. *Of course she would look right past that.* But her friend's question was a good one. "That's the other strange thing. He didn't react. Not at all. He just sat in one of the new chairs and played with his video game as if nothing was different. And that's not the only time this has happened. In fact, these past few nights he's been dreaming about a big dog and *a man with long white hair*! And look what happened last night!"

Brooke grabbed her shoulders firmly. "Okay, first off, don't panic. Lots of people have precognition to one degree or another and lead perfectly normal lives. Like yourself, for instance. You still have dreams sometimes, don't you? And feelings in advance of things. What would it hurt if Fox had those, too?"

"If he did, it might well be a good thing," added Aidan, gliding seamlessly into the conversation. He carried a heaping plate of pancakes and a couple of extra forks, which he pushed into the center of the table before taking a seat. "Our Fox isn't fond of surprises. A little warning might be a great favor to the lad."

Lissy turned that over in her mind. "You know, I hadn't even thought of that. Getting a heads-up on stuff *could* be pretty positive for Fox. I've just been scared that he might get the entire *Santiago* gift, all of it, and he—we—oh, hell, *none of us* needs any more things to worry about."

Brooke patted her arm while deftly stealing a finger of whipped cream and chocolate from the topmost pancake. "I totally agree; you sure don't need the stress of wondering if Fox is going to be a full-fledged *brujo*. But your mother hasn't said anything like that, has she?"

"I'm wondering if Mama's been hinting, and I just haven't wanted to hear it. She keeps saying he has *strong gifts*."

"Well, for one thing, she's a very proud grandmother. And *gifts* could mean a lot of things. He's über-smart, he's artistic, he has an affinity for rocks. And what about his way with animals? They all love him, even that humongous faery dog last night."

"Aye, I wish Fox had been with *me* yesterday. I had a wild beast at the forge that needed taming." Aidan held out his left hand. Thick gauze engulfed his thumb and first two fingers from the very tips of them all the way down to his wrist. Duct tape held the generous dressing together.

"Omigod, I didn't even notice that. Did those raccoons come back again?" An entire family of them had moved into Aidan's blacksmith shop one winter. They'd been chased out but made regular attempts to reclaim the building ever since.

"'Twas no raccoon did this. Tina came by to pick up a few things for the camp and brought her little dog along. I reached down to pat him and near to lost my hand. Couldn't get the little *ddraig* off."

The big man was from Wales, and Lissy knew that *ddraig* meant "dragon." *It suits Jake to a T. Especially if dragons have bulldog tendencies.*

Brooke leaned over to her. "Aidan finally had to dunk him in the water barrel in self-defense."

"It cools off red-hot metal, so I thought it might do the same for Jake." He shrugged. "He let go quick enough then. That's why I wish Fox had been there. He sweetens the bitty devil's temper considerably."

"And anyone who can do that *definitely* has a gift!" Brooke laughed.

"Amen to that." Lissy smiled, but her mind was still full of questions. "But Fox seemed to be able to talk to that big dog last night. *Really* talk. And he said that Jake tells him stuff."

"We've seen him do that with the cats. I'm sure they really *are* communicating, but again, it's more normal than you think. Remember that animal psychic who helps at Morgan's clinic now and then? It's just not major wizardry, hon. Besides, where's the downside? Some kids have to be taught to be kind to animals and considerate of their needs. Fox has that naturally. You know he has a big heart."

Brooke's words made sense. "I guess you're right. I'm probably just overreacting," she said. "But that faery last night seemed to think there was something special about him, especially after Fox said that weird thing about the dog being the guy's brother."

Her friends exchanged looks, and it was Aidan who answered. "I have reason to know that grims are not always what they seem. And this dog may not be a true grim, but he is no ordinary dog, either. It's possible he's a man under enchantment."

"You mean he really could be that fae's brother?" Lissy frowned. "But how on earth would Fox know a thing like that? You didn't know. I didn't know. Nobody did, just Fox. And after you took him away, he—the faery—called Fox a *young adept* and asked me who was in charge of his training."

Now it was her friend's turn to frown. Behind her, Aidan growled. "'Tis seldom a good thing when the fae take notice of a child. Lucky for us, this one rides with the Wild Hunt."

"And you trust those guys?"

"I do not trust the Tylwyth Teg, but Lord Lurien has his own sense of honor. I trust his word," explained Aidan. "As for his Hunters, they are dangerous—and they know it. They have no need or desire to prove their strength by preying on the innocent. During those months I rode with them, they never once strayed from their purpose."

"Okay, I'll bite. What the heck *is* their purpose, besides scaring people with big dogs?"

"I don't fully understand how they do it," said Brooke, "but the Wild Hunt keeps the balance between our worlds." Her husband nodded.

*So the guy I met has a mysterious but important job. Like a superhero or something.* Lissy looked at Aidan thoughtfully. "Would you have recognized the faery who was here?"

"Maybe, maybe not. It was a few years ago now, and Lurien was trying to patrol two places with not enough men, plus serving as the Queen's Right Hand at the same time. Only a handful of his riders were on this side of the waters. 'Tis why he had need of my service."

"Did you ever ride *here*? In the park?"

"Never. I've not seen the Hunt in this place or I wouldn't have allowed my woman and my friends to camp here—"

A look from his wife had him backpedaling somewhat. "I mean, I would have *expressed concern* about the location." His brow furrowed deeply, and he stuffed half a pancake into his mouth.

"What my caveman hubby means," said Brooke, "is if that great dog hadn't been attracted to our Fox, he's certain you'd never have seen a Tylwyth Teg here at all."

"Yeah, but we *did* see him," said Lissy. "All of us. I thought that only certain people could see the fae."

"Only certain people can peer through their *magic*," Aidan explained with his mouth full. "That's a rare gift. As for the rest of us, once the fae have revealed themselves to you, they can't ever hide from you again."

"Revealed themselves? I don't think the dog was interested in hiding at all! And as for his owner, he didn't seem to give a damn what we saw. Like it didn't matter, because we were mere humans, or maybe peasants, and not worth the effort." In fact, the fae's regal attitude *still* grated on her. "I want to know why the dog was so interested in Fox in the first place."

The big man shrugged and swallowed his pancake at last. "Simple curiosity, I imagine. There's little that's novel or new to creatures as ancient as the mountains themselves."

"That tall guy I spoke to didn't look any older than me."

"They don't age as we do. Their queen is among the oldest of all, and yet her beauty would break your dear heart in two," said Aidan. "Ask Morgan. Gwenhidw yet visits her from time to time."

"I'll do that," she said. *But not today.* Right now, she wanted nothing more than to keep enjoying an exceptionally good day with her friends and her son and not give another thought to faery *anything*.

If only she knew how to get that exquisite male face out of her mind. And if only her mind would stop trying to remember how to say his name . . .

~

The dog was in his room. Not the small, pale image that the moon sometimes showed him, but the real thing—and the animal looked even larger in Fox's small bedroom than in the wide-open air of the campground. He reached up and rubbed its wrinkly muzzle. "You're too big for my bed," said Fox. "But you can lie next to it on the rug and put your head up here. Not on my pillow, though. Okay? And dude, do *not* lick Squishy Bear." The dog said something inside his head. It was just like talking with Jake or with Auntie Brooke's cats, only they didn't use as many words as Braith did. "You don't use pillows or blankets or *anything*? That must suck. I can't sleep without my pillow."

The great animal made himself as small as possible beside the bed and rested his chin on the edge. "I can read you a story," said Fox. "I've got lots of good books. *Sky Raiders, The Hunt for the Secret Papyrus, Captain Underpants, Diary of a Wimpy Kid* . . ." What would a magical dog from the faery world be interested in? "I know! I've got one about brownies and stuff. It's kind of a baby book, 'cause Auntie Morgan gave it to me when I was really little. But it's still pretty good."

The dog inclined his big head.

"Thermin Nodkin was a brownie . . ."

Lissy put away the last of the camping supplies, stuffed a load of laundry in the washer (after checking all pockets thoroughly for more rock "specimens"), and cleaned up the kitchen. Despite the strange events of the night before, today had truly been one of Fox's best. Though he'd been a little wound up, he was far more social than she'd ever seen him. It took a toll on his energy, of course, and before lunchtime he'd retreated to his tent to look at rocks again with Squishy Bear and Jake and ended up falling asleep in a heap with both.

When her son woke up, however, he'd wanted to go home right away. Lissy understood. Fox had had enough stimulation for one day and needed to *return to base*. She didn't mind. She was so damn proud of this rare social success; plus she'd gotten the chance to have an unhurried visit with all her friends. Had that *ever* happened? It didn't mean her son would never get overwhelmed in a grocery store again, but it did mean that he was developing skills, and sometimes those skills actually worked.

Closing the door on the dishwasher, she turned the dial to "On" and let it hum. She was tired, but she never minded the mundane tasks at night after Fox had gone to bed. It was quiet then, the chores required no brain cells, and it helped her unwind before she sat down to go over her lessons or mark papers. Tonight, however, there were no more papers to mark, and she had a respite from lesson prep for a whole two months . . .

The idea of having so much unscheduled time was mind-boggling. *I've been so busy; I haven't given much thought to what to do this summer. Or even what I'd* like *to do.* She was going to wake up Monday morning with no particular agenda. That would be a treat for a few days, just hanging out with her son and puttering around her little townhouse.

Not many staff members needed a place to live, but still, the residences had a waiting list, and she was lucky to have gotten one of the newer ones just before Fox turned four. He'd resisted the change, of course, as he resisted all changes. In fact, it had taken three whole months to persuade him to sleep overnight in the place! But Lissy had no intention of living with her mother for the rest of her life, and the townhouse was not only right on the campus where she worked, it was only three blocks from where Fox would attend preschool and kindergarten, and four blocks from grade school.

As for herself, she loved the bright open kitchen and the modern colors she'd chosen for the walls (with a nod to Fox's preference for citrus green). With all this time on her hands, she could organize her office (a job that seemed to need doing on a regular basis), maybe rearrange her bedroom. She might even shop for a piece of art to hang over the sleek fireplace . . .

In other words, she had about a week's worth of projects and two months to do them in. Plus, in mid-July, Fox was enrolled in a three-week-long day camp for Asperger's kids. Assuming she could persuade him to attend—she'd been talking about it with him for months so he'd be as prepared as possible—what on earth was she going to do while he was gone?

Lissy plopped onto the couch, stunned to discover that she had absolutely *no frickin' idea.* She adored her son and her career, but it had been necessary to focus on them to the exclusion of everything else. Hadn't it? *Omigod, maybe Mama had a point. Guess I need to get reacquainted with Lissy Santiago-Callahan and see if I can remember who she is. It wouldn't hurt to expand my horizons a bit.* Of course, the little voice in her head argued that as soon as August came, those horizons would once again close in as she fell into the familiar teaching-parenting loop. Fox was getting older, sure, learning and growing. Just look at today's unprecedented success! But he was still going to need a great deal of her time and coaching.

*I'm just going to be grateful for this summer and make the most of it. For both of us.*

Looking down at her hands and clothes, Lissy decided right then and there to have a long, leisurely hot bath. *Maybe even with candles and bubbles, like they do in the magazines.* She had a gift pack from a couple of Christmases ago that she'd never used, but hey, Mama said it was time to do something nice for herself, right? If she'd had any wine in the house, she might have poured a glass of that, too, just for the hell of it. *Oh, well, next time. For now, we soak!*

# EIGHT

The stiffly manicured grounds and unimaginative landscaping offered little cover, but a minor enchantment easily camouflaged Trahern and his horse. He stood leaning against Cyflym as he studied the upstairs windows of the strange little row houses. Truth be told, he was disappointed that the woman and her son lived in such a place. The idea of dwelling so close to others repelled him. It was like a pysky colony, only these buildings were unnaturally angular and lacking in any adornment whatsoever. Beauty was an essential ingredient in every structure in the fae realms. Did these humans lack an appreciation of it? *Other* humans, he corrected himself. Because while most of the covered entrances were bare or cluttered with dull furniture, there was a definite acknowledgment of nature by the woman's door: many vibrant flowers growing in colorful pots; a clever copper wind chime that struck pleasing notes in the breeze; a tray of seeds on the railing to attract birds; and along the front of the porch, beneath silvery green bushes, a half dozen red-capped figurines that reminded him of the coblynau at the tavern. He scrutinized them with a frown, sensing a strange energy. A sudden discordant gliss from the wind chime prickled the hair on the back of his neck. A charm of some sort was at work here, but it wasn't fae in origin. In fact, it seemed designed to *repel* fae. It might have worked, too, had Trahern been a lesser sorcerer.

*It will not keep me from my brother.*

With a finger, he drew a small circle in the air and peered through it like a glass. The spell allowed him to scan the second floor without the impediment of walls. *There!* The woman was in one tiny room, the boy in another, separated by an absurdly short hallway. And just as Trahern had suspected, Braith was with the boy.

Why?

The child was speaking—had he somehow spelled Braith to come to him and compelled him to stay? *He might be untrained yet still have discovered how to do a few such things on his own.* Gathering molecules of air with his fingers, Trahern quickly shaped a transparent seashell, broke it in half, and sent one part drifting upward to the boy's open window. The other he pressed to his ear.

"The bad mice chewed through the walls made of sticks and carried away all the brownies' food for the winter. Everyone was angry with Thermin because his idea had not worked. 'Now we will starve,' they said. 'And it is all your fault. We should never have listened to you . . .'"

Trahern frowned. What kind of spell was this? *"Drawsleoli!"* he shouted. Instantly, he appeared in the room, fully prepared to wrest control of his brother's mind from this young *ddewin*, this *sorcerer*—

The fair-haired child sat cross-legged on his bed with a small book. Trahern snatched it away from him at once, only to find his arm abruptly clamped inside an impressive set of teeth. His brother glared at him with bright golden eyes.

"Hey, dude, give it back!" said the boy. "Braith and I are still reading."

The great dog increased the pressure, but Trahern was determined. He inspected the small volume, awkwardly turning a few of the pages with his free hand.

"It is just a tale," he said at last.

"You mean like a story? Yeah, it's my favorite. Well, it used to be when I was a kid. I can read it to you, too, if you want."

"I—I thought you were casting a spell on my brother."

"Dude, why would I want to do that?"

The boy looked at him as if he were the seventh kind of idiot. Not only was that a new experience for Trahern, he even *felt* like an idiot. "It seems that I judged in haste." Carefully, he presented the book to the child, and the dog's massive jaws released his arm with a disgusted chuff. Braith resumed his position by the bed without another glance at his brother.

"You made me lose my place. I hate it when I lose my place!" Suddenly frantic, the boy leafed through the pages until Braith nosed his small elbow. "I know, I *know*. The mice ate the stick walls, but I can't find the page. I can't find it!" He shoved the book back at Trahern. "*You* find it!"

There had been a time when he obeyed the Matriarch of the House of Oak. Since then, his obedience was owed to the Lord of the Wild Hunt. Save for the commands of those two powerful individuals, no one had *ever* given him orders in his entire life. They would not have dared.

Were all children like this?

Trahern sat gingerly on the edge of the small bed and leafed through the little book. The illustrations were cleverly done, but the artist had obviously never seen a true brownie. It didn't seem like a good time to mention that, however. Instead, he quickly scanned the story until he found the phrase he'd overheard. "Here it is."

The book was yanked from his hands, and the boy made a show of getting comfortable. "You should sit over *there*," he said at last, and pointed at a chair in the corner. "I don't like people on my bed. It squishes the mattress in the wrong places."

Trahern got up at once. It was like rising from a pool, the boy and the dog flowing back into their former positions like so much water. The reading of the tale continued as if he'd never entered the room.

He'd been *dismissed*. By a *child*.

Declining to sit as directed, Trahern stood by the window. The room was nothing but a tiny box, and the square glass pane likewise diminutive. A far cry from the spacious accommodations he was accustomed to. Even though he no longer lived as one of the House elite, as a Hunter he lacked for nothing, not even privacy. Perhaps the woman was poor? That might explain why she and her son lived like this . . .

The idea bothered him. Surely someone who shone as brightly as she did should have only the finest and loveliest of everything. Judging by the character of the mortals taken prisoner by the Wild Hunt, however, the human world was not so very different from the Nine Realms. The strong took the best for themselves, not only ignoring the needs of the weak but actively preying upon them.

At least the energy of the room was pleasing. The walls were the green of sprouting ferns. Most of the furnishings were natural wood, and while several shelves were devoted to books, others held many types of interesting stones. A large plant—a tree, really—stood in a corner, reaching from its bright clay pot to brush the ceiling with brand-new leaves and lending to the harmony of the small space. The only discordant items were tiny figures, strangely made of copper and twigs, standing in rows upon the small desk . . . Like the wind chime outside and the odd red-capped figures in the flower bed, there was something belligerent about them, almost hostile—

"And the brownies made Thermin their king, because he had saved them from the bad mice," the boy read. "And the bad mice were never seen again. The end." He closed the book, and the dog wagged his tail as if applauding.

"Let us be on our way, Braith. No doubt your young friend requires his sleep."

Raising his great head, his brother seemed somehow apologetic as he regarded Trahern for a long moment, then rested his chin on the edge of the bed again and closed his eyes.

"He doesn't want to go," said the boy, as if Trahern failed to understand the message.

*But . . . but he has always been with me.* They had lived their entire lives together. And after Braith's transformation, they had followed the Hunt together for centuries as mortals counted time. *How can he not wish to accompany me? I have done him no wrong—*

Except failed to find a cure for his curse. And if it hadn't been for this mortal child, Trahern would never have guessed that Braith's essence still existed, that he was yet aware of himself as a man trapped in a grim's body.

Perhaps Braith preferred the company of someone who could *hear* him, as Trahern had once heard him.

It was the boy's fault. Everything had been perfectly fine until *he* came along. Suddenly incensed, Trahern strode down the hallway and flung open the woman's door. "This must stop at once! Your son is unduly influencing—"

She was naked. And wet. A hammerblow of arousal jolted his entire body, numbing his surprised brain until a solid blow to the head with a rubbery object on the end of a short stick announced that she was attacking him.

*"Get the hell out of my house!"* she yelled, swinging the strange club again. This time he ducked, but the confines of the ridiculously small room kept him from avoiding the blow completely. It glanced off his shoulder and bounced into the side of his face. Instinctively, he tried to retreat, to leave the way he had come, but the narrow door slammed shut behind him. It gave the woman a chance to bludgeon him squarely in the nose.

"I have no wish to harm you!" Trahern had barely succeeded in slapping the weapon away from her before she seized upon a heavy candle and bashed him repeatedly with it. As he fended off the blows, he finally regained his wits enough to use a spell—and the door momentarily dissolved into nothingness, spilling him into the hallway.

"Get out of my house!" she repeated, deftly yanking on a robe before snatching up a long-handled brush. The door solidified just in time for her to run smack into it.

*"Tylluan!"* hissed Trahern, and winged his way down the hallway as a great gray owl. It probably wasn't his best choice, considering the size of the window at the turn in the stairs—he had to perch awkwardly on the sill, gripping its frame with his talons so he could squeeze beneath the raised pane. But moments later, he was once again seated on his horse, watching unseen and listening intently as several humans burst from their homes and rushed to the woman's house.

"I'm really sorry for all the fuss. There was an animal upstairs. It surprised me, that's all."

Lissy sat on the couch with Fox, thankful that her son was apparently too deeply involved in a handheld video game to be bothered by the crowd. She wished she could be that detached. Campus police were searching the house, and assorted neighbors milled around the living room. Some—led by Claire Emsley from two doors down—even wandered through the kitchen and laundry room. *You'd think I was having an open house.* Of all the people Lissy would prefer not to have in her home, Claire topped the list. Did being an avid busybody make her a better teacher of information systems? The woman was all South Carolina sweetness on the outside, but she was known for making frequent complaints about her neighbors—including Lissy or, more correctly, *Fox*. The woman knew nothing about Asperger's Syndrome and appeared to have no desire to learn. Sighing inwardly, Lissy stuffed what she'd *really* like to say to Claire into a compartment in her head and nailed the door shut. "You know, I'm wondering if that creature got in through the window in the stairwell. I've been asking Maintenance to replace the screen on it ever since we moved in," she said, hoping the woman would take the bait.

Claire gave a knowing nod. "Everything's all catawampus over there ever since Ralph Oberhausen retired. The new manager could mess up a one-car funeral. Why, I had to phone three times last week just to get the paint on the front door touched up."

"Hmpf! I've been waiting for my damn air-conditioning to get fixed since last summer!" added a gray-haired man who lived in the end unit and was hardly ever seen. *Murray? Murphy?* All Lissy could remember was that he taught history.

"There now, you see?" Claire pointed a manicured finger. "And now our Melissa's been attacked by a wild animal. Why, any one of us could be next! We simply *must* take a petition to the residence board."

*It wasn't a wild animal; it was that damn faery from Palouse Falls.* When he surprised her in the bathroom, Lissy hadn't exactly had time to think about it. In retrospect, he'd seemed seriously pissed—although being beaten with a plunger may have had something to do with it.

A pair of uniformed men walked briskly down the stairs. "All clear, ma'am. Whatever it was, it must have gone out the same way it came in," said the older one. His name tag said HANSON. "We've had several young raccoons behind the main cafeteria lately, trying to get into the garbage, so they're definitely around. There's some fresh scratches on the window frame, and I noticed there's a downspout from the rain gutter right outside—it'd be an easy climb for them, and they're pretty curious."

"Make sure you keep your distance if you see another one," warned the other officer. "They look cute, but raccoons can inflict a nasty bite, and they also carry rabies."

Hanson nodded. "I'll make sure a copy of the report goes to Maintenance, and maybe it'll light a fire under their butts about that window screen."

"I'll cross my fingers it works." Lissy laughed. "Thanks so much for coming, all of you. I'm embarrassed it was something so silly, but it's good to know I have neighbors who would react if they thought there was a problem." *Even if one of them is Claire.*

"If the critter comes back, just call us," said Hanson, and saluted by touching his flashlight to his forehead.

When everyone had finally filed out, Lissy turned to regard Fox—and his brand-new *friend*. Not a single person had perceived the giant dog sitting quietly behind the couch, looming over her son like a protective lion. In fact, although the canine had seemed solid enough to Lissy's touch at Palouse Falls, Claire had walked right through the creature more than once. *Too bad she couldn't see it. Wouldn't* that *give her something to talk about?* Of course, the woman would probably waste no time filing a report on a "no pet" violation . . . The dog looked up at Lissy and grinned, exposing a flash of very large teeth even as his bath-towel tongue lolled out like a Labrador's.

"Dude! I didn't get to see the raccoon." Clad in his second-favorite pair of Scooby-Doo pajamas, Fox still didn't look up from his game. He should have reacted to the sudden influx of strangers and neighbors into the house. In fact, her routine-oriented son should have reacted, and *badly*, to the disruption of his bedtime routine—it was past eleven o'clock, after all. Instead, he focused solely on the game as if nothing else was amiss.

"There wasn't any raccoon, sweetie. All those good people came to help us because they thought we were in trouble—but I couldn't tell them about your big dog or his brother because they can't see them like we can." *And isn't that six kinds of weird?* "Besides, if I told them a faery man walked into my bathroom, they'd spend all night looking for him, and they'd never find him." Worse, they'd be looking at *her* like she needed serious help.

"Yeah. They wouldn't get any sleep," said Fox, continuing to play his game. "And they'd have a really bad day tomorrow." He understood because that was exactly what would happen to him. Except for the great blue-gray dog watching intently over his shoulder (and Lissy didn't know what the hell to do with the creature other than offer it a blanket and a steak), things seemed okay with him. She felt herself start to relax.

Until the tall fae appeared right in front of her—and he *still* looked pissed.

"You again! I told you to leave!" Lissy snatched up her cell phone from the coffee table and speed-dialed Brooke. "You have no business being in my home. I didn't invite you in here!"

"Of a surety, good lady, I have no wish to be here. Please instruct your child to release my brother."

*Pick up, Brooke, pick up!* "My child is not keeping your d—I mean, your *brother* here."

A sleepy voice sounded in her ear at last. "You okay, Liss?"

"I'm having a close encounter of the faery kind," said Lissy. "Guess who's in my living room right now?"

"What?" She could almost *hear* Brooke snap fully awake. "I'm on my way. Um—remember we talked once about hospitality being really important to the fae? Just treat him like a guest, and try to play nice till I get there."

*A guest?* Her house was being invaded and she was supposed to play frickin' *hostess*? Mentally, Lissy counted to ten, reminding herself that her best friend was the expert here. If Brooke had instructed her to sing karaoke or play Pictionary with the guy, Lissy would do it without question. *I just need to keep everyone calm so that Fox is safe, right?* That shouldn't be too hard. Didn't she already spend every day of her life trying to keep things on an even keel for her son's sake? Once she'd reframed the situation in her mind, the next step came easily.

"I'm sorry that I don't remember how to pronounce your name. But please come into the kitchen and sit down. It's silly for us to stand here being angry over something we don't know how to fix yet." Even as she said it, she realized it was true. The man clearly didn't want to be in her house any more than she wanted him to be there. A faint shiver in her core announced that at least part of her *very much* wanted him there . . . which was crazy and annoying, and she shut those feelings down at once. "My friend is coming over to try to help us," she said. "While we're waiting, I'm going to put on some tea and make up a snack for us."

Behind that veiled gaze was the flicker of surprise she'd seen once before. A moment later, he unfolded his arms and followed her.

# NINE

Unlike the rooms upstairs, the woman's kitchen was of a reasonable size—if you were a coblyn, that is. He approved of the pleasant wall color, though—green again, a vivid shade reminiscent of budding leaves. Open shelves displayed bright plates and bowls, and the windowsill boasted an assortment of colored glass bottles that would capture positive energies—even spirits—when daylight shone through them. Clear jars of spices and herbs marched along the back of the counter, like ingredients in an alchemist's study. An upright metal cabinet—*no*. He corrected himself. The cabinet was a human *machine*, a cold box for storing foods, and its bland surface was nearly covered with layers of her son's paper artwork—and one of the uppermost drawings boasted a gray dog with golden eyes very much like Braith.

The dog in the picture was smiling. *Smiling!* Trahern resisted the impulse to scowl.

Meanwhile, the woman motioned him to a rather plain chair. *At least it is made of wood, not metal.* Tracing the fine, clear grain of the tabletop with his finger helped him to center and calm himself in this cramped human habitation. But it wasn't the surroundings that were causing the near-constant hum of electricity beneath his skin, and he knew it. As she had issued her invitation, color had burned along her cheekbones, a natural ruddiness unbidden by magic.

Was the invitation for something more?

*I must say something.* He was being offered hospitality, an extremely rare thing from a mortal, and there were age-old courtesies to be observed. Basic manners, at the very least, but the eloquence that he'd once relied upon at Court had deserted him. "I am Trahern," he said at last, cursing himself for such an unoriginal beginning.

She tried to pronounce his name without success, and she laughed at herself. The sound was spontaneous and guileless, far from the practiced amusement of females of the Court. "I'm sorry," she said. "There's a sound in there that I'm not quite getting. Is it a Welsh name?"

"Not originally, although I hear it is sometimes used in Wales. Tra-*hern*."

"*Tra*, like in *trajectory*," she said. "I can hear the beginning just fine, but the end confuses me."

"The sound you are missing is much like *hair*." He seized a tendril of his own and held it up.

*"Hairn. TraHAIRN,"* she practiced. "Accent on the last syllable?"

He nodded, even as he thought it extremely odd that his name should sound so pleasing from a human tongue. There were other pleasing things about her as well. She was clothed now, but he would not forget what she looked like undressed. As she pulled plates and mugs from an upper shelf, the soft curves of her body fascinated him, beckoned to him . . . He shook his head to clear it and recovered his voice. "And your name, good lady?"

She stopped slicing bread and turned to study his face with those dark-brown eyes that bespoke intelligence and strength—and that saw entirely too much. "I've heard that names have power. Am I going to regret telling you?"

*Wise as well.* "I have already gifted you with my true name. Because of that, it is I who have given power to you in this situation."

She snorted at that. "It's not power if I don't know how to use it!"

*Very* wise. "If it sets your mind at rest, then I offer my oath that I will not harm you or your son in any way." Trahern didn't intend to say more, but the words sprang out unbidden: "Nor permit harm to come to you if I can help it."

"All right, then. My friends have told me that the fae keep their word, and I believe my friends." She appeared to take her time slicing the last of the bread, and he understood that she was giving him time to absorb that she didn't trust *him*, at least not yet. Finally, she set the bread on the table, along with a pot of butter. "My name is Melissa. But it's usually just Lissy for short."

"*Melissa* sounds much like our word for *sweetness*. But what is this short name?"

A plate of cheeses and apple slices joined the bread. "Don't you have nicknames in the faery world?"

He frowned. "I do not know this term."

"If a name is difficult or long, your friends and family might shorten it. I might call you *Tray*, for instance."

"Do not do that! You spoke the truth when you said that names have power. They should not be tampered with."

She didn't repeat it, but there was a mischievous quirk to her lips now. "You know, sometimes people pick out a feature or an attribute and make up an entirely *new* name for you. For instance, I have a student in my class whose name is Elizabeth Rose, but she's been known as *Deets* most of her life. It's because she's so detail oriented. Someone might look at that gorgeous white hair of yours and nickname you—"

"You are a teacher?" He seized on the chance to change the subject. The mere thought of name changing made him very uncomfortable. Did humans not realize the magical implications of such actions? Who knew how her life had already been affected by the alteration of her name?

"A teacher of science, yes. Geology and physics mostly."

Trahern buttered a slice of bread that was fairly bursting with interesting seeds and grains. "I have heard of this *geology*. You study the structure of the earth on the mortal plane?"

She frowned in puzzlement, and he decided he liked the way her forehead creased just *so* between her brows. "I study the earth. Period. All of it."

"Ah, but you cannot study all of it. You have not been to the Nine Realms, and human sciences would not make sense of it if you did." He waved the bread at her. "This is quite good."

"It's from this great organic bakery I found, but it must seem pretty plain to someone like you."

"I have dined on exotic fare." *In another life.* "But I have found that plain foods often satisfy better. This would make a fine meal after a hunt. What animals provided milk for the cheese?"

A teapot whistled, and she whisked it away from its heat source. "Dairy goats. My friends, Caris and Liam, keep a herd of about forty."

He nodded. "I have seen goats in your world. They are very tiny and tame compared to those that live in mine. In fact, one of our Hunters prefers a great black goat as his mount. It is as large as my horse." *And even more dangerous.* With six horns and red eyes, the creature bore closer resemblance to a demon than to the benign animal that grazed on mortal farms.

"A goat big enough to ride? Now that would be something to see!" She poured the steaming water into two large mugs and set one before him.

"Most who do see it, regret it. The Hunt usually reveals itself only to those who have betrayed human or fae laws." He sniffed his cup, studying the fragrance of the steeping herbs. "Rose hips. Chamomile and blackberry leaves. A flower—*hibiscus*, I believe it is called. A fruit of some kind and a single spice as well, but I do not know your names for them."

She picked up the box she'd taken the tea from and squinted at the words on it. "Orange peel and cardamom," she supplied. "But everything else is exactly right. That's a pretty good trick. How did you do it?"

"If you mean, did I use some form of deception or pretense, the answer is *no.* A sorcerer must be familiar with countless plants, in both worlds. I have often gathered ingredients from this realm to use in a spell or a potion." He didn't mention that they had been for Braith's sake. "The sage that grows in this area is especially potent for magic work."

"Spells and potions. Magic." A cloud passed over her fine features as she sat across from him. "That's what this is really about, isn't it? That's why you're here? There's some sort of magic attracting your dog to my son."

"He is my brother, not my dog."

Her hand flew to her mouth in an honest gesture that charmed him. "I'm so sorry that I keep saying that," she said. "Your *brother.* I didn't know he was in my son's room—I found him after you, uh, *left.*"

It had not been a dignified exit. Nor had it been a courteous entrance. "I did not give adequate consideration to my actions. I was intent on retrieving Braith."

She snorted. "Is that supposed to be an apology? Because it's not a very good one."

"I explained myself."

"Yeah, but you didn't get to the *I'm sorry* part. You know, for breaking into my house, violating my privacy, scaring the hell out of me, stuff like that?"

Growing up a prince of the House of Oak, he apologized to no one. Nor did he in his second life as a Hunter—not even when Lord

Lurien once inquired about his stolen horses. So why did he find himself wanting to say something more to this human woman? "I regret my intrusion," he managed at last, even as he was quite certain he didn't regret its outcome. The woman's company was undeniably pleasant . . .

"I guess that'll do. And I get that you were worried about your brother. If mine were in danger, I probably wouldn't be too polite, either. Is it okay to ask—I mean, is he under a spell or something?"

"You may ask," he said. Few had dared to. "Of a surety, his form has been changed by a curse."

"That's horrible. It must be very hard on both of you." She eyed him appraisingly. "Probably worse for you."

"Why do you say that?" It wasn't pity he saw in her expression but something he couldn't define. True emotions were hard to understand, never mind navigate—and in his experience, humans emoted a *lot*.

"Because if someone is hurt or has a problem, it's always harder for the people who care about them."

*It . . . has been difficult.* The thought caught him unguarded, but she did not press for more. Instead, Lissy moved away from the topic as if skimming over a wound. As if she knew there *was* a wound.

"Fox said his name is Braith. Am I saying that right?"

"Fox is your son?"

Her gaze snapped to his as she realized her mistake, and Trahern saw again the ferocity with which she would defend her child. After a moment, however, she nodded and relaxed.

"An auspicious name for a powerful sorcerer," he declared. "It will serve him well."

"He's not a sorcerer."

"Why do you say that?"

"Because he's not; he can't be. It—it just can't happen, that's all."

"But it has already happened. Can you not see the magic that surrounds him? I have never seen the like of his aura, not even in the Nine Realms. It is why I asked you who is charged with his training."

To his surprise, she paled considerably before dropping her head in her hands. "This is *so* not happening," she said, more to herself than to him.

"I do not understand your distress."

"No. No, you couldn't possibly understand. Magic is something you live with all the time in the faery world, but it's not so common here. Don't get me wrong, I know about magic. I've witnessed it my whole life because my family possesses a gift, but I didn't inherit much of it myself."

"As it did not fully come to Braith. Power chooses for itself upon whom it will rest."

"So I've heard. But I was glad that it didn't come to me, you know? I didn't want the burden and the responsibility of that power. And I certainly don't want that for my child."

"It is true that the possession of great power implies great responsibility. But are you not proud of such rare aptitude? Fox's gift is very potent. He will be truly spectacular."

"Spectacular is not what we're going for here. Normal, calm, ordinary, everyday. And did I mention *normal*? Look, it's not like a talent for music or a flair for art. Those gifts are easy to encourage, and they would bring my child a lot of self-expression and satisfaction. They'd enhance his life, improve it."

"You think there is no creativity, no fulfillment to be found in sorcery?"

"Sorry. I'm not trying to be insulting. It's just that Fox has—well, he has *issues*. And magic would only complicate his life to an unbearable degree."

Trahern studied her. "And if he suffers, so would you."

"Yes."

"That is exactly why he must be trained to control his power, to manage it and himself."

"Are you kidding? Managing himself is all we ever focus on. It's what we *have* to focus on. It's the only thing that's going to help him cope with a world that is too busy, too fast, too loud, too stimulating, too *everything* for him."

"The child has an illness?"

"No. Yes. No. I don't know how to explain it to you. Fox has Asperger's Syndrome. It's a form of high-functioning autism. Sensations, sounds, and other stimulation easily overwhelm him. He doesn't cope with change, with transitions, very well. He needs structure, routine, predictability. And he needs help in interpreting and understanding not just the world around him but people in general. For instance, he often misses important cues in others' words and behavior."

Trahern struggled to reconcile her words with the perceptive child in the other room. "Your son is very intelligent, and wise beyond his years." *Like his mother.*

"It has nothing to do with how bright he is. You want to talk spectacular? Well, Fox is spectacularly smart to the point of being brilliant." Her smile was genuine, but there seemed to be sadness as well as pride behind it. Trahern had never seen such an expression. "And what's even more important? Despite his difficulty in reading others, he has a truly compassionate heart," she declared. "Like when some people came to the door one day collecting donations for the food bank, and I gave them a couple of cans of tuna and a jar of peanut butter. Afterward, Fox asked me why, and I had to explain to him that some people just don't have enough to eat. I didn't think any more about it at the time, but it must have really bothered him.

"A few days later I came downstairs in the morning and found half the food in the house bagged up and sitting by the front door—and I do mean exactly *half*. If we had two cans of beans, he kept one for us and put one in a bag. If we had four cans of peas, two stayed and two went. He had a terrible time when we had an odd number of something . . . But the point is, once Fox knew, once he understood that someone needed help, *he absolutely had to do something.*"

"You permitted him to give away your food?"

"Well, of course I did." She looked at him askance. "Not only had he stayed up all night working on it, I wanted to encourage his kindness."

Most of the Tylwyth Teg regarded kindness as a weakness. No one *encouraged* it, least of all in the House of Oak . . . but it didn't seem prudent to mention it. "Fox is truly unique," he said instead, then added silently to himself: *And so are you.*

"I know, right? But so few people get to appreciate Fox's good qualities. They just see a child in the grocery store having a tantrum when really he's just reached the limit of his ability to cope. I—"

A light, frantic knocking sounded, and Trahern heard the front door open. "Hey there, Fox. Hi—uh—hi, *Braith.* Hey, Lissy, where are you?" The voice reminded him of the healer he'd seen the night before, the woman with the short black hair who had cleverly prevented the child from revealing his name. "Aidan's at the forge, so I brought reinforcements, just in case!"

A new voice piped up. "Well, now, 'tis a fine big dog you've got there, Fox. And will ya be needin' a charm to keep this great beast in line?"

"That's my cue," said Lissy. "Feel free to take your time with your meal. You can join us whenever you're ready." She left to greet her friends.

Trahern took her at her word and remained behind. Although he ate the bread and cheese on his plate and drank the rest of his tea, what he really wanted was a few moments to think. He couldn't even pretend to understand what she'd been describing. She spoke as if the child had some sort of deficiency, and yet there was nothing wrong with Fox that Trahern could discern. If he had possessed a physical deformity, then sorcery would amply compensate for it. If he were somehow lacking mentally? The magic would have passed by him, unable to make the sure connection it required. He could understand that Fox was sensitive to his environment—all good sorcerers were. But Lissy seemed to think the quality extreme.

*A puzzle indeed.*

As it was obvious the woman had no servants, he moved the plate and cup to the sink—but he didn't like leaving them there. A flick of the hand wove a minor restorative spell, punctuated by a soundless flash of rose light. All the dishes were now clean and dry and (he assumed) in their proper places. Satisfied, he reentered the living room. The healer he'd seen before was indeed there. There was no mistaking the lock of white in her short black hair, a sure sign of a long-ago spell gone awry. Behind her open, friendly face, she was as alert and watchful as if he might turn into a dragon at any moment. *Wise. And a most loyal companion.*

Lissy gestured in his direction. "Brooke, this is—"

She stopped there, and he realized she waited for permission to reveal his name. The consideration touched him. "Trahern," he supplied, and added a small bow.

"Okay, good." Lissy sounded relieved. "And this is our dear friend Ranyon."

As he rose, Trahern caught sight of a knee-high creature glaring at him, its knobby brown arms folded defiantly over a bright-blue tunic bearing some sort of bird emblem. An odd blue hat with the same embroidered bird sat at a rakish angle on thick braided hair that sported leaves, and its wizened face appeared carved from knotted wood. *By the stars of the Seven Sisters, an ellyll!* He hadn't seen one since old Heddwen disappeared—

"What business brings the likes of you here?" demanded Ranyon, all but vibrating with barely leashed anger. "Bad enough yer of the Tylwyth Teg, but better a snake had crossed the threshold than a treacherous son of Oak!"

# TEN

Trahern was taken aback as the ellyll spat on the floor at his feet. "Why insult me, good sir, when it pleases me to see you?"

"Don't be *good sirrin'* me. And it would please *me* ta be callin' down lightnin' where ya stand." He pointed a long twiggy finger that glowed like a white-hot ember.

Energy sprang instantly to Trahern's palms, but not before a thunderous roar shook the glass in the windows. The great gray grim leapt in front of him, showing every one of his long teeth at the ellyll—

And abruptly vanished.

"What have you done with my brother?" shouted Trahern, holding aloft an apple-size sphere of crackling green light. If Braith were injured in any way . . .

The ellyll adjusted his strange blue cap, jamming it down on his long braided hair until a handful of leaves went whirling to the floor. "I sent your great calf of a pet to Tir Hardd." He put up his little knobby fists in front of him and bounced from side to side on his woody toes. "Yer lucky I didn't send him clear to the Nine Realms, but I'm savin' my energy fer *you*, ya *fradychwr*!"

"I am no betrayer!"

"You're a son of Oak! A sprout from a tainted tree! Deceivers and assassins all!"

"A sorcerer does not prey on others."

"Ha!" snorted Ranyon. "A sorcerer, are ya? Came fer the boy, I'll bet, but yer not gettin' him or his power." He jabbed at the air with his clenched hands. "I'm ready fer ya. Let's see whatcha got!"

"I came here to retrieve my brother. Return him at once!"

"Return my family, ya greedy traitor!"

"Whoa, whoa, *whoa*!" Lissy inserted herself between them, seizing Trahern's arm with both her hands before he could throw the sphere. "Hold it right there, *everybody*. No one's having a wizards' duel in the middle of my goddamn house!"

"The House of Oak destroyed my entire clan!" protested Ranyon. Brooke knelt beside him and tried to calm him, but he was past listening.

Lissy eyed Trahern with suspicion. "It was *you*?" She gripped his arm tighter.

"Nay! It was an ill business, and one I had no part of," he declared aloud, then turned to mind speech in an effort to reach her. *Do I seem such a monster to you?*

Her hand relaxed somewhat. "Well, then, who *was* responsible?"

Not only had he not expected the question, he was unaccustomed to being questioned at all. Yet something about this woman made him want to explain, to have her understand. Trahern extinguished the sphere of energy in his palm and lowered his hand. He lowered his voice as well. "Eirianwen has led the House of Oak longer than anyone can remember. She craves power and status and the expansion of her territory, and lays her plans accordingly. The Ellyllon are not fae but elementals, the only beings in the Nine Realms whose magics exceeded her own, and they refused to lend her their talents."

"The wicked *wrach* demanded we help her make slaves out of the Dragon Men! A'course we said no!"

Trahern nodded. "After that, Eirianwen regarded every ellyll as an enemy. Rumors were spread at Court that the clan was preyed upon by migrating bwganod at a gathering—"

"Lies!" Ranyon shrieked. Brooke gave up trying to soothe him and simply locked her arms around his waist from behind and held on. He seemed not to notice. "Lies and treachery!"

"There were many lies and much treachery, and I was privy to none of it. What was done to your people was never revealed to me, or indeed to anyone. It took a very long time, and considerable coin, before I finally uncovered the truth—that Eirianwen had found a way to infiltrate the Ellyllon lands."

"There was a battle?" asked Lissy, releasing his arm at last.

"There was no fair fight, or we'd have kicked yer sorry arses and sent ya runnin' with yer traitorous tails between yer legs!"

"There was no fight at all." Trahern's voice was subdued. "There were no soldiers, no army. Only a venomous plague of small orange *wenwyn* toads gathered from the bottle trees in the easternmost realm. Their poison stops the heart instantly, and they can bite many times." Lissy was silent, and horror dawned in her sable eyes. He wished he could stop now, leave the rest of the sorry tale to the imagination . . . *But only truth will honor the dead.* "There were countless numbers of the dangerous creatures hidden in every house, every barn and tree, every tavern and well. Eirianwen's magic not only cloaked the toads from sight, it controlled them and suspended them in waiting. At the next dark moon, in the deep of night, she loosed them all."

"But—but what about their own magic?" Brooke looked from him to Ranyon and back. "Why couldn't the Ellyllon defend themselves?"

Ranyon's voice was bitter, and tears ran down his angry face. "To kill one elemental is to weaken all, dontcha know. To kill so many, so fast, so sudden . . . We were overwhelmed where'er we were, and most were in their beds!" Unable to contain himself, he broke free of Brooke's arms and flew at Trahern, beating on him with furious fists.

"*Lofruddio bradwr! Murdering traitor!* The foolish Court believed your lies because the bodies were gone," he cried. "But their bodies were fed to the bwganod in Coedwig Swamp to hide the proof of the plot!"

*By the Seven Sisters* . . . He hadn't known that part, hadn't been able to determine why all of the villages were empty. It made sense that Eirianwen wouldn't want the bodies left behind to be examined—and any remains that did turn up would be in a bwgan nesting ground, adding credence to the rumors. The sobering revelation wrung a sigh from Trahern, and he simply stood still, accepting the little ellyll's blows without defending himself. Ranyon's knobby hands stung like the hooves of a hunted hart, but the ellyll had clearly suffered far more—

A sudden high-pitched wail rent the air. Trahern had forgotten about Fox; indeed, everyone had. The child hugged his knees, rocking violently back and forth on the couch with his eyes squeezed tightly shut, keening in distress.

*"Now look at what you've done!"* Lissy whispered fiercely.

"We did nothing to harm your son," protested Trahern.

"Nothing except argue and yell and threaten each other in front of him. Now for heaven's sake, everyone be quiet so I can think." She took a deep breath, and he could see her gather herself as if for battle. "Brooke, could you go find Squishy Bear for me? I think Fox left it—"

A sudden determined knocking at the door made everyone jump. "Melissa? Melissa, honey, is everything all right in there?" The caller resumed knocking loudly.

"Oh, for the love of little fishes!" Lissy made a peculiar motion as if to pull her own hair out, then headed for the door, whispering quickly to Brooke as she passed.

The healer moved fast, seizing Trahern by the shoulder and Ranyon by the hand. She steered them into the kitchen more by sheer force of will than physical strength. Trahern was unaccustomed to taking directions from humans, never mind being handled by them, but part of him sensed it would make things easier for Lissy if he complied. *No doubt the ellyll is of the same mind, or he would refuse to be in the same room with me.* The visitor couldn't see either of them unless they permitted it, of course, but their presence might interfere with Lissy's attention.

Brooke put a finger to her lips, but she needn't have bothered with that, either. All three of them scarcely breathed as they listened to the exchange at the front door—which wasn't easy with Fox still howling and moaning in the same room like a lost soul.

"Whatever was that ungodly ruckus earlier?" demanded a woman's voice. "Why, I thought a tiger was in here!" Trahern silently cursed Braith for his determination to defend him from the angry little ellyll.

"Goddess help us, it's Claire," whispered Brooke. "Lissy's nosiest neighbor."

". . . and I'm sure I heard a hellacious argument." There was a pause, and it wasn't hard to imagine that the woman was staring at Fox. "My goodness, is that boy all right? That's quite a fit he's pitching."

"My son's just had too much excitement tonight," said Lissy smoothly. "I turned on the TV hoping for a cartoon to take his mind off things, but there was a Godzilla movie still in the DVD, and the volume was all the way up. Scared us both, actually."

"Good save, girlfriend," whispered Brooke, and Ranyon nodded in agreement.

"I'm really sorry you were disturbed a second time," Lissy said. "In fact, I'm surprised the whole neighborhood isn't at my door with torches and pitchforks."

"Why, bless your heart, you know we're just *worried* about you, hon. You're carrying so much on your plate with a full-time teaching position plus a handicapped child to look after."

"Fox is not handicapped. He's brighter than most of us, and quite functional, thank you." For all that he was unfamiliar with human emotions, it was easy for Trahern to hear the tight control in Lissy's voice and sense the anger that bubbled beneath it. The annoying woman, Claire, didn't appear to notice. At least, her *words* indicated that she didn't notice. He couldn't help but think she'd fit in rather well with the Royal Court . . .

"Well, of course he is, sweetie, and you're so brave for thinking positive. But sometimes even kids who are *special* need a firm hand, and it's just too bad he doesn't have a daddy to help straighten out his attitude. Anyway, I just wanted to make sure you're okay. I can see you've got a hide to blister, so I'll just head on home now."

"A hide to blister? For real? You honestly think I should spank my child?"

"Well, now, everyone in the complex thinks so, hon. They just haven't said it to you, so as not to add to your burden."

"*My son is not a burden!* And hitting him for something he can't help would be as useless as slapping you to make you less ignorant!"

"Well, I'll be! That is truly ugly, and so unlike you, Melissa—"

The front door slammed so hard that the kitchen tools swung on their hooks. Fox wailed all the louder, drowning out every other sound. Trahern risked a small wordless spell to enable himself to hear Lissy's next words. "Don't listen to her, Fox," she said. "She's a rude and nasty woman. I love you, and I'll always love you, and I would never let anybody hurt you. Maybe you can read me a story when you're feeling better, and then I'll feel better, too."

*Love again.* Trahern didn't get a chance to ponder it because Lissy was suddenly right in front of him. Fury blazed along her cheekbones, and righteous anger crackled like flames in her dark eyes. Still, she fought to keep her voice low. "You, and especially *you*!" she hissed, pointing first at Ranyon, then at Trahern. "What the hell do you think you're doing? Fox has trouble coping with a lot of people at once, but it's much harder for him to deal with anger and contention even if it doesn't involve him. *Thanks to the pair of you*, my son is upset. And even worse, I've just had to lie my face off in front of my child!" Lissy folded her arms and continued in the same ferocious tone. "I don't know what the history is between you two, and right now, *I don't care.* Whatever your problem is, take it somewhere else! Blow each other up with magic if you have to, but you're not disturbing my son again!"

Ranyon stared at the floor, rubbing one foot with the big knurled toe of the other. "Aye, I shoulda dealt with this traitor outside."

Trahern ignored the slur. "I regret that your home has been disrupted, good lady, and that Fox has been upset by my actions," he said. Even though it wasn't entirely his fault, he found himself wanting to express some sort of contrition to Lissy. "That discourteous woman was wrong. Your son is a very intelligent and talented child." His words did nothing to appease her, however. If anything, he'd somehow succeeded in upsetting her further.

"Oh, blow it out your ear. And I'm not your *good lady*, either. I may not have a whole lot of magical powers myself, but even *I've* heard that it's unlucky for a human child to be complimented by a faery," she said. "And you've said just a few too many flattering things about him tonight. I don't know what's going on between you and your brother, but I want both of you to leave."

"Aye, and so do I," added the ellyll, balling up his slender hands into knobbly fists again. He was about to say more, but Lissy shook her finger at him.

"*Ranyon!* You know I love you dearly, and I know you've been through a lot, but you've done nothing but make this situation a whole lot worse tonight!"

"But I've—but he's a—"

Trahern used their distraction to return to the room where the boy still howled, a lost and despairing sound. Brooke hovered protectively a few feet away from him, humming a soothing tune that Trahern recognized as a gentle calming spell. It wasn't working in the least, of course. He narrowed his eyes until he could see the discordant vibrations Fox was throwing off. They pulsed at odd angles through the air, effectively blocking the healer's spell. "Pardon me, Lady Brooke," he said. "I believe that Lissy requires a moment of your time in the kitchen. And I must attempt to contact my brother."

Brooke eyed him suspiciously, but he was unconcerned by her scrutiny. He trusted in the empathic abilities of a true healer to inform her that he harbored no ill intent. Just to be certain, however, he underscored Lissy's fictional *need* of her with a magical suggestion of a type that Brooke was unlikely to detect. She left the room at once, and Trahern glided to the boy's side. With the forefingers of both hands, he drew a glowing arc in the air over Fox, while quietly pronouncing the five words of a *distawrwydd* spell.

# ELEVEN

Lissy eased herself into a kitchen chair as Ranyon apologized for the third time, complete with tears that squirted out of the corners of his bright-blue eyes. She handed him the dish towel from the nearby oven handle and tried not to flinch as he loudly blew his ample nose on it. *I feel so bad for lecturing him. What happened to his family was horrific, and he had every right to be upset—but what was I supposed to do?* Her son's well-being had to come first, and right now Fox alternated between shrieking and crying in the other room. She supposed she'd have to haul him up to his room like a newly roped steer and let him sort himself out on his own. Right now, though, it felt like her son's bedroom was ten flights up instead of only one. Was this weird-ass day ever going to end?

Brooke appeared in the kitchen. "Are you guys all right?"

"Nay, I've been naught but a proper *dihiryn* and given dreadful offense to a dear friend." Ranyon sniffed as fresh tears spurted.

Lissy ordered herself not to roll her eyes. She knew the little ellyll wasn't being melodramatic—*much*. He just felt what he felt very keenly. "Yeah, we'll be okay," she answered. "Now if I could just figure out what to do with Fox so we can both get some sleep, that'd be great."

Brooke put an arm around her. "He'll settle eventually. You know he will."

"*Eventually* can be an awfully long time when he's this far gone. The grocery store on Saturday was nothing compared to this. He's stimming, and you know he hasn't done that for a very long time." In fact, Fox hadn't curled up in a ball and rocked himself—if you could call it *rocking* when he bashed himself against the back of the couch with as much force as his nine-year-old body could muster—since he was six. And that wasn't even the worst of it. "On top of that, I never should have pissed off Claire. She's going to report us to the residence board again for sure." She pressed the heels of her hands to her eyes. "But did you *hear* what she said about Fox? How can anyone, least of all an *educator*, be that uninformed in the twenty-first century? Or that rude? Usually I can ignore it, but this time I let her damn condescending tone get to me."

"You're right, it's not that she doesn't understand," said Brooke. "I can feel it. She understands perfectly well; she just enjoys causing trouble. It makes her feel powerful. You can't let her get your goat—it's exactly what she wants."

"She's trying ta steal yer goat?" Ranyon jumped off the chair, his melancholy temporarily forgotten. "I'll be teaching *her* a thing or two about that!"

"Figure of speech, bud. Just a figure of speech." Brooke made calming motions with her hands. "I meant that Claire deliberately tries to upset Lissy by saying mean things about Fox."

"Aye, I heard the *ffiaidd* insulting our boy." He shook his fist, and Lissy had a sudden brain wave.

"Ranyon, would you like to do something to make things up to me tonight?"

His whole demeanor brightened. "A'course I would! You've only ta name the task."

"Well, then, what I need most is for you to help me with Claire." She held up a cautionary finger. "I don't want her hurt in any way, understand. But I need her to forget everything she saw and heard tonight. Oh, and I'd love it if she never speaks or writes our names." That ought to cover any complaint forms Claire might fill out or phone calls she might make. *But why stop there? Here's my chance to really fix this problem once and for all.* "You know what else, Ranyon? I don't want Claire to ever hear a sound out of this house again, no matter how much noise we're making. And it'd be fantastic if she completely forgot she ever met us. So, what do you say? Can you manage all that?"

The little ellyll rubbed his twiggy hands together. "I have charms aplenty fer that and more! And I'll be gettin' right to it, too." He disappeared, and Lissy sat back in her chair with a sigh.

"I sure hope I don't end up regretting that."

"Naw," said Brooke. "You were pretty clear. And if he gets it a little wrong, that miserable woman is due for a lot of karma anyway. So, what should we do now?"

*Good question.* Lissy had the beginnings of a headache, and her ears were starting to ring, yet her son could easily carry on for another hour or more. His record was three hours, thirty-two minutes, though that had been when he was much younger. She'd asked Ranyon before about a charm for meltdowns, but he'd explained—with almost as many tears as tonight—that Fox repelled most of his type of magic. "The poor little lad seems to need to work through his troubles on his own," Ranyon had said.

*Wait a minute . . .* Something twigged at her mind, but she couldn't pin it down. It was too hard to think about *anything* with all the racket coming from the next room.

Brooke sat beside her. "I tried relaxing Fox with a gentle spell, a lullaby, really, but as usual it didn't work. I just hate that I can't seem to reach him when he's like this."

Lissy patted her friend's arm. "It's not your fault you can't fix it. I'm his mom, and I still don't know of anything to do except wait it out. It's discouraging, though," she admitted. "I keep thinking we're making progress and then, *bam*, he totally loses it."

"Oh, but you're making tons of progress—both of you," said Brooke. "Holy cow, I remember when it was practically Armageddon every day!"

"Yeah, but we went almost three weeks this time. Three whole weeks without an incident! He was fine, then without warning he lost it at the grocery store on Saturday. Now *this*."

"Lissy, you *know* you can't count tonight. It hasn't been a normal night. It wasn't even a normal *weekend*. Look at it from a kid's perspective, any kid. Fox did a lot of things outside of his comfort zone—camping, hanging out with a whole bunch of people, tasting a s'more even when he thought it looked yucky—and he coped with it *all*."

"Yeah. Then he meets a giant faery dog, plus the big frowny faery who goes with it," she said.

Brooke laughed a little. "You have to admit, it's a miracle Fox didn't melt down hours ago—"

The sudden silence was almost as intense as the noise her son had been making. She was in the living room in seconds, her brain taking in the scene at once. Trahern sat on the couch, cradling Fox in his lap. Her son's eyes were closed, and he appeared utterly limp.

Lissy's heart stuttered in her chest. And then she recovered. "Hey! What the hell did you do to my kid?" She raced over, intending to snatch the child away—and collided with something hard enough to knock her backward. If Brooke hadn't been right behind to catch her, she would have landed on the floor. Clutching her head, she glanced wildly around, searching for what she'd hit, but saw nothing.

Trahern frowned. "Have a care, good lady. I do not wish you to injure yourself."

*I'll show you some injury, dammit, as soon as I get my hands on you!* Lissy reached out and walked slowly forward, feeling around until she connected with something. Whatever it was, it was cool to the touch, like glass. She tapped on the invisible wall with her fingernail, then her fist. Hard as concrete. "What have you done to Fox?" she demanded. "Let him go!"

"I have done nothing to your child. I used no magic on his person. I merely created a *distawrwydd*—a bubble of silence—around him to relieve him of stimulation for a time."

"If you didn't do anything to him, then why isn't he moving?"

"The boy fell asleep at once. I believe him to be exhausted."

*Him and me both.* She exchanged glances with Brooke. If there was negative energy present, from mild envy to petty spite to full-blown malice, her empathic friend would sense it immediately, just as she had with Claire. But Brooke only shook her head. Lissy took a deep breath, reaching for some shred of calm, and looked again at Fox. He seemed so fragile against Trahern's tall and powerful frame—but she could see the steady rise and fall of his small chest beneath the Scooby-Doo pajamas. *He's okay.* Relieved, she felt her gaze wander slightly to Trahern's chest. She couldn't see it beneath all that elegant dark leather, yet she sensed its shape and form as surely as if she had run her hands over it. The fae's hair had escaped its braid, falling over one shoulder like a white silk cape. What would it feel like against her skin?

*Whoa!* Her cheeks flared with sudden heat. Where on earth had those thoughts come from? Mortified, she made the mistake of looking directly at the suspected source—and found herself staring into eyes that were first purple, then blue, then green, then colors she didn't even know the name of. *Are you putting ideas in my mind?*

*Why would I do such a thing? Your own thoughts are interesting enough.*

That velvet voice in her head produced a whole-body shiver that culminated in a soft, decadent warmth between her legs. Lissy tried to swallow, but her mouth had gone desert dry. *Just get out of my brain, okay? I'm overtired and not thinking straight, and I don't want you listening in.*

*Very well. I will not intrude. But it is pleasing to know you can hear me.*

She gave herself a mental shake and tried again to focus on the issue at hand. "Look, Trahern, you shouldn't do things like this with Fox without asking me first," she began, then decided he probably deserved a *little* appreciation. "Thanks for trying to make things easier for him, though."

Long twiggy fingers suddenly seized her elbow. Ranyon had reappeared at her side. "Are ya daft?" he asked, his gnarled face further contorted by sheer alarm. "'Tis dangerous to be thanking a fae! Especially *that* fae!" He stood on his tiptoes to address Trahern, although he still wasn't eye to eye. "What is it yer up to, son of Oak? I'll be tying yer snowy locks to a bwgan's prickly arse!"

"I am attempting to undo the difficulties I may have contributed to this night. And I certainly *do not* take advantage of genuine courtesy," retorted Trahern. "I have no need to bind anyone to my service or return ill for good intentions." He turned his attention to Brooke. "You are a human healer. Do you think the child will remain asleep if I move?" he asked her. "I do not wish to disturb him now that he has found some peace."

"Fox usually sleeps very soundly after an episode," Brooke replied. "Frankly, I don't think he'd notice if a herd of elephants stampeded through here."

Lissy caught the puzzlement in Trahern's mind. Either there were no such animals in the faery world or they were known by some other name.

"Aye, now there's a brammer of an idea," Ranyon declared. "I can call up some elephants right now if you don't give Fox back to us!" Brooke shushed him at once.

"Truly, I have not taken Fox from you," said Trahern, but he looked at Lissy rather than the ellyll. "I only sought to give him a few moments of respite. I understand more clearly now what you meant when you said he was sensitive to his surroundings." He drew a strange symbol in the air that glowed for a split second, then vanished.

Lissy reached out and discovered that the barrier had also vanished, as if it had been nothing but a soap bubble. Her initial impulse had been to grab Fox and rush away with him, but a very different instinct directed her now. That strange energy was once again in play, that impossible sense of recognition she'd experienced the first time she'd met this man, this *being*. It was so strong and deep that she surprised herself by deliberately sitting on the couch right next to Trahern. As she held out her arms, the fae carefully deposited the sleeping child into them.

Braith suddenly reappeared from wherever Ranyon had sent him, with Squishy Bear dangling from his enormous mouth. His pendulous lips were drawn back, and the exposed sharp teeth held the toy as carefully as if they were tweezers. Gently, the dog deposited the stuffed toy next to Lissy before lying at her feet. Brooke sat across from them. Ranyon remained standing a few moments longer, his branchlike arms folded across his Blue Jays T-shirt and his brow so furrowed that his eyes were barely visible. Finally, he sighed and clambered up beside Brooke. Lissy was grateful he didn't say anything more to Trahern. She didn't have enough energy left to play referee or to ponder the strangeness of the group now gathered in her living room. All she wanted was to hold Fox for a while, dammit. When he was exhausted like this, it was the only time she got the chance to simply cuddle him. *You wouldn't let me if you were awake, sweetie,* she thought as her fingertips brushed the pale blond hair from his forehead.

*Fox does not like to be touched?*

*You're reading my mind again*, she chided Trahern. *But yes, touch is usually too intense for him. Sometimes he'll come and sit close to me, maybe even lean on me. He never wants me to hug him, though.*

*This saddens you.*

*What can I say? I'm a mother. I naturally want to hold my child, and kiss him and hug him. Touch is a vital way of expressing love. But I have to find other ways that are meaningful to Fox without causing him stress. Love him the way he* wants *to be loved, you know?*

Trahern only shook his head. *Love is not known among the fae, not even between parents and their offspring. For most of us, it is only a myth, albeit a pleasant one.*

The idea was so startling that she risked looking at his perfect face, meeting again that ageless gaze that seemed to see right through her. She wanted to look longer but gave herself a mental shake. *It's late, and way past time to be direct*, she decided. "I don't want to be rude, but are you and your brother planning to leave soon? Fox needs to go to bed, and so do the rest of us mortals."

As if in answer, the grim shifted his great bulk so he faced away from Trahern. No emotion registered on the outside, but Lissy detected confusion in Trahern's eyes—and something very akin to hurt. Nevertheless, he rose smoothly to his feet.

"I regret troubling all of you this evening. It is obvious to me that my brother intends to remain with Fox, and I must respect his wishes."

"Wait just a minute," protested Lissy. "What about *my* wishes? I'm not allowed to have dogs in this building!"

"I'm certain your ellyll friend has informed you that most humans do not see us. A scant few have a gift and cannot be prevented from perceiving the fae, and even fewer are deliberately permitted to do so. Braith will be imperceptible to all else."

Lissy's insides unexpectedly turned to liquid as his voice blossomed in her head. *I thank you for your hospitality, good lady. I will return soon to see if Braith has changed his mind.* Flustered, she couldn't think of anything to say before Trahern simply disappeared.

"Good riddance!" declared Ranyon.

"And good grief! Looks to me like you have a new pet," said Brooke. Her mouth quirked as if trying not to laugh.

"This isn't funny." Still holding the sleeping Fox close, Lissy regarded the enormous blue-gray beast on the floor. Lying down, his broad back was level with her coffee table and nearly as wide. "Not funny at all. What am I going to do with him?"

"Well, at least you don't have to feed him. Grims don't eat." Her friend looked thoughtful. "And he did fetch Squishy Bear without being asked. Maybe he'll be helpful with Fox. You know, like a service dog or some kind of companion. After all, Fox seems to be able to communicate with him. And who knows, Braith might even keep him safe."

"Safe? No one is safe as long as a son of Oak is involved," declared Ranyon. "He could be a spy, dontcha know!"

Brooke leaned over to the ellyll. "Paranoid much? Exactly what great secrets are we hiding here? Look, I feel nothing but positive, even *happy*, energy from that dog. I think he loves Fox. And Trahern wasn't exactly pleased that Braith found Fox at the campground in the first place. I don't think he had any secret plans to infiltrate our ranks with a canine agent." She stood and picked up Fox so Lissy could get to her feet.

"Give it a rest, Ranyon. Trahern came here tonight on a rescue mission. He thought Fox was holding his brother prisoner," explained Lissy, taking her son back into her arms with a groan. Carrying him when he was asleep *should* have been a lot easier than when she'd hauled him thrashing and wailing from the grocery store. Instead, Fox's ultrarelaxed state made him about as easy to lug as a duffel bag filled with Jell-O.

"Let me help you," offered Brooke. "We could each take an end? Put Ranyon under the middle?"

Picturing that made her smile. "Naw, I got it." She heaved him over her shoulder and headed for the stairs. The massive dog rose and followed her. "You're coming, too? I should have known. Remind me to fit you with a sling so *you* can carry him next time."

Fox seemed peaceful when she eased him into his bed, but his eyelids had that bruised look again. She wondered if she looked the same. *Meltdowns are hard on us both, bud*, she thought as she tucked his Scooby-Doo blanket around him and kissed his forehead. Just as she moved to the door, Braith lay down beside the bed with his chin on his paws. For a moment, the massive dog looked like one of the great marble lions guarding a famous library . . .

"I guess nothing's going to get past you, huh?"

A large tail thumped on the carpet twice.

When Lissy returned to the living room, she found her friends avidly discussing the giant canine. She had a few things of her own to discuss, but for the moment she simply curled up on the couch across from them.

"So Braith is Trahern's brother," said Brooke. "What's the scoop on that?"

Lissy shrugged. "All Trahern said was that he's been cursed—he didn't say how or why."

"Aye." A little of the indignation faded from Ranyon's gnarled face. "He's a fledgling grim. And all grims begin as a mortal or a fae."

"So it's like what happened to Aidan and Rhys," said Brooke, leaning forward.

"Well, he's not a pure grim, mind ya, or he'd be black as Hades itself. I'm thinkin' someone interrupted the spell before it could fully change him. But Aidan and Rhys were human, dontcha know. They could be freed."

"Lucky for Morgan and me." Brooke grinned.

"Yeah, but what about Braith?" asked Lissy. "How do we free him, too?"

The ellyll shook his head. "It takes very little magic to transform a mortal to a grim. But changing a fae"—he spread his skinny arms wide—"takes enormous power. Such a spell is seldom used, and 'twas never designed to be undone."

"What, it's permanent?" Brooke sounded horrified.

Even Ranyon seemed a little subdued by the prospect. "Aye, it is," he said at last. "He might be of the House of Oak, but there are only a few I'd wish such a fate upon."

No one spoke for a few moments. No one *could*. Lissy shivered inwardly, then gradually put that subject aside. There was something else that needed discussing, something that the quiet had finally allowed her brain to piece together. "Speaking of wishing fates on people, let's talk about magic, shall we?

"Ranyon, just how long have you known that Fox has power?"

# TWELVE

Though he could barely see over the tops of the tables, Fychan the tavern keeper wended his way through the boisterous crowd effortlessly, delivering yet another large silver tankard of coblyn ale to Trahern's table without spilling a drop. He gathered up the empties but refused to accept a proffered coin. "Thee knows the auld proverb: *naught for a Hunter, naught from a Hunter.*"

Of course, Trahern knew the superstitious saying. Everyone did. If you didn't charge a Hunter for your services, you'd never find yourself judged by a Hunter. At least, that's what many in the Nine Realms liked to believe. He'd never taken advantage of that belief before. In fact, he didn't know of any rider who would.

"My coin has fit in your hand rather well on other nights."

"Thee hast never drunk this much on other nights. I figure thee for sorrow. Ne'er a good practice to profit from sorrow. Brings poor luck. May *thy* luck change, and if ale won't help it along, I'll bring thee something stronger." Fychan touched his woolly red cap in respect—not an easy task with his arms full—and headed off to the kitchen as the empty tankards clanged like bells.

Trahern stared into his ale. His luck had already changed, and not for the better. Why else would he have retreated to a coblyn tavern? It wasn't a favorite of the Hunt's riders. It wasn't a favorite of any Tylwyth Teg he knew of, for that matter—not only did they seldom choose to associate with other fae, but coblyn ceilings tended to be uncomfortably low. Yet there was something about this noisy, bustling establishment that often appealed to him. Tonight, however, neither the clamor nor the copious amounts of ale had silenced his thoughts in the least, and he doubted that a stronger drink would help. Not only was it cursedly difficult for a fae to get falling-down drunk, a sorcerer such as himself was duty-bound to keep both his judgment and his abilities reasonably unimpaired.

*Duty.* That's what it came down to, didn't it? *Duty and loyalty.* Trahern had not only shouldered the responsibility of keeping his brother safe but had also committed himself to unlocking the spell that bound him. In the first, he had succeeded, and in the other? Utterly failed. He hadn't even known that Braith was still *Braith*, and he had mistaken his brother's lack of mind speech for lack of *being*. A foolish assumption, and one that no doubt lay at the heart of why Braith had elected to remain in the mortal realm.

*No. I know him. He would forgive me, though I cannot forgive myself.*

The true problem lay with the human child. While Fox hadn't bespelled Braith, as Trahern had first suspected, he had nonetheless captured Braith's loyalty. His brother had chosen Fox.

Just as magic had chosen the boy.

Trahern pinched the bridge of his nose as a rare headache began to kick him in the forehead. He could spell it away, but on some level the pain suited his mood. *Duty again.* Among most sorcerers, there was an unspoken rule, a code of sorts, by which he was obligated to help guide the newly endowed. And those in his family who possessed the gift—save Eirianwen of course, who held herself above such mundane duties—had indeed helped him along. Once he'd learned just enough so that he wasn't a walking hazard, however, he was left to his own devices. *Did my mother plan it that way?* His abilities were strong, but his potential would never be realized without continued instruction. Fortunately, his desire and determination to learn had been even stronger than his gift. At first he'd studied in secret from whatever he could get his hands on, from sentient books that inched over the floor of his bedchamber to ancient scrolls of fireproof dragon skin. When he was old enough to take over the reins of trading with other realms on behalf of the House, he could justify traveling to the most distant reaches of the vast kingdom. With Trahern's clear talent for creating agreements that fattened the coffers of his clan, no one questioned the amount of time he spent away from home. Nor did they suspect he'd spent most of that time plus his own wealth seeking out teachers among every tribe and clan, every known fae race—plus a few whose existence was only legend.

His mother hadn't known the lengths to which he had gone to hone his gift, the sacrifices he'd made for knowledge. *Or perhaps she did, and that is why she fears me.* Braith, on the other hand, had no power, save one. Perhaps he had foreseen a distant future in which Eirianwen did not rule, and that was why she had struck him down . . .

The future . . . Trahern hadn't thought about his brother's rare ability for a very long time. *Braith has seen something in* Fox's *future!*

"I have been an idiot," he muttered, shoving the untasted tankard away so that the ale sloshed over the rim. An aged coblyn—a woman—appeared almost instantly to mop up the mess, though her small size obliged her to hop up on a chair to do it. She shook her head, causing her faded curls to flail about like springs from under her shapeless red cap.

"Nay, sir, thee hast not been an idiot yet. The building is yet standing. People are yet breathing." She winked before hurrying off to attend another table.

Unknowingly, she'd hit on the very crux of the situation, he thought. Fox had been endowed with terrifying potential. It wasn't a dog's affection for a child that had compelled Braith to attach himself to Fox.

It was a seer's concern for the future.

*The boy will be a very formidable sorcerer.* If *he does not destroy everything and everyone around him first.* And that left just one course of action for Trahern: return to the mortal world and persuade Lissy Santiago-Callahan to let him train her son in the very magic she did not wish him to have.

~

Lissy was tired beyond tired, but sleep was just going to have to wait. "Out with it, Ranyon," she ordered. "How long have you known that my son has magic? I heard what you said to Trahern. You knew he was a sorcerer, and you immediately accused him of coming for Fox *and his power*."

The ellyll swung his spindly feet like a guilty child as he sat perched on the couch beside Brooke. Finally, he sighed deeply. "He's rightfully inherited his family's gift. But 'tis not the only power to come to him, Lissy dear. He's got something more, dontcha know."

Lissy clutched the last fraying strand of her patience. "No, I do *not* know. Explain, dammit."

"Fae magic." Ranyon's voice was almost a whisper, as if he feared being overheard. "*Royal* fae magic. Our Fox was born with it."

"*What?*" blurted Brooke and Lissy at the same time. Brooke recovered first.

"Ranyon, that is so not funny."

"Aye, there's not a thing fun about it, but there you are."

Lissy's mind worked furiously. *A faery dog shows up out of nowhere and appoints himself Fox's bodyguard. And the dog's brother just happens to be a wizard? Trahern says Fox has a powerful gift. Wait, that's not quite right—he said Fox would be* spectacular. *I just assumed he meant my own family's magic had . . .* "No. No way. I'm not buying into this, Ranyon." She tried to adopt a reasonable tone, even though she wanted to scream. "Where on earth would my very human little boy get faery powers?"

"Why, from yer good man, Matt, a'course," said the ellyll. "'Twas in his blood."

Lissy snorted. "Give me a break! Fox's dad grew up in Los Angeles. That's a helluva long way from Wales."

"Um—not as far as you might think." Brooke moved over to Lissy's couch and put a gentle hand on her shoulder. "Matt's last name was Lovell," she said. "It's one of the surnames adopted by the Kale, the gypsies who lived in Wales. I've traced Matt's lineage back to them." Her friend paused for a moment. "It was going to be a surprise, Liss, but I've been making a family tree for Fox since the day he was born. I was hoping it might be finished by the time he graduates high school. I thought—well, I thought he'd want to know where he came from."

"Really?" Despite the tumult in her brain and the gravity of the ellyll's revelation, Lissy was astounded and touched. Knitting an afghan would be a major project in her books, but a whole genealogy? "That's the sweetest thing I've ever heard. No wonder you're my best friend." She squeezed Brooke's hand and ordered herself not to cry. *Not now.* There were still some big questions to be answered, dammit, and *somebody* was going to answer them. She sniffed a little as she took a deep breath, then another, composing herself. "Okay, Ranyon, so there's a long-ago connection to Wales," she said as calmly as she could manage. "But you're not going to tell me that Matt had fairy dust in his veins."

"A'course not! The fae are many things, but they're not a bit dusty," said Ranyon.

*One day I'm going to remember how literal he is . . .* "Then what is it you're saying?"

"That yer man was heir to a powerful line of magic. One of Matt's ancestors wed a fae woman, dontcha know. Nerilda of the House of Thorn. She was one of the most powerful sorcerers to come from the ruling family. And despite her high station, she followed the old ways and was faithful to her calling—a rare thing among her kind, dontcha know."

Brooke sat abruptly. "Holy cow, you knew her."

"Aye, she healed me of a poisonous wound from a *llamhigyn y dwr*."

"A what?" asked Lissy.

"A water leaper. 'Tis like a great bulbous frog with leathery wings and eyes like glowing green lamps. When its mouth opens, it seems like its ugly head has split in two, but that's not the most dangerous part. The creature's long tail ends in a deadly stinger." Ranyon shuddered. "Jumped me, it did," he said. "'Twas when I was mournin' my family and blunderin' too close to the Lake o' Loes."

Suddenly Lissy wondered if perhaps the grief-stricken ellyll had *blundered* near the water on purpose. She found herself wanting to jump up and hug him, but if she didn't keep him on topic, she'd never get the answers she needed about her son. "Okay, so Fox has two gifts, one from my side of the family and one from his father's," she said aloud. "And you didn't think you should tell me?"

The ellyll looked decidedly uncomfortable. "Well, 'twould seem there's a mite more than that to his gifts."

"More?" *Of course there's more. There's always more.* "More what?" Lissy could almost hear the *twang* as what had to be her very last nerve snapped like a broken guitar string.

"Ya put two types of magic together, and they either explode or they make something new. And they didn't explode."

"Are you talking about synchronicity?" asked Brooke. "Greater than the sum of its parts?"

"Bigger, surely, and different, too. I've never seen the like."

Lissy suddenly felt tired right down to her bones. Even her goddamn hair was tired. She was out of energy, out of patience, and out of resilience. "All right, guys, that's enough discussion for tonight," she said with far more calmness than she felt. "I'm done like dinner. I don't want to hear another word. I can't hear another word." She glared at Ranyon when he put up a twiggy hand. "Not. One. Word." The hand fell back into his lap. "But tomorrow? I'm coming over to the shop tomorrow afternoon, and you are *so* going to tell me every single thing you know."

"But that could take years!" exclaimed Ranyon.

Instantly Brooke grabbed his hand and steered him toward the front door. "She means about *Fox*!" she hissed.

"Oh, aye. *That*."

Though her brain was on overdrive after the night's ruckus and revelations, Lissy fell asleep almost instantly. Nightmares, frequent visitors when she was stressed, did not plague her. Instead, she found herself wandering a strange, exotic garden under a moon that hung like a bright-orange slice in a deep-blue sky. Unknown constellations, even the tiny spiral arms of far-off galaxies, pinwheeled high overhead while the air around her was thickly redolent of honey, gentian, licorice, and something oddly akin to nutmeg. *The flowers*, she thought. The rich scents emanated from the vibrant blossoms all around her, intoxicating her to that perfect point of carefree euphoria as if she'd drunk a glass, or maybe two, of dark Mourvedre wine. She reached out a hand to a poppylike bloom—but no poppy was ever this size or had such vivid petals. Her fingers came away with pollen that glittered like diamond dust a moment before it vanished into her skin, and suddenly she could taste spices on her tongue.

When knowing hands began to unbutton her blouse from behind, she didn't resist. Instead, Lissy laughed and leaned backward until strong arms caught her and bore her away . . .

Trahern laid her down on a thick bed of soft golden violets, cool and vanilla-fragrant as they crushed beneath her. He was already naked, his marble skin warmed with color by the apricot moonlight. A myriad of intricate symbols, signs, and strings of words, each inked in amber, wound their way over lean muscle, from the straight line of his shoulders to his narrow hips and long legs. Every detail of his body was there for her to see, to appreciate. Even his long white hair was bound back so she could easily see the telltale scar across his throat. Nothing was hidden from her—

Save his face.

*Is this a game?* The exquisite half mask was finely crafted of flawless copper, inlaid with semiprecious stones. The high cheekbones mirrored Trahern's own angular features, but the visage was completely expressionless. She reached for it, but at a word from him, her hand fell away and would not obey her again. "Hey!"

"My touch is for you. All for you," he said.

"But I want to touch you, too! And what's with the mask?"

He shook his head. "It matters not. For now, relax and feel. Allow me this."

Her arm was her own again. "All right." Lissy smiled and settled deeper into the violets, a tremor of anticipation tingling through her entire body. "But next time *I* get to wear the costume."

*Look at me*, he said in her mind. Lissy obeyed, determining that this time she would finally discern the color of his eyes—at least she could see *those*! But his irises shifted and changed even as she stared. *Gold? Blue?* Whatever their color, Trahern didn't take his eyes from her face as he slowly undressed her. As each inch of her skin was gradually revealed, he drew light spirals upon it with the brush of a masculine fingertip—and the clothing left her body in very tiny, teasing increments. No kisses, no fondling. Only the lightest of touches that electrified and soft, feathering strokes that devastated.

By the time her blouse and jeans had disappeared, Lissy trembled with sensation. Was he creating a tactile memory of her form? He never seemed to need to look at what he did in order to coax a fresh flush of excitement from her body, another frenzy of tantalized nerve endings. Her nipples rubbed impatiently against sheer fabric as his relentless fingers traced the outline of her bra . . . then slipped beneath its edges to tug gently at the confining material. She wanted to scream at Trahern to *rip it off, dammit*, when suddenly the offending garment was gone. Just gone. The thick night air caressed her breasts even as his inexorable touch ringed them with designs as finely detailed as those on his own skin. Perhaps the patterns were the same . . .

Lissy's body throbbed and pulsed, ached and arched. Wanted more and couldn't bear any more. Arousal lifted her to unimagined levels, and she knew there were still greater heights ahead. Yet something was missing. Trahern still held her gaze, and although she'd given up on ever knowing his eye color, she found herself suddenly looking deeper, past an unnamed barrier, to the man within. Saw the emotions he struggled to understand, the feelings he resisted, the truth he hid from.

In one fluid movement, Lissy sat up and tried to pull the mask from him. *Let me see you*, she shouted in her mind. "Let me in," she whispered aloud.

He pulled away from her. "I cannot. I am *gaethiwyd*. My will is not my own."

"Then let me set you free—"

Instantly she found herself sitting on her bedroom floor, wide-awake, naked except for a tangle of blankets, and definitely alone. All was dark, save for the glowing numerals on her alarm clock: 3:45.

*Crap.*

# THIRTEEN

In Trahern's former life, his finely honed talent for negotiation made him both highly respected and successful in trade. Now he had to negotiate some sort of leave from the Wild Hunt. Was such a thing even possible?

He had no idea how his petition would be received—not only was a human involved, but Braith had already acted on his own and left the Hunt. Did that negate Lurien's protection? The dark fae was truly a law unto himself, and no one, not even Eirianwen, dared cross him. Retribution was swift and terrible and certain. But Trahern also knew that Lurien held himself to a strict code of honor. He treated his Hunters well and, unlike many of the Tylwyth Teg, was both approachable and reasonable. Most of the time . . .

*There must be a way to convince him.*

With the queen still in residence in Tir Hardd, the Lord of the Wild Hunt could only be at the old capital, as far away from the monarch as possible. Eventually, Trahern found his leader on a broad knoll in the Black Marsh, inspecting a trio of strange young foals. All three were dark as night—until they moved. Pure-blooded fae horses were rare, and they often possessed unusual attributes. Trahern's own mount boasted horns and clawed hooves. *But these . . .* In his former life, he would have traded half his wealth, perhaps even most of it, to possess them.

"They're exquisite," he breathed. "Triplets?"

"Indeed. A ternion birth, rare and propitious."

Trahern couldn't help himself. "May I?"

At Lurien's nod, he stepped close to one of the beautiful creatures, passing his hands lightly over its withers and back. Instead of the fuzzy coat of a weanling, the young horse had smooth, overlapping scales that were as soft as shadow and just as black. That is, until its hide twitched. A dazzling wave of iridescent colors swept over the spot, fading from sight as the skin ceased quivering.

"I've never seen such horses."

"Nor have I, and I will not see them again. They are a gift from the ruler of the Dragon Men and, as such, will be returned."

*Returned?* How could anyone let go of such a prize? And then Trahern realized who the giver was: *Aurddolen*. A stunning and clever woman, she'd made no secret of her desire for the Lord of the Wild Hunt, nor of her goal to share with him the dominion of her vast, wild territories if he would but relinquish his much-rumored desire for Gwenhidw. *The legends say that love binds souls together—yet I see only division. If such is love, for what did Braith sacrifice himself? What purpose did it serve?*

Trahern wisely refrained from voicing such dismal thoughts and turned his attention back to his objective. His carefully prepared arguments proved unnecessary, however.

"Any mortal possessing such power is a serious matter," said Lurien. "But a young child with such abilities cannot be left to his own devices."

"Exactly. I believe he poses a great peril to those around him."

"In the human world, most assuredly. But this child—" The dark fae paused, expectant.

"Fox," supplied Trahern, feeling a surprising amount of discomfort as he did so. Lissy would be deeply troubled to know he had spoken the child's name to another in the faery realm. *But the Lord of the Wild Hunt is the most powerful ally we can hope for.*

Lurien nodded as if he, like Trahern, approved of the child's unusual name. "This young *Fox* is highly dangerous to our world as well. I felt his power the day he was born. Before he even received his name, I witnessed for myself that great magic had chosen him for its own."

"You *saw* him?"

"And hid the boy's energy as well as I could, knowing even as I did so that others would sense his power sooner or later. Some factions in the Nine Realms will surely seek to take him, hoping to use him to further their own goals and ambitions." He appeared to come to a decision then. "It is better that we know exactly where he is. The Hunt can protect him if necessary, and if we are fortunate, perhaps we will have some influence on him. You must train Fox before he attracts the wrong attention."

"His mother has great courage and is much devoted to her son. What if she does not agree to this?"

"While free will is to be respected among mortals and bravery honored, a human cannot be allowed to endanger the Nine Realms. If the woman will not acquiesce, then you have no choice. You must take the child elsewhere."

Trahern fervently hoped it would not come to that. "And what of my duty to the Hunt?"

Lord Lurien motioned to a fluttering of pyskies to take two of the horses away. "As I told you from the beginning, you are quite free to walk away from us at any time. But since your services have proven rather valuable, I would prefer not to lose you. And I'll wager that you'd rather not lose my protection."

"True enough."

"Then let both purposes be served. I hereby *command* you as a member of the Hunt to undertake a specific mission: to teach this human child all that you can. Use what resources you will. And as for duration, the mission will take as long as it will take."

"The boy will be instructed to the utmost of my ability, and I will withhold no knowledge from him," he said. *Not as my family sought to blunt my own training.* "But I cannot be faithless to my brother. I cannot stop searching for a way to free him."

"You have labored long. According to pysky chatter, when the Hunt takes its ease, you study and work, worrying at the puzzle of Braith's transformation like a hound gnaws a bone. Hast thou found the key?"

The answer was as a physical weight, crushing down on his entire body. "Nay." He waited for his leader to rebuke him for his failure. Instead, Lurien's voice was thoughtful.

"It is highly possible that by aiding the young child, you may aid your brother as well."

*What?* "How so?"

"In the contemplation of one problem, the answer to another often presents itself, does it not? Focus on the child, Trahern. And that you might do so fully, I will assign someone to guard you both. Braith will fill that role rather well, I think." The dark fae looked amused. "And, most conveniently, he is already in place."

"Yes, my Lord." *Of course he knows. He knows everything . . .* But there was *one* truth Lurien might not be aware of, and Trahern lowered his voice to a whisper as he revealed it. "The future is not hidden from my brother. I know not what he saw, for he is unable to tell me, but he sought out Fox immediately and has refused to leave his side since."

The Lord of the Wild Hunt was silent for a long time. "Make haste to train the child," he said at last. "It's been a long time since a mortal with such potential has appeared. A *very* long time. Not since my friend Myrddin was born."

Though Merlin was human, there wasn't a sorcerer in the Nine Realms who did not know of him and envy his abilities. And Lurien was his *friend*? Trahern struggled to keep the surprise from his voice. "I—I have heard he yet lives."

"Indeed. With mortals, the greater their exposure to magic, the longer their life. After mentoring Arthur, he paired with Coventina, a sorceress of the Undine, and has made his dwelling in the seas ever since. He walks upon the land or even between the realms at will but always returns to her." Lurien finished with the young horse and sent it away with its brothers. A fleeting expression of regret passed over his dark features, but whether it was for the gift or the giver, Trahern could not guess. "When last I spoke with Myrddin, he was yet content," continued Lurien. "He loves Coventina well and truly."

*Even Merlin? Does no one perceive the foolishness, the futility, of love?* However, the Lord of the Wild Hunt had lived far longer than Trahern. Perhaps he possessed some insight, some illumination, on the subject. "What is this love that both fae and mortals speak of?"

The Lord of the Wild Hunt released a long, deep breath—a sigh?—and a faraway look appeared in his depthless black eyes. "Love is truly an affliction and a great vulnerability. Yet it is the most desirable of all things in all worlds."

He vanished without another word, leaving Trahern with more questions than ever. The *affliction* and *vulnerability* parts he understood. But desirable? The queen would never love anyone but her dead king. And while Lurien might have affection for Aurddolen, he would never love her as she wished. *Three powerful people made miserable by their belief in love, and trapped by their desire for it.*

Just like his brother.

Yet Braith appeared pleased, even happy, in his new role as Fox's companion and guardian. *He has fresh purpose. Perhaps teaching the child will grant me this also.*

All Trahern had to do was gain Lissy's permission. And avoid the complications of his unexpected attraction to her . . .

Did she feel it as well? Her thoughts suggested as much, and she had said aloud that his hair was *gorgeous*. It wasn't a word used in the fae realm, but he hadn't been able to resist doing a little research. It meant "striking," "elegant," even "magnificent." He'd never had anyone admire his hair before, other than when he was a child and his relatives approved the color as meeting the high standards of appearance set by the Royal Court.

But it was just hair. What about the rest of him?

Love might not exist, but pairing was as natural as breathing in the fae world. The Tylwyth Teg reveled in pleasure as frequently as possible, and at Court, every type of carnal sport was commonplace. Frequent festivals there called for elaborate costumes that exposed more than they disguised—and sometimes no costumes at all. Charmed music was designed to heighten desire, and dances almost always concluded with more than a few naked couplings on the polished quartz floor of the grand ballroom. Little attention was paid to such, except to jest or wager. Or join in.

Having grown up in such an environment, Braith and Trahern had likewise indulged freely whenever the opportunity presented itself. And since the brothers were heirs to the House of Oak, opportunity had presented itself often. Even when he traveled to the far-off corners of the Nine Realms seeking both trade opportunities and new knowledge, the chance for indulgence was ever present.

Eventually he came to understand that pleasure had its limits, particularly when one lived long. *Small wonder that novelty is often esteemed above wealth.* Bored and desperate for ever-greater heights of sensation, many among the excitement-hungry fae used their ethereal beauty to lure humans to the realm for the express purpose of bedding them. Rumors claimed the experience to be exotic, far more interesting than sex with other fae, and possibly even addictive. Which made mortal lovers extremely valuable—as long as they lasted or until their novelty wore off.

Rumor *also* claimed, however, that a few fae harbored something rather like affection for their human pets, even forming an attachment. Heddwen had told him a story as a child, something about a fae lord taking a human to wife—a *briodferch o ddail*, or *bride of leaves*, so called for her mortality. And like a leaf, she eventually withered and died, to be mourned forever by her faery husband . . .

Such a thing would never happen in the House of Oak. Unlike other clans of the Tylwyth Teg, most with Oaken blood would never stoop to touch someone from a family of lesser status, never mind couple with a mortal. Humans were an altogether inferior species.

*As I once believed as well . . .*

Until he'd encountered Lissy.

Unarmed in any way, she'd confronted him in defense of her child. And when he surprised her in her home, she'd been as fierce as a warth, fighting with anything that came to hand.

*Novelty*, he tried to tell himself.

Her aura burned bright with intelligence, and her forthright personality held tremendous appeal after the artifices of courtiers.

*Simple novelty.* Nothing else.

Physically, Lissy's unique beauty set her apart from any female in his own world. Her hair, her skin, her eyes. *And her scent . . .* Minute vibrations suddenly thrummed in his blood like music, hummed along his skin until it burned, drummed between his legs until his *gwyllt* awakened.

The rush of true desire wasn't a novelty; it was a *revelation*. The mere thought of a woman had never excited him so! Was this part of the mystique that surrounded mortal lovers? Trahern shifted uncomfortably in the saddle and spelled his riding leathers to ease his arousal. He was sweating like an earthly horse run to ground.

*I cannot permit such distraction. The only thing that truly matters is obtaining Lissy's leave to train her son.*

If he failed to get that, he needn't be concerned about the effect she had on his body. He'd be too far away to be troubled by it. Too busy instructing Fox on the secrets and disciplines of sorcery.

*And too regretful for having stolen Lissy's child from her.*

The morning sun was impossibly bright as Lissy opened one eye. 7:39. *7:39?* She was on her feet in a heartbeat. And still naked, not having bothered to put on her favorite pajamas again before she climbed back into bed in the middle of the night. She glanced around for them—they were blue with little cartoon penguins, the soft material faded and almost threadbare in spots. If there was a less sexy outfit on the planet, she couldn't imagine it. And yet she'd managed to have a dream that simply blew everything she'd ever experienced or imagined right out of the water.

Apparently, it had blown her pajamas off as well. Lissy finally located the bottoms behind the corner chair where she must have flung them. The top turned up wedged between the mattress and the headboard. She didn't remember undressing herself, but the alternative was impossible. No goddamn faery had been in her room, she was sure of that. Okay, maybe *not* so sure—especially with her brain in desperate need of caffeine at the moment—but she was going to cling to the notion until proven otherwise.

Clutching the crumpled nightwear in front of her, Lissy stuck her head out of her bedroom door and listened. No cartoon soundtrack assailed her ears, so the TV wasn't on. And if the TV wasn't on, then her son was still safely in bed. He never began his day without a little screen time. Other parents might disapprove, but the truth was that morning television helped Fox keep track of time, something he had immense difficulty with otherwise. By portioning his routine into tidy thirty-minute segments, he could manage to adhere to a schedule that worked for them both. For instance, breakfast had to be finished by the time *SpongeBob* was over. When *Henry Danger* started, Fox got dressed and brushed his teeth. When *The Thundermans* began, it was time to leave the house for school. Lucky for her, though he liked the show, he didn't fuss about leaving it . . .

Relief washed over her as she realized she didn't have to get her son ready to go anywhere this morning. *Gotta love summer*, she thought. *Fox gets to sleep in, and I actually get a shower I don't have to rush through.* She balled up the pajamas and threw them into the laundry basket on her way by. Under the spray, however, she discovered that last night's dream wasn't yet finished with her. Every inch of her skin was still hypersensitized to touch. In fact, it would take very little to tip her over the edge. *Oh, hell, why not?* She opened her legs to the pulsing water and circled her fingers between them until the ferocious pleasure buckled her knees . . .

# FOURTEEN

The coffee can was empty. It took two cups of strong black tea and part of a third before her head finally cleared. Lissy had checked on Fox before coming downstairs, but he was still sprawled with an arm around Squishy Bear and softly snoring. And yup, Braith was still there, too, awake and alert, though he remained beside Fox's bed. He thumped his tail and appeared to grin as he recognized Lissy, just as any family dog would do. *If any family dog was a great gray grim . . .* She had no idea what Braith would do if someone tried to mess with her son, but surely just becoming visible to them would be deterrent enough.

After draining her cup, she rooted around in the freezer for an organic breakfast burrito to heat up. Tea was really not her drink, and so much of it on an empty stomach was never a good idea, but last night's erotic dreams (not to mention this morning's shower-powered orgasm) seemed to have shorted out most of her brain cells. And when a few finally revived, they got busy rehashing everything her mother had said lately about needing to get out and have a life. Maybe even meet someone.

Lissy pressed the buttons on the microwave emphatically as her thoughts picked up speed. She really didn't want to shoehorn a relationship into her already jam-packed life, but the powerful dream had effectively demolished her oh-so-logical reasoning. *I guess my subconscious is trying to tell me something. Or else I was just really overdue for that orgasm.* No grown woman wanted to admit that her mother had been right all along, but . . .

*I should call Mama and let her tell Vincente that I'd love to get together with him—*

*Gack!* She slapped the side of her head. Just because her mother might—*might*—be right didn't mean Lissy wanted her to know it. And she wasn't about to dip a toe into the dating scene (coffee . . . it was just for coffee!) with an enthusiastic Olivia practically watching over her shoulder. *For heaven's sake, I* know *Vincente. Kind of. We did go to the same high school, though he was a couple of grades ahead of me.* Her memory dredged up a skinny, nerdy guy with braces, fixated on chemistry and little else. *He certainly didn't talk to girls.* That was a long time ago—maybe he was just a late bloomer. *So, couldn't I just drop by the store and pick up a few things and just sort of casually run into him? And see what happens. Maybe nothing. Maybe coffee.*

Just *coffee.*

If she did that, hopefully her subconscious would stop hooking her up with oversexed faeries. *Why Trahern?* Her brain shot back, *Why not?* After all, wasn't he the first single guy she wasn't related to who'd actually been inside her home? Sat at her table? Talked about her child? And of course, it didn't hurt a bit that he was drop-dead gorgeous, and even the subtly alien angles of his perfect face were appealing. *I wonder why he wore a mask in the dream?* Ha, that had to be her subconscious again! Probably telling her that Trahern's presence in her dream was just filling a role. He could be anybody—well, not just *anybody*—but there was a definite gap in her life, a space, a vacancy that needed to be filled.

And sweet Jesus, she didn't want to think about what else she'd like filled . . . Shaking those incendiary thoughts from her head, Lissy got out the mundane ingredients for waffles and scrambled eggs.

When Fox came downstairs, she'd make breakfast for him (and more for herself, too. That silly little veggie burrito just wasn't going to cut it today). She'd check out how Fox felt, give him a decent amount of playtime, help him organize all his rock specimens from Palouse Falls if he wanted to, and then broach the subject of going to Handcastings after lunch. Good thing he loved visiting Brooke's shop, because she had a helluva lot of questions for her friends there.

A-a-a-nd if Ranyon just happened to want to atone for keeping secrets, then he could watch Fox for an hour or so while Lissy ran an errand to the pharmacy to pick up a few things . . .

Maybe a little male companionship.

*Dammit, it's just* coffee*!*

~

Flame spurted from the pwca's stallion nostrils, and he stamped his black hooves until they wrung ominous bell-like tones from the dented pavement. Thick rubbery lips sliding over long sharp teeth should not have been able to articulate words so well, but the pwca spoke clearly in the old language. "Do not challenge me, Hunter!"

His hand resting easily on his light whip, Trahern maintained an expression of polite disinterest, as if the discovery of a potentially deadly fae creature in the very midst of a human city was an everyday occurrence. As if finding this flesh-loving shapeshifter feasting on lilac blossoms like a cow but half a league from Lissy's home did not fill him with foreboding. By all the stars, why was it here?

Around them, cars traveled the smooth streets like great shiny beetles, their passengers intent on their destinations. A few people walked in the morning sunlight on the other side of the street, oblivious to the confrontation on this shaded sidewalk. Whatever happened, at least Trahern would not have to deal with their panic—

"Man, that is frickin' *awesome*!"

A young man had just emerged from a shop. His dyed red hair was long on one side and shaved on the other. White letters on his black shirt boldly proclaimed SCIENCE DOESN'T CARE IF YOU BELIEVE IN IT OR NOT. "Is your giant horse a puppet or a robot?" he asked, the words tumbling over each other in his excitement. "Gotta be a robot, right?"

The creature bellowed like a dragon, replete with smoke and flame. The man ducked—and just in time—but bounced back up and clapped his hands together.

"Wow! *So* frickin' lifelike! Hey, did you make it yourself? You got mad skills for sure, bro. Really like how you scaled it up, too. A mega-horse! That is just frickin' epic!" Too excited to wait for an answer, the man kept on talking.

And man he was. Every sense Trahern had told him that the stranger was mortal to the bone. While it was still possible for humans to be born with the ability to perceive the fae, the gift had become increasingly rare in the human population. But far more surprising was the pwca's reaction. It had ceased to bare its teeth and now sat upon the sidewalk like an oversize dog, its long mane and tail pooled around it. Golden eyes glowed with interest, and formerly flattened ears were pricked to full attention as it leaned forward eagerly to watch the man. *Not as potential prey but as entertainment.*

"I fool with computers and stuff, but I been looking into changing schools, getting into robotics. I mean, like, robots are future and all, you know?"

"Remember us as street performers," said Trahern, adding an undertone of compulsion to his voice. "Walk away in peace, be inspired by what you've seen this day, and learn to create your robots. Walk away *now*."

Still beaming, the man gave them an airy salute before heading down the sidewalk. The breeze carried back snippets of words: *Amazing! How the hell did he* do *it? Most awesome thing ever!*

"Truly, mortals are both strange and fascinating." The pwca shook himself all over, his long mane snapping within inches of Trahern's face. "What is a row-bot, Hunter?"

"Perhaps a simulacrum of some sort."

In answer, the horse became a snarling warth, a heavily muscled bull that stamped the ground until it shook, an elk swinging treelike antlers, and more, all in quick succession. Every creature as black as Hades itself and each with the same golden eyes. Finally, a powerfully built fae with skin the color of coal stood with folded arms before Trahern and grinned. "I am Cadell, and I can take any form that pleases me. I will have to find a row-bot so I can learn its shape as well." The pwca became the giant stallion once more. "But I find that this form pleases me best. I think the mortal admired it greatly."

"And since you did not attack him, you have earned a few more moments of my patience. What business have you in this world?"

The fae creature appeared to shrug, a strange and impossible gesture had he been a real horse. "My kind are both restless and curious. I have seen all there is to see in the Nine Realms, and it changes not. But among mortals, now, there is always something interesting going on. Countless nights in countless forms have I wandered freely on the human plane above our world. *Wales*, they call it now. I've watched how humans live, how their farms and forests grow, how their kingdoms rise and fall and rise again. They plant, they build, they *do*. They are never still, as I am never still."

All this Trahern knew and more. While other fae sought to amass wealth and power, pwcas gleaned information. Perhaps it helped fuel their limitless energy. Pwcas could even absorb the wisdom of the creatures they devoured, which unfortunately included the occasional mortal. But while they didn't bother to turn their boundless knowledge into gain, they'd seldom pass up a chance to use it to create a prank. Pwcas were not only shapeshifters, they were master tricksters.

Few could outwit their quick minds. "You have yet to answer for your presence *here*," he said.

"Did the queen not invite all to Tir Hardd? It is a good place, as Gwenhidw said it would be. Different, as she also promised. I find much to observe here as each clan finds its feet and builds for whatever future it imagines." Restless now, it whipped its long tail and danced upon its hooves. "But *my* kinsmen do not build. We are a free people, and seldom do our feet rest upon the ground. Curiosity compels me to visit the human world. And restlessness drives me to seek a place where I might outrun even the whirlwind." The long, dark muzzle suddenly hovered close to Trahern's ear, and the bold voice lowered to a whisper. "But I will tell you there is something *else* here, Hunter. An itch beneath my skin. A peculiar energy that pulls at me like grasping fingers. I came into the city thinking I might discover its source, for it is new to me."

Sudden ice snaked along Trahern's spine. Though he felt like cursing, he simply shrugged as the pwca drew back. "This entire world is peculiar. What would you do if you found it?"

"Do? I have no interest in *doing* anything." A true horse could not frown, yet the creature's forehead wrinkled deeply as if puzzled that Trahern would ask such a thing. "A question answered is as a thirst that is quenched, a fire doused, a desire sated. The satisfaction is all in the knowing."

*Truth.* Trahern could feel it, and he relaxed somewhat. The pwca would pose no danger to Lissy and Fox. But if it had sensed the boy's power, then other fae could as well.

"Am I to be sent back to Tir Hardd now?" The creature's bottom lip protruded slightly.

Normally, that was exactly what a Hunter would command. But those were not the words that left Trahern's mouth. "The rolling hills in that direction"—he pointed to the east and north—"have much open land, and the grasses and sage are as a silver sea beneath the moon. I ride there myself on occasion. Swear only that you will visit no harm upon a human, and I will pretend that I did not see you here this day, or any day after."

"So do I swear." The pwca ducked his big head quickly in a nodding bow. "I will also pledge to remember *you*, Hunter." It bent its long neck around and neatly plucked a trio of hairs from its ebony tail with astonishingly nimble lips, then proffered them to Trahern. They were longer than the fae was tall. "Use these to summon me should you have need." The big animal pivoted neatly on a single hoof and bolted down the street, up and over the tops of cars and trucks, leaving a wake of vibrant yellow flames that faded quickly to nothingness.

Though pleased with Cadell's gift, Trahern permitted himself a sigh as he carefully coiled the glittering hairs and secreted them in an inner pocket. As more faery beings inhabited the new territory of Tir Hardd, more appeared in the mortal plane above it. Across the ocean, the fae had wandered freely in the human world for as long as anyone could remember. But here? So far, the Wild Hunt had acted quickly to turn them back or retrieve them. It was apparent that this method would not work for much longer. *We cannot hope to contain them all. There will have to be laws put in place, boundaries and conditions set, as there are in the Nine Realms. Perhaps even a treaty made. I will have to consult with Lurien again soon.*

But first he had to speak with Lissy. The need to train Fox was far more urgent than he had first thought.

The large sign in the window read **HANDCASTINGS—MAGIC FOR A MODERN WORLD**. A smaller sign hung below it: **PAGAN, WICCAN, AND FENG SHUI SUPPLIES, ENERGY THERAPY, TAROT READINGS, AND MORE**. Lissy had barely parked her car before her son was out of his booster seat and tugging at the door handle. Once freed, he raced down the sidewalk to the door, just as Brooke's giant of a husband, Aidan, stepped out. Fox hammered home a fist bump, though his pale hand looked tiny and fragile against the master blacksmith's enormous knuckles.

"What up, dude?" he hollered at the top of his young lungs.

"You're up!" Aidan swung him effortlessly to his shoulder. If anyone else had swept him up like that, Fox would likely have gone rigid and started screaming. It had taken *four years* of unflagging patience on Aidan's part before Fox finally agreed to try the game. Now it was a comfortable tradition for them both.

Fox still refused to hug Aidan, though, just as he didn't hug Lissy. *But who knows, maybe I'll get a fist bump, too, someday . . .*

"That's a brammer of a dog you have there," Aidan said to the boy on his shoulder, and winked at Lissy. He already knew all about the grim—as much as any of them knew—but waited patiently as Fox introduced him. "Let's take your big friend to meet our cats." He ducked low with his excited cargo to enter the bright-purple double doors, with the enormous dog at his heels. Lissy followed the trio, shaking her head.

They didn't have far to go. Morning light splashed across the black-and-white tile floor, and Brooke's three cats were sprawled full-length to enjoy it. The dark one, Rory, was lying on his back like a sunbather at a beach.

"Rory! Hi, Rory!" yelled Fox from above her. "Bouncer, Jade, look at me! I'm way tall now, dudes! And I've got a dog, too!"

Braith sat down at a distance and wagged his great tail politely. *Can they see him like we can?* If they did, Lissy was certain the felines would head for the hills. Instead, they immediately bounded over to the monstrous fae dog, sniffing and rubbing against him—then casually sauntered back to their sunning spot as if meeting lion-size canines were an everyday occurrence.

"Hey, you three, look at the *fox* I've caught for you!" boomed Aidan. "I think you should eat him up!" Lissy's son giggled as he was gently deposited among the lazing felines. He stretched out on the tiles among them immediately, chatting as easily as if they were human friends. Bouncer, the big spotted one, batted playfully at the boy's hair with a carefully sheathed paw.

"Brooke's just finishing a healing ritual with her last client," Aidan said to Lissy. "She'll likely be another twenty minutes or so. And Ranyon's not here yet, but he'll be along soon. The shop's closed for the rest of the day, and I'll be keeping a good eye on our Mr. Fox." He reached into his pocket and produced a handful of long white turkey feathers. "I'm sure he'll think of some way to entertain these poor bored cats."

Lissy laughed, but her brain was suddenly abuzz. *Brooke's busy for a few minutes . . .* Before she could talk herself out of it, she put a hand on Aidan's heavily muscled arm. "Would it be okay if I ran a quick errand? It's just a couple of blocks from here."

He looked surprised and pleased. "You get little enough time on your own, girl. Off you go. I'll tell Brooke if she comes out before you get back."

She stood on tiptoe and kissed his cheek, then leaned in Fox's direction. "I'm just going to the store. Are you okay here without me for a little while?"

He was far too engrossed with his furry friends to even look in her direction. "I'm going to take that as a yes," she said, and bolted for the door before she changed her mind.

# FIFTEEN

The pharmacy was five blocks over and two blocks down. Lissy decided to walk, hoping it would give her time to think of an approach. Should she go up to the dispensing counter with a question of some kind for the pharmacist . . . and then act surprised that the pharmacist was Vincente? *Not really my style.* Maybe she could just browse, then look over and catch his eye. *Better, but what if he doesn't look up?* She crossed the last street and stood in front of the shop windows, pretending to be interested in a display of orthopedic sandals. Finally, she straightened her blouse, adjusted her cross-body handbag, and headed inside.

Pharmacies always seemed to have a certain aroma to them, like sniffing a bottle of aspirin. This one seemed to have a fruity potpourri mixed in. There were the businesslike aisles of cold and stomach remedies, vitamins and ointments, diapers and tissues, plus an entire section of feminine-hygiene products. *Definitely not going to browse there.* Glass shelves ran along the east wall, however, with pretty giftware. A candle and scented-wax display was probably the source of the potpourri smell. And facing it was a colorful bank of greeting cards. Relieved, Lissy decided to do some real shopping and pick up something for Tina's birthday.

She had just selected a card with a wiener dog on it that looked a lot like Jake when a voice near her made her jump.

"Melissa, *bonita*! I was just telling your beautiful mother the other day that I hadn't seen you in years." It was Vincente, but not the quiet, gangly youth he'd been in senior high. He'd filled out—and maybe even worked out—and his confident smile displayed even, movie-star-white teeth. Contacts had replaced the wire-framed glasses she remembered, and his wavy hair was slicked back into a carefree *GQ* style. "And here you are in my very own *farmacia*!"

"I-I just ran in to get this." Lissy held up the wiener dog card almost defensively. "So, this place is yours?" she asked, deciding to feign ignorance.

"Bought it last year, lock, stock, and barrel." He waved an arm to encompass his surroundings, and she wondered if he were flashing his expensive-looking watch on purpose. Nope, he was aiming to put the other arm around her . . . She danced just out of reach, pretending to select another card, and if the man noticed, he didn't let on. In fact, he continued without missing a beat. "Great location, huh? We do as much business here as any of the local chain stores, yet we remain completely independent. Plus, I've converted the entire upstairs into a high-end office space. Not a single vacancy—in fact, we have a waiting list of prospective tenants!"

She smiled weakly. *Talk about trying too hard to make an impression.* Maybe he just needed to show her how much he wasn't that shy boy in twelfth grade anymore. Still, something about this exchange made the hair on the back of her neck stand up. Could her own awkwardness be causing such uncomfortable vibes? "That's wonderful," she managed. "It must keep you very busy."

"Of course it does, but I can always make a little time here and there. That's the advantage of being the owner." His smile broadened as he suddenly seized her hand in both of his. "For instance, I could take you to lunch right now, *florecita*, and we could get reacquainted.

I'm thinking we could start with some Manzanilla sherry and raw oysters at this great little place I know."

Oysters? *You gotta be kidding me. He can't possibly be unaware of how that sounds.* She tried to ease her hand out of his grip without seeming rude. "That's really kind of you, Vincente, but I'm on my way to an appointment in a few minutes."

If anything, he looked more hopeful, and he gripped her hand tighter. "Is it medical? Because a trained pharmacist can often give you great advice. Doctors don't always have the time to really listen to you and administer to your true needs."

*Ugh! My true needs are to get my hand back and leave*, she thought. "Look, Vincente, I—"

"Ah, there you are, Lissy. It is imperative that I speak with you." The new voice came from close behind her and must have startled Vincente as well, since her imprisoned hand fell free. She turned—and found herself completely speechless.

*Tall, dark, and handsome* did not do justice to the man standing in front of her. An upscale executive suit had been admirably dressed down with a smooth-fitting T-shirt, the gray jacket left open as if to tease her with the hard definition of his chest and abdomen. His thick sable hair fell carelessly to his collar, and expensive sunglasses softened the angles of his lightly bearded face. *Esquire*'s photographers would probably walk a mile on their knees just to put him on their next magazine cover . . .

She wasn't fooled, however. Surprised and possibly drooling a little, but not fooled by the elegant facade. *Trahern!*

*At your pleasure.*

There was no mistaking the fae's voice in Lissy's head, self-assured yet intimate. How had he managed to disguise—no, *humanize*—his appearance so dramatically? More important, why?

*What the hell are you doing here?* She directed her thoughts squarely at Trahern, confident now that he could hear her.

*I came to speak with you about your son.*

Her heart missed a beat. *Where's Fox? Is he all right?*

*Your son is well, and precisely where you left him. But it is needful that we speak privately.*

"Where—where did you come from?" Behind her, Vincente's protest sounded high and thin. He cleared his throat twice, then seemed to recover himself. "Sir, my tech behind the counter will be happy to assist you. At present, I am engaged in serving this fine woman."

"Truly? You appear to be doing her no service at all."

The pharmacist's face darkened. "It is impolite to interrupt."

"Then please cease to do so. My matter is urgent."

"Melissa, do you know this, this *maleducado*?" He seized her upper arm possessively—and won himself a solid punch in the shoulder as she pried her limb free.

"For your information, he is *not* a rude man." *Although we are* so *going to have a chat about the finer points of human customs.* "And I know him very well." Walking up to Trahern, she tucked herself neatly under the tall fae's shoulder as if she did it all the time. "Vincente, this is my dear friend *Tristan*. He's with an international law enforcement agency and—and he's on a case right now." *Work with me here, will you?*

Trahern looked down at her. His unusual eyes weren't visible through the dark glasses, but one eyebrow arched high above them for a long moment. Then he slipped long, strong fingers around her waist, carefully drawing her closer as he regarded her former schoolmate with feigned interest. "In my haste to perform my *official duties*, I appear to have forgotten my manners. Vincente, is it?" He did not offer a hand.

Neither did the pharmacist. "How could I not know you are an officer of the law? Of course you are. Look at you! I didn't see you come in here, and it startled me, that's all. Forgive me, we get so many shoplifters who try to hide behind the displays." The man's confidence was nowhere to be seen now, and a droplet of sweat trailed down his temple.

"Plainly, the loveliness of our mutual friend has enchanted your senses," said Trahern. "I entered the front door directly behind those women over there." He pointed to a trio of seniors in workout gear appraising exercise drinks in the cooler. Vincente turned to look.

Lissy looked, too, until Trahern tipped her chin up with a finger and kissed her.

It should have been a simple kiss, a friendly kiss, at the very most a frivolous mistletoe kiss. Yet the warm press of his lips seemed to speak to something within her, awoke something long-buried . . . and that *something* raged to be set free. Every intense sensation from her dream came back to her, and a deliciously icy shiver ran from the top of her head to the tips of her toes. His mouth smiled against hers—did he know?—before traveling on to softly skim her cheekbones, her brow, her eyelids.

*He smells like the air after a thunderstorm . . .*

Lissy reached for him then, twisting her fingers in his hair as she tasted the wild sky on his elegant mouth and the faint tingle of lightning on his skin. She breathed him in, and a cool, clean breeze seemed to waft right through her, carrying away all the little gray bits from the dark, dusty corners of her soul. How had she not noticed them before? She felt light, lifted, on the verge of taking flight herself. And with her, heartbeat for heartbeat, was Trahern. Her fingers outlined his shoulders, traced their way around his body, feeling the surprisingly hard muscle beneath the glovelike leather—

Leather? It surprised her just enough that she opened her eyes, and whatever pleasurable zone she'd been floating in dissipated like morning mist. Trahern's disguise—the glasses, the suit, the dark hair, the styled beard—had indeed disappeared entirely in favor of his own striking features, and her heart beat even faster at the sight. Surely it wasn't fair for anyone, human or otherwise, to be that good-looking!

His snowy mane fell long and loose, feather-soft as it brushed over her bare arms. Lissy bit back the sigh that the sensation drew from her and shoved away the memories it triggered, but she couldn't keep her skin from quivering. *What just happened?*

*It is difficult enough to maintain a glamour when someone has already seen my true form. Impossible to do so when you touch me. I cannot hide from you.*

She hadn't been asking about the sudden reversion to his natural appearance. Lissy had seen enough magic in her life to be unfazed by something so minor. But . . . he hadn't exactly been talking about his appearance, either, had he? Trahern's gaze on hers was unfathomable at first. She still couldn't tell what color those incredible eyes were, but as before, the longer she looked into them, the more she could see. He was . . . shaken? Fair enough—she felt a little shaken up herself. Lissy hoped like crazy that he hadn't sensed that strange, wild part of her that even she hadn't known existed. What the hell was that anyway? *Who* was that? Not her, surely.

Yet here she was, still in his arms and making no effort to leave. She may have broken off the kiss, but her body was still firmly fitted to his—and most surprising of all was how easy it was, how natural it seemed to be so close to him. As if they had danced to this song before and would again . . .

*You did not give him my name.*

*Names have power, right? Why would I want to hand over your power to someone like Vincente?*

Trahern smiled with genuine warmth and brushed back a curl from her face. *I see that Fox has acquired his considerate nature from his mother.*

In the back of her mind, Lissy was vaguely aware that Vincente was wide-eyed and indignant, his mouth opening and closing as if he couldn't find any words. It was of no importance to her. All that mattered in this moment was trying to figure out this strange new connection with Trahern. He leaned his forehead to hers, and part of her hoped that he might kiss her again. He didn't. Instead, she became aware of a strange sensation in the back of her head, something between the fizzing of a soda and the buzz of electricity—

And found herself standing on the sidewalk on another street entirely.

"What the hell did you just do to me?" Lissy wriggled out from under his arm but immediately stumbled. If he hadn't caught her elbow, she might have fallen.

"Stand still!" ordered Trahern, and frowned when she pulled away anyway. "You are not accustomed to magic."

"Ya think?" She put a hand to the back of her head as if it hurt. "You can't—you can't just go poofing people from place to place!"

"I just did. And it is called *translation*, not *poofing*. It is efficient. It is how one travels in haste."

"It is how one pisses off people in a hurry," she retorted. "And to think I defended you to Vincente! I take it back. It's rude enough when you zap yourself inside my house without being invited, but you don't get to move me from place to place like mindless luggage."

*Rude?* He didn't understand all the nuances of the human language, but this word was plain. Rudeness was something to be avoided at all costs. The entire language of the Royal Court was one continuous dance of courtesy, the rituals of which served to veil the less savory thoughts and machinations that almost always lurked beneath the hauntingly beautiful exteriors. Although he, Trahern, heir apparent of the House of Oak, had witnessed rude behavior many times in many parts of the fae realms, he'd certainly never been accused of it! Even as a Hunter—for the Hunt cared not how they were viewed by others—he did not stoop to discourtesy.

Yet clearly he had done so with Lissy. *I am not in my world; I am in hers. If I am to secure Lissy's permission to train her child, then I must observe the rules of behavior that apply here.* He suspected it was going to make a challenging task all the more difficult, however. So was the attraction that all but sparked in the air between them. *By the Seven Sisters, this cannot be the product of mere novelty.* Something else, something much more powerful, was surely at play here. And he had no idea what it was.

"It has never been my intention to give offense," he said at last. "What is it you would have me do instead?"

Lissy eyed him suspiciously, as if he might be mocking her. "Right now? For starters, you should have asked permission before you beamed me out like that. At the very least you could have warned me. And what about Vincente? He's going to be traumatized for life after seeing us vanish like that."

"The man remembers nothing," said Trahern. "I cast a mild spell so he would forget the incident." *Including that you were ever in his shop.*

"I guess that's for the best. Now about my house . . ."

"Your house?"

"Yeah. Most people come to the goddamn door and wait outside to be welcomed in. Even Claire knows that much, and her manners wouldn't fill a teaspoon."

*Wait? Outside?* Trahern was long accustomed to going where and when he pleased. In his former life, his presence might be formally announced as he entered either house or palace, but he would never be required to wait. As a trader, there was nowhere in the Nine Realms that he could not enter at his own pleasure. And as a Hunter? He need not beg entry from anyone, anywhere. And not long ago, he would never, ever have done so for a mere human.

But Melissa Santiago-Callahan was no ordinary human . . .

*My brother would surely laugh if he knew how acutely my perception has been altered.* He shrugged as if he didn't care one way or another. "I will linger at the door in the future," he said at last. The concession should have grated on him—but strangely, it didn't.

"Thank you. And no more poofing me without warning."

"That I will not promise. You pretended to have an intimate connection to me in order to divest yourself of that man's unwanted attentions," he said. "I am not all that familiar with human culture, but if we were truly paired, then surely I would remove you from a situation you did not wish to be in."

"*Remove me?* Who on earth talks like that?" She paced in front of him, then stopped suddenly and put her hands up. "Nope, this one's squarely on me. Although I can see that we've got some serious cultural differences to work out, this time it's my fault. I put you on the spot, and I'm sorry."

"How can any fault be yours?"

"Because I shouldn't have involved you. I didn't need to be rescued—I'm not helpless! If you hadn't surprised me, I would have finished telling Vincente I wasn't interested and simply left on my own."

Trahern folded his arms and studied Lissy, more for pleasure than anything: he already knew she was right. "What you say is true. But surely it was far more gratifying to see the man gaping like a fish when we kissed."

She blushed suddenly, a warm wash of color from throat to cheek that fascinated him. Fae women could not blush unless aided by a glamour. And none had ever favored him with such a conspiratorial grin. "Okay, I have to admit that *was* pretty good," she said. "And he won't ask to see me again because he doesn't know he saw me in the first place, so that's good, too."

*Very good indeed.* He hid his thoughts from Lissy but could not hide them from himself. Nor could he understand them. Why was it so pleasing to imagine turning that pompous, self-important human male into a fat, toothless *afanc*? His sorcerer's code prohibited such action against a human who was merely annoying rather than guilty of a crime. The law of the Hunt precluded it as well (although a temporary prank would likely be considered). Yet the most powerful deterrent was the fact that Lissy herself would not approve. She prided herself on self-reliance, and to interfere in her affairs would be insulting to her. He grasped that now. *I was a fool to think that a woman who would defend her child from a grim with only her bare hands would require protection from a mere shopkeeper.*

*And am I also a fool for wanting her back in my arms?* He needed to talk to Braith—if only his brother could respond! Trahern was so focused on his own thoughts that he missed most of what Lissy said.

". . . and of course, we won't be doing any more kissing."

The words were like the sudden rap to the head that old Heddwen occasionally gave him when he didn't pay attention as a child. It wasn't the child in him that reacted now, however. "You did not like it?" he blurted.

"You know full well that I liked it very much. But that certainly doesn't mean we're going to do more of it."

"Why not?"

"Look, I'm sorry I may have given you the wrong signals. I don't know how things work in your world, but in mine—at least in my own life—I usually don't kiss men unless I have some sort of relationship with them."

"You told Vincente we were *dear friends*."

"I exaggerated. You and I are barely even acquaintances. And then your faery magic overcame my better judgment."

It took him a moment to realize what she meant. "You believe I used magic to coerce you?" Many of the Tylwyth Teg would have done exactly that, yet he found the idea distasteful and more than a little offensive.

"Well, of course I do! That wasn't like any kiss *I've* ever experienced."

Trahern shook his head slowly. "Nor have I experienced such. Shall I accuse you of ensorcelling me?"

Her sable eyes grew very wide. Twice she started to say something, and both times she stopped. "Just—just don't do it again," she managed at last, and walked away without looking back.

Disappointment—that was what this new emotion must surely be. He wondered wildly why it should even matter to him that Lissy didn't want his attentions. Countless women across the Nine Realms had offered him every pleasure possible and would happily do so again. How could a single refusal be so, so . . . Trahern could find no words in any language that described what he felt. *It doesn't matter*, he told himself, not believing it for an instant. *It must* not *matter*, he corrected. *The only important thing is the boy.*

His longer strides quickly brought him alongside Lissy. "We still must speak of Fox and the powerful magic that has come to rest upon him. Your son cannot continue without a teacher."

She kept walking. "Oh yeah? What if he doesn't want one?"

"I—but—he must be tutored!"

"He *must* do nothing." She stopped to face him. "You don't even know if he's interested in magic. In fact, you don't know *him* at all. For your information, Fox already has hobbies. He loves rocks and animals and video games. He's crazy about superheroes and bugs and Scooby-Doo. He's never even mentioned magic or expressed the slightest desire to learn about it. Not once. So don't tell me he *has* to learn about it. Believe me, he has other skills he needs to work on."

Trahern swallowed his first response, considering it best to say nothing for a time. He might not be fully acquainted with other human emotions, but anger was common to both mortal and fae—and Lissy was obviously irritated. She didn't say another word to him but took two steps to one of his, moving briskly and quickly as they crossed numerous streets and made their way through small clusters of people here and there.

Finally, they stopped in front of a tall brick building with bright-purple doors. "I have an appointment," she said simply.

"You are yet annoyed with me." He sought to hear her thoughts and lightly touched her shoulder to make a stronger connection. The mere fact that she didn't shrug his hand away afforded him a peculiar sense of relief.

"You'd better believe I'm annoyed, but it's not personal. Not yet anyway. I think you mean well."

"As Ranyon undoubtedly meant well when he did not reveal what he knew about your son."

Her eyes flashed beneath her frown. "Dammit, you can stop reading my mind right now, mister, or I *am* going to be truly, personally, very much annoyed with you."

"You do not understand, I—"

Both of them froze as a high-pitched shriek knifed the air, ululating from all directions at once. Lissy clapped her hands over her ears in apparent pain as the shrill wail continued. "What the hell is that?" she shouted, stumbling toward the shop entrance.

Trahern was already there. "*Agored!*" The double doors flew open before him as if blasted. His light whip flashed in his hand as he ran inside.

# SIXTEEN

*I have to get to Fox!* The noise was not only deafening but dizzying, driving her to her knees with vertigo. Nevertheless, Lissy fought her way inside the building, crawling along the smooth black-and-white tiles. If anything, the sound was even louder in here. There was no sign of anyone in the main shop, no one hiding behind any of the counters or under the table of a booth. *The storeroom.* The last time she was here, Aidan had helped Fox build a fort out of boxes . . . Lissy clamped her jaws shut against the nausea that roiled her stomach, as her fear for her child drove her onward.

She'd nearly reached the black paneled door marked **STAFF ONLY** when Ranyon appeared at her elbow. Quickly, the ellyll placed his strange twiggy hands over her ears and muttered something she had no hope of hearing over the din—

And then suddenly she *could* hear. The wailing seemed no louder than a teakettle whistle—aggravating but not debilitating—as if the little elemental had dialed down the volume on it. The nausea and the vertigo dissipated quickly.

"Omigod, Ranyon—"

"Shht! There's a hungry *cyhyraeth* in there," he whispered. "Ya don't be wantin' her attention. She uses her wail to stun her prey so they cannot flee."

"Where's Fox? *Where's Fox?*"

The ellyll didn't get a chance to answer before Lissy was on her feet and fighting with the old door latch. "Hey!" she yelled as loudly as she could. "Leave my son alone!" She burst into the storeroom—and stopped dead.

Furniture, crates, books, and papers were plastered to the walls as if a massive explosion had taken place. Aidan lay in a pile of boxes as if he'd been thrown there. The great gray grim was sprawled in another corner of the room. And in the very midst of the chaos, Trahern stood with his light whip wrapped around an apparition from hell. The form was that of a woman, but there all resemblance ended. Huge leathery wings were crumpled behind the gray-skinned creature, bound to its bony body by the whip's crackling coils, yet the cyhyraeth floated near the ceiling as it fought against its lightning-charged tether. Long, twisting ropes of seaweedlike hair framed a skeletal face, its mouth a wide, dark hole filled with black needle teeth. Glittering white eyes flashed as they caught sight of Lissy, and loud shrieks gave way to venomous hisses. Just as it spat at her, Ranyon shoved Lissy aside with surprising strength. A flaming glob struck the floor where she'd been standing and proceeded to burn through it.

*The child is safe! Get out of here!* Trahern's voice was loud inside her head, and although Lissy couldn't take her eyes off the creature he held captive, she allowed herself to be half led, half dragged by the determined ellyll. She'd barely reached the doorway when the fae shouted aloud: *"Ddod fel llwch!"* With the skill and strength of an accomplished fighter, he leapt and spun, jerking the whip so that it tightened around the cyhyraeth—

And brought it crashing to the floor in a silent flash of violet light.

Ranyon, bless him, had been faster to cover her eyes than she had, throwing his beloved baseball cap over her face. When she pulled it away, the screaming creature was gone—and she was nearly knocked down by Brooke racing by her to get to Aidan. More than a little stunned, Lissy walked slowly into the room, studying the debris. Searching.

"Where's Fox?" She trusted the fae's word that he was safe, and something in her gut, perhaps what tiny bit of precognition she possessed or maybe just plain mother's instinct, affirmed it—but she'd feel a helluva lot better seeing for herself that her son was okay.

Trahern turned at the sound of her voice, and his appearance shocked her. His fair skin was even paler than usual, with a decidedly gray cast to it, and he seemed unsteady on his feet. Lissy was at his side in a moment, inserting herself under his shoulder and supporting him. "Omigod, are you hurt?"

"Nay, my strength is merely depleted. Rest and food will cure it. It is the duty of the Wild Hunt to send trespassers back to the fae realms—but some such as this are a danger in both worlds."

"Hmpf," said Ranyon. "Then 'tis a shame you reached the monster first. I didn't find sending your great lump of a dog back to Tir Hardd to be difficult at all."

Trahern's face was expressionless as usual, yet Lissy sensed his deliberate effort to exert patience. "While it is true that an elemental possesses far more magic than any sorcerer may aspire to, I did not send the cyhyraeth to another realm. I destroyed it."

The little ellyll suddenly looked uncomfortable. "Aye, well . . . good riddance to that troublesome creature fer sure. We'd best be tendin' to the others." Quickly, he headed over to Brooke and Aidan. Thankfully, the big man was already on his feet, though he held his arm.

Confident her friends were in Ranyon's good hands, Lissy helped Trahern walk to where the great gray grim was sprawled. The steady rise and fall of the enormous dog's sides assured her that he was breathing. But where was Fox? Surely Braith would not have left him?

"You said my son was safe," she prodded Trahern. "Where did you send him?"

"I did nothing. It was my brother." The fae knelt by the dog and placed his hand on a muscled gray shoulder. After a moment, the dog opened his eyes and raised his great head, panting heavily—and appearing to grin. He rolled to his feet to expose a wide-eyed Fox, curled up in a deep cavity amid the broken boxes.

"Dude!" Her son bounced to his feet and reprimanded his canine friend. "That's not how you play hide-and-seek! You're not supposed to tell where I am!" Three cats popped their heads out of a nearby box and likewise glared at the unrepentant dog.

"Omigod, sweetie, are you all right?" asked Lissy. She wanted to hug her son so hard and tight . . . but even as she placed a hand on his shoulder, he shrugged it away.

"He told you where I was!" he yelled. "Tell him he's not playing the game right!"

*Nope, he wouldn't welcome a hug right now at all.* "Um, Braith just didn't understand the rules, hon. Your new friend's not from around here, so he probably never played hide-and-seek before." She watched as Fox took a breath, then another. Shifting his weight from side to side. Considering.

"Maybe he needs someone smart like you to teach him how," she added softly.

Fox rubbed his head rapidly with both hands, leaving his blond hair in wild tufts, and gave an exaggerated sigh. "I guess so. But we're going to have to start *all* over again." He headed for the main shop with three cats trotting close behind him. Before Braith could follow, Lissy threw her arms around the dog's huge neck.

"Thank you for looking after him," she whispered in his velvety ear. "Thank you." The big washcloth tongue caught her full in the face before she could dodge, and she fell back sputtering as the dog ambled after Fox.

*This may be of aid.* A square of bright fabric floated into her view, and she accepted it gratefully. After drying her face, she smiled up at Trahern.

*Thanks to you, too. I can't believe you faced down that demon by yourself.* Her thoughts seemed to flow more easily to him now, as if a pathway had been made. *You saved us all.*

His face didn't change, nor did he acknowledge the compliment. "I fear it is but the beginning. Fox and your friends are only safe for the moment."

"You said you destroyed the monster."

"The cyhyraeth feeds on magical energies. Just as this creature was drawn here by your son's powerful aura, others will be attracted to Fox as well. I have already questioned a pwca in the city this day. It is why I interrupted your visit with Vincente earlier."

"But—but my son *can't* be attracting these things!"

"He can, and he is." Trahern paced then, a little stiffly. "How do you think Braith discovered Fox in the very beginning? And by the stars of the Seven Sisters, it is truly fortunate that my brother found your child first."

"Now wait just a—"

"Good lady, waiting is no longer possible. Not for me, not for you, and certainly not for Fox. That night at the waterfall, I watched you defend your son against impossible odds. Just now, you had every intention of doing so again, though you knew not what you faced."

"Any mother would do the same."

A shadow passed over his features, vanishing as quickly as it had appeared. "Fortunately for you and for Fox, what you found the first time was my good-natured twin. But your courage would not have prevailed against the cyhyraeth." Trahern spread his hands. "You and Fox would be dead, your mortal friends as well, and the fault would be entirely mine. Because you *are* mortal, I have delayed telling you all that I should have."

Lissy stilled. *Is there a goddamn sign on my head that says, Don't tell me important stuff?* She already had one confrontation scheduled with Ranyon. Maybe Trahern should take a number . . . "And just what is it you think I should know?"

"Fox is in danger at this very moment. Magic has chosen him, a more powerful magic than you have ever witnessed or, indeed, can imagine. If he does not learn to control his power, others will come here from the faery realm who will seek to control *him*. They will take him and use him, or they will kill him."

The world abruptly narrowed to a pinprick—then expanded again with too-bright light. Lissy swayed a little, but Trahern's grip on her arm kept her from going down.

"Sit," he ordered, and instantly she found herself in an elegant yet comfortable wing chair. Embroidered birds of every type and color graced its soft, rich fabric. She knew that Brooke and Aidan didn't have any furniture like it. And if they did, it sure wouldn't be standing at ground zero in what was left of the storeroom. "This—this is beautiful," she murmured while she tried to gather her scattered thoughts.

"You appeared ill. Perhaps I was too blunt—"

"Too blunt?" The last of the fuzziness left her brain. "A couple of days ago, I was looking forward to a happy, peaceful summer with my son. Now you show up, and suddenly Fox's life is on the line through no fault of his own, and I'm trying to cope with one weird-ass thing after another. How do I know that monster didn't show up because of you? Maybe you're the one who attracted it here!"

"That is not possible. A cyhyraeth would avoid such as I because I possess the power to—"

"Exactly! You. Have. Power. That's the point. It makes me think I've been a little too quick to trust you. For all I know, you staged the whole damn thing to make me agree to let you near my son." She gripped the arms of the chair and rose to her feet. "You can't possibly need an apprentice or an assistant badly enough to choose a human being. What is it you really need him for, Trahern? A spell? A ritual? You know, I've heard that *some* faeries steal away children!" As soon as she said that, she wished she hadn't. But the ethereally handsome being before her not only wasn't like her, he wasn't even the same goddamn species. Who knew what the hell she was dealing with? Only one thing was certain: she would go down swinging rather than allow anyone or anything into Fox's life that might harm him.

Trahern was silent for a long moment, seeming to draw inward. "You were correct when you said we were but acquaintances," he said at last. "If we were indeed friends, then you would know the insult you have just offered me."

"I'm not trying to insult you. I just want my son safe and—"

He cut her off with a gesture of impatience. "You and I shared bread in your kitchen, and I gave you an oath. You claimed to believe me then. As for the rest, what need could I possibly have for a human child? I who have ridden the sky itself with the Wild Hunt for several of your lifetimes? I who have called down black fire in the midst of the Royal Court? Melissa Santiago-Callahan, you may fight the truth all you wish. But magic has chosen Fox, and as a sorcerer it is my responsibility to teach him, if only to be able to defend himself. That is the way for him to be *safe*."

Lissy became aware of Brooke on her left. On her right, Ranyon slid his strange, skinny hand into hers. Their silence and their solidarity spoke volumes, confirming her worst fears: that the fae's chilling words were absolutely, immutably, and irrevocably *true*.

She took a deep breath, then another, willing herself to accept what she would rather not. And wishing, too, that she could take back some of her words. "I'm really sorry for what I said to you, Trahern."

"I hold you blameless." His words seemed careful—even gentle. "This matter has come to you with great suddenness, and you are accustomed to neither fae nor magic. You would not have recognized the signs in advance."

"Oh, but I *did* see some signs. Fox having dreams. Fox communicating with animals. Fox seeing things before they happened. I didn't want to believe it; I didn't want to know. What kind of a mother hides from what's right in front of her?" She hadn't hidden from the words of the autism experts, the doctors who'd identified Asperger's as the source of Fox's strange behaviors. She'd embraced it all, from the extra work it meant for her, to the daily frustrations and the little victories. But she'd closed her eyes to any possibility of magic, of any kind. "Was I protecting Fox or myself?"

"Perhaps both, but not without cause. I have witnessed for myself that your son is highly sensitive. You have told me that he is easily upset by change. It could be frightening to introduce something new and potentially disruptive into your lives."

Beside her, Ranyon snorted. "'Tis exactly why I've held my tongue!"

"And did your friends no service by trying to spare them." Trahern's voice gained an edge as he confronted the ellyll. "You knew of the child's talents from the beginning and said *nothing*, when you might have prepared Fox and readied his mother for what was to come!"

"Now don't be judgin' the complications! Ya weren't here, son of Oak, and if yer great calf of a dog hadn't shown up, ya *still* wouldn't be here!" Watch gears and marbles fell to the floor from beneath his shirt as the ellyll shook his knotty fist at the fae. Brooke's efforts to shush him were in vain. "'Twould suit me if ya weren't, too! We've already got an elemental and a masterly witch. Why do we need *you*?"

*Not this again.* Lissy leaned over and whispered fiercely, "What would have happened to Fox today if Trahern hadn't been here? When no one else with magic was close enough to get there in time?" Ranyon's mouth opened as if to speak, then closed again, his lips compressed into a thin line. His body language spoke for him as his slumping shoulders made his Blue Jays T-shirt sag.

Lissy made a mental note to take her leafy friend aside later and give him a hug, then turned her attention back to the issue at hand.

"It's true that we have an elemental and a witch. We *also* have a fae and a mom. I can see it's going to take all of us working together as a team to help Fox understand the magic he's inherited." She looked up at Trahern. "You're absolutely right about my being reluctant to rock the boat. I think I've spent the last nine years of my life trying to keep things as calm and level as possible, with no surprises." She switched to mind speech. *It's not just how Fox survives, you know. It's how I coped when my dad died, and again when my fiancé died.*

*I did not know of your losses. And your fiancé . . .* She could feel him struggling to interpret the word. *Your betrothed? He was Fox's father.*

*Yes. He died before Fox was born.*

*Then he has missed meeting an intelligent and talented son.* Trahern inclined his head. *Nor has he seen what a fierce and devoted mother you have become.*

Lissy willed herself not to tear up as she continued aloud. "Sometimes despite everything you try to prepare for, you get surprised anyway, and this is one of those times." *On more than one level!* "So, Fox and I will adjust. It'll be hard, but we'll get through it. But I have other, bigger concerns."

"You are worried about Fox being safe," supplied Trahern.

"There are different kinds of safety, and many ways to harm someone," said Lissy, feeling her way along. "I could use some reassurance that you fully understand that. For instance, Fox has needs, and it's usually not a good idea to take him out of familiar surroundings. I don't know where you thought you'd hold these lessons of yours, but some deep, damp wizard's cave in the middle of nowhere is completely out of the question."

*Magic does not require dampness.* Was he teasing her? "I am quite capable of instructing your son wherever he is most comfortable, including at your home. I will defer to your judgment on the location."

She nodded, trying to sort her thoughts. There was one thing above all, one thing more important than everything, and she struggled to find a way to express it, even to herself. And then the right words welled up inside her, quiet but sure.

"I told you about my son's heart, that one of the most wonderful things about him is how kind and compassionate he is," she began. "So I need to know that you will do nothing to change him." *I will fight for this.* Lissy held Trahern's gaze as if challenging a tiger, but there was no answering challenge in his ever-changing eyes. Only steadiness and reassurance now, as certain as if he held his hand out to her. *I need to hear it from you*, she persisted. *Say the words. Say the words now in front of my friends.* "Tell me that magic is not going to change who my son is."

"To change Fox would be to harm him, and I have already vowed not to do that. I will train him so that he will not become a helpless slave to his own power or a puppet to another's desires. Instead, Fox's magic will serve him as he truly wishes, and what he wishes will be his choice and no one else's." Trahern drew an ornate silver dagger from his waist and pricked his left wrist with the tip. "Permit me your hand, good lady," he said. "*Llaw chwith*—the left."

Lissy didn't know what was coming, but *no way* was she going to look afraid. She thrust her hand toward him, and his strong fingers were gentle as he turned it palm up.

*"Rwy'n addunedu ar fy mywyd."*

As he spoke the strange syllables, he allowed nine large, dark drops of his own blood—*omigod, it's blue!*—to spill upon her palm, then folded her fingers back upon it and held them in place for a long moment. "I will take my leave for now and scout our surroundings for any further dangers," he said. "Later, you and I will agree upon a plan for Fox's lessons."

He vanished from sight then, leaving Lissy still holding her hand out in front of her. *I sure hope faery blood's not a biohazard to humans!* Slowly she opened her fingers, expecting a fistful of blue yuck. Instead, she discovered a curious design upon her dry palm. Its intricate curves glowed like the fire within an opal for a moment, though she felt nothing but a cool tingle. A heartbeat later, it was simply a deep sapphire pattern in her skin. "Goddammit, he tattooed me!"

"Nay," said Ranyon. The little ellyll's expression was uncharacteristically solemn as he and Brooke both examined her hand. "He's given you his very life."

"I don't understand."

"It's as literal as you can get. His life is in your hand if he breaks his oath," explained Brooke. "Morgan told me it's the most ancient and powerful contract in the faery realm."

"So if he screws up, I get to kill him? Come on, he's got to know I wouldn't do such a thing no matter how much I wanted to." *And I'd want to if he ever hurt my son.* Of that much she was certain.

Ranyon removed and replaced his baseball cap, adjusting it with both hands as if trying to rearrange the thoughts beneath it. "Lissy, dearie, ya won't be havin' to do a single thing. If Trahern breaks his promise to ya, he'll simply die."

Shocked, she stared first at the ellyll, then back at the design on her palm.

It was Brooke who finally broke the silence. "Yeah, I might be going out on a limb here, Lissy, but I think Fox is pretty safe with this guy."

# SEVENTEEN

Most rooftops in the downtown area were hot, dusty places, with strange vents and stranger posts and poles, all crisscrossed with wires. The top of Brooke's building, however, was a lush oasis in the middle of a barren desert. Lissy passed the large greenhouse and a wall of rolling carts supporting raised garden beds. On another day, she would have been content to remain among the soothing greenery. But there was more to the rooftop beyond the sea of plants. She looked in that direction and—*dammit!* A moment's inattention allowed a stray melon vine to bring her down, skinning her left elbow in the process. She sat for a moment, picking tiny bits of grit and roofing tar from the wound and catching her breath. And wasn't that just like her life with Fox? Things would go along fine for a while, then *bam!*

This whole magical thing was one of the biggest surprises she'd ever had, though. As Lissy got up and dusted off the knees of her jeans, she wished again that it could all be a mistake. *No magic here, he's just an ordinary boy.* Well, as ordinary as a brilliant kid with a big heart . . . and as ordinary as the world would permit a child with Asperger's to be. Still, those challenges seemed very small compared to what she and her son now seemed to be facing. *Could the universe just cut me a break for once?*

She paused to peer over the edge of the raised skylight that illuminated Brooke's second-floor apartment over the shop. Aidan and Fox—plus three cats and a giant grim—were currently piled together on the big couch in front of the TV. Everyone looked happy enough, even Aidan with his arm bound up in a sling. Man and boy were laughing over something . . .

Normally, Lissy tried not to hover, but it had been damn difficult to let her son out of her sight again so soon. Yet how could she talk freely in front of him? *Not about this stuff. Not yet. Hell, maybe never.* She'd lingered for several minutes after Brooke and Ranyon left, and it was only the knowledge that Trahern patrolled the neighborhood and Ranyon had painstakingly reinforced the wards on the building against evil intent that permitted her to walk away at all. *Even a housefly with a bad attitude couldn't get inside now.*

For that matter, the ellyll had used his magical talents to "set the storeroom to rights," as he called it, restoring everything from boxes of stock to furniture to the walls and floors themselves. There was no longer the slightest sign that anything had ever happened, no hint that a creature from hell had nearly destroyed the place. Yet Lissy knew that no one was going to go in there alone for a very long time . . . except perhaps Fox. He seemed completely matter-of-fact about the whole incident. *"Braith said the monster was just hungry,"* he had told her. *"And then Trahern came in and blasted it, just like I do in my games. He didn't get any gold coins or energy stars, though."*

She didn't know whether to be grateful for her son's video games or concerned that he played *way* too many . . .

As Fox and Aidan began wrestling with Braith, Lissy pulled herself away and continued to a pretty terrace of terra-cotta tile. Large clay urns burgeoning with fragrant flowers defined the space, helped by an L-shaped wall of vine-covered latticework. Somewhere a hidden fountain provided the soothing sound of tumbling water, and in the midst of it all, an enormous copper-colored umbrella shaded a glass-topped table and half a dozen comfortable chairs. Brooke already sat in one while Ranyon teetered precariously atop a stack of very old phone books. *They just don't make a booster seat that'll suit an ellyll. Especially one that never sits still.* Normally it would have brought a smile to her face. In fact, *normally*, all of them would be smiling and laughing together. But nothing felt normal to Lissy, not now. She simply took a seat and nodded at her friends across the broad table. Though she already knew the answer, "How's Aidan doing, for real?" was all she could think of to say.

"His arm is broken, but he's not in any pain. Ranyon worked a charm with it."

"It'll be bright as rain in a day or two," said the ellyll, and neither Lissy nor Brooke bothered to correct the idiom.

"And you're absolutely sure he's up to having Fox hang out with him?"

"Hey, you saw it yourself. The guys have all the raw materials for male bonding—food and movies galore. Besides, I told Aidan to ask Fox how to play Minecraft." Brooke said it lightly, though Lissy could tell her friend was as rattled as she was. Maybe more. "They'll have a great time together."

Lissy forced a smile. *Better than we will.* "Are you sure *you're* okay?"

"Yes. No. I don't know. I still don't know how that *thing* got through my wards and protections—you *know* I've put safeguards on this building against the fae." Brooke put her hand over her heart and closed her eyes for a moment, as if calming herself.

"'Twas not yer fault," declared Ranyon. "Yer protections are still strong. Someone dug away the salt and herbs from a basement window, is all. They even pulled all the iron nails from the frame and smudged away the ward that ya drew on the glass."

"Someone human?" asked Lissy, and the ellyll nodded.

"Aye, a fae creature couldna touch it. But some could charm a scurrilous mortal to do it fer them," he said.

Just as Lissy tried to think if *scurrilous* was a real word, Brooke suddenly burst into tears.

"It *is* my fault!" she said. "Ever since that horrible faery tried to kill Aidan and George, I've checked our perimeters every day and reinforced the spell just in case. *Every day.* But I was so tired this morning that I must have forgotten." She sucked in a sobbing breath. "I screwed up, and Aidan and Fox could have been killed!"

Lissy put her arms around her friend. "Honey, you're pregnant. Of course you're tired!" She got an idea. "Maybe it's time for someone else to take over, just for a while until after you have the baby." Sure enough, Ranyon piped up right on cue.

"I could do that for ya! Lissy has the right of it, ya need to take care of yerself and that wee son o' yers."

Brooke shot a look at him through watery lashes. "You can't really tell what it is—"

"Well, a'course I can! It's a brawny boy, and he'll be just the image of Aidan." The ellyll looked genuinely perplexed. "Didn't ya know?"

She laughed a little then and leaned her head on Lissy's shoulder. "Not yet. I was still trying to decide whether to work a spell to tell me, ask the ultrasound tech, or just be surprised. Omigosh, Aidan's going to be over the moon about this. He'd dote on a little girl, too, you know, but he's *old school* enough to be extra excited about a son."

"It's definitely a guy thing," agreed Lissy. "But about the wards here, why don't you take Ranyon up on his offer? You know he'll do a terrific job."

He puffed out his little chest beneath the bright Blue Jays shirt. "Aye, there's nary a creature nor a mortal that'll want to tangle with one o' *my* charms."

Brooke frowned. "True enough. But you have to go home to Leo in Spokane Valley in a few days. How are you going to—"

"Pffft! Distance is nothing. Ya know that yerself, sending out protections and wards to those who need them. And I'll just be takin' over that job, too—ya need yer rest, dearie." Ranyon suddenly stood on his chair with his spindly hands on where his hips must be. "Where is that high-and-mighty son of Oak?" he demanded. "Shouldn't he be attending this meeting o' the minds?"

Lissy rubbed her palm, the one Trahern had marked, on her jeans. There was no question that the fae's blood vow to her had vastly improved Ranyon's attitude. "I guess he's still busy." For her part, she was just as glad the fae wasn't present. Not only did it seem unfair to question Ranyon about the past in front of a stranger, she wanted a chance to hear and digest his answers first. Especially when she had a feeling she wasn't going to like those answers very much. "Let's just get started."

"Well, all righty, then. But it seems to me, ya can't tell a story properlike if you don't have good food to help things along!"

"I really don't think—" That was as far as Lissy got before the empty table all but groaned under an inviting spread: giant latte cups piled high with foam, a steaming French press of rich coffee, and thick slices—make that *slabs*—of chocolate cake generously festooned with dark frosting and cherries. And there was so much more. Lissy counted three kinds of fruit tarts, a plate of at least a dozen cheeses, a tray of cold meats, a basket of buttered bread, and, last but not least, a bowl of the biggest dill pickles she'd ever seen in her life. They towered upright in a crock near the center of the table like a dwarven patch of saguaro cactuses.

Brooke looked as stunned as Lissy. "Good goddess, Ranyon! I only asked you to bring up the snacks I left on the kitchen table."

"Aye, and they're all right here with not a thing forgotten. I just filled in a bit of a gap here and there, like a proper pint of ale fer meself. And pie. And fixins for sandwiches, a'course. And everyone knows ya can't be havin' sandwiches without pickles!"

"Was that *bit of a gap* the Grand Canyon?" asked Brooke. "How many people are you feeding?"

"Well, all of us, a'course! I put the same on the table fer our boys downstairs."

Lissy shook her head. Maybe it was lack of sleep, maybe she'd finally gone insane, or maybe it was simply the tension falling away from her shoulders after the attack of the vicious cyhyraeth, but laughter abruptly burst from her lips, and soon her friends joined in. Moments later, she took her first full breath in what seemed like hours and reached for a tall iced latte. "I don't know if you're trying to distract me or bribe me, Ranyon. But just because the food is good, and you happen to be cute, doesn't mean you can keep secrets from me. I'm still upset about that, you know."

"Me, too." Brooke grabbed her hand and squeezed, even as she directed her words to the ellyll. "I'm not sure you realize just how serious this is."

"I promise ya that nothin's been done save to protect and defend our Fox," said Ranyon, and lifted his tankard. "We're all of us friends first and always."

*Tough to argue with that.* Whatever the story was, at the bottom of it would no doubt be an enormous desire to help. Of course, good intentions could sometimes cause more harm than good . . . "You know darn well we're not just friends. We're family," she corrected. Ranyon's strange, woody skin dappled with flecks of color, his version of a blush. One twiggy hand shot forward to seize the biggest pickle, but not before Lissy spotted the quick swipe of his eye with the other hand. Sitting back, the ellyll made a show of getting comfortable, thoughtfully munching the big brined cuke as if trying to decide where to begin. Lissy was biting her lip by the time he finally began to speak.

"Our Fox, ya see, was born on Samhain."

"He was not! His birthday is November twelfth."

"Mortals who still celebrate Samhain do so on Halloween, but 'twas not always so. Old Samhain falls on November twelfth, when the Seven Sisters rise."

"The Pleiades," supplied Brooke. "That cluster of stars in the constellation of Taurus."

"I *know* what it is. But what do stars have to do with my son?"

"'Tis not about the stars, Lissy dear. 'Tis the season they mark, when magic is at its most powerful. The gates between the worlds, all worlds, are open wide, and spirits roam where they will. The Wild Hunt is strongest then, too, dontcha know. Did ya not see the storm that night?"

That night . . .

*She'd barely passed the eight-month mark when a strange thunderstorm erupted in the autumn night, its black clouds smoldering with green fire and fierce lightning. A storm seemed to erupt inside her, too, and her water broke.*

*Everything after that was a blur.* Almost *everything . . .*

"Yeah," she said quietly. "Come to think of it, the weather *was* pretty weird." During the frantic ambulance ride, it had seemed like the end of the world both within and without.

"The Hunt was in the neighborhood, so to speak. And the Lord of the Wild Hunt paid a visit to our new little Fox, just afore the sun rose."

Green flame consumed the bodies of the water leapers, reducing them to their most basic elements and bearing them away in a swirl of smoke. It didn't take away the stench, however, an unholy blend of warth piss and rotted fish. The smell would dissipate. The danger would not.

Arms folded, Trahern waited by the sign that named the pleasing collection of tall trees and winding paths as Pioneer Park. A moment later, a small flock of barn swallows swooped out of the sky and landed along the top of the sign, all bobbing and bowing their tiny cobalt-and-russet heads. They reminded him of the blue passerines that circled the uppermost turrets of the Royal Palace. With a careful spell, he'd conscripted them to help him search for fae creatures in an ever-widening circle around Handcastings.

The swift birds soon found the nest of venomous creatures under a small concrete bridge. Each *llamhigyn y dwr* carried enough poison to kill many humans, and the largest one attempted to sting Trahern before he dispatched them all with a word and burned their remains.

He released the little swallows with a blessing and a quick glance toward a gathering of women playing with their children on the other side of the park. The mortals saw and heard nothing, of course, but the young man who had so easily spied the pwca earlier had made Trahern wary. *At least nothing else has wandered here from Tir Hardd this day.* But it was only a matter of time. Not only were more faery beings certain to cross to the mortal plane, they would be drawn directly to this place, to the city where Fox lived. There was no denying that his unique and powerful energy had become a magnet for all things nonhuman.

Any other member of the Hunt would have taken the child away by now. So, too, every wielder of magic who had ever instructed Trahern would have elected to spirit the boy from this place immediately. Even Lurien himself had declared that the safety of the Nine Realms must be placed above all. *It would have been much simpler to remove Fox.* A spell would have rendered Lissy cooperative and trusting. A strong enough spell could even cause her to forget her son completely.

Instead, he'd made a vow to her with his own life as surety, and sealed it with blood.

Sighing, he regarded the dark-blue design on his palm, the twin of the one on Lissy's shapely hand, and wondered at it. Although important treaties and accords had once been sealed with the *adduned gwaed*—the blood pledge—as a matter of course, it had fallen out of use among the Tylwyth Teg long before Trahern was born. Even his mother had never utilized such a permanent pact. But then, Eirianwen much preferred to keep both her allies and her enemies guessing. Not only would she not tolerate the slightest risk to herself, but to give so much power to another was completely unthinkable in the Royal Court.

And yet the gift had sprung freely, even easily, from somewhere deep within him. He had *wanted* to do it. For Lissy. By all the stars, his words alone had not been enough to convince her of his suitability as a teacher. Or of the pressing need for Fox to receive instruction at all. Even after she witnessed Trahern destroying a cyhyraeth, she didn't seem very reassured of his ability to help her with her son. *She admonished her friend Ranyon when he protested my involvement. And she spoke of working together.* Yet Lissy's own thoughts revealed how overwhelmed she felt at the prospect of raising a child with such powers. And how hesitant she was to turn to Trahern for aid. No matter how much he wanted her to.

Bright sunlight filtered through the leaves of the trees as he walked the winding paths, ending up at the pond in the park's aviary. Only the wire enclosure prevented the ducks from gathering at Trahern's feet. Using simple magic to fill his palms again and again, he tossed grains to the hopeful birds. Curiously, it seemed to help him think.

*I do not regret my pledge.* Though it was immutable by any known power, he would do it again. But surely it was strange that he feared hurting two humans more than he feared for the security of both mortal and faery realms! It made little sense considering the immense danger, yet Trahern had to admit that the relationship between Lissy and Fox was a source of wonder to him. The thought of interfering with it was more than merely distasteful. It was nearly unbearable.

His own family would laugh at such foolish sentiments.

*Braith would not.* The impression came to him as gently as a flower petal on the breeze. His brother would heartily approve of respecting the bond between this mother and her child. Of keeping them together in their own world. Braith hadn't snatched Fox away or tried to take him to a safer place. Instead, he had abandoned the Hunt and left Trahern's side to devote himself to the boy on the mortal plane.

*Very well, then. The bones are cast, and the pledge is made. I must instruct the child here, and Braith and I will both guard him to the utmost of our ability. But more is needed.*

The Wild Hunt was needed.

From a pocket inside the breast of his dark leathers, Trahern produced a tiny silver horn. It lay curled in his palm like a toy—until he breathed on it. It trembled at first, vibrating with energy, then grew rapidly until he was forced to grasp it with both hands. Sunlight gleamed on the heavy silver. Fae horses and hounds chased a myriad of creatures around and around the great double coil, and antlered figures danced about the broad bell. He hefted the ancient instrument and pressed it to his lips.

The steady tone was long and low, a cadence formed not of notes but of starry nights and full moons, rustling tree limbs, and lowering clouds, thunder rolling and staccato lightning strikes. And beneath it all, the beat of horses' hooves thrumming the air like wings and the full-throated baying of hounds.

The air shimmered, and Wren appeared astride his monstrous black bucca. The tall goat rolled its red eyes, stamped and blew, and shook its formidable horns as its rider merely grinned. "What quarry, Trahern?" He nodded at the park's aviary. "Surely these fat birds are not giving you difficulty?"

They clasped wrists as Trahern explained what he wanted. A pair of riders in the city by day and a patrol of four by night, until the mission Lurien had charged him with was fulfilled. Trahern did not, however, reveal what that mission was. The fewer who knew about young Fox, the better, even the trustworthy Wren. And to his credit, the Hunter did not ask.

"All will be as you require." Wren touched his coiled whip to his forehead, even as he reined his bad-tempered mount in a tight circle. "Nodin will join me now. It will be a novelty to hunt in mortal sunlight. Perhaps I will need a pair of dark spectacles as the humans wear." He laughed. "Hyleath will choose her own Hunters for the moon hours. I daresay she will enjoy the assignment. Until anon, Trahern. *Hela da!*"

*"Hela da,"* he replied. *Good hunting.* Wren spurred his bucca, and they bolted across the park, leaping unseen over an older couple who grabbed their hats to save them from the sudden gust of wind. Goat and rider vanished from sight among the streets beyond.

Trahern threw a final handful of grain to the eager ducks and whispered a spell that sprouted new grass in the barren dirt of their enclosure. Lurien had said to *use what resources you will.* And what better resource to deal with the fae creatures that might creep into the city? His fellow Hunters were experienced and efficient, and none would escape them.

All that remained was for him to fulfill his mission.

*If I am to honor my vow, then I must make no further mistakes with Lissy.* For that, he needed information. Long-ago trade negotiations had taught him the value of subterfuge, and he didn't hesitate to use it now. A wordless spell took him to the roof of Handcastings. Concealed by a powerful glamour he'd learned from a draigddynion mage, a spell that even an ellyll like Ranyon would be unlikely to detect, Trahern sat upon the concrete parapet to listen to the woman and her friends.

# EIGHTEEN

The coffee cup tumbled from Lissy's hand. She barely heard the noise of it shattering on the tiles over the tumult of her thoughts. "You can't be serious, Ranyon. Lurien? *The* Lurien showed up at a human hospital?"

"Aye, his very self. The Lord of the Wild Hunt came strolling down the hallway in his great leather boots as if he did it every day, and not a single mortal noticed him. He passed that place where they line up all the babes in a row like pastries in a shop window, and he never gave it a glance. Instead, he came straight into the nursery for the very wee ones like Fox. I was there, minding yer own business and making up some more charms for our brand-new boy, when—"

"What kind of mojo did you put on Fox?"

"Well, my very best, a'course!" he retorted. "Protection, first and foremost, his being so new and all. And then a few to make him hale and hearty."

"Healthy and strong," said Brooke. "Fox was premature. If Ranyon hadn't done it, I would have done it myself, Liss."

*Safety, health, and strength. Basic and positive. He loves Fox, and he would never harm him.* But it was all too clear that magic had been part of her child's life since day one, while she had totally failed to suspect a thing. Lissy forced herself to take a deep breath, then two.

"Thank you for doing that for Fox, Ranyon. But what the *hell* was the Lord of the Hunt doing there?"

"Why, he brought our boy a gift for his naming—though we didn't know what his name would be yet—and wished him *tynged da*."

"I know *da* means good," said Brooke. "I learned that from Aidan. But I'm not sure about the rest. Good *what*?"

The little ellyll furrowed his already wrinkled brow. "Well, it's sorta like fate, dontcha know. Ya might even say future. Or destiny!"

Brooke turned to Lissy. "Not exactly *happy birthday*, but I guess somebody important like Lurien would be formal about the whole thing."

*And that's the problem*, thought Lissy. "*Somebody like Lurien* doesn't bring presents to human kids. I don't know much about him, but I do know the leader of the Wild Hunt isn't goddamn Santa Claus! So I want to know *why* he did it. And what it was."

Ranyon sighed and rested his chin in his twiggy hands as he stared at the half-eaten pickle on his plate. "Well, there's just no hidin' anyone with a *maes ynni* like that, dontcha know. I tried my very best."

Lissy frowned in confusion.

"He's talking about Fox's *aura*," explained Brooke. "When he was born, his energy field was so vivid, it practically lit up the place. I was sure every doctor and nurse in the hospital would see it or feel it, whether they believed in the existence of auras or not. Heck, I figured little Fox would be visible from the *space station*, if anyone was looking. But luckily, no one seemed to notice."

"No one human," added the ellyll.

*Like me.* Despite how weak and ill she had been, Lissy had sensed good energy—bright, delightful energy—from her new little son. She'd chalked it up to her own giddiness and wonder. But to actually *see* auras, the vitality that surrounded every living thing, required a gift that she simply didn't have. It was silly, she knew, but she felt just a little left out. "You could see it."

"I saw it, Ranyon saw it. And your mother certainly saw some of it, even though Olivia's abilities aren't as strong."

"And Lurien saw it like a great beacon from a long ways away," said the ellyll. "We're lucky 'twas him and no one else."

Lissy didn't feel very lucky about it. Not yet. "He saw Fox," she prompted. "Then what?"

"Well, a'course his Lordship could read my attempts to camelfloss our boy—"

*"Camouflage,"* supplied Brooke.

"Aye, that's what I said. I'd been trying to disguise our boy, and along comes the Lord of the Wild Hunt and makes a spell of his very own. Weaves a veil o' power and throws it over Fox like a blanket, he did. That was his gift, ya see, and a finer one couldn't have been given."

Lissy was half-amazed and half-frustrated—where did the fae get the right to interfere as they pleased? She recalled Trahern's imperious words: *I require no rights from you. I ride with the Hunt.* "What did this, this blanket do, exactly?"

"Why, hide Fox, a'course!"

"Omigod, that's why his aura changed!" said Brooke, putting her hands to her temples. "After being so brilliant, it was as if someone had used a dimmer switch and toned it down. I couldn't figure it out, but you're saying that *Lurien hid it*!"

"It's just as that bossy son of Oak said, there're things that dwell in the faery realms 'twould love ta feed on such energy or turn it to their own use! And some of them creep into this world from time to time, like that cursed cyhyraeth downstairs!"

Brooke shivered. "Aidan told me that one of the purposes of the Wild Hunt is to send back creatures that don't belong in our world. He says there's been a lot more of them in the past few years."

"Aye, 'tis exactly what the Hunt was about the night Fox was born," continued Ranyon. "Chasing a pair of great cranky bwganod that had settled into one of the little lakes hereabouts. They'd gobbled down most of the fishes and—"

"Let's try to focus on Fox, shall we?" said Lissy. "You still haven't told me the whole story about Lurien. He put some sort of protective blanket on my son?"

"A many-layered spell, and one that I'd never seen the likes of. He warned me, though, that it wouldn't last but a dozen mortal years, maybe more, maybe less. *Strong magic has chosen this child*, he said, and it would leak through the spell eventually like water from a cracked cup."

Lissy pulled her chair close and placed her hands gently on the ellyll's shoulders, trying to ignore how odd and angular they felt beneath his habitual Jays shirt. "Okay, Ranyon," she said, looking hard into his bright-blue eyes—the only ones she'd ever seen that authentically twinkled. "Tell me if I've got this straight and if I've left anything out. Fox has magic, a lot of it, something even bigger than what came to Brooke. Big enough to attract the attention of someone powerful like Lurien and . . . and somehow different from anything we know. At least from what *I* know. Plus, Fox's magic isn't coming to him when he's older, like it does in my mother's family. He *already has it*?"

"Aye, that's the way of it. I don't know what we'd have done if Lurien hadn't happened along when he did. He kept the aura from being seen by other fae. Kept the magic out of our boy's reach as well. Ya don't be handin' lightning to a babe, and that's what Fox's powers woulda been to him." He sighed deeply, and his whole body seemed to droop. "My charms are the very best, dontcha know, but their strength isn't what they once were. The more ellyllon there are, the more power each ellyll has. And there's nary a one of us left."

Brooke put an arm around Ranyon and said something kind and comforting. At least, Lissy assumed it was—after all, that was what her BFF was best at. In actuality, Lissy couldn't hear anything above the tornado of thoughts that swirled inside her beleaguered brain. "You didn't mention any of this when Fox was born. Not a word," she managed at last. "I took my baby home from the hospital and never knew a damn thing."

"Why ever would I tell ya then? With grief o'er yer beloved Matt still weighing on yer shoulders plus a new babe to care for?" Ranyon asked, wringing his twiggy hands together until Lissy was sure he'd never be able to untangle his fingers.

"So you kept it to yourself," said Lissy. "And while I can see why you didn't say anything at first, it's been nine whole years now. *Nine!*"

Ranyon blinked in confusion, and she suddenly realized that nine years must seem more like nine *minutes* to a long-lived creature like an ellyll. "Well, ya see," he said, "I figured by the time Lurien's spell wore off, our boy would be a mite older. And it would seem to everyone that he'd naturally come into the family magic. Then I could tell ya the rest gradual-like. But now the magic's starting to leak through."

Brooke glared sharply at the ellyll, who had the grace to look abashed. "Exactly how long has it been 'leaking'?" she demanded, making air quotes around the word.

"I guess it'd be about six o' yer mortal months now," he said.

"Dear goddess." Lissy's friend looked at her with stricken eyes. "That's about how long you've been noticing new things happening with Fox—the dreams, the precognition, the heightened senses. And here I've been brushing them off as pretty much normal—at least *normal* for a child from a gifted family—and telling you not to worry. I had no idea, none at all, what we were really dealing with, and I am so, so sorry!"

"You don't have to be sorry, Brooke. I didn't want to notice those things, and you made me feel a lot less scared about them. It's not your fault there was more to the story."

"Nay, 'tis my fault," said Ranyon, removing his hat and clutching it with both hands to his chest. "And I'm as sorry as a one-legged cricket. I didn't see how ya would feel about it, how it would look. I shoulda told ya the whole of it from the beginning."

"Yes, you should have." *But when it comes right down to it, I wasn't ready.* It had taken a major shake-up—like a giant faery grim and his good-looking brother crashing into her life—to force her to see what had been right in front of her all along.

"Mind ya, I haven't been resting on my bunions," he continued. "I worked a fresh protective ward every night and sent it winging away on the breeze to yer house. And I've always made my very best charms to watch over our Fox."

Lissy frowned. Ranyon had brought many gifts to her house over the years. *A wind chime . . . and then there were those garden gnomes and . . . the little figures on Fox's desk!* The ellyll had created them the same way he made almost everything else—with bits and pieces of household things and natural materials bound together with copper wire. Strange figures. Crazy animals with feet of marbles and metal washers and tails of feathers and springs. Whimsical men with chestnut heads and arms and legs of bent spoons and twigs! Come to think of it, Ranyon had brought one along almost every time he visited (ever since her son was old enough not to put the creations in his mouth). And Fox loved them all and named every one, even though there were practically enough for an army now. Bean. Rufus. Tinny. Donut. Toothy-Cat. Croco-Bite. Larry . . . "The toys were for *protection*!"

"Every one o' them," Ranyon said solemnly.

*I'm such an idiot.* Lissy's energy drained away like water from a bathtub. She'd been so self-righteous, felt so justified in demanding to know what the little ellyll knew and when he knew it—and now that she did, what difference did it really make? *Everything that happened these past few days would still have happened. And I wouldn't have been able to foresee it or prevent it. Meanwhile, he's been working overtime from day one to keep us safe.*

"Okay, I can't deny that I've had a lot on my plate since Fox came along," she said aloud. "Looking at it from your point of view, I would have hesitated to hand me a brand-new problem, too. And I'm grateful for all the protections. But could you just promise not to keep secrets from me again?"

The little ellyll was hesitant. "Are ya still gonna let me visit with Fox?" he asked, his lower lip trembling.

"Good grief, Ranyon, you didn't rob a bank! But you just can't hold back information anymore. If you know something, you have to tell me so we can work *together*. Promise me?"

The little ellyll stood up on the stack of phone books and planted a hand somewhere near where a liver might be. It could be over his heart for all Lissy knew—after all, he wasn't human. "I swear to it," he said solemnly. "And a sure sight easier it'll be than keeping secrets!"

"To no more secrets." Brooke lifted her cup.

A fresh latte appeared in front of Lissy, and she drank gladly enough, but her mind raced. *What do I do now? I can barely teach Fox enough coping skills to manage everyday life. We're still working on stuff like grocery shopping, for heaven's sake! I don't know how to teach him to control magic!*

A familiar voice slipped into her head, steady and calming.

*I do.*

And then it was gone.

# NINETEEN

The tall fae stared at the door with furrowed brow, as if it were personally responsible for his discomfort. He was determined to align himself with human custom for Lissy's sake—but in the absence of servants, he was uncertain how to announce his presence. No bell ropes hung from the small porch roof, no embroidered pulls along the walls in either direction. The annoying neighbor had banged on the door and shouted Lissy's name like a kobold selling fire salamanders in the marketplace. *Surely that cannot be right . . .*

As he pondered what to do, a scraping sound above made him take a few steps over to look past the roof. A blond-haired boy folded his arms on a second-story windowsill and rested his chin on them as he regarded Trahern. Braith's massive head hovered over him like a great lion.

"Dude, how come you're still on the porch?"

"I'm observing the rules of courtesy and waiting to be granted entrance."

Fox frowned. "You mean like waiting for somebody to let you in? Braith says you've been here a long time. You know you're supposed to knock on the door, right?"

"Your mother did not appear to like it when Claire knocked."

Fox rolled his eyes. "Duh! That was too loud. And she yelled, too. My teacher, Mrs. Fletcher, says yelling's only for when there's an emergency. Like if the school's on fire, you know?"

As Trahern attempted to digest that, the boy rapped his knuckles on the windowsill. The sound wasn't disagreeably loud yet had an urgent pattern to it, like a coblyn might use to lead human miners to richer veins of coal.

"Kinda like that," continued Fox. "If you do it too hard, though, people get mad at you. I know because Mr. Murray next door yelled at me for it. I said yelling was rude, but he just got madder." He shrugged. "People are hard to understand. I like animals better." He pulled his head back in and shut the window. Braith's great head lingered on the other side of the glass, incorporeal for a few moments, with his jaws grinning widely as if laughing at his twin below. Then he disappeared as well.

"That was illuminating." Trahern turned his attention back to the door and mimicked the boy's knock.

Lissy opened the door almost immediately. "Trahern! I thought I heard Fox talking to someone."

"I was being instructed in the finer points of human etiquette."

"I see." Her beautiful full mouth twitched. "You're doing very well. Please come in." As he crossed the threshold, she waved a hand at herself. "Sorry about the pajamas and wet hair. It got kind of late, and I hadn't heard from you, so I took a shower. I'm not exactly presentable for company anymore."

As she walked in front of him, he thought she looked extremely presentable, at least to him. The loose fabric of her tunic and leggings boasted a pattern of tiny colorful owls—what female among the Tylwyth Teg would wear such whimsical garments? Lissy's damp hair and skin left a trail of scents in the air. He discerned soaps and perfumes and a faintly pungent compound common to human water.

But over it all lay her own unique scent—warm and earthy, salty and sweet. Like an exotic spice, he would recognize it anywhere.

"I came to instruct Fox," he managed.

"At this time of night?" They sat across from each other in what he now knew was oddly termed a *living room*. "I'm guessing that you don't know it's a little late for a lesson," she said. "Fox only has an hour left before bedtime, although he certainly seems full of energy tonight."

Trahern cursed himself inwardly. Mortals lived with the burden of set hours that measured out their lives. He would have to adopt the concept of *time*. "The moon is nearly full, and its influence is potent. Perhaps Fox simply feels constrained by being inside."

She sighed. "I can understand that. As a geologist, I'd much rather work outside than indoors."

*Perhaps we should visit out of doors, then.*

*That's a nice idea. But why don't you visit with Fox now? Maybe you could set the stage for his future lessons or something, give him a little introduction. That way, he'd be able to have his snack and get to bed on time.*

As before, Lissy made the transition to mind speech smoothly and easily, as if she had done it all her life. Trahern decided he liked this intimate communication with her. Her warmth and humor—and even her occasional irritation—evoked a pleasing sensation in his mind that he would be hard-pressed to describe. Most unexpectedly, it also filled the terrible void left by his brother's silence.

"There's one thing I should tell you," she said aloud. "I explained to Fox about how you'd like to be his magic teacher. And he didn't quite understand, so I used a movie he knows to help make the point. I don't suppose you've seen *Harry Potter and the Sorcerer's Stone*?"

"Who is Harry Potter? Is another sorcerer seeking to interfere with the child?"

She laughed and shook her head. "No, no, *no*. Harry Potter is a character from a famous series of books written by J. K. Rowling. He's a little boy who finds out that he's really a wizard and gets invited to attend a wizarding school. They made the whole series into eight wonderful movies—those are stories you watch instead of read, kind of like a play."

"A form of entertainment," he supplied.

"Yes! The problem is, I could never get Fox to watch more than one of them."

Her words brought up a wealth of questions, but Trahern forced himself to focus on the issue. "Why would that be a problem?"

"Fox just wasn't very interested in Harry and his exciting magical adventures. The only character he really liked was Hagrid, the man who talked to animals." She sat on the edge of the couch with her hands folded on her knees. "You know, a little of it might be because Hagrid lives by himself in a house near the forest. Fox would be very attracted to that—he does better with peace and quiet, and the fewer people around, the better. But most of all, my son definitely has a *thing* about animals."

"A thing?"

"An affinity. It's more than just liking animals, he's *comfortable* with them. Fox would really rather be with animals than people."

"So he has said to me."

"Well, he's also mentioned more than once that they talk to him. I made the mistake of chalking that up to a child's imagination. Now I think that he really can communicate with them, all of them, just like he seems to do with Braith."

Trahern committed Lissy's words to memory. "Knowing such details may prove helpful as I instruct him."

"I just don't want you to be disappointed if he isn't interested in your instruction."

"Any disappointment I might experience will be the least of our concerns. I must find a way to encourage Fox to learn. And I must make a beginning." They stood, and he took a step toward the staircase. Stopped. "Do you require your son to remain in his room?"

"Of course not! He ate supper, and then he said he wanted to play with some of his toys. That's pretty normal for a nine-year-old." She shrugged. "And his room is kind of a sanctuary for him—he likes it a lot."

"This night, with such an auspicious moon, I would like to work with him outside. If he is willing, of course," he added quickly. "We would remain close to your home, and—" Trahern paused for a long moment. "It is possible that I may be more successful in gaining Fox's attention if you are not present. Will that cause you concern?"

She shook her head. "Not at all. I trust you. How about our backyard? It's not very big, but it's completely private, and there's even a fire pit if that's something you need. Although it's pretty small, too."

*I trust you.* He heard little else. Words possessed power, and these were words Lissy had not spoken before. The truth in them shook his senses. Trust was no light thing between mortal and fae, but he hadn't been expecting the relief that washed through him like a cool mountain stream, and a kind of giddiness took hold. Before he formed the thought, he'd already pulled Lissy to him and pressed his lips to hers.

Sight and sound fell away, leaving a world composed solely of subtle sensations. They were no less powerful for their simplicity. Lissy's delicate breath against his cheek and the spicy-sweetness of her mouth. The warmth of her skin and the softness of her hair. He nuzzled her face and throat, kissing, licking, indulging in her scent that had so captivated him. Her arms slid around his neck and pulled him close, even as he molded her gently rounded body to his angular one as tightly as he dared. By all the stars, he wanted more, all, everything—

Something hit the side of his head. He barely gave it any heed before several more *somethings* pelted him in quick succession—and stung like fire-bees! Trahern pulled back midkiss, instinctively placing his body between the mysterious attack and Lissy, just in time to be hit squarely in the center of the forehead. He threw up a spell, and a dozen small objects struck an invisible wall and clattered to the floor.

Acorns?

"It's about time ya came up fer air, ya lecherous son of Oak!"

Ranyon stood on the back of the living room couch, twiggy hands planted on his hips, his strange blue cap on backward and his gnarled face screwed up into a frown of epic proportions. "You'd best be steppin' away from her!"

Self-control and discipline were the greatest powers a master sorcerer possessed, and Trahern found himself exerting a great deal of both to keep from tossing the ellyll out the nearest window. "I see no reason for your concern," he began as soon as he got reliable control of his voice. Too late. Lissy had already marched around him and confronted the ellyll practically nose to nose.

"What on *earth* do you think you're doing, and why are you in my house?"

"Well, no one answered the door, now did they? I looked in the window fer fear that ya might be in danger, and here ya are snoggin' with a fae!" he sputtered. "He's Tylwyth Teg—yer lucky he didn't steal yer breath like a shadowcat!"

"Ranyon! I can't believe you'd say such a thing!" She thrust her palm out, displaying the blue symbol. "I trust my *child* with this man, and you yourself said Trahern could not break his oath."

"Well, I didn't say he couldn't break yer heart, now did I?" The ellyll folded his arms in front of his bright-blue shirt and harrumphed loudly.

Her voice rose. "Listen, mister, I'll damn well *snog* with whomever I want to, and it's none of your business!"

"None o' my business? None o' my business?" he shouted, and threw his bright-blue hat to the floor. "Lissy, darlin', ya said yerself we're family. And as family, I can't be watchin' ya mourn again."

"For the love of little fishes, my own mother is giving me a hard time about not trying harder to meet men. Now *you're* upset because I'm actually enjoying a little male companionship?"

"No, I'm givin' ya the fifth degree because he's not a man, he's a *fae*!"

"It's *third* degree, buddy. And you don't have the right to—"

"Dude! How come everybody's yelling?"

The three of them froze. Lissy turned slowly to see a wide-eyed Fox standing on the staircase.

# TWENTY

*This must be how the Grinch felt when little Cindy Lou Who surprised him . . .* Unfortunately, she had no Christmas tree to hide behind. "I'm sorry, Fox," she began. "We were disagreeing, and we got carried away."

"Braith says you were *kissing* Trahern!"

*That Braith is a tattletale.* She threw a glare at the dog looming behind her son, but the great creature simply wagged his tail. Her cheeks reddened—she could feel the heat—as she scrambled for something, anything, to say to her son. *Great. I got nothing.*

Trahern, however, wasn't as tongue-tied. "Your mother is a remarkable woman," he said with a lot more calm than she could have managed. "And I have a great liking for her." Ignoring the loud raspberry from Ranyon, he continued. "Therefore, I kissed her."

Fox made a face. "Dude, that's so *gross*!" He bounced the rest of the way down the stairs, with Braith following him like a silent gray shadow. "Can I have ice cream?"

Either he was satisfied by the fae's explanation or he was as mercenary as every other kid Lissy had ever met. *Nothing like exploiting a parent caught in a weak moment.* "We don't have any ice cream right now. But you can have three cookies and a glass of milk before bed." She waved a hand at the fae next to her. "Trahern actually came over to . . . to visit you!" Lissy almost said *give you a magic lesson*, but that sounded incredibly weird. And maybe off-putting considering her son's lack of interest in the subject.

He shrugged. "Yeah, okay." Fox ambled over to Trahern and stared up at him. He was barely half the fae's height but didn't seem intimidated in the least. "Your brother says you want to teach me how to do cool stuff. What kind of cool stuff?"

"Perhaps you could show me where the *backyard* is. We can sit out there while we talk about it."

"Can we have a fire? We can look at the stars, and I know where the Big Dipper is, too!" said Fox, grabbing Trahern's sleeve and towing him toward the kitchen where the back door was. Lissy was shocked. Her son didn't often touch people, not even their clothing—

"And I'll just be goin' with ya!" The ellyll jumped from the couch, picked up his hat, and dusted it off before jamming it over his strange leafy hair. "If a fae is going to be tutoring our boy, then someone's got to be keepin' an eye on things."

"Ranyon!" began Lissy.

Trahern stopped, although Fox continued trying to move forward with his small feet sliding uselessly on the smooth floor. "I do not require supervision."

"Aye, so ya say. But I'm bettin' ya don't know the first thing about human children."

Lissy put a hand on Trahern's arm before he could answer. *Remember that we talked about not arguing in front of Fox? You have no idea how lucky we are that he didn't get upset when he came downstairs. The last time we were all in this room together, you had to put a spell on him to get him to settle down.*

He nodded. *So I recall. You wish me to acquiesce to the ellyll?*

*I wish you not to argue with him! Look, I know you don't need any assistance at all from Ranyon, and I honestly don't know why he came here, but maybe he'd feel better and leave you alone once he saw what you planned to do. Can you put up with him for a little while?*

His eyebrow rose, and she had a sudden silly wish to trace it with her finger. *What does it mean to put up with him?*

*Tolerate him.*

*For you, good lady, I would tolerate an audience of drunken bwbachod.*

*Um, sure. Thanks. I think.* As Trahern again permitted Fox to drag him from the room, followed by the silent Braith, she stepped squarely in front of Ranyon. "Hold it right there, mister. If you're going to be part of this, then there are going to be ground rules," she whispered fiercely. "And number one is there will be no more arguing. None! You will not attempt to undermine Trahern's efforts in any way, or distract my son, or encourage my son to obey you instead of him. I love you, Ranyon, but you're going to work *with* Trahern or you're going to stay away when he's here. *Capiche?*"

For a few seconds, the little ellyll rubbed a toe on the floor in front of him and wouldn't look at her. Finally, he sighed and rearranged his hat upon his head as if rearranging his attitude at the same time. "Aye, I'll agree to yer terms."

She sighed. "Look, I just don't get what the problem is. Aren't you the one who told me how important this was for Fox? Why are you acting like this now?"

"Why, the thought of you and Trahern, a'course! I'd rather be marrying a basilisk myself than see ya with one o' the traitorous Fair Ones."

"That might be, but you know that Trahern is different." Her voice softened, and she knelt to hug him. "Of all the people in the world, you have ample reason to hate the clan he came from, but *he is not them*. I'm asking you, for Fox's sake, to just work with Trahern. And if you really can't, then I'm asking you to keep out of his way. Okay?

Because he's setting the foundation for you and Brooke to teach Fox later."

"Aye. But Lissy, dear?" His bright-blue eyes in his gnarled face were earnest. "Promise me you'll be as wary as a mouse in a tree full of starvin' owls. Faeries and mortals live apart fer a reason, dontcha know. Trahern might not harm ya, and Braith surely won't, but what about their relations?"

"You mean their family? The House of Oak?"

"'Tis exactly what I mean. Where are they? Maybe ya need to be askin' some questions, is all."

"Okay, Ranyon. I hereby promise I'll ask a whole *bunch* of questions. And I'll be very, very careful."

Lissy watched him make his way slowly to the kitchen, head drooping, as if he walked his last mile. It was all she could do not to hold her breath until she heard the *squeak-clunch* sound of the back door closing. *Finally! If I have to referee anyone else today, then I want a goddamn whistle!*

She dropped into an armchair like a rag doll, completely and utterly spent.

"Fox, do you understand why I'm here?" The three of them sat on the smooth wooden benches beneath slender young birch and mountain ash. Trahern was pleased with the choice of trees. Birch was useful for healing, and the other was a tree of great power. Ivy had overgrown the fence in one corner, a natural protective ward. The entire green space—the *yard*, as Lissy called it, though he could not understand the term—was more of a grassed-over garden, really, and small indeed, but otherwise it was an ideal space in which to work magic. Tall cedar fencing surrounded it, offering additional ambience and energy, as well as privacy. Trahern took the extra precaution of veiling the entire area so that *no one*, human or fae, would see or sense them.

The heat of the day yet lingered in the air. Perhaps that was why the child seemed to forget about the fire he'd been so eager for. Instead, he'd taken great delight in pointing out constellations, reminding Trahern of a time when he and Braith were young and old Heddwen had named some of the stars in the changeable skies of the fae realms. It wasn't long before Fox fell silent, though, his eyes on the rising moon. Trahern had witnessed great golden hares in the fae realm that became almost hypnotized by the bright orb and danced in its pearlescent glow. Yet Fox was far from moonstruck. Rather, his face was serene, with a hint of a smile, as if the moon was a cherished companion sharing a secret. Without looking away, he shrugged in answer to Trahern's question. "I dunno. Something to do with magic, I guess. But I don't really wanna be a wizard."

"Why do you say that?"

"Dude, because they're always fighting each other! Somebody *always* wants to be the boss, and then they hurt people."

"What is a *boss*?"

"You know, the person who tells everybody what to do."

He couldn't disagree with the boy's astute assessment. "Sometimes that is true."

"More like *most* o' the time," snorted Ranyon, but Trahern ignored him.

"If you do not learn to use and control magic, Fox, then a boss might try to control *you*."

The boy turned to him then, his small brow furrowed. "Like Meagan and Brianna at school? They push me down a lot, and then they laugh."

The ellyll muttered something about *tasting their own medicine*, even as Trahern nodded at Fox. "Like that or worse. So you see, it is important that you pay close attention and learn as much as you can. Tonight, we will begin with a basic history of sorcelling. First—"

"*First,*" interrupted Ranyon, "the lad would probably like to do something interestin.'"

Trahern swallowed his initial response. As he had promised Lissy, he would not risk distressing Fox by arguing with the ellyll. And as much as it irritated him to consider Ranyon's words, it was true that the boy had not grown up surrounded by spells and powers as Trahern had. *Perhaps I should attempt a different approach—but what would be of interest to a mortal child?* He had no answer for that. The Lord of the Wild Hunt had charged him with Fox's training, and his own responsibility as a sorcerer demanded it, but for the first time Trahern wondered if he was up to the task. As he floundered mentally, one of old Heddwen's sayings came to him: *'Tis a foolish man who asks no questions!* He'd rather not ask Ranyon any questions at all—but perhaps the child himself could provide insight.

"Fox," he ventured. "Is there something that you wish to do with magic?"

The boy seemed surprised to be asked, but his little brow furrowed as if considering. Suddenly he jumped up and ran into the house.

Ranyon threw up his spindly arms. "Now ya done it! Ya didn't even get started and you've scared the lad away!"

"I did not frighten him! You called the lesson into question before I had even begun!"

"Well, you'd *begun* by being boring." The ellyll shook his head. "Dry old *history* of all things! Have ya not been around children at all?"

"No," admitted Trahern. "I was simply going to begin as I was taught at his age. Fox is intelligent and talented."

"And a lively young human boy. Easier to teach a wild kelpie to love dry land than force-feed Fox something that doesn't appeal to him."

"A sorcerer must learn discipline! By rights, he should have been taught the basics long ago." He shot Ranyon a pointed look. "And now we are behind. How can he control the forces of magic within him if he has no solid foundation?"

"Pish—I know all that. I'm sayin' ya gotta give the lad a reason to want to learn. And it's gotta be a reason that's important to *him*. Ya can sneak in the vegetables between the cookies, dontcha know."

Before Trahern could ask what that meant, Fox dashed from the house at full speed and abruptly stopped in front of him, holding up a small blue cylinder.

"Can we make my flashlight better?" he asked breathlessly.

"What is a *flashlight*?" asked Trahern, ignoring Ranyon's barely smothered snicker.

Fox clicked a button on the side, and the device delivered a weak glow. "I use it to read at night sometimes, but the batteries don't last very long."

"Now we're talkin'!" The ellyll was triumphant. "Let's—"

"*Let's* do something better," interjected Trahern. "In the faery realm, we don't have to use *flashlights* when it's dark."

"You don't?"

"Not at all. We use our magic instead, and our magic is always with us." Trahern cupped his hands together and blew into them. When he opened his fingers, a sphere of light shone bright enough to make both Fox and Ranyon squint. He blew on it again, and the light dimmed to a pleasant glow. "You may make it large or small, and it will last as long as you wish."

"Dude, that's awesome! Can I do that? Can we start now? You can teach me, right?"

"Yes, you can do it, and yes, I'll teach you." Trahern glanced over at Ranyon and gave him a slight nod. The little ellyll had been right.

~

Lissy tossed the TV remote onto the couch cushion in disgust. Although there were a couple of programs she normally might have watched, nothing held her interest tonight. She'd gotten up at one point, folded laundry, vacuumed the second floor, even taken a stab at organizing her office, only to return to her spot on the couch. Beside the remote lay two books, the latest issue of *GSA Today*, and a basket of papers to sort, all relatively untouched.

Her son was learning to wield magic.

Lissy didn't have anything against magic per se—how could she when members of her family and some of her best friends were so adept at it? But the idea of training her impulsive child to control such power made her glad she was sitting down. *Thank heavens I have help!* What if she hadn't met Trahern? Brooke had enough on her plate. And Ranyon, who would have been her own first choice of tutor, had grudgingly conceded that the tall fae was exactly the instructor Fox needed because of the type of fae magic he'd inherited.

But what if her son didn't want to learn? Fox had immense focus and patience for the things that were important to him but very little for subjects that didn't interest him. With magical power already pulsing through him, what if Fox resisted Trahern's efforts to train him? Right now, she had to cope only with supermarket meltdowns. What if her son *blew up* the grocery store the next time he became frustrated?

A vibration at her hip had her digging for the phone in her pocket. It was Brooke.

"Good timing," said Lissy. "I've already run out of ways to keep myself busy."

"You? You're the last person on earth I expected to hear that from! Everything going okay?"

"Well, Trahern and Ranyon haven't killed each other yet, so there's that. I have no idea if Fox is learning anything."

"What's Ranyon doing there?"

"Supervising. And expressing his disapproval because I kissed Trahern."

"You *kissed*—oh, honey, we have to sign you up with a dating service, and fast."

"Why can't you guys just be relieved that I'm showing some interest in the opposite sex? You've dropped enough hints over the years."

"Duh! Because he's a different *species*, Liss!"

"Oh, come on, it was just a kiss. I know the difference between attraction and anything more. He's a fae. I'm a human. I get it." *Love is not known among the fae*, Trahern had said. *For most of us, it is only a myth.* No danger of involvement there, although a little voice in her head reminded her of that odd sense of connection she'd experienced.

"Do you know if you acted of your own free will? Are you *certain*?"

Considering the look on his face when she practically accused him of coercing her, Lissy was *very* certain. "You don't have to worry about me."

"As your BFF, it's my sworn duty to worry! As long as Trahern is Fox's teacher, you're going to be spending a lot of time around him. And the fae, they're—he's—well, he's a *hot* fae. Hot as Hades. Supernaturally hot. *Dangerously* hot."

"Yeah, he is." She sighed. And because it was Brooke, she admitted the rest. "And I'm enjoying the hell out of it."

"Okay, spill. I want every juicy detail. What's it like to kiss a fae?"

An hour had passed by the time Lissy ended the call. No one had come back into the house (thankfully) while she indulged in some serious girl talk with Brooke. But there was no sound from outside, either. Was everything okay? More important, was every*one* okay? Fox was bright and quick to learn—but also easily frustrated. And what if Trahern became impatient with Fox? He'd be in for a surprise if he expected her son to be a perfect pupil. And, of course, Ranyon was a wild card. Despite his promises and his very best efforts, it was still possible for the ellyll to get carried away again and compromise the lesson.

*Damn.* She'd promised herself she wouldn't hover, wouldn't look outside, would let whatever happened happen—but surely it was past time to check on things. Wasn't that what a good mom would do?

Thankfully, the kitchen light was already out as Lissy crept to the window. *Sheesh, I feel like a spy!* Drawing a corner of the curtain aside, she could see the string of tiny yard lights faintly illuminating the curved path to the fire pit, but no one sat there. As her eyes adjusted, she finally spotted the trio in the shadows only a few feet from the house. Ranyon stood on a bench next to Trahern. Both were bent so their heads were close to Fox's—

And suddenly a soft bluish glow sprang into existence in their midst, seemingly from within Fox's small cupped hands. Lissy completely forgot about hiding and pressed her face to the glass to get a better look. The glow brightened, shifted colors from blue to gold, and grew into a sphere the size of an apple, illuminating the threesome like a lantern. Approval shone in the faces of Trahern and Ranyon, and the ellyll began bouncing up and down in his enthusiasm.

But it was the expression of sheer wonder on her son's face that filled her heart and reassured her as nothing else could.

# TWENTY-ONE

Lissy dumped the hot popcorn into the last bowl and drizzled butter over the fluffy kernels as snatches of dialogue from *Harry Potter and the Sorcerer's Stone* could be clearly heard in the kitchen. She'd have to turn the volume down again—if she could pry the remote from her son's hands. Balancing four bowls in her arms, she headed to the living room and paused in the kitchen doorway to appreciate the view from behind the couch.

Braith sprawled on the floor in front of it as usual, but his hindquarters and tail extended comically beyond it. Next, over the back of the cushions, she could just see a tiny patch of bright blue that was the top of Ranyon's baseball hat. After that was an untidy thatch of blond hair: her son. And on Fox's right, Trahern's wide dark-cloaked shoulders loomed large, and his long braid of white hair lay along the top of the couch. *Who'd have thought that I'd be hosting movie night for such a diverse audience?*

It had been her idea. Although Fox's first three lessons had gone surprisingly well, subsequent ones had been more challenging for the hunter-turned-teacher. He was confused by some of her son's questions and responses, particularly when Fox kept asking why Trahern didn't have a wand. Lissy understood exactly where those ideas were coming from. *Time to bring Trahern up to speed on pop culture.*

The TV might be loud, but Fox had finally ceased to compete with it. He'd started out by giving a play-by-play of every detail to Ranyon, Trahern, and Braith, but thankfully his first bowl of popcorn put an end to that: it was hard for him to talk and eat at the same time. He was fully absorbed now, perhaps because magic had a brand-new meaning for him, and he accepted the fresh bowl from Lissy without even taking his eyes off the screen—or noticing that she'd traded the popcorn for the remote. Ranyon and Trahern had thanked her for the treat the first time, but they, too, were now completely immersed in the film, and she practically had to shove the bowls into their hands. Lissy resumed her own seat, a niche next to the tall fae (which felt a lot more comfortable and right than she wanted to think about). His thoughts weren't reaching out to her at the moment, however. Ranyon, she knew, watched a great deal of TV with his dear friend and roommate, Leo, but the old man was more a fan of police dramas and baseball games than fantasy. But was it Trahern's first experience with modern media? Did they even have anything like it in his world?

Heaven only knew what he thought of the story.

Thankfully, she'd managed to negotiate with Fox to watch just *one* movie tonight. He needed his routine and, most especially, his sleep. *There'd be no survivors if Fox stayed up all night!* It had been a challenge, of course. Like all kids, her son drove a hard bargain, and having Asperger's made him even less able to be flexible. But in the end, they settled on watching the other seven films in a row, one per night. Her son had been sold on the idea of a weeklong Harry Potter marathon with his unusual friends. *I sure hope Ranyon and Trahern are up to it!*

As it turned out, Fox sank lower and lower in his seat until he eventually slid off the couch completely to lie full-length on top of Braith. That's where sleep found him sometime during the last half hour of the movie. When the credits rolled, Lissy moved to pick him up, but Trahern put a hand on her arm. *The child is heavy. Permit me to carry him up the stairs for you.*

*Thanks, but I'm used to doing it.*

*If not me, why not my brother? Fox is already on his broad back, and Braith is undoubtedly heading to the boy's room as well.*

She hesitated. The grim probably wouldn't even feel Fox's weight, but . . . *He'll fall off!*

*A little magic will prevent that.* "Braith," he said aloud. "Would you kindly bear young Fox to his bed?"

The great blue-gray dog rose easily to his feet and ambled over to the stairs. Lissy hurried after him, but there was no need for alarm. As Braith mounted the steps, Fox didn't slide so much as an inch. Instead, he remained on the dog's back as if glued there, arms and legs dangling limply over the sides. The grim made his way to her son's room and stood alongside the bed like the most faithful of mounts, and Lissy was a little surprised that it was suddenly easy for her to roll the softly snoring child onto the mattress. She tucked him in and kissed his blond head, then put her arms around the great dog's neck.

"Thanks, big guy," she whispered, and laughed as she successfully dodged his massive tongue.

There was no one in the living room when she came downstairs. "Trahern? Ranyon?"

*Ranyon left to help Brooke with her nightly rituals. I am outside.*

Lissy grabbed a sweater and headed to the backyard. It was a tiny affair, but Fox loved it, and so did she, and many marshmallows had been roasted—or, more often, *charred*—over the diminutive fire pit. Trahern stood off to one side, looking up at the moon through the trees. Round and full now, it was crossed by long, thin streamers of cloud like so many waves.

"My mother would say *la luna está bajo el agua*," she said as she approached. "The moon is underwater."

"So am I, according to Ranyon." Trahern turned toward her with a wry smile. "He assured me from the beginning that I am *in over my head* in this situation. I understand some of what he meant after viewing the moving story."

"Movie," she corrected. "And yes, Fox has a lot of preconceived notions to unlearn. Did he ask for a flying broom or a wand?"

"I thought he might, therefore I prepared to explain how fae magic is different. Instead, you were quite correct. The animals are what fascinate Fox the most. He feels quite well equipped to be a wizard now that he has my brother as his companion."

"You said *wizard*! I can't believe you're using the *W* word."

"And Fox has used the word *sorcerer* twice tonight."

She tried not to roll her eyes. "It's in the title of the movie."

"I will accept victory wherever I can find it," he said wryly. "We have far more pressing concerns. Magic is challenging work, requiring focus and concentration and a lifetime of study. More, a solid foundation must be established upon which we can build, and many basics simply *must* be memorized. So far your son resists this."

"He has the same challenges at school. His best subjects are math and science because he likes them, but it's taken a long time to talk him into putting any effort into other subjects. It's true of most kids to a degree, but with Asperger's, Fox tends to be obsessed with specific topics to the exclusion of everything else."

"Such as rocks?" There was amusement in Trahern's eyes. "I am lectured about them frequently."

Lissy laughed. "*Especially* rocks." She thought for a moment. "You know, a couple of years ago, his teacher's aide and I came up with some flash cards to help him memorize facts in his weaker subjects. Fox is a visual learner." At Trahern's puzzled expression, she explained the concept further until finally he nodded.

"Such cards may prove very useful. I would like to create a set for herbs and plants. Not only must he be able to identify them all, he must know their properties and uses."

"That's an awful lot of *musts* for any child, never mind one like Fox."

"I find I must do something as well." He smiled and moved closer. "I must kiss you again."

She put her finger on his lips to stop him, but he simply took it into his mouth. Lissy shivered as her nipples tightened and her core suddenly clenched. Hard. "Okay, not right now," she managed, clearing her throat with difficulty. "We're still talking about Fox."

Trahern released her finger slowly, with a teasing expression. "Very well. But I will have *two* kisses later. What else about your son?"

*Focus on Fox, focus on Fox.* "Homework—schoolwork you do at home—used to cause him a lot of anxiety. It can be hard for him to settle down and start things. Sometimes I've had to sit beside him with a whole pocketful of little crystals and rock specimens and dole them out as a reward for each completed question or task. Over time, having something pleasant to anticipate has helped Fox to be less stressed about it."

"I have not carried stones in my pockets since I was a child myself. Perhaps I will have to do so again if it will encourage him to learn." He sighed. "In truth, I have perhaps as much to learn as your son."

"That actually gives me a lot of hope."

"Why? I am responsible to train your child, and I have just admitted to weakness."

"Some people say that's the beginning of wisdom. And you're not too proud to be willing to address the problem. A child like Fox requires *constant* learning—I'm always having to make adjustments."

"How can that be? You are an excellent mother!"

"Thanks, but I'm very far from a perfect one. I just won't give up, that's all."

He brushed his fingers over her hand then, the one with the symbol in her palm. "Nor will I give up."

"I don't believe you will," she said, her voice barely above a whisper as that cool tingle of connection sparked like an electrical charge between them. She shivered suddenly, and he frowned.

"You are cold." Trahern strode to the center of the yard. "*Tân*," he murmured, his hands palm down over the fire pit. "*Tân araf.*" Tiny tongues of marigold flame suddenly appeared from the cold, gray ashes. The rising glow haloed him as he turned back toward her, and Lissy caught her breath. For an instant, he was an angel in sleek black leather . . . It distracted her just enough that she didn't even get a chance to protest before Trahern had already scooped her up and sat on the bench closest to the tidy blaze.

Lissy had to admit that the radiant warmth was welcome. The side of her that pressed against Trahern was warm as well, however, and another kind of heat sprang up within her. *Good grief, Brooke was right. This guy's* dangerously *hot.* "What do the words mean—the ones you just spoke?" she asked, seeking a diversion while she tried to decide if she should get off his lap. She certainly didn't want to, but . . .

"There are many kinds of fires. I simply called a small and steady one. Are you uncomfortable?"

*More like too comfortable.* "I don't really need to be carried, you know."

"At least I did not *poof* you."

She laughed and gave in, even allowing herself to relax into him. Was it so wrong to just enjoy being close to a man—even if he was a fae? Trahern wasn't manipulating her in the least; she was sure of that. Her physical reaction to him was to be expected . . . and perhaps even appreciated. It wasn't like she was in danger of falling in love with him. And if fae women were as exquisitely beautiful as she had heard, Trahern would not be looking for anything serious with an ordinary human like her. All things considered, it might be ideal to have an uncomplicated and temporary relationship to practice with. *Heaven knows I'm not ready to dive into dating. Yet.*

The fire gradually grew, flickering with tongues of color—green, blue, violet, magenta. "You've seen where I live," she ventured. "Tell me about your land. I don't know anything about the faery kingdom."

"One kingdom, true, but many lands. Most are very beautiful."

"Okay, then tell me about the last one you saw."

The thin smoke above the flames solidified into a round, opaque cloud. Trahern blew lightly at it, and the strange smoke swirled around, opening like an iris to reveal a window filled with vivid greens and jewel-bright hues. As Lissy watched in wonder, the colors coalesced to form a clear image.

"The forest of the Silver Maples," he announced. "Ten thousand were planted a hundred of your centuries ago. There are many more now."

The giant trees, obviously named for their dense canopy of glittering leaves, were far larger than any maples she'd ever heard of. *This place could give Sequoia National Forest a run for its money.* "It's beyond beautiful," Lissy said, wishing for words worthy of such majesty.

"As with most things fae, danger hides beneath the beauty," said Trahern, and traced the long scar across his throat. "I have this to remind me of the place."

"Is it okay if I ask what happened?"

He nodded at the image. Dark, lanky shapes with long tails trotted through unseen paths in the dense underbrush. Suddenly, one leapt upon a fallen trunk, running easily on clawed feet to emerge above the thicket. Striped and glistening with scales rather than fur, the powerful predator pointed its long, narrow muzzle into the air, releasing a series of rapid staccato yips as if calling its fellows. Lissy shivered at the glimpse of serrated teeth, and Trahern's arms drew her closer. "What *are* they?"

"Warths. A large pack pursued my brother and me when we escaped," he said. "There were too many to outrun, even with fae horses, and agents of the House of Oak were close behind. A warthen claw caught me in the neck during the fight. But death was preferable to capture."

Hadn't Ranyon warned her about this guy's relatives? "So—uh—I take it you don't get along with your family. They're not the ones who turned Braith into a dog, are they?"

The vision of the faery forest and its predators dissipated until once again there was only smoke rising from the flames. Trahern was quiet for so long that she wondered if she'd overstepped a boundary. Then he shook his head. "No," he said, his voice suddenly hoarse as if every word was dipped in sorrow.

"I did that."

# TWENTY-TWO

"You turned your own brother into a *grim*?"

"No—yes—no." Trahern released her and stalked away from the fire to an overgrown corner of the yard. The wild tangle of ivy resembled his thoughts at the moment. "It is complicated."

"I'm sure it is." She rose and followed him. "And I think you'd better explain it to me."

"The hour is late for you. I should take my leave and return tomorrow."

"Not a chance, mister." Lissy put a hand on his arm as if to stop him. *As if she could . . .* yet he did not move.

"There's no room for secrets in a relationship, whether you're friends or—or whatever the heck you and I are to each other," she continued. "You don't get to drop a bombshell like *that* on me, and then just walk away!"

"You are not Tylwyth Teg. You would not understand." The instant the words left his lips, he knew he'd made a serious mistake. Those wondrous sable eyes that never failed to mesmerize him now flashed with the same fierce temper he'd admired when he first saw her. And as before, that anger was directed squarely at him . . .

"I *understand* that Braith's a dog because of something you did. And not just any dog, but some kind of never-eating, never-sleeping giant of a hellhound. Now *you* understand this: my son loves Braith, and if you want me to continue to let them hang around together, or continue to allow *you* to be my child's magic instructor, you'd damn well better give me the full details." She folded her arms. "So did you change your brother on purpose, or was this some kind of horrible magical accident?"

"There was no accident. To save his life, I was compelled to help cast the spell that transformed him into a hunting hound. An *ordinary* hound, nothing more."

"Something *did* go wrong, then?"

"No. The spell worked as intended, though it was very painful for him." *For me as well.* He recalled Braith's agonizing transformation as if it were mere heartbeats ago. Daggers of guilt, regret, and sorrow pierced him anew. Meanwhile, Lissy's gaze softened as she once again saw far too much.

"Trahern, your gifts are amazing. Because of my family and friends, I thought I knew something about magic. But you can do things that I've never dreamed were possible. What on earth, *who* on earth, could force you to do such a terrible thing to Braith? I know you care about him."

"No one *on earth* has such power, but in the fae realms, some do. Like Eirianwen. As the grand matriarch of the House of Oak, she condemned my twin for disobedience—nay, *treason*. His crime was that he would not accept a pairing with a woman she had selected for him, one who would add to the political influence of the family."

"An arranged marriage?" asked Lissy.

"Braith loved another and refused to comply."

"Loved? *Loved?* Am I hearing that right? I thought you said love was a myth among the Tylwyth Teg."

"My brother believed otherwise. Her name was Saffir."

"So this Eirianwen person punished him for having a mind and heart of his own. In doing so she punished you, too. Sounds to me like she wanted to control you."

He paused, appraising her for a long moment. "I was incorrect when I said you would not understand."

"I *want* to understand." Lissy was well aware that he read her thoughts as if testing her sincerity. For once, she didn't seem to mind. *I want to know all of it. Tell me.*

"Very well. But seeing is far easier than words," he said at last, and lightly pressed the tips of his fingers to her temples. His mind brushed against hers, asking, just asking. Lissy trembled but did not shy away.

*There's a tickling in my head. It feels like you're teasing my brain with a feather.*

*It is a spell called* cyswllt meddwl*—our awareness will join.*

*What's that weird buzzing sound? Hey, this better not be like the last time you used magic on me! I—*

Lissy fell silent as the spell engaged and their thoughts were suddenly one . . .

Together they beheld the palace garden. It surprised him to see his own memories through her eyes, to feel her awe at the exquisite flowers, the vivid trees, and sublime statuary. And her voice in this strange shared state was even more familiar than in mind speech. *There! I can see you,* she said to him. *And that must be Braith, right?*

Any intention he might have harbored to censor those images, to pick and choose what he would share, vanished like a water droplet on desert sands. Was it that the past demanded to be acknowledged, or was it the esteem he had for Lissy—even trust? Because Trahern held nothing back. Not only that, but he experienced his memories anew as the woman before him experienced them as well . . .

*Frustration and anger tightened Trahern's shoulders, sharpened the pain in his heart, and intensified the already bitter taste in his mouth. It had sickened him to the core to lend his own magic to Braith's blood-chilling transfiguration . . .*

*Not so the grand matriarch of the House of Oak. By all appearances, she'd enjoyed the spectacle immensely as her son's screams fell on willfully deaf ears. After what was left in Braith's place was dragged away, she took further delight in tormenting and testing Trahern. Knowing that his position required him to remain in attendance at her side, she had deliberately lingered at Court. Only for his brother's sake had he maintained appearances by carrying out his duties to their mother, as she welcomed the fawning admiration of many. Rage roiled in his gut for what she had done, for what she had forced him to do. It mixed uneasily with fear as keen as an obsidian blade because Trahern still could not reach his twin through mind speech. Was Braith yet unconscious? Dying? Dead? The thoughts beat at him, bruised him, like a stone hawk's wings when it was flushed from the rocks—yet he permitted no concern to cross his features. Instead, Trahern played his expected role perfectly, artfully affecting an air of well-mannered patience and exchanging superficial pleasantries with self-serving courtiers. He even smiled as if he enjoyed himself, though every particle of his being fairly screamed at him to seek out his sibling at once. It would be exactly what his mother expected, however . . . and so Trahern kept his apprehension locked away, his raw anger caged, even as she found new ways to goad him further.*

*It wasn't long before she'd gathered a large audience, charming them with clever conversation. Merrily she jested that they ought to watch her remaining son lest he show any signs of contagion from his brother. Somehow, he found it in himself to laugh along with the courtiers, even as he knew they would take the joke seriously and be Eirianwen's eyes and ears in hopes of winning her favor.*

*None of this showed on his face, of course. No one survived at Court without developing a flawless mask, and Trahern had mastered that skill early. Yet his mother turned to him more than once with a self-satisfied smile on her golden lips, as if she knew exactly what he thought . . .*

Lissy jerked and tossed like a sleeper in the grip of a dream. Instinctively, Trahern wrapped his arms around her, echoing their mental embrace as it rocketed them forward through countless remembrances until at last they neared the present. When they beheld Braith leaping the bonfire the night they met at Palouse Falls, Trahern shook himself free and severed the connection.

"Omigod!" Lissy's hands shot to her head. "Omigod, omigod. Your own *mother* did this to you? Your *mother*? It was so damn cruel!" To Trahern's horror, she burst into tears.

"No! I did not mean to give you pain!" He cupped her face with both hands, trying to brush the tears away with his thumbs, to kiss them from her cheeks, her eyes. The tide could not be stemmed, however. Lissy slid her arms around his neck and buried her face in his hair—and he suddenly understood that the terrible grief was for *him*. All for him.

Shocked, all he could do was hold her tightly to him until her shoulders stopped shaking and her breathing eased.

"Sorry about that," she said at last, her face still pressed to his chest. "I really wasn't prepared for that little revelation, although I don't know how anyone could be."

"It is I who should apologize to you. I did not realize you would feel so deeply on my behalf." Though he wished he was not the cause of her distress, Trahern couldn't help but be fascinated anew at how mortals lived their lives not only with rich emotions but with those emotions unmasked. And perhaps because of their recent connection, he could even *feel* Lissy struggling to digest the information. Truly, as a mother who openly cared for her child, it would be difficult, even impossible, for her to comprehend the machinations and intrigues, the continual plays for power, that characterized the leading Tylwyth Teg families.

"Why did she make the spell permanent?"

"That I do not know." Bitterness welled up inside Trahern like bile. "As you saw, by the time I reached him, it was too late."

"You had no choice, no choice at all," she said, and looked up at him. "You blame yourself, but I saw you devote every spare minute to trying to *change him back*. All the work, all the study, all the experiments, all the sacrifices. And you still do it. You've never given up."

"Nor have I ever succeeded. I will never stop trying, but it is increasingly difficult to have hope."

Lissy reached up and stroked his brow as if she knew that every word he uttered was like pushing heavy rocks off his heart. *And she does know.* Trahern stood frozen for a long moment, a maelstrom of unfamiliar emotions whirling within. The sheer wonder and relief of being understood brought with them an intimacy he had never imagined. His mouth sought hers, intending perhaps a gentle thanks for such a rare and wondrous gift—he would never know. Because everything changed the instant their lips met. Without warning, the attraction that had flickered between them from the beginning ignited. He was in the very heart of a star, blind and burning with need.

*And she is ablaze with me.*

Lissy already had her hands knotted in his hair as she drank in his kisses and gave back with a kind of tender ferocity that erased language of any kind from his fevered brain. Words and spells were replaced with the urgency of sensation. He drew her warm breath into his lungs as if it were more life-giving than the night air itself, and he sought her heated skin beneath her clothing. The soft weight of a rounded breast filled his hand, the press of the nipple insistent in his palm. His other hand fumbled with his own garments, seeking to ease the confinement of his *gwyllt* when suddenly she rocked her shapely hips and rubbed herself against him . . .

With that simple action, the ground seemed to drop away beneath him. He lifted her then, and her legs wrapped around his waist, anchoring and claiming him as surely as he was adrift and wanting. Trahern carried her to a bench by the fire while he could yet walk.

Straddling Trahern's hard thighs, Lissy pulled back from a bone-melting kiss just long enough to peel off her shirt and bra. She might not be a flawless faery princess, but she was damn well comfortable in her own skin. Pleasure shivered down her spine, and dampness blossomed between her legs as he bent to her, as his lips and teeth slowly worked their way down her throat, lower, lower . . . And all the while, his unbound hair skimmed across her sensitive skin. In her hands, his hair felt like silk. Now it seemed different—softer, finer, more like the luxuriant brush of winter fur. Scents teased at her senses, the high, clear air of a mountain, the petrichor of rain, the tang of ozone before a lightning strike.

At last he arched her backward to give his mouth full access to her breasts. She locked her legs around his waist again for balance and this time made full contact with the bulge in his leather pants. Lissy groaned deeply in pure anticipation—and found herself abruptly pulled upright. Concern was written all over Trahern's elegant face.

"Are you well?"

"Of course I am!"

"That sound you made—"

"I make a lot of different sounds when I'm aroused." She grinned wickedly. *Want to hear more?*

His mouth twitched, and an answering grin appeared, the first she'd seen from him, and it delighted her. *You look like a pirate.* She could feel his puzzlement and enjoyed that, too, as she reached for the intricate fastenings on his tunic. The strange closures, so far removed from mere buttons, should have stymied her, yet the memories she had shared with Trahern guided her fingers. It was quick work, then, to push apart the leather to reveal his chest. The firelight caught the amber patterns that warmed his marble skin, symbols and spirals and what could only be words, perhaps sentences, in an unknown language—

In wonder, Lissy reached out to touch one that she recognized, tracing the spiraling design from beginning to end. It glowed slightly wherever her fingertip made contact. *I dreamed of you, of us. I've seen these, all of them. They cover your whole body, but they're not tattoos, are they? Not ink.*

*No. These are* ledrith, *and no hand placed them there, not even my own. For those born to sorcery, each one appears when a certain complicated spell has been mastered.* He took her hand and, as before, slowly drew a finger into his mouth, setting off a whole-body shiver that might have caused her knees to fail if she'd been standing. *With such spells embedded into the skin, they can be enacted with a single thought, a word, a gesture. Many are weapons that require little more than reflex. It is efficient, especially in times of danger.* He lifted his head suddenly, his eyes uncertain. *Do they trouble you?*

"Not at all. I think they're beautiful, like artwork." She retrieved her hand and pulled him closer. Her mouth roamed along his jawline to just behind his left ear, where the old warth scar began. He flinched when her lips first touched it—was it sensitive? Or was he sensitive *about* it? "History can be art, too," she murmured, and placed soft, openmouthed kisses along its silvery length. Surprise and confusion flared in his mind, and she could feel the sheer will he exerted to permit her to do as she pleased. By the time she reached the end, just below his right collarbone, there was only a grudging pleasure, as if he had not expected to enjoy it.

Maybe she could find something else he'd enjoy even more.

"Mmm—sit back a minute," she murmured, giving his shoulders a tiny push. Obligingly, Trahern leaned back along the bench, resting on his elbows. He watched her intently as she used her tongue to outline a serpentine design on his chest. When it ended at his bluish nipple, she was satisfied to see it quiver . . . and then she placed a firm hand on the bulge that presently nudged the vee of her legs. Squeezing gently at first, she increased the pressure until he said something that sounded suspiciously like a curse, and all their clothes vanished.

Lissy found herself with a rampant cock in her hand that might have been sculpted from alabaster. Fascination trumped surprise. His blood was blue; therefore, his sensitive parts were bluish as well, she realized. Stroking the seemingly polished head, she admired its pale-azure shade—

Until the sound of a window closing in the next house had her throwing her hands over her breasts in a futile effort to cover herself. "Omigod, the neighbors!" How could she have forgotten where she was?

Trahern sat up at once, his arms encircling her protectively. "They see nothing, not even the fire," he reassured. "Before I began working with Fox, I shielded this place from all eyes and ears, fae or human. The spell will not fade unless I will it so." He shrugged as he easily anticipated her next question. "Your son is asleep, and Braith is at his side. Even if they were to come outside, they, too, would see only a darkened yard. But . . ."

Lissy looked up into his perfect face. "But what?"

"We can stop if you prefer."

She laughed, easily reading what *he'd* prefer. "I want this," she said, and kissed him slowly and deeply, even as she ran her fingers up and down his cock. "All of this." *Now.*

The heat of the fire played across her naked backside as she rose and settled, as they began to move together. She spared an instant to marvel at how at ease she was with this man, as if they'd been here before, loved before, many times. And then his fingers touched where they joined, and there was no more thinking . . .

# TWENTY-THREE

Thank heavens the neighbors hadn't heard any of *that*. Lissy couldn't help but grin as she stretched languidly and snuggled closer to Trahern on the feather-soft surface. The bench was gone, having been magically replaced with a broad divan in the instant that he rolled her underneath him the second—no, the *third* time they had come together. Her body felt gloriously well used and satisfied right down to the bone. *I'm never going to be able to get this smile off my face.*

She paused, wondering if Trahern had heard her thoughts, but he remained sound asleep. He'd told her that the fae didn't need to sleep often, certainly not every night as humans did. And she knew from his memories that he seldom slept at all, spending most of his downtime searching for a way to restore his brother. *He thinks the fae do not love.* Considering his horrific experience with his mother, she could see where he got that idea. But Trahern's devotion to Braith showed otherwise.

And what of his tenderness with her? There'd been enough passion between them to burn down the entire yard, yet he had been gentle and considerate. *Maybe he thinks humans are fragile. I guess we might be, compared to his people.* It was more than that, though.

He hadn't handled her like she was made of glass but, rather, as if she were *precious.*

She still didn't know what to make of the profound connection she felt to him. How could this man, this being, be so familiar? There was nothing about him that reminded her of Matt. Was it simply that there hadn't been anyone in her life since? Because there was no denying that the encounter with Trahern had hit her hard and fast, like an oncoming train.

*Sex-deprived,* she decided. *It's no surprise that I wanted to sleep with him.* After all, the vibrator in her nightstand certainly didn't stack up against a sinfully hot flesh-and-blood man. Her eyes roamed over the long, lean muscles of his arms and legs, the well-formed abs and chest, his half-relaxed cock. He was beautifully made. With his white skin and hair, he might have been a statue in repose, a work of art. A heathen god, inscribed with the strange amber symbols of another world entirely . . .

And she knew him. He was alien and *other* and yet inexplicably known to her heart. What she had felt when they came together had gone far beyond the physical. It made no sense at all. But then, how could anything about this situation make sense? *There's a giant faery dog in my son's room, and here I am in bed with a card-carrying member of the Wild Hunt.*

Did he feel the same? Did he feel at all?

Mentally she gave herself a head smack. *Get real, Lissy. He's Tylwyth Teg, practically an immortal. What could you be to him but a friend at best—even if it's "friends with benefits"?* Trahern would teach Fox some things, and then what? Someone who rode the sky certainly wasn't going to stay with her in her very ordinary world.

As if to underscore that depressing thought, Ranyon's words came back to her: *I didn't say he couldn't break yer heart, now did I?*

Damn. The smile she thought couldn't be wiped from her face faded into something bittersweet, even as she made her decision.

She'd chosen this, and she would not regret it. As for the future, she'd take what was offered for as long as it lasted—five minutes, five days, five *whatever*. She'd enjoy every bit of it.

And she would not hope for more.

Trahern was aware of Lissy before he opened his eyes. Her aura, warm and bright, still melded with his as she lay curled against him. He could feel the rise and fall of her breath and the soft tumble of her long dark hair on his skin. And beneath his palm was the pleasing fullness of a naked breast. It was more than pleasant to simply lie together in peace—and entirely new to him. Had he ever known a lover who lingered?

Court dalliances had always been shallow, but now they seemed vulgar and repellent. There had been other females in other parts of the realms who had not been as cold and indifferent, yet they were still self-serving. Bedding an Oaken prince was cause for a temporary elevation in status among their peers, not to mention the possibility of costly gifts they might receive. None of Trahern's experiences had allowed him to consider the existence of love when his brother spoke of it. If not for the long-ago influence of old Heddwen, he'd be hard-pressed to believe in affection and caring, either.

Now he found himself questioning everything because of this mortal woman. He closed his eyes for a moment and simply savored the curve of her fingers around his. Listened to her steady quiet breathing and to the profound silence of her understanding. He waited for a revelation, for some bestowal of wisdom, a deeper insight. Anything at all . . . but as expected, he was left with only his own tangled thoughts.

He glanced up to see ash leaves silhouetted against the moon, relieved somehow that neither belonged to the Nine Realms. The flowers and plants of this human plane were not as exotic, yet they appealed to him. There were roses on the night breeze, purple evening stocks, and a type of primrose. *This world is not without its charms.* And the play of moonlight on Lissy's dark curls reminded him that the most enticing of those charms was within arm's reach. He turned and kissed her awake.

They lay tangled, still aglow with the heat of passion, and Trahern mused that perhaps they had melted together. It was difficult to discern where her skin ended and his began. Her head nestled on his shoulder, and he breathed in her scent as they talked beneath the stars.

"Why is it that I can hear you so well in my mind?"

"I do not know. Perhaps because you are a twin. Do you not speak with your brother, George, like this?"

"Yes and no. It's not as clear. It's more like I feel what he feels, even now that he lives in California. If we're together, I can guess what he's going to say." She shrugged. "Often, we finish each other's sentences, but that's about it. What about you and Braith?"

"I can use mind speech with him and no one else. It is not common among the Tylwyth Teg, and I do not believe our mother ever suspected we had the ability. Sadly, the longer Braith was in the form of a grim, the less I could hear him. I do not hear him at all now."

"But Fox can. Why is that?"

"His own gift plus the strength of his magic. As you suspected, he can speak with most living things and be understood by them. I am glad that my brother once again has someone to communicate his thoughts to, although I miss talking with him."

"How could your mother not care about her own sons?" She sat up and circled her knees with her arms. "Surely she must have shown you *some* love when you were a child."

"No. But as children, we never expected that she would." He searched for a way to explain. "You show frequent affection to Fox and give much consideration to what he thinks. It is not so in the circles of power. Few of the Royal Court bear offspring. When they do, they are merely assets."

"Like—like *property*?"

"Similar. If you are royalty or otherwise titled, children can be kept in reserve for succession."

"With fae life spans so long, I'll bet that doesn't happen much."

"True. And intent can change over millennia."

"So now your mother sees you as some kind of threat? Who *does* that?"

"Such is the nature of fae nobility. If a child is not required for succession, then he or she might be used to cement a valuable alliance. I have even seen offspring from the noble houses used as trade items to barter with for other resources."

"That's horrible! It's—it's so *cold*. Doesn't anyone have children for *love*?"

"It is not love but mutual advantage and loyalty that holds high-ranking families together." And Trahern had been loyal to a fault: obeying, appeasing, even defending Eirianwen no matter what latest horror she had inflicted on someone else. It sickened him still. "Or so I once believed."

Lissy was quiet for several moments. "Did you hate her?" she asked softly.

"Not growing up. Understand, I knew nothing else, expected nothing else. But later, yes. Later, when I dutifully stood in attendance at her right hand after Braith had been taken away, I hated both her and myself." Trahern remembered wondering if Eirianwen's enemies would someday remove her beautiful head from her shoulders—and wishing he could do it himself. "Of course, our mother is accustomed to being hated. I believe she even relishes it. To be hated reinforces her sense of power, and in the Royal Court, power is the only thing that truly matters."

"Not to you."

"My brother matters to me. But until Eirianwen left the palace, I had to pretend that he did not."

"When we shared minds, I saw you do it, and I understood why. But I can't even imagine how hard it was." It was several moments before she spoke again. "I hope this isn't too personal a question, but I need to know. Why didn't you turn out like your mother? If you didn't have love in your life, if the Royal Court is so cutthroat and callous, then how did you and Braith become decent men with a sense of honor? How did you become kind or considerate or . . ." She struggled for words. "Or *anything*?"

A very good question, one he'd asked himself long ago. "If I have any sense of fairness and honor, it is no doubt due to Lord Lurien's example."

"I've heard Aidan speak highly of him."

"The Lord of the Wild Hunt is extraordinarily dangerous, yet never without cause. The innocent have nothing to fear from him." *Unlike Eirianwen, whom everyone fears.* "I have come to believe that sorcery should be like that as well. Those who taught me to wield magic—not of the House of Oak but teachers I sought out in other realms—ascribed to certain principles, even ideals."

Lissy nodded. "Brooke has a code that she follows."

"Exactly. Many find magic to be stronger if handled with appreciation and respect, in harmony with living things as much as possible. I think I grasped that because of the influence of old Heddwen. She was an ellyll, like Ranyon, and my twin and I were in her care from the time we were born. I saw very little of my mother—we were dressed up and shown off occasionally, but never for very long. Heddwen was the constant in our lives."

"No wonder you seemed so happy to meet Ranyon."

"He was not pleased to meet me. And I cannot blame him."

"Give him some time. I think he'll come around eventually. But right now, I want to know more about the ellyll who took care of you."

What to say? How did you condense someone into mere words? "Heddwen was strict but fair, and she had an endless supply of stories to both amuse and teach us. Indeed, I thought of her tales much when we viewed the movie tonight. I often wondered why she stayed, as my mother did not treat her well. But then, Eirianwen treats no one well."

"With someone like Eirianwen in charge, maybe it was important to Heddwen to try to be an influence for good on the next generation," said Lissy. "You know, to make things better for everyone in the future."

"I had not considered that. My mother's main concern was that we behave properly at Court. Heddwen was tasked with instructing us in protocol, but she took it upon herself to teach much more than that. Heddwen would not tolerate unkindness or selfishness between us, and she tried hard to instill a certain respect for living things. I remember Braith being scolded severely for injuring a bird in the garden. I'd never seen her so angry. She insisted that he nurse it back to health, and it made a deep impression on us both."

A gentle hand tugged his hair, and he looked down.

"You said love does not exist among the fae. That it's a myth. You're wrong."

"Do you speak of Braith and Saffir?"

"Nope." The moon glimmered in her dark eyes as she held his gaze. "I'm talking about you. We're not so different, you know. We both have people we love very much and we'd do anything to protect. You watch over your brother like I watch over Fox. You would give your life for him. In fact, you already have. I can't even imagine the number of years you've spent trying to find or create a cure for him."

"Loyalty binds us together," he began—then saw in her eyes just how foolish that sounded. It suddenly seemed foolish to him as well. Whatever he felt for his twin, loyalty was far too weak a word.

"And didn't you ever think that maybe Heddwen loved you? That she stayed because she cared for you and your brother? You miss her. I can see it."

"It was . . . *difficult* to be without her. She was the first to recognize that magic had come to me and encouraged me to learn. My very first spell was one that she taught me. I owe her much." He managed a smile, for Lissy's sake and to honor Heddwen.

"So where is she now?"

*I wish I knew.* "My brother and I were old enough to be presented at Court, that we might be officially named by Eirianwen as her heirs. There was a ceremony and a grand gala, and we were gone for several suns. When we returned home, Heddwen was gone. Simply gone, as if she had never been. I am certain my mother was responsible, but she would not reveal what became of her. Nor have I ever been able to discover the answer." *Braith and I missed her sorely.*

"Was it when . . ." Lissy trailed off, but he already knew what she was asking.

"It was just before that cursed day, and I know not if she escaped."

"I'm so sorry." She slid her arms around his waist and held him. Simply held him. As when they coupled, her bright aura infused his with warmth and something more . . . Trahern gave in to the temptation to rest his cheek on the soft curls of her long dark hair. It was strangely *comforting*, though he had never been comforted before. The ancient travesty was unchanged, yet Lissy's closeness allowed him to breathe in a sort of peace along with her scent.

A tiny trio of green shooting stars careened across the blue-black sky.

"Did you make a wish?" she asked.

"I do not understand."

"It's traditional to make a wish when you see a shooting star. You know, wish for something you really want. A heart's desire."

Trahern stared at the sky for a long moment. "I would wish for my brother to be free of his curse. I would wish for *all* of Eirianwen's terrible deeds to be undone."

# TWENTY-FOUR

Close your eyes. Then draw the energy to you."

"Dude, do I have to close my eyes *every* time? It's boring."

Trahern directed a look at Braith. The big dog stretched out in the ivy-laden corner of the yard, watching with what looked suspiciously like amusement. Fox's expression changed with his brother's unspoken cue, however, and Trahern knew they communicated. It was hard not to feel a pang of—what? It wasn't envy so much as a wistful sadness that he couldn't hear Braith's words in his own head anymore. *I miss it . . . I miss* him.

"Yeah, I guess so," Fox said, responding aloud to whatever Braith had said in silence. "But just *one* more time, okay?" He heaved a dramatic sigh and closed his eyes, then tried once again to do what was asked of him.

Instantly, Trahern sensed currents of energy beneath his feet. Tiny trickles grew into rivulets, joining, expanding streams. Energy was being drawn from all quarters of the property and beyond—perhaps even from the entire neighborhood now—and Fox still had his shoes on. He seemed to require no contact with his skin at all in order to pull power to him. Magic responded to Fox almost like a faithful pet. It came when he called, and the more he practiced, the faster it responded.

If only he could learn to control it once he had it . . .

"Good. Now send back the energy I give you—"

The boy's eyes flew open, and he suddenly threw a furious volley of punches and kicks at the air. "*Tiger Ninja!* Hey-hee-*yah*!" He leapt around the yard, adopting strange and extreme stances, until finally he pounced on Braith and wrestled his arms around him. "Surrender! You can't defeat Master Fox!"

The dog rolled and pinned him neatly with hardly any effort at all.

"Dude! No fair!"

This lesson wasn't going the way Trahern had planned. Few of their sessions together did. *Just go with it*, Lissy had told him. *Use whatever he gives you to make your point.* He rose from the bench and nodded at his brother to let the boy up. "Very well, Master Fox. You must now use your ninja abilities to deflect the—the *deadly mega-force bombs* I throw at you."

Now he had the child's attention. Carefully he formed a small clear ball in his hands and caused it to glow vivid red before he tossed it directly at Fox. The boy jumped to meet it and smashed it with his small fist, whereupon the ball vanished in a brilliant flurry of multicolored fish. They swam in the air briefly before vanishing.

Trahern could almost hear Lissy's voice: *When you have to correct him, frame it in a positive way.* "Excellent coordination! However, instead of absorbing the energy, I want you to deflect it."

Fox's puzzled look told him he might have phrased it positively, but he'd failed to explain it clearly.

"*Deflect* is a word that means to push something away from you," said a voice behind Trahern. Lissy appeared and sat on the bench near him. "You know, like in that game where Super Igor uses his shield to bounce lightning right back at Dr. Frankenstorm."

As understanding bloomed on the boy's face, Trahern lobbed another ball of energy, a green one, in his direction. This time Fox kicked out a foot. The ball wobbled backward several feet before it lost momentum and hovered in place.

"Good! Very good," said Trahern, and he meant it. He threw a blue one then and had to duck when Fox returned it with unexpected velocity. It struck the side of the house and exploded in a bright flare of light. "Once more." He began to form another sphere—

And ended up flat on his back in the ivy in the far corner of the yard.

Lissy ran to him. "Omigod, are you all right?"

He laughed where he lay. "My fault entirely—I should have been ready." Trahern sat up and waved a hand at Fox, who looked a little scared. "Well done!" he shouted. "That is precisely what you needed to do." In Lissy's mind, he added: *I told you he would be spectacular.*

*So you did.* She gave him a hand up, and they walked back to her son.

"Do I get another crystal?"

"Fox!" protested Lissy. "Shouldn't you be asking if he's okay?"

"I am quite fine, thank you," Trahern supplied as if the boy had indeed inquired. "And I think you have earned the right to choose one." He held out a hand with five gleaming stones in it. Fox bounced up to consider each, then finally chose a smooth agate with bright bands of color.

Lissy admired it as it was thrust into her face. "Congratulations, sweetie. There's a sandwich and an orange on the table for you."

"Is it the smooth peanut butter?"

"Absolutely."

"Did you cut it right?"

"Yes."

"Did you take all the white stuff off the orange pieces?"

"Dude!" she said, mimicking her son. "Do I ever forget? Yes, everything is just the way you like it. I've got the TV set up to play *Tiger Ninja* in about two minutes. You can eat in the living room if you want to."

The child raced into the house, and Braith trotted after him. Trahern sat on the bench next to Lissy. She put an arm around him.

"I assume things are going better today?"

"In truth, much better. I suggested to the ants that they remain underground." Yesterday Fox had spotted a troop of ants dismembering a dead cricket, and Trahern was unable to draw his attention away from the tiny spectacle. In the end, he'd sat on the ground beside the child and conjured a round pysky glass into existence that allowed Fox to observe the creatures much more closely. His hopes that the boy would soon tire of the distraction and be receptive to a lesson, however, proved fruitless. "True progress has been made this day. If Fox closes his eyes, he focuses better. He can draw energy to him without effort when he is concentrating. Now, thanks to your timely explanation, he *deflected* energy for the first time. And as you witnessed, he learned very quickly."

"What's so important about pulling and pushing energy?"

"The very foundation of magic itself is the manipulation of energy. To enact a spell requires a great deal of energy, much more than the physical body naturally possesses—hence you must be able to draw it from your surroundings as needed. And to protect yourself from magic, you must be able to send it away from you at will. If he masters nothing else, he *must* master these basic skills."

"Hmmm. You know, that doesn't sound like the person who told me that Fox had to memorize plants and learn the history of sorcery before he could do anything else."

"Your friend Ranyon may have helped me to see a different path," he admitted. "Applied instruction better captures Fox's interest." He didn't say, however, that although the Hunt patrolled the city, the danger of the boy encountering a fae creature still existed. Privately, Trahern had decided to focus on self-defense first and leave all else until he was satisfied that the boy could protect himself.

"So tell me, did watching *Tiger Ninja* yesterday help?"

His mouth quirked. The strange and colorful little story was undeniably Fox's favorite. "It provided me with some language I could use, yes."

"That explains a lot. I didn't think *deadly mega-force bombs* was in your everyday vocabulary."

He kissed her before she could laugh at him. She pulled away and laughed anyway.

"I have things to do. Are you coming in for lunch?"

"I believe I will remain here for a time and contemplate possible strategies for the next lesson. And I must inform the ants they are free to leave their nest now."

"How did you—"

"I told them it was raining."

She kissed his forehead and headed to the house. Sunlight brightened her long dark curls, and she was always pleasing to gaze upon, but he found himself thinking of another Lissy, the one revealed by firelight. Glints of gold were unveiled in her hair and eyes, and the flames' glow warmed her naked skin to honeyed mead. His body stirred anew at the very thought, and he sighed aloud. The first time they had come together as lovers, he'd been undone by the unexpected tenderness, the way she generously gave of herself. Hers was not the artful stroke or the trained caress traded for the same. Instead, she seemed to put her entire self into the act, withholding nothing—wholly, gloriously *present.*

*And she laughs often.* At him, at herself. No mockery, only delight. Only the purest enjoyment of the moment. He'd never known such a thing, never imagined such a thing. Trahern fingered the scar across his throat. Imperfections were something to be shunned in the Court, yet Lissy had kissed it during their first night together and several times since, without reservation. He felt accepted—

He *felt.*

For no good reason, Trahern looked at his hands, as if they might belong to someone else, as if *he* were someone else. Perhaps he was. Had he not changed, slowly but surely, ever since Lissy Santiago-Callahan had confronted him at Palouse Falls?

Perhaps his brother had been right all along. Perhaps love did exist. But surely he had not succumbed to it. Indeed, he was still very certain he could *not* love. Lissy believed that he did, but his feelings for old Heddwen were no more than fondness. Not love. And although he wanted no other woman but Lissy, it was simply affection, was it not? Braith had paid a heavy price for his love of Saffir. If Trahern also yielded to love's siren call, disaster would surely follow. *Love leads to ruin.* Who would watch over Braith then? Teach Fox?

Worst of all, what would happen to Lissy?

He'd revealed his past to her with a touch. He hadn't told her that the veil over her own past had been drawn back as well. The grief she'd experienced over the sudden death of Matt Lovell had been wild, soul-scorching, and raw.

*If we continue on this present path, will I cause her heart to sunder anew?*

There was a bounce in Lissy's step as she headed downstairs, her mood as sunny as the morning light streaming through the windows. Summer had developed an unexpectedly rich and satisfying pattern. She spent time with her son over breakfast, then allowed him to watch *SpongeBob* and *Henry Danger* with Braith before the pair headed out to the yard for Fox's first magic lesson of the day.

Through trial and error, Trahern had refined his approach to teaching her son. First, the lessons were broken up into several brief sessions a day, no more than fifteen or twenty minutes each. Fox had to complete at least one lesson per day in exchange for Trahern watching an episode of *Tiger Ninja* with him. *Two* completed lessons were rewarded by activities that Fox chose for himself.

But hours later, when Fox was sound asleep, it was Lissy's turn to meet Trahern in the garden . . . And in the near-triumphant afterglow of incredible sex, they often talked until the morning star rose. Still, when she finally withdrew to the house, what few hours of rest she got seemed more than adequate. *I really shouldn't feel this refreshed on four hours' sleep. I wonder if it's a spell?*

He certainly seemed to have a spell for everything else. He surprised her by creating a new bed for them in the yard every night, some stunningly beautiful, others outrageous and even silly in design. She would never have suspected Trahern had a playful side to him—and she'd bet money that he hadn't known, either. He seemed to delight in bringing her gifts, rare and beautiful specimens of rocks and crystals, as another man might bring flowers. Except another man wouldn't watch with fascination as she examined his gifts with a hand lens and named them. It became a game for Trahern to try to stump her, but he'd managed it only once with a neon-blue variety of tourmaline that was native to Paraiba in Brazil.

After lovemaking, there were exotic foods for her to try as well (although she drew the line at the tiny orange fruits that *moved*), since she was invariably famished. Perhaps they were even the source of her unusual energy.

Or maybe she was just plain happy. Certainly, Fox seemed to be. Some of it was no doubt due to the continual calming influence of Braith—boy and grim had proved to be inseparable friends. The big gray creature accompanied them everywhere, even to the grocery store. And there hadn't been a single meltdown there or anywhere else. Perhaps being tutored in magic had something to do with it, too. Over the past few weeks, Fox had seemed more confident, more grounded. He hadn't changed who he was, and his likes and dislikes remained. Lissy wasn't about to receive a hug or be permitted to hold him. And he still insisted on calling her *Dude* instead of Mom. But there was a self-assuredness that hadn't been there before.

*It's certainly not because the magic lessons always go perfectly.* She'd come back from an errand on Monday morning to find the entire yard reduced to smoldering ash, from the back steps right up to the charred fence boards. Fox still stared at it in openmouthed shock, and Lissy could swear that both Trahern and Braith looked sheepish. Somehow, she summoned the restraint to go back into the house without asking any questions. And that evening, when she met up with Trahern, there was no sign of the earlier devastation. In fact, if anything, her yard looked *better* than it ever had. Were the trees taller? The ivy thicker? Reaching down, she tugged on the lush grass to make sure it was real.

It was. And so, unfortunately, were her feelings for Trahern.

"You're *sleeping* with him?" Brooke's eyebrows disappeared entirely beneath her black bangs with the telltale white stripe, and she had to make a grab to save the stack of new tarot decks she'd been pricing from tumbling off the table.

"Shhh! Not so loud—what if a customer comes in?"

Her best friend didn't seem to hear. "Are. You. Insane? How long has this been going on?"

"Since the very first night he came to teach Fox. Ranyon left to go help you, and we got talking, and then, well . . . things got physical. It wasn't planned; it just happened. And by the way, I let it happen. On purpose. My choice."

"Gah!" Brooke bounced out of the corner booth and began to pace the tiled shop floor. "That's practically a month! More than a month! This is not good, girlfriend, not good at all."

"I'm not expecting anything," said Lissy. "I'm just trying to enjoy it while it lasts."

"He's fae!"

"So I've noticed."

"What about Fox? How is *he* taking this?"

"He caught us kissing only once, the night that Ranyon came over. Trahern handled it well—explained very matter-of-factly that he was showing affection to me because he liked me—and Fox doesn't seem to have given it another thought. Since then, we've been very careful not to show anything more than friendship to each other around him." She sighed. "Fox already has a faery as a teacher and a grim as a sidekick. I figure that's enough change in his little life."

"Okay, I guess you haven't gone completely crazy, then. But you're still on the pill, right?"

"Of course I am!" She glanced around in case a customer really did lurk somewhere, but business was thankfully slow on Tuesdays. "I've been taking it for the past couple of years as a just-in-case measure, thanks to your own urging." More like nagging, but she wasn't going to say that. "It was either that or wear one of those hairy bracelets you make."

"It's called a gris-gris, and it would have worked very naturally."

"By creeping out any guy who looked at it! It had *bones* in it!"

"It was a *root*, and there was only one," said Brooke. "So, okay, I get that you have that subject covered. And Morgan says that humans and fae can't conceive without a deliberate spell anyway. But Lissy, promise me you'll be careful. Like maybe *hire a bodyguard* careful. Aidan explained about the different faery houses the other night—and the House of Oak is like a Mafia family. They're scary powerful."

"I know, I know. Ranyon warned me." And then disappeared. Despite the shared success of teaching Fox to produce light in his hands, the little ellyll hadn't been back to her home since. It could just be that he wanted to spend time with his dear friend, Leo, now that the old man's grandkids had finished their visit. Yet Lissy had the distinct impression it was simply too upsetting for Ranyon to see her with Trahern. *And that was when I'd only kissed him . . .*

Brooke sat down again and took Lissy's hands across the table. "Can you blame us? We love you, and we don't want anything to happen to you. And we *really* don't want you to get your heart broken."

"If I dated a nice normal human banker or a doctor or a construction worker or even another geologist, I could still get my heart broken. There aren't any guarantees in relationships. Do you want me to date Vincente so my heart will be safe?" The thought alone nearly made her gag.

"Goddess, *no*! You'd really be crazy then!"

"Well, at least we're on the same page about that." Lissy took her hands back and placed them in her lap so she could fiddle with the hem of her blouse. "You're my best friend. I was hoping I could confide in you because I really need to talk to someone."

Brooke's demeanor changed completely. "Oh, honey, I'm sorry I gave you the third degree—"

"Hey, it was better than the fifth degree that Ranyon gave me." They laughed a little, and the tension eased.

"Honest, I think my hormones are in overdrive with the baby and all." Brooke looked amazingly guilty for a moment. "I chewed out Aidan yesterday for not stacking the dishes in the sink just right. Lissy, you know that I don't even care about things like that, but *bang*, I went from zero to sixty on the angry scale. And then I started bawling for yelling at him. I'm lucky he's so patient."

"And thick-skinned."

"That, too. Let me guess, this thing with Trahern started out as some kind of summer fling, and now it's something else?"

She nodded. "I thought it was just practice, like training wheels or something while I got my mojo back. But there's this connection that I felt from the first time I met him. I mean, at Palouse Falls I was so mad at him I almost punched him, yet there was still this funny feeling of familiarity. I chalked it up to infatuation at first, but the more I've thought about it and analyzed it, it's not chemistry at all, it's *recognition*. As if I've known him for a very long time, so long that we're at ease with each other, that we understand each other." Her friend nodded, and Lissy continued. "Like I said, I don't expect anything. I know he's probably going to walk away the moment he figures his obligation to Fox has been fulfilled, but . . ."

"*But* your heart has already run ahead of you." Brooke's voice was softer now, the healer in her coming to the forefront. "Did you ever think it might be right?"

"What?"

"No, really. You claim you don't have magic, but you've always had amazing instincts, gut feelings about things. Forget about the stupid lecture I gave you. Maybe you need to listen to your own intuition on this one." Brooke riffled through the stack of tarot decks she'd just priced and pulled out a leafy green box titled FAERIE ENCHANTMENT. "I think it's a good time for a card."

"You want to do a reading?"

"Not exactly. Remember what your mother taught us about using the tarot during stressful times?"

It came to her at once. "Mama always said that a single card could sometimes give more focused guidance, like an entire reading condensed into one image."

Brooke handed her the box.

The clear plastic wrapping came away in Lissy's hand. She took a moment to handle the cards, running each through her fingers and finally pressing the deck to her chest to make sure it connected with her energy, her aura, her essence. She shuffled and drew.

*Knight of Wands.*

As lithe and powerful as a jaguar, the faery knight sat comfortably astride a rearing stallion that boasted strange horns and clawed hooves. In his hand was a wand—not a magician's pocket-size instrument but a tall wooden staff topped with a fiery globe—and he wielded it like a weapon. His long hair flew wild, the icy color of frost despite his youthful face. *That face.* With features that better belonged to an angel, his eyes stared out from the card with lifelike intensity—

The touch of Brooke's hand on her arm brought Lissy back to herself. Shakily, she placed the card back in the deck and put it aside. "Okay, no question who that represents. Now what does it mean?"

"The Knight of Wands can bring many things." Her friend's face was solemn. "In other types of readings, we're usually talking about change—travel, new opportunities, new challenges—but whatever change he's got for you, it happens fast."

*There's an understatement.* Trahern's abrupt appearance had heralded a ton of sudden changes in her life. "But?"

"In this context, it can also be very literal, as in *a man has come into your life*. It can even mean love."

"Should I be reassured or worried? Is it real? This isn't like a hit-and-run thing, is it?"

"The relationship? I just don't know. It's a positive card in any reading but not one for preserving the status quo—it often turns things upside down. All I can say is that it kinda looks like Trahern is supposed to be in your life right now. Not Fox's life, mind you. This card is strictly for you."

*Just for me*, she thought. *But I don't know why . . .*

# TWENTY-FIVE

*By all the stars, it should have gone well.*

Trahern had planned carefully for the morning's lesson. With Fox advancing in leaps and bounds with energy manipulation, surely he might be ready for an introduction to plant lore. Trahern had taken Lissy's suggestion and created a set of vivid illustrations that would function as flash cards. The backyard had been seeded with select specimens that would grow and bloom before Fox's eyes. Colorful stones filled Trahern's pockets, motivation for effort and rewards for achievement. And when Brooke came by to invite Lissy to shop, he urged her to go, assuring her that he would take excellent care of her son.

Instead, Fox now thrashed on the ground, wailing like a lost soul. Cards and stones littered the yard as if they had hailed down from the skies.

Next to him, Braith lay motionless with his great head slumped on his large paws. He whined softly, but Fox didn't seem to know he was there, and certainly Trahern's own efforts to speak to him had been ineffective. The child was clearly in a state where he could not hear or make sense of their words. *Overstimulation?* He didn't know. As he had in the living room that first night, he whispered the words of the spell that would create a bubble of serenity around Fox. A few moments later, as if it took time for the boy to realize he was no longer being assaulted by sensation, the wailing devolved into small hiccupping sobs. *Quieter. But he does not seem eased . . .*

Kneeling on the grass beside Fox, he noticed for the first time that the child's face was flushed, and beads of sweat made the blond hair stick to his temples, though the air was cool. He didn't get to form another thought before Fox rolled over with a strangled heaving noise—

And vomited all over him.

~

Lissy came in the front door and kicked off her shoes gratefully as she set her purse on the shelf. Before she forgot, she hung her keys on the hook—then allowed herself a hearty sigh. "Talk about shopping till you drop! It was fun, though. There are *so* many more cool things on the market for babies now than when Fox was born."

Brooke had already flopped on the sofa, with newly bare feet propped up on the old ottoman. "I just wish I could make up my mind about what color to paint the nursery. I want something unique and fresh and happy. Pastels just don't say any of those things to me. And don't get me started on neutrals! Well, except maybe that crisp, cool gray . . ."

"It looked really good with the turquoise accents," agreed Lissy. "We should go to the building store together, see if we can find that shade."

"So far I've been avoiding the paint department. I just can't deal with the sea of paint chips."

*Yeah, it does sound kind of overwhelming.* "What if we skipped the chips and went straight to the little jars of samples. I'll bet we could narrow it down to four or five in less than half an hour and start painting swatches on the walls. If none of them do it for you, we'll get five more the day after."

"That's a really good idea. You just made an onerous task sound totally doable."

Lissy laughed. "It's what I do. Everything in my whole life has to be broken down into little steps to keep Fox on an even keel. Want some tea?"

"Sure. Where are the guys?"

"Probably in the backyard still. That's where Trahern holds most of his lessons." In the kitchen, she filled the teakettle and plugged it in, then leaned over the sink and pushed aside the curtains to look. Nobody. Just in case, she went out on the back porch. No one was in the yard, but there seemed to be a lot of papers scattered around . . . *That's weird.* Fox liked order, so he didn't usually make much of a mess. *He's got to be the only nine-year-old boy with a perpetually tidy room.* But she sure couldn't imagine Trahern leaving a trail of debris.

Unless something was wrong. It wouldn't be unusual for Fox to decide he wanted to hang out in his favorite sanctuary with all his favorite things instead of cooperating with his teacher. She made the tea and took a cup to Brooke. "I'm just going upstairs for a minute."

As she approached Fox's room, she heard Trahern's voice asking a question.

"What does the dragon do when he's tired?"

"He sleeps," answered Fox.

"When the dragon is angry?"

"He breathes."

"And how does he breathe?"

"Deep and slow. Deep and slow." Fox demonstrated noisily.

"Very good. What does he do when he's restless?"

"He walks."

She stopped dead in the doorway. It was midafternoon, but Fox was in bed with the covers drawn up to his chin. Beside him, Trahern's tall form sat, or rather *perched*, on the child-size chair from

Fox's desk. And Braith's great gray bulk seemed to sprawl over the entire floor. "Omigosh, what happened?"

"I threw up," said Fox, almost cheerfully.

"I'm sorry to hear that, sweetie. Are you okay now?" she asked, but in her mind, she spoke to Trahern. *Are* you *okay?*

*Why would I not be well? Fox is the one who was ill.*

*Because . . .* She scrambled for the right words. *Because dealing with sick children is difficult. And it can get messy.*

*True, and it was. Very. But magic helps a great deal in such situations.*

*You just poofed away the mess, didn't you? Speaking for all moms everywhere, I officially hate you.*

*A jest?*

*Maybe.* But whatever his methods, he'd dealt with the situation. He'd looked after Fox, and both had survived. Once again, Trahern had surprised her.

"Trahern gave me a cool dragon!" Fox waved his arm at her, and she stepped over the obstacle course that was mostly dog to get to him. The image of a blue baby dragon curled playfully around his wrist, its stubby little wings and too-big yellow eyes making it utterly adorable.

"Wow, that's really, *really* nice."

"His name is Jake."

"Like Aunt Tina's dog?"

"Jake's my friend. And the dragon's my friend," he said simply. "So now I can have *two* Jakes!"

The reasoning was a bit of a mystery, but if it made sense to Fox, so be it. "I'm sure Aunt Tina's Jake will be very proud to have a dragon named after him." And a lot of her friends, including Tina, would get a kick out of it, considering the dachshund's cranky temperament. She squinted at the image. Was that paint? Ink? "This'll wash off, won't it?" *Jeez, I sound like such a mom!* "Or wear off?" But it sure didn't look promising, and even more damning was the fact that no one answered her question.

"I can talk to it, too," offered Fox.

"That sounds like fun. I'm going to get you some ginger ale for your tummy, okay? You just rest until you feel ready to get up," she said out loud. Her thoughts were a whole lot louder and directed at Trahern. *A tat? You gave my kid a tattoo? Do you know what the school will do when they see this? Do you know what Child Protective Services is?*

She tried to stay calm as she headed downstairs, but Brooke looked up from her mug immediately. "What happened? What's wrong?"

Lissy dropped into a chair with her head in her hands. "I'm going to prison, that's what's wrong."

"You are unhappy about what I have done." Trahern descended the staircase and entered the living room. With a nod to Brooke, he sat directly across from Lissy. "My gift to Fox today is not what you think."

"Just tell me it comes off, and I'll be fine," said Lissy, though she felt anything but fine.

"Hear me first." He leaned forward, capturing her gaze and holding it. "Do you know when you are ill? Or tired? Or hungry?"

Lissy frowned. "Yes, of course I do. What does that have to do with—"

"Fox does not know these things about himself—at least, not immediately. Instead, he is uncomfortable without understanding why, and the discomfort builds until he cannot bear it and loses control."

"Omigod, he had a meltdown, didn't he?" She could feel the blood leaching away from her face. "He threw up *and* he had a meltdown. And you're still here."

He reached out and took both of her hands in his. "Where else would I be?"

"Trust me, most people would have run screaming down the street."

"There was already enough screaming. My own screams were unnecessary."

Brooke snorted, nearly spilling her tea. Lissy simply stared at Trahern as if seeing him for the first time.

"I searched for something that might be assailing his senses, but all was quiet and calm," he continued. "Nor had I urged him beyond his bounds. Plainly, something else was amiss."

"This is my fault. He took a long time to eat his breakfast this morning," said Lissy, pulling her hands from his so she could sit back. "And then he didn't finish half of it. I should have thought he might be sick."

"But Lissy, honey, he didn't *act* sick, and he couldn't tell you that he didn't feel well," Brooke said. "You always have to guess."

"I believe that even Braith has to guess," added Trahern. "He would only know what Fox is able to tell him."

"See?" Brooke seemed excited now. "That's precisely the biggest problem we have in a nutshell. And so what you said before makes an amazing amount of sense, right, Lissy?"

"That Fox gets overwhelmed because he lacks awareness about *himself*..." Not only did it make sense; it would account for an awful lot.

"And that is why I placed an *anifail un drych* on his arm," Trahern explained. "In your language, it is something like *mirror animal.* I chose a dragon for Fox. It is young like he is, and it will reflect his own condition at all times."

"Wait a minute. You're telling me that the tattoo—I mean, the *picture*—changes?"

"That is its purpose. And as you once told me, Fox has a compassionate heart. Because of this, I do not doubt that he will care for the dragon's needs, and in so doing, care for his own. If the dragon is ill, he may not know how to help it—but I believe he would seek help for the creature by asking one of us."

"Okay, my mind is officially boggled," said Brooke.

*Mine, too*, thought Lissy. "Does *Fox* grasp this lofty concept?"

"He will come to understand it better over time. For now, the dragon is simply his companion. If it is hungry, he must feed *himself* to get food to it. If the dragon is tired, the boy must sleep to replenish him."

Brooke no longer reclined on the sofa but practically bounced on the edge of it in her excitement. "Holy cow, it's like those virtual pets we had as kids!"

"Sounds like it." Lissy considered. "Maybe it could even be a *Fox barometer*. Because I can look at the dragon, too, right?"

"You can guess at your son's state by what the dragon is doing. But Fox will know its nuances far more intimately. And he will respond."

Lissy held up her hands, palms out. "Whoa, I'm not so sure about *that* part of the equation. When my son is zoned out playing video games or absorbed in his rock collection, he's not going to remember to look at a picture on his arm."

Trahern was silent for a long moment, as if considering his words. "Fox cannot ignore it because it is not a picture," he said at last.

"Okay, it's a *magical* picture," she amended, but he shook his head. "The dragon is very much alive."

*Alive?* Shock gave way to action. Lissy gathered herself and stood, grabbing her best friend's hand and pulling her to her feet. "Come on, we're going upstairs." She glanced at Trahern as she hurried by with Brooke in tow. "You too, mister."

There wasn't a lot of room for three adults to crowd into Fox's bedroom, even when Braith somehow became incorporeal so they could walk through him. It was even harder to do it quietly, since Fox was asleep, and no one wanted to disturb him, least of all Lissy. Fortunately, his left arm was still lying on top of the blanket, the *not a picture* fully visible.

Brooke's voice was hushed—and awed. "You didn't tell me it was cute!" It was. But it had changed. A lot.

The baby dragon's eyes were closed. No longer wrapped around the boy's wrist but coiled in a bright-blue ball near the inside of his elbow, its little body rose up and down ever so slightly—

*You are doubting your sight.* Trahern's voice was gentle in her head, and his hands on her shoulders drew her back against him.

*It's moving. It's breathing!*

*Yes. And you need to breathe, too.*

Lissy hadn't even realized she'd been holding her breath. She sucked in air abruptly, noisily, and clapped her hand over her face to muffle it.

"He likely will not wake until the dragon does," Trahern said aloud.

She whirled on him, glaring up into that strong ethereal face and gripping the sleeves of his leather tunic. "Is that thing controlling him?" she whispered fiercely. "Because if it is, you'd better get it off him right now!"

"Fox is in control, not the dragon. I merely meant that he may well have decided to sleep until the dragon feels better."

*Fox decided?* Her protective fury ebbed at that, and she looked over her shoulder at her son's arm. The dragon lazily opened one bright eye, as if to check what was going on, then closed it again. Her grip on Trahern tightened as a wave of dizziness washed over her. For the first time in her parenting career, *she* was the one who was overstimulated.

"I think I need to go back to the living room and sit down . . . possibly with a drink."

# TWENTY-SIX

It's a toaster. It makes toast," said Lissy. He watched as she opened a window to let some of the acrid smoke out of the kitchen. She opened the back door as well—there was a *lot* of smoke.

Trahern eyed the small metal box dubiously. "It makes nothing. It applies heat to bread you already have."

"Yeah, well, in this case it makes charcoal out of that bread if you turn the timer all the way like that. In fact, I think you broke it. Don't you have any appliances in the faery realm?"

*They would look very much out of place there.* "There are no machines in the Nine Realms. We have no need of them."

Lissy looked surprised. "None at all? No phones, no laptops, no refrigerators? How do you *live* without technology?"

"How do you live without magic? You create machines to do for you what our magic provides for us. But as fascinating and clever as your devices are, they are still very limited."

"You think magic is better."

"Let us say it is more *efficient*." He raised a hand and fanned it once. Instantly, all the smoke vanished, and with it the pungent smell. "With magic, we have everything we need. And as I explained to Fox, magic is always with us; therefore, everything we need is always with us."

"But not everyone in the faery realm is a sorcerer."

"No. True sorcerers are rare, but every living being possesses magic to some degree. If someone needs something they cannot create for themselves, they have only to purchase or trade for a spell."

"Look, I've witnessed magic—small *m*, mind you—my whole life. But the idea that there's an entire world that operates on it is kinda tough for a scientist to wrap her head around."

"I know what science is," he said. "And I know that magic is simply science you do not understand. Yet."

"Some famous humans have said the same thing." She laughed. "So, are you going to teach me?"

"Perhaps I can show you instead. Would you like to visit my world?"

The words were out before Trahern considered them, but he allowed them to stand—with a slight amendment. "I can take you to Tir Hardd for a short time."

"Really? Holy cow, I'd love to get a glimpse of the faery world!" He caught her as she bounced up to throw her arms around his neck—and he laughed as she punctuated her words with kisses. "It's underneath ours, right? Can I bring instruments? Can I take samples? It'll be like a field trip! Omigod, *think* of the rock formations down there . . ." Trahern silenced her with a longer, slower kiss.

"When?" she asked as soon as they drew apart. "I'll need to leave Fox with Brooke and Aidan."

"Ask them when it is convenient, and that is when we will go. Perhaps warn them that I cannot predict precisely what hour we will return. Time does not work the same in the fae realms."

"That's okay. Fox will sometimes agree to stay overnight there because of the cats. If he doesn't want to, though, they can just bring him here." She kissed him again and hurried from the room, leaving Trahern with a profound sense of wonder. Who knew that it could be so singularly satisfying to make a woman happy? It made him want to do even more for her, greater and grander deeds, anything at all just to see that delight on her face as often as possible . . .

~

"You expect me to get on one of *those*?"

The sun was a rosy glimmer along the eastern horizon, casting just enough light to see the two tall horses standing on the campus lawn in front of Lissy's house. They were much bigger than she expected—eighteen hands? More?—but *big* she could probably handle. *Weird* was something else entirely. The gold one sported honest-to-God horns that spiraled up from its brow as if it were an exotic antelope. The smoke-colored one was just plain spooky, with its jutting tusks and strange milk-white eyes. A loud snort from it had her taking an involuntary step backward—

Straight into Trahern, who rested his hands lightly on her shoulders as she continued to stare at the creatures. "Cyflym and Cryf are blooded fae horses from Lord Lurien's own stables," he said. "There are very few finer than these."

"This is your usual mode of transportation? What happened to magic?"

"You said you do not like *poofing*."

"I'm reconsidering."

"It would be much more uncomfortable for you to be translated over such a distance."

Recalling how she felt after being zapped out of the drugstore, Lissy sighed inwardly. "I guess I'm riding. Which one is—nope, lemme guess. I get the prehistoric thing with the tusks, right?"

"His name is Cryf. His gait is smooth, and he is fearless in nature."

"Does he bite? Kick? Disembowel his rider?"

"He would never be so ill mannered. You will be safe with him." Trahern stepped forward and knelt before the horse, apparently looking for something in the grass. When he rose, there was dry soil in his palm, which he rubbed over Cryf's nose and face. The horse's nostrils flared as the tall fae spoke sharply: *"Dychwelyd yma!"*

With one hand on the horse's neck, Trahern extended the other to Lissy.

"What did you tell him?" she asked, allowing him to draw her close to the animal as its ears pricked with interest.

"I instructed Cryf to return to this place. He will not forget where to bring you should anything occur to separate us."

Swallowing hard, she touched the broad gray forehead, allowing her hand to slide down the center of the horse's face until her palm rested between the protruding tusks on its big dark nose. It was surprisingly soft, and she stroked it with gentle fingers until Cryf raised his great head and nibbled at her hair with questing lips.

"Does he like me, or do I just taste good?"

"Possibly both."

"That's not as reassuring as I'd like."

Trahern chided him, and the animal stepped back. That's when she noticed Cryf's feet weren't touching the ground . . . Turning slowly, Lissy saw that it was true of Cyflym as well. While both animals were truly tall, at least some of their imposing height was due to their hooves barely brushing the very tips of the grass. Speechless, she simply pointed until her companion caught on.

"They are not mortal creatures, good lady. Faery horses belong to the wind and the sky."

Lissy found her voice then. "Please tell me we're not flying."

"Not this day. Perhaps another time."

*Okay, that's something.* She walked around him to survey Cryf's ornate black saddle trimmed in silver. Finely crafted, its spare, clean lines reminded her of an English saddle but with a high cantle and tall front swell. Embroidered hunting scenes raced around the flap, and the slender silver stirrup was cleverly shaped like a dragon with its tail in its mouth. Clearly it was the most beautiful tack Lissy had ever seen, but all the riding she'd done with Morgan as a teenager wasn't going to help her mount a creature this tall—or this buoyant! "I think I need a ladder."

"Place your hand *thus*." Trahern lifted her hand and set it on the horse's withers.

Immediately the great horse knelt on all fours. Lissy scrambled into the saddle and tangled her fists in Cryf's long, pale mane as he rose again to his feet. It was more than strange to look down on Trahern! *If I fall off, I'm gonna break something for sure.*

*The saddle is enchanted, and you will not leave it unless you wish to.*

*You really thought of everything, didn't you?*

*I will not risk your well-being. And that is why you will be disguised as well.*

A strange buzzing sensation covered her skin from head to toe, as if suddenly coated in humming bees. *"Hey!"* When the bizarre feeling ceased, Lissy's jeans and sneakers had been replaced with fine boots that laced up to her thighs over pants as supple and soft as doeskin. A long, dark tunic, tastefully appointed in silver, fit her curves perfectly. Even in her wildest dreams, she would never have worn an outfit like this, yet it was as comfortable as a second skin. Lissy caught Trahern eyeing her with speculation. "Don't get any ideas, mister. I'm not sure whether to say thank you for the gorgeous outfit or yell at you for dressing me without permission."

"You appear as a Hunter now. If a human were to be seen in my company, it would draw attention and perhaps suspicion."

*I didn't think of that.* "I'm guessing they don't get many humans in the faery world."

"In the Nine Realms, more than a few. But in Tir Hardd, no." *At least, not yet.*

Her hair tickled her face. Absently, she raised a hand to brush it back and froze. "What did you do to me?" The strands in her dark-gloved fingers were shining white and smooth as silk, much like Trahern's. Before she could think to ask, the air in front of her shimmered and solidified into a mirrorlike surface, and in it she saw the porcelain skin and exquisitely fine features of a fae woman—with her eyes rounded in shock and her mouth hanging open. Lissy closed her mouth, and the woman in the reflection did the same. She patted her face and stared intently, trying to determine what color her own eyes were. As for hair, the snowy stuff hung in a long careless braid over her shoulder. She tucked some loose wisps back into the plait, knowing they would work their way out almost immediately. "All I can say is that this had better not be permanent," she said as the conjured looking glass faded away into nothingness.

"It is but a glamour, a strong one. Sadly, even I cannot see your true form, but better to be overcautious than not enough. As I said, *I will not risk you.*"

He leapt into his own horse's saddle effortlessly, though Cyflym was as tall as Cryf. Just as Lissy realized that neither seemed to have reins, Trahern's golden mount headed off across the campus grounds. Her horse followed as if tied by a string, keeping perfect pace.

Few people other than dog walkers and joggers were out this early, but none of them turned to look at the riders. Lissy adjusted her posture to post while trotting and found that Cryf indeed had a smooth gait. There was no bouncing, no jarring, at all. Was it because he didn't touch the ground?

All too soon they left the grassy lawns for the busy street beyond. Cyflym broke into an easy canter, and Cryf followed suit down the center line between the moving traffic. Lissy knew she could trust Trahern, but it was damn unnerving. What would they do if a car turned into their path? She didn't have to wait long for an answer. As they crossed an intersection that brought them out on Isaacs Avenue, a delivery truck started to make a left-hand turn off Roosevelt.

Yanking Cryf's mane and shifting her weight into the back of the saddle didn't affect his forward progress in the least. Diving from his back would throw her in front of oncoming traffic.

"Trahern!" She braced for impact—

It didn't come. One moment Cryf stepped in front of the grill of the truck, and the next, the truck headed down its intended street. *As if I hadn't even been here.* Putting a hand to where her heart attempted to escape her chest, Lissy tried to slow her breathing—and jumped when Trahern took her arm. She hadn't even seen him ride up alongside her.

"Are you well?"

"No, I am *not* well." The only thing keeping her from punching him was the truly surprised expression on his face. "What the hell happened? How come I'm not dead? Or am I dead and I don't know it yet?"

"I regret that I did not think of how this might appear to you." He waved a hand at the traffic around them, and she realized they were still standing in the busy intersection. Cars and trucks passed back and forth, some pouring from a turning lane as the lights permitted them, and none of them so much as brushed against the dark-clad riders in their midst. "We are not presently on their plane of existence."

Lissy clamped her teeth to keep her mouth from falling open again. *A different plane? We're in another dimension?*

"All fae beings are. It is why so few humans can perceive us."

"But I'm not a *real* faery, I'm just disguised as one."

"You ride a fae horse, and its powerful aura shields your own."

Thankfully, her heart rate had slowed down. "Okay, so I don't have to worry about colliding with anything in the human world?"

"You will pass through anything created by mortals." Trahern walked his horse beside her. She hadn't even realized that Cryf was moving! "However, some trees and most rocks exist in both realms."

"Check. Don't go charging into a mountain."

"A wise strategy. We will leave the road behind us soon." He galloped his horse ahead, and again Cryf kept perfect pace. Gradually their speed increased until the fastest thoroughbred would be unable to keep up with them, yet Lissy felt secure in the saddle. They left both the city and the highway, heading due north. Over fields and forests, hills and streams, through fences and farmyards . . . no matter the terrain, she felt strangely in sync with Cryf, anticipating his every motion and moving with him. A fierce, wild joy surged through her, an exhilaration that sparked in every cell. Was this what Trahern felt when he rode with the Hunt? Just as she wondered what it might be like to ride through the very clouds, the ploughed fields of wheat gave way to rocky land dotted with sagebrush. Jutting basalt bluffs told her exactly what their destination must be.

Palouse Falls.

"Stop!" yelled Lissy as they topped a rust-colored ridge. Any fear she might have had that Trahern wouldn't hear her was instantly allayed. He was at her side before the horses even slowed to a standstill—but he didn't get to say a word before she pointed her finger at him. "You're heading for the falls, aren't you?"

"Of course. It is one of the main portals to Tir Hardd, and the closest."

A cold shiver zipped down her spine despite the morning sun. "Look, I saw you—when we first met, you—after you left us, I—" She gave up and covered her face with her hands, fighting to find her calm and failing utterly.

"You are worried about the precipice?"

"Seriously? That waterfall is nearly two hundred feet, and you jumped your horse over it without hesitation before disappearing into thin air. How could I not be worried about that?"

In answer, he held out his hand. When she took it, she found herself suddenly seated in front of him, his hard thighs on either side of her legs and his strong arms wrapped securely around her.

"Ride with me," he said, and she nodded. Cyflym sprang forward into an easy gallop across the arid landscape toward the park. Several campers were up and about but paid no heed to their passing. The faery horses crossed the parking lot and banked to the left of the bowl-shaped gorge beyond. Rather than follow the worn trails, however, they headed overland to the Palouse River, hidden from view behind the basalt columns and cliffs. A voice sounded inside her head: *Do not be afraid.* Lissy trusted Trahern, but her heart still tried to climb into her throat as the horses picked up speed and ran along the top of the river as if it were a highway. Ahead she spotted the strange columns of the Castle formation and belatedly realized Trahern had chosen this route so she wouldn't see where they were going until it was—

They rounded the bend and hurtled over the lip of the falls.

# TWENTY-SEVEN

A scream rose in her throat and stayed there. There was no sensation of falling, no sensation of gravity, no inner warning of being up or down or *anything.* As far as her equilibrium was concerned, nothing was out of the ordinary—except for the terrifying view and the deafening roar as they rode straight down the back of the plunging cataract! The green-blue water below was a fast-approaching wall . . .

And then it stopped. Everything around her stopped. The surging water that pounded beneath the horses' hooves, the wind and spray that numbed her face, the thunderous rumble and crash of the falls that shook her bones. All soundless. All still. Yet the horses galloped on, seemingly unaffected. By now they should have struck the great rocky basin of water, shattered like glass against concrete. Instead, distance had changed, shifted, lengthened into the strange vacuum of silence.

*I'm glowing!* We're *glowing!* Lissy stared hard at her hands knotted in Cyflym's long mane. Despite the bright sun, it was impossible to miss the bizarre phosphorescent green that emanated from every detail. For an instant, she remembered the strange luminosity that had surrounded Trahern when she'd witnessed him riding off the edge of the falls the night they'd met. Then her attention was seized wholly by a far more vivid glow in the water ahead, as a vortex of light opened up like a camera iris. The horses leapt through without hesitation. For a long moment Lissy could see nothing but the brilliant blue-green light, as flesh and bone seemed to be pulled and squeezed and stretched to its limit.

Abruptly it was all over. She gasped and blinked as if surfacing from underwater—and indeed she had expected to do just that. Instead, she was still mounted on Cyflym as he slowed to a walk and stopped *on solid ground*. At least she thought it must be solid ground as ordinary sensation flooded back into her overwhelmed brain: the smoothness of the saddle that molded itself to her, the protest of her cramped fingers, and the extremely welcome feel of Trahern's arms and legs still sheltering her. She realized she was already leaning back against his hard body—okay, *plastered to it* was more like it—and sat up a little as her fingers unclenched.

"Are you well?"

It took her two tries to find her voice. "I'm alive," she managed at last. "I'd call that a win. Sorry to be such a scaredy-cat."

He was out of the saddle in an instant, his hands gentle as he lifted her down. "Do not apologize. You showed great courage." He kissed her forehead as he rested his hands on her shoulders.

"Are you kidding? White-water rafting is going to be *easy* after this. I was scared out of my mind!"

"Is that not what bravery is? Doing what you fear to do? You were already frightened, yet you agreed to ride with me without hesitation. And you did not close your eyes but met your fate head-on."

"Good thing I didn't scream, then. It would have spoiled your big brave image of me."

"Never."

Lissy couldn't resist stamping her feet a little to test that what was under them really *was* solid ground. *Yup, terra firma—or is it faeryland firma?* "Remind me to get my brother, George, to take you on a roller coaster one day. He knows where the wildest ones are."

He narrowed his eyes, but there was amusement in them. "Do I detect a desire for vengeance?"

"You know it, mister." She let him kiss her anyway—she wasn't *that* vengeful—long and deep and sweet, until something bumped the back of her head. And bumped it again, harder. Lissy turned around to find herself nose to nose with Cryf.

"He believes we should go, and so do I. Time does not move the same here as in the human world, and you would not be pleased to return home a week hence."

Cryf seemed content to pace alongside Cyflym, which left her completely free to look, *really* look, at their surroundings. The broad pebbled trail wound gently through tall grass dotted with vibrant blue flowers. Giant trees towered to skyscraper heights overhead, and tiny flashes of bright, glowing colors swooped and soared from limb to limb with trilling calls. Horses and riders seemed infinitesimal in scale, vastly insignificant. Amid the coastal redwoods of her own world, Lissy had felt herself a mouse in a cathedral. Here, the forest was a *universe*, and she was a speck of stellar dust.

"So beautiful . . ." The interlocked branches were too far away for her to discern the outline of their leaves, but the shape of the trees themselves didn't seem to match the image Trahern had conjured in the smoke of her backyard campfire. "This isn't the Silver Maples forest at all, is it?"

"I would not take you to such a dangerous place. Do you see the white bark? These are ash trees, not unlike the little ones outside your own home."

"My home could fit inside one of these incredible trees. I think my whole townhouse row could fit inside some of them!" She continued to gaze upward in purest wonder. A steadying hand suddenly rested on her shoulder, and she blinked rapidly and waited for a wave of dizziness to pass before meeting Trahern's eyes. Belatedly she realized the horses had stopped. "I guess I got carried away. The trees are utterly magnificent. And even that word doesn't do them any justice. They must be incredibly old to be such amazing giants."

"Not at all. These ash trees began as seedlings sent from the Nine Realms by Gwenhidw herself and were planted not long after Aidan rode with the Hunt."

Lissy caught herself before she protested the impossibility of such a claim. This was a very different world—a different *dimension*, even—and it probably didn't operate on the same principles as hers. *I wonder what my university professors would think?*

A single pinnate leaf spiraled downward, and Lissy caught it in her outstretched hands. Its vivid green leaflets were tipped with red and magenta and seemed to glow before her wondering gaze.

"A blessing of protection for you. You've pleased them with your admiration," said Trahern.

"They—they *heard* me?"

"Of course. The ash trees possess awareness. All trees do, in both worlds. They vary only by degree."

The knowledge stunned her, and hard on its heels was a revelation. "Fox! When he was little, Fox started patting trees with his hands and talking to them. He—he still does with some of the bigger ones on campus."

Trahern simply nodded as if he'd expected it, then rode close enough to pass his palm over the great leaf. It vanished from her hands, and its bright colors reappeared within a crystalline disk on a fine silver chain around her neck. "It is no light thing when a tree bestows its favor. Now it cannot be lost." Without waiting for a response, he rode ahead.

Lissy stole a moment to admire the lovely pendant, then quickly tucked it inside her tunic to make *doubly* certain she wouldn't lose it.

"Thank you," she called out to the white branches so impossibly high over her head as Cryf trotted after Cyflym.

She wasn't a scientist anymore. She was a child in a make-believe storybook. Any thought she'd entertained of taking rock samples or studying specimens dwindled and vanished as the day bloomed with unimagined wonders. Transparent flowers that chimed in the breeze. Tiny red salamanders that burst into flames when startled, then ran off as if nothing had happened. Exotic scents that rose up from black sands along the shores of an amethyst lake. And in a darker forest, beneath a looming sky, the arches of an ancient stone bridge crossed a slow-moving stream of glowing blue lava. Everywhere she looked, there was something new and profoundly amazing. And when they traveled on open land, she could see for herself that even the sky was strange and unpredictable; the sun rose along its expected arc, then traveled back the way it came until it was joined by a larger twin. And all the while, a fat orange moon floated in a midnight sky on the opposite horizon . . .

There was no *how* or *why*. No explanation could possibly suffice. There was only what existed, what was experienced, in the moment.

At the edge of another forest, their horses stopped abruptly, and Trahern put his finger to his lips. *Be still and watch*, he said in her mind. She could see nothing beyond save smooth hills covered in compact golden-green moss. The air itself changed, however, alert with tension as if a storm approached. Lissy strained to hear something, anything. Instead, it was a sudden vibration in her bones that alerted her to the approach of something mighty.

"*Rhai corniog*," said Trahern, as fifty or so shaggy animals suddenly topped a hill and thundered down its sides.

*Unicorns*, she thought, but these were far from the dainty and delicate creatures of legend. The size and heft of heavily muscled Clydesdales, the animals fairly radiated power. Great cloven hooves were skirted with long jet hair; dark roan coats were speckled with blue and gray. Their single horns were not slender spirals but thick and curving blades that tapered up from their broad foreheads and flashed in the sunlight. A tangy scent filled Lissy's senses, a strange blend of lathered sweat, hot iron, cool earth, and (of all things) *rosemary*. The unicorns paid no attention to the riders but galloped on, tossing up huge chunks of moss as they passed. They vanished behind a rise as suddenly as they'd appeared, and in their wake, the ground was not merely trampled but churned, and perhaps even a little charred in spots. Yet blushes of velvet green were already appearing like a new crop in a plowed field.

"They renew the soil," said Trahern. "When next we pass this way, the moss will again cover the hills." He looked at her expectantly, but Lissy couldn't think of a single question to ask. Not one. Her brain could only vaguely wonder if sensory overload had finally taken its toll. Perhaps that was why she didn't notice Cyflym sidle close to her own mount until Trahern reached out to her. His strong hand stroked the side of her face, then slid beneath her hair to cradle the back of her neck. His long, cool fingers made luxuriant circles along the muscles there, until relaxation made her shoulders drop. Her guard dropped as well. She might be in an alien wonderland in an unknown dimension, but not only did her body know Trahern's touch, it recognized his energy as surely as if it were visible. Magic had nothing to do with how grounded and centered she felt when close to him. Somehow, he always brought her to herself.

Brushing his lips over her face, her eyes, her mouth. Lifting her from the saddle and bearing her away from the horses, the path. Into the forest through a tall bower of blue-leafed bushes to a clearing—and a bed of golden violets. The scent of vanilla rose around her as the cool flowers bruised beneath her, beneath Trahern.

She had been here before, in her dream. In that night vision, however, she hadn't possessed sleek white hair. And her lover hadn't held up a strand of it and frowned.

"*Yn wir*," he said.

The strange vibrations that buzzed over her entire body didn't startle her as much this time, but the sensation was just as weird. When the hum lifted, however, she was still a little surprised to find herself to be . . . well, *herself*. Not only was she naked, but a glance at her hands and arms confirmed that she was no longer faery pale. Trahern, resting on an elbow beside her, drew out a lock of her hair and released it. The dark curl sprang from his fingers, and he smiled.

Lissy smiled, too. "Are you sure you wouldn't prefer me to be fae like you?"

"Have I ever given you cause to think I would?"

"Not even once."

Her bare skin quivered beneath the long, light stroke of his hand as he bent to kiss her, carefully tracing the outlines of her lips as if memorizing them. *I can think of no word in your language save* beautiful, *but it is hardly adequate to describe you.* When he finally raised his head to look at her, it was still impossible to discern the color of his eyes, even in the sunlight. But there was something new in them, something unexpected and—

Trahern's clothes vanished as well. They'd loved many times in the glow of firelight and beneath the moon's pale rays. Now, sunlight warmed his marble skin, and the many glyphs and symbols glinted like liquid fire. There was fire in his touch, too, and she was wet for him long before his heated lips found their way to her breasts. He kissed them carefully, reverently, paying homage to each, worshipping her nipples with tongue and gentle teeth before working his way even lower. His breath was hot on her belly, low, lower . . . until his thick white mane spilled unbound across her thighs in a rush of silk, and his burning mouth found her aching clit. The abrupt storm of sensation shot her into glorious overload. Lissy seized his hair and pulled his face hard against her as she came.

Then drew him onto her, welcomed him into her. Slick. Deep. Hard. Again she climbed, gasping at the dizzying height, reaching for that high, clear edge of pleasure—

And took him with her as she tumbled over the brink.

Still naked, they lay together for a time, her head pillowed in the hollow of his shoulder and his arm around her. As she often did, her fingertips traced the outlines of his *ledrith.*

"Will Fox develop these, too, as he learns more magic?"

"I do not think so. Power has come to him through his bloodline, yet he is not fully fae."

*Not fully fae—but partially.* She hadn't looked at it quite like that. "Well, less for me to explain to the school, at least." Because she was pretty sure that while the little dragon image was invisible to ordinary humans, the *ledrith* were not. She kissed the one closest to her, intent at first on following its spiral with her lips—then giving up and laying her head back on Trahern's shoulder with a sigh. "I dreamed about this place, you know."

"I am not surprised. You claim to have no magic, but you have more than you realize. You sense things all the time."

"I dreamed about us. Right here, flowers and all."

His voice in her head sounded intrigued—and not a little pleased. *And what were we doing?*

"Pretty much what we just did." She laughed. "But the real thing was much better. Besides, I didn't like the mask you were wearing in the dream."

"What mask?"

"It was copper, with stones set into it. A half mask, really."

Trahern was silent for so long that she turned her face to look at him. "There is a marketplace close by. It has a tavern with good ale, where we can rest and eat," he said.

"I know a change of subject when I hear one. So, is it a real thing, this mask? You said in the dream that your will was not your own."

"Such a mask exists, and I would not speak of it here and taint what we have just enjoyed. Let us go to the tavern—we have traveled much this day."

She wasn't fooled. More like *she* had been traveling a long time and he'd merely been out for a warm-up. It was all too obvious by the horses' behavior—Cyflym was always dancing around as if anxious to be given his head. Cryf often craned his great head around to look at her. Despite his strange white eyes, she had no trouble sensing his dismal puzzlement at his new role as tourist transport. *Like a prize rodeo horse demoted to kid's pony. Poor guy.* Lissy laughed. "Okay, okay. It's kind of you to try to make me believe we're all ready for a break, but I'm well aware it's just the wimpy mortal who needs a rest."

"What does *wimpy* mean?"

She didn't get a chance to answer as the shifting sunlight revealed golden eyes amid the lobed leaves as something large emerged from the brush. A tall green buck with polished jade antlers stood staring at them, a thick cape of long emerald hair covering its neck from ears to chest. Lissy held her breath. The magnificent creature had to be as big as the bull elk she'd once seen in Yellowstone—and probably just as dangerous. She gasped a little when it suddenly pawed the ground and snorted loudly with flared nostrils.

*It will not hurt you. The Green Stag only seeks to remind us that it rules this particular forest.*

*Are you sure? Because it looks like it wants to stomp all over us.*

*If it wished to do us harm, it need only brush our skin with its antlers. Every tine is tipped with venom.*

*Every tine, huh?* The heavy rack was a hunter's dream, at least twenty points, maybe more. *That is* so *not comforting.*

Trahern's arm suddenly tightened around her. *Whatever happens, do not move.*

*What* . . . There was no time to even think. The stag charged right at them, leaping at the last possible moment. Lissy held her breath as its deep-green underbelly and knife-point hooves soared high over them, coming to rest at the opposite end of the clearing. With a final snort over its shoulder, the emerald animal bounded away among the trees.

"An interesting omen, and a good one." Trahern stood, rising to his feet as gracefully as a panther. "Are you well?"

"You keep asking that for some reason."

He grinned and held out a hand.

Trahern chose the best seats in the house—*best* according to a Hunter's way of thinking. From their table in the farthest corner, he could see all who came and went while shadows hid his own features. Lissy was likewise veiled. Instead of sitting across from him, he had seated her at his side so she, too, could study the crowded tavern. He had renewed her glamour before leaving the flowered glen, but though her form was once again disguised, her own vibrant spirit shone through as she watched the diverse clientele with interest. He was proud of her. She'd embraced her many new experiences in the faery realm with wonder and delight. And neither the plunge over the falls nor the lengthy ride had brought a complaint to her lips—

And would those lips taste the same while disguised?

Trahern resolved to find out, but not here—though his body stirred at the thought. It was rare enough for him to be seen in the company of another Hunter, never mind a female. The coblyn child who had waited upon them had already cast sidelong glances at Lissy as if she were a novelty. Perhaps it was because she smiled at the boy—after all, Hunters were not known for their friendliness.

*Should you ever meet any of the Tylwyth Teg, hide your feelings*, he cautioned her.

*Why?*

*They do not experience emotion as mortals do, and therefore do not read it well. If you do not demonstrate your feelings to them, you have an advantage.*

*This is how you live in your world?*

*No, only how I survive.*

It wasn't long before a broad silver tray, heavily laden with food and drink, appeared to escape the kitchen, bobbing and weaving around the tables and their occupants and narrowly missing a towering bwbach heading for the door with a wooden keg tucked beneath its hairy arm. The tray came to a halt before Trahern and Lissy, and wide, stubby hands slid it onto their table, revealing the red cap and smiling bearded face of Fychan himself.

"'Tis about time thee graced my doorway again," he said to Trahern. He bobbed his head to Lissy, who nodded back solemnly—though Trahern could sense it was difficult for her to repress her natural warmth.

"I have been on Lord Lurien's errand," he said.

"As I thought. I could not figure thee no longer cared for my cooking or my ale!"

"Never that."

Fychan made a show of accepting Trahern's coins, then leaned forward with a lowered voice. "Three suns ago, someone came asking about thee. We don't get many Tylwyth Teg here, only Hunters like thyself. Drove away half my customers that night. Wanted to know if I'd seen thee."

"What did you tell him?"

Fychan laughed as if he'd heard a good joke. "Told him he'd have to ask Lord Lurien himself, as I was but a poor tavern keeper and not worthy to serve the Wild Hunt."

"House?"

"He wore no colors, so I could not tell. Not a commoner, though—he spoke much like thee, save I could tell he didn't care to be talking to me at all."

"Truly, it was his loss," Trahern said, and passed Fychan two more coins. "I am indebted to you as always." The man grinned and touched his cap, winked at Lissy, and strolled away.

"Is something wrong? Who would be looking for you?" she asked. "Your family?"

"It would surprise me greatly if one of them ventured to Tir Hardd." *But who else could it be?* More important, what did he want? What would cause Eirianwen to send someone to the new colony that was so eschewed by the nobility? Lissy was disguised well enough that no one, not even his mother, would know her for a mortal. Still, Trahern would have to take her away from here as soon as possible. *I do not want her involved in whatever business the House of Oak thinks it has with me.* "Perhaps someone sought the aid of the Wild Hunt." Though remote, it was a possibility, and therefore not a lie. It made him uncomfortable just the same.

"Do you think he'll come back?"

"I do not know. If it is the Hunt he seeks, he will find riders at other taverns. Perhaps he has found Hyleath and Iago already. They often drink together not far from here."

Knowing it would delight her, Trahern passed her a plate made of polished agate sliced so thin she could see through it, then pushed the enormous platter closer to her so she could take whatever she wished. The coblynau had produced a tidy feast, and he could tell by the color of the ale in the silver tankards that Fychan had opened one of his better barrels. "Eat what you will, but drink only a little of this—faery ale is very strong." Trahern signaled another coblyn. "Bring us water as well."

"What about the old stories?"

"What stories?"

"That if you taste any food or drink in the faery realm, you can't leave."

Trahern couldn't help but laugh. "I promise you, there is no such enchantment. Food is merely sustenance, whether you are mortal or fae. The only concern is whether or not it is poisoned. And this is not."

"Well, that's a big relief."

Lissy appeared to enjoy the meal. As for himself, he could not stop thinking about Fychan's words. The House of Oak had no power that could trump that of Lord Lurien. Trahern belonged to the Hunt, and nothing could change it. Still, was Lissy's dream a warning?

Having finished her meal, Lissy reached again for the ale, but he was quicker. The tankard floated out of her reach and circled around to Trahern for inspection. Almost a finger's width of the potent drink was gone, and he set it on the tray of a passing server.

"Really?" she said. "It's *that* strong? I thought when you said to drink just a little, I could at least have the mug."

"The mild flavor is deceiving. A mortal—even your friend Aidan—could not drain the entire cup without losing consciousness. You would not wish to return home to Fox in such a condition."

"Good point. Thanks for the save. I'm not going to pass out from the food or anything, am I? Because I really enjoyed it."

He heard nothing more. The tavern was busy as always, yet a movement at the door had captured his attention. There, a short figure in an earthen-colored dress seemed to have stepped from his memories whole. Every detail was just as he remembered, from the braided hair with many shiny charms woven amid its brown leaves to the bright eyes in a softly wrinkled face. Her slender fingers appeared more like twigs than flesh as they reached for the great brass handle—

*"Heddwen!"* Trahern rose so quickly he nearly upset the table. But the little ellyll didn't even glance up as she hurried outside. Forgetting entirely that he could have cleared a path for himself with a single word, he dodged patrons and servers, stumbled over an inebriated basilisk, and almost knocked Fychan himself down. Reaching the door at last, Trahern flung it open.

And leapt back to avoid the poisonous horns of the Green Stag that lay dead across the threshold.

# TWENTY-EIGHT

There was no scent of burning leaves, no stench of magic of any kind. Indigo blood, heart's blood, stained the fine green pelt and ran down the steps to pool on the street below. The stag had been felled with a single obsidian arrow—*and the arrow was fletched with amber and claret.*

"We are leaving. Now." *There is no time for the horses,* he added silently. It was all the warning he could give her before he gripped her hand and hurtled them both through what must surely appear to her as a tunnel of stars . . .

They burst onto the mortal plane amid an army of small spruce trees that marched in rows as far as the eye could see. Trahern caught Lissy to him and held her tightly until she stopped shaking.

"I really, really hate that, you know," she muttered into his tunic.

"I know."

With one last shudder, she pushed herself away from him—still clutching his tunic with one hand to steady herself—and looked around. "Where are we?"

"Your world."

"That's a little broad. My world, *where*?"

"Keckler's Christmas Tree Farm, in the historic town of Cape Elizabeth. In Maine." Despite the circumstances, he enjoyed her surprise. No need to mention that his greater height enabled him to read their location from a distant faded sign visible just above the stubby trees. "Whoever is searching for me is dangerous, and it was imperative to take you away, not only from the tavern but from Tir Hardd, as quickly as possible," he explained. "I dared not take you directly to your home."

"In case he followed us," she finished. Lissy released his tunic and walked away a short distance, hands on hips as if deep in thought.

*"Yn wir,"* he murmured, removing the glamour as before—though regrettably it was more prudent to leave her clothed in this prickly setting. Still, the sunset now glinting gold in her long dark curls afforded him something akin to relief. Her features, and only hers, both charmed him and steadied him. When she turned back to him, however, her sable eyes were filled with questions he had little time to answer.

"Who was it, Trahern? Do you really think you saw Heddwen?"

"At the time, I believed that I did. She appeared to be opening the door to leave. You saw no one?"

"The door didn't open," she said gently. "And there was no one there."

The disappointment was surprisingly painful. "An illusion, then. A strong one." *Bait for a trap.* Only a handful of people could have known that an image of the old ellyll would capture his attention. And while the arrow's colors had meant nothing to Lissy, Trahern knew them all too well. The House of Oak had sent a clear message in the death of the Green Stag. *Come to us or die.* He intended to do neither. "They seek only me," he said before she could reply. "You and Fox will be safe with Braith. Call Ranyon to you to be doubly certain."

"Wait a minute, aren't you—"

Lissy didn't have a chance to finish before he sent her home. *She is a brave woman and will be angry with me for forcing her to leave.* But he had to know she was safe. With great care, Trahern erased any evidence of magic, any trace of Lissy's essence, from the elements around him. No one would know she had been here, never mind where she had gone, but he was grateful for the protective safeguards he'd left over her house and yard just the same.

Satisfied, he returned to Fychan's tavern. The Green Stag must be properly burned, its magic returned to the forest.

And then he would hunt.

~

*At least I'm dressed.* Lissy sat in the midst of the ivy in the corner of the backyard, grateful there was a layer of denim jeans between her and the prickly vines. There was still a ringing in her ears, but the dizziness had passed quickly this time. *Maybe I'm finally getting used to being poofed.*

No way was she getting used to his doing it without her permission, though. How dare he send her away like a child? Far worse, however, was that Trahern hadn't *poofed* with her. Where had he gone? Someone who rode with the Wild Hunt certainly wasn't going to hide out in a bunch of holiday trees. *Please be safe*, she thought, and focused on the memory of Trahern destroying the monster in the storeroom at Handcastings. He was intelligent, strong, and powerful—she had to believe he would be all right.

*I believed Matt would be all right, too.* The unexpected thought stabbed her like a knife, leaving her breathless for a long moment. Fear and hurt made her angrier than ever, though, and she wrestled those feelings into an inner closet and slammed it shut. *Fox. Just focus on Fox.* Seeing her child, witnessing for herself that he was okay (although he could hardly be anything else with Brooke and Aidan and Braith looking after him) would steady her. Just being with her son, going through all their little daily routines, even some of their ongoing struggles, would crowd out most of her worry over Trahern. *Maybe.*

From the angle of the sun—which thankfully could be counted on here—it must be around suppertime. Her friends would soon be sitting down with Fox, and undoubtedly Brooke had made the special grilled-cheese sandwich that he always asked her for. No crusts, cut in perfect halves, a single pickle slice beside each (but not touching the bread), though he never ate the pickles. *He just likes the way they look.* The simple familiarity reunited her with her world at last and galvanized her into motion. Lissy rose, dusted herself off, and noticed that her shoes were on the wrong feet. She'd tease Trahern about that little goof later. As long as it was just the shoes and not her actual feet that were transposed . . .

Unfortunately, her house was silent and empty. *So much for the reunion.* Her phone was on the kitchen table, and a text informed her that Fox was at Handcastings playing pirates with Rory, Bouncer, and Jade. So far, he was enthused about staying overnight (especially since they were going to binge-watch *Tiger Ninja* together), and he'd actually managed it a couple of times before. As Lissy smiled and sighed, however, her peripheral vision caught sight of a shadow at the screen door. A very short shadow. "Ranyon! Why are you standing out there?"

"On account of ya told me I was to be knockin' afore I came into yer house." He stood with his thin branchlike arms folded huffily in front of his ubiquitous Blue Jays shirt. "And I haven't decided to knock yet."

*Don't smile, don't laugh,* she ordered herself. "Please come in. And thank you for waiting."

The little ellyll immediately appeared in the kitchen, perched on the edge of a chair, swinging his strange knobby feet. His gnarled brow frowned like a ledge over his bright-blue eyes. "Brooke said Mister Son of Oak took ya on a picnic in the fae realm."

"There was no picnic." *Well, not of food.* There had been a glorious feast of sensation in a forest clearing . . . and Lissy hastily stashed those thoughts for later. "But Tir Hardd was amazing. I didn't collect a single rock!" In fact, no aspect of geology had even crossed her mind. Tomorrow she would kick herself for not asking more questions, for not trying to observe more of the formative features of the fantastical land, for not even scraping up a teaspoon of that aromatic black sand or pocketing a pebble from high up the banks of the stream of blue lava. Today, the faery world had been too vivid, too filled with life, too overwhelming. Even now, she had no hope of describing it. But maybe she should reveal what happened at the tavern? Trahern had said to *call on Ranyon* . . . though the ellyll would be sure to blame the fae for everything. Given a choice, she'd probably keep quiet. But there was Fox to think about, and if there was the slightest possibility of danger from a fae source, then she needed everyone—*especially* Ranyon—on board. "Can I make you a sandwich? I have things to tell you."

His bright-blue eyes sparked with interest, though his brow remained furrowed. "Well, now, I might be able to manage a bite or two."

The *bite or two* turned into four large sandwiches (all different) and every dill pickle in the house. Chewing was interspersed with dark comments about Trahern's power-hungry family and the tragedy of the Green Stag. "A desecration, that's what it is," he said, and more than one tear ran over his gnarled face to plop onto his plate. "'Twas an ancient creature, the very life of the forest it guards. Many sought it for favors and blessings, though very few received."

*Trahern said it was a good omen.* It certainly hadn't been favorable for the stag. "You're certain it was the House of Oak?"

"No one else would commit such heartless sacrilege." Ranyon finished the last bite of the last sandwich and sighed. "Another stag might rise up to take the place of the old one. But it'll take a very long time, and the trees may dwindle in the waiting." He drained his last juice box, too. Six of the little crumpled containers, all apple, lay on the table. "So exactly where is Mr. Son of Oak now?"

"I wish I knew," she said. "I know he's strong and capable, but if his crazy family is involved? I'm scared for him."

The ellyll looked uncomfortable for a long moment, then finally offered: "He'll be all right, dontcha know. That Trahern is pretty clever with his magic. Fer a fae."

She came around the table and hugged her friend. "Thanks." Standing on the kitchen chair, he returned the hug heartily, though those long branchlike arms were always surprisingly gentle—

And strong. He threw her to the floor just as a blast of blinding white light disintegrated the screen door and struck him. There was no time to move, to scream, to run. Ranyon's beloved Blue Jays hat was still spinning in the air when men with long white hair and sharp, pitiless features entered the empty doorway. The tall invaders encircled her but didn't touch her. Instead, their leader spoke a single word, and Lissy found herself hovering about a foot off the kitchen floor. She didn't remain upright, as Cryf and Cyflym did, but bobbed weightlessly in all directions as if gravity itself had ceased to exist for her. Upside down at one point, she made a fruitless grab for Ranyon's sprawled form. With his hat gone, his wild braids were askew, and a flurry of brown leaves, buttons, and trinkets surrounded his woody features. If it wasn't for his beloved Toronto Blue Jays shirt, he might have resembled a tangled pile of fallen twigs. She couldn't seem to control the rest of her weightless body but managed to turn her head, keeping her eyes fixed on Ranyon until she was satisfied that his little baseball shirt really *was* moving ever so slightly. *Keep breathing, bud. Please be okay—*

Another fae word sent her floating helplessly out the door into the twilight. Though she swung and kicked at her captors, she couldn't make contact—it was like being inside a bubble. Instead, she called them every name she could think of and (although she knew they wouldn't comply) demanded to be freed. Either they were deaf or they didn't care how much noise she made, and she made *plenty*. They wouldn't even look her in the eye as they approached a group of fae horses under a pair of campus trees.

Suddenly a lone figure appeared, walking briskly in high heels along the sidewalk. Claire Emsley headed for her own house, just two doors away!

"Help! *Help!* Tell my friends what happened!" It was hard not to use names, but Lissy wasn't about to give her kidnappers any more power than they already had. "Look at me, dammit! I need your help! Call someone!" To her horror, Claire simply stood on the doorstep of her townhouse, rummaging in her large, expensive purse for her keys. Lissy didn't expect the woman to see the Tylwyth Teg or the group of fae horses that waited for them—after all, she'd walked right *through* Braith that first night in Lissy's living room—but those sharp ears that had heard every sound that Fox made inside his own home should have been able to hear Lissy now. *Crap. I asked Ranyon to make her forget us! How could I have been so stupid?*

But then, how could she have anticipated being taken prisoner by a gang of fae?

*At least Fox is safe with Brooke and Aidan.* She drew comfort from that. As for herself, though, how would anyone ever know what happened to her? Where on earth—or, more likely, *below it*—was she being taken?

~

The kitchen door was not merely open but missing entirely. A wild wind stirred eddies of papers from a sideboard, plucked pictures and drawings from the refrigerator door, and wrested clothing from the coatrack. Fierce gusts through the window had made ragged sails of the curtains over the sink, yet Trahern's mind processed none of it. His attention was wholly on the silver dagger thrust deep into the blackened door frame. Pinned by its blade, a long claret sash edged with amber fluttered in the air like a mocking banner. The odor of burnt leaves stung his nostrils, the scent of recent magic.

Lissy was gone.

*Eirianwen has done this. This . . .*

It was his first and last coherent thought before a tsunami of raw emotion slammed into him. No mere grief or despair, this. Nothing as tame as anger or even pain. In fact, the sensations were beyond anything he could have imagined, buffeting him with bruising intensity, until it seemed as if his very essence would be shattered.

*This!*

A geyser of white-hot fury erupted from depths he'd never known existed. His blood pounded and raged that Eirianwen would seek to control him by laying hands on an innocent and fragile mortal. But hard on the heels of the heat was icy anguish. Frost bloomed in his bones at the certain knowledge that a mortal was unlikely to survive long in his mother's hands.

*My* mortal. *My* woman. *My* Lissy.

After a long lifetime of denying love's existence—and more the fool for it—he'd finally accepted its presence, marveling that it could be both rich and powerful yet also subtle and gentle.

The absence of that love, however, was a genuine horror: a flaying of the mind, a tearing of the heart, an agony that threatened to sunder joint and marrow. Yet his suffering had nothing to do with himself. True, it would likely have felt as if his most vital organs were being cut out if Lissy had rejected him—but at a single word from her, he would have walked away to ensure her happiness and hidden his pain all his days. He still would.

No, the demon-clawed emotions that now ripped through him were all for her. The thought that she might be frightened or hurt made him wild. She could be dead already—

A croak from the other side of the room stopped his heart. He flung the table aside, revealing not Lissy but *Ranyon*. Trahern knelt by him at once, passing a hand above the still little form while whispering a seeking spell that might reveal his injuries. A crimson glow radiated briefly from the ellyll before disappearing.

"Lie still, friend. Your magic is gone." More like *ripped away*. Whoever came through the door had expected Trahern to be with Lissy and planned to incapacitate him. "It will return with rest and time."

"Couldn't stop 'em," rasped Ranyon. "Took her."

"It is not your fault. Lissy is alive, and I will find her." Of course she was alive. His shrewd mother would never kill such a valuable bargaining chip. But there were far worse things than death, and Eirianwen knew how to inflict every one of them. "Tell Brooke not to bring Fox back to this house. I am sending you to her for healing." The ellyll tried to protest even as he disappeared.

Deadly calm descended over Trahern like a dark cloak as he rose to his feet. The wind stilled abruptly like a quieted horse, and the torn curtains fluttered into motionless shrouds. At his glance, violet flames consumed both the oaken sash and the glittering knife, leaving no spark or ash behind. Trahern studied and flexed his hands as magical energy crackled over his skin—building, gathering, eager for greater release.

*Lissy Santiago-Callahan, by all that is hallowed in your world or mine, I will find you and free you.*

And there would be neither help nor mercy for anything or anyone who stood in his way.

He stalked outside but didn't mount Cyflym. Eirianwen would have ordered Lissy to be taken all the way to the Nine Realms beneath

Wales, to the very heart of the House of Oak. As faithful and swift as his fae horse was, Trahern needed something far faster. He could translate there, of course, but doing so over such a distance would cost him energy that he might not have time to recoup. More, he desperately needed a plan of action.

*Think!*

By all the stars, he had to fight to do so. Unfamiliar emotions, raw and raging to the point of overpowering, called for him to simply blast away the walls of the grand matriarch's sanctum and loose his full powers upon her before she could react. Satisfying, yes, but short-lived because she would not be alone. Her camarilla of sorcerers would be there to add their magic to hers. His own power was sufficient that he might best his mother if he caught her by surprise, but he could not hope to win if he had to face all of them together in a head-on assault. He would die or be captured before he could free Lissy.

*Think!*

Diplomacy he was skilled in. Sorcery he excelled in. But it was stratagem he needed right now, and not the usual games and machinations that were the lifeblood of the careless Court. Eirianwen was a brilliant and ruthless tactician. The situation called for some unexpected maneuver, an unconventional ploy, a trick—

A trick.

*Who better to devise a trick than a trickster?* Trahern reached into an inner pocket and withdrew a coil of glittering pwca hairs.

# TWENTY-NINE

Lissy opened her eyes to find herself facedown on a polished stone floor, the smooth surface cool against her cheek. She didn't dare move—not yet—though she was stiff, sore, woozy, and utterly *furious* that her captors had knocked her out for the trip to wherever the hell she was. *Not a dungeon, at least.* Small splashes of sunlight here and there struck dragonfly hues of green, gold, and blue from the seamless stone. The flashy iridescence automatically identified it to her inner geologist as a feldspar—*labradorite*—though she'd never seen it in such quantity.

Listening intently, she heard nothing except far-off birdsong and her own heartbeat. Finally, she risked raising herself on her elbows. A rough serpentine shape filled her field of vision, and she was forced to sit up to take stock of her surroundings.

The shape belonged to a massive tree root, just one of hundreds that pierced the stone floor, rising upward and coming together to form a cleverly stepped platform. Glancing around to ensure she was alone, Lissy slowly got to her feet to peer over the edge. There, the fused roots had been highly polished to reveal rich honey-colored wood beneath, and they formed a stagelike surface large enough to accommodate dozens of people. At the back of the dais, the remainder of the rugged roots coalesced into a gigantic trunk as wide as a city bus. Her gaze followed it up and up and up, until she realized the entire wall and vast vaulted ceiling were formed of an airy network of interwoven branches. She turned around then, surveying the immensity of the Hall. Roughly the size of a football field—if football fields were round—its entire dome sprang from this single massive tree. *I'm definitely in the faery realm.* Not much of a surprise there.

In the high canopy, bright-furred creatures with big ears and long grasping tails glided from limb to limb, reaching for hovering clusters of jewel-toned butterflies. Here and there, shining white birds sang as they clung to the rough bark—until one took flight and revealed them to be not birds at all but bats. Glowing eyes stopped to peer at her as a parade of glassy lizards marched along a branch. She ignored all of them. As sunlight dappled like gold coins through the thick clusters of foliage high above, she held her breath, her periphery darkening to a narrow circle as she squinted to make out the shape of the leaves . . .

*Oak. It's a damn oak tree.*

All sensation, all emotion, all thought, came to an abrupt stop. She sat unmoving on the cold stone floor below the dais, breathing shallowly, unable to process anything, until a glittering leaf spiraled down to land beside her hand. Its silent arrival was enough to jolt her into taking a deep breath. Then another as she regarded the fallen object. No leaf, this, no blessing bestowed by a friendly tree, but a single torn butterfly wing. And didn't that just sum up her situation nicely?

If this was the House of Oak, odds were that she might not see Fox again.

The horrific thought galvanized Lissy into action. She began walking the lengthy perimeter, inspecting the living wall for any gap she might be able to fit through. There was no entrance that she could find—*who builds a room without a damn door?* And worse, there was some sort of barrier between the open branches. Light shone through unfiltered. Cool, fresh air flowed in and out freely, bearing the fragrance of outside flowers she could see plainly. But when she tried to stick her hand through, it met an invisible wall as solid as the stone beneath her feet. She tried them all anyway, every opening she could reach. Finally, she climbed the rough crisscrossing limbs as high as the physics of the dome-shaped room allowed to see if the barrier went all the way up. Sadly, it did. She repeated the climb in several places until her hands were scraped and filled with splinters, peering through the higher apertures to get a feel for what lay beyond. The great vaulted room that seemed so enormous to her was merely a small building high atop an immense castle—but not like any castle she'd ever seen in a book. Expanses of formal flower gardens, including multitiered crystal fountains and even a few full-size trees, stretched to cover the entirety of the vast roof, hemmed only by an ornately carved parapet of the same flashy stone as the floor below her. Elaborate watch walls jutted out from the parapet at regular intervals, furnished with stone tables and benches. It was like an extravagant and fanciful version of Brooke's little rooftop sanctuary in the city—if Lissy were trapped in her greenhouse! There appeared to be no way down, however, no convenient doorway or staircase or even a rickety ladder or a rope. Even more disappointing was the dense forest beyond and below the castle. If she somehow managed to escape and reach the woods, would she be in worse danger from whatever lived there? *I'll take my chances.*

She sat on the floor for a few moments to rest her aching arms. Studying the creatures in the canopy offered no useful insight, save that none of them appeared to fly, climb, or crawl outside the room. *Great. Everyone's a prisoner here.* Lissy picked a few tiny pieces of bark from her stinging palms, then got down on her hands and knees to scrutinize the monstrous tree's root system beneath the sprawling dais. The sun's rays deepened to orange, then red, as she inspected every inch of it that she could reach. There seemed to be no open space beneath the platform at all. She watched wistfully as a few red salamanders scuttled through the dark columnlike roots that were much too close together to allow her entrance.

Twilight washed the immense room in shades of violet, and she sat in the very center of the floor. For some reason, it comforted her to have as much space around her as possible. Maybe it seemed less of a prison that way.

The gaps between the branches overhead soon revealed an ink-black sky pinned in place with strange stars. The white bats stopped singing and left their perches to hunt glowing insects. The colors fled the stone floor, its dark surface broken only by faint silvery shimmers as if fish swam beneath it. Like the memories that now swam through her mind, occasionally breaking the surface with their images. Not the *life flashing before your eyes* kind of thing but simply a random collection of defining moments and foolish ones, the serious and the silly. An emotional audit of sorts, in no particular order. She'd lost an awful lot for one person, beginning with the sudden passing of her dad when she was still a kid. Matt's death when she was a grown woman had devastated her anew. Her unexpected pregnancy brought even more pivotal changes to her life. And with Fox's diagnosis came another kind of loss—the parenting experience she'd *expected* to have. Still, somehow, she'd gotten up after every knockdown, and her heart had faithfully repaired itself after every grieving, even when she was certain it would never be mended again. Change happened, *shit* happened, but she adapted. She still believed in life. *And love*, she thought. *I've experienced a lot of love. I have it now. I've got Fox, I have my family, and all my friends.*

And Trahern. He'd collided with her life with all the unpredictability and sheer force of a meteor strike. Then insisted on becoming part of it and changed it forever. Because of him, Lissy had gotten another chance to choose to love and give it freely, without reserve. And with that thought came the only real regret she had. *I should have trusted him enough to tell him how I felt and let the chips fall.* It wasn't right to keep a thing like that a secret. Or to decide for him how *he* felt.

Did Trahern know where she was? Or was he still in Tir Hardd somewhere and didn't yet know she was missing? A little part of her hoped for a rescue because it didn't look like she'd be able to get herself out of this one. Mostly she hoped like crazy that Trahern would stay as far away from this place as possible and keep an ocean between him and the family who had wrought such a cruel spell on his twin. Besides, Fox needed a teacher, right?

Her thoughts circled back to her son then. Her beautiful blond-haired boy with those serious blue eyes. Trahern would teach him magic, and Braith would guard him. Mama and Brooke and Aidan would raise him, and the new baby would be like a little brother for him. The rest of her friends would continue to be loving aunts and uncles. All of them together would help buffer him from the world that so often overwhelmed him. And all would help him find his balance. *Fox'll be okay if something happens to me. He'll be okay.*

*But I'm damn well not giving up on trying to get back to him. I just have to figure out how. I just have to figure it out . . .*

~

No spell was required to summon the pwca. Trahern had barely formed the thought before a column of flame and smoke burst up from the ground in front of him. When it died away, an enormous black hare with golden eyes looked up at him. And grinned with wickedly pointed teeth. "Your need must be great, Hunter."

"I would call on your strength and speed, Cadell," Trahern said. "But more than that, I need your knowledge and your talent for a very dangerous trick." Quickly, he explained.

"The Wild Hunt cannot aid you in this?"

"Nay. They are a law unto themselves in many things, but they may not stray beyond their ancient charge. Betrayers are their lawful prey, as well as trespassers from other realms. The defense of the queen, above all. They do not concern themselves with petty squabbles." *Were they to pursue all those who scratch and scheme for power, the entire Court would be ridden down in an instant.*

Cadell was silent for a time, pacing and shaking his head in a manner more suited to a caged warth than a hare. Trahern was accustomed to patience, and when he didn't feel patient, he knew how to mimic it perfectly—but this time, waiting was agonizing. Every heartbeat spent here was another moment Lissy was a captive of the House of Oak . . .

Finally, the pwca stilled and faced him. "Eirianwen is formidable, commanding magic few can oppose, plus the loyalty of your Oaken brethren. She is rightly feared for her ruthlessness, and many whispers claim that she has slain countless innocents."

"The stories are all true, though she is clever enough that no trace is ever found that points back to her. I would hold you blameless for refusing the task," said Trahern.

"Nay, I would not be left behind in such a venture. Think of all the things to be learned!" Once again, Cadell was the huge black stallion that Trahern had first met, nearly twice the size of Cyflym. Flames blew from flared nostrils, and an enormous front hoof struck sparks from the pavement. "You need a mount, do you not?"

He vaulted to the pwca's broad back and knotted his hands in the long black mane. "You once said you sought to outrun the whirlwind. Show me now."

# THIRTY

This is the mortal?"

Lissy's eyes flew open, and she glanced around wildly. The melodious voice seemed to come from everywhere at once, but there was no one in sight. Every lilting word possessed an alluring musical quality, and she found herself automatically yearning to hear more—until some warning instinct kicked in. *It's magic. Someone is using magic on me.* The realization seemed to break the enchantment because when the voice continued, there was no crystal chime at all but a chilling undercurrent of broken glass and shards of bone rubbing together in a fast-running stream . . . "You are quite certain it is the one I seek?"

Hearing nothing more for a time, she stood stiffly. Every muscle protested as she straightened. *Serves me right for falling asleep on a rock.* Turning in a circle, she scanned the room carefully.

A faint shimmering—not unlike a heat wave rising from a summer pavement—drew her attention to the very center of the great dais. As Lissy turned to look at it, the exposed golden wood abruptly heaved and grew upward, as fluid as a fountain, shaping itself into a broad seat. Substantial arms developed and curled into wide knots and spirals, seamlessly blending into the high, curving back, reminding her of Celtic art. But the chair's beauty was marred by deeply carved scenes of armies clashing, battles with horrific monsters and predatory beasts. Violence covered every inch of it—and moved sinuously as if alive. Blue blood ran amid haunting horrors. *For intimidation, no doubt.* It was certainly working on her.

And then the great chair was no longer empty.

A slender fae woman who didn't look more than twenty in human years regarded Lissy from beneath long lashes tipped with gold. Exotic features seemed divinely sculpted from purest marble, the impossible beauty almost hypnotic in its perfection. Though she needed no improvement, her apparel was likewise mesmerizing. The pale claret skirt of her trumpet-shaped gown was richly embroidered with an entire golden forest, with countless wine-colored gemstones forming fruit on the finely wrought boughs that waved in a nonexistent breeze. Wine-colored animals ran and leapt and stalked among the trees as if alive. The animated design extended to the long train that spiraled as neatly about her gold-slippered feet as if arranged by invisible hands. Long filigree talons capped her delicate fingers as they grasped an oak branch with gilded leaves—surely symbols of her station. Eight men in wine-colored robes now stood in a half circle a few paces behind her. Guards, advisers, or simply enforcers, they were likewise a testament to her supreme position.

*Eirianwen.*

Lissy searched for some resemblance to Trahern in the woman's face, without success. Her glistening white hair, wound high into an intricate headdress before falling to her waist like a waterfall, was as thick and lustrous as Trahern's own. And as with him, it was impossible to discern the color of her irises. But similar attributes also belonged to the fae who surrounded her. Perhaps the coloring was typical of all Tylwyth Teg. Even Lissy's disguise in the faery realm had featured the same.

But she certainly hadn't possessed the imperious gaze that now appeared to examine her like a bug in a collection. Lissy stood quietly, tucking her annoyance into a mental drawer and locking it, saying nothing. Instead, she focused on returning the ruler's stare without flinching. And as she did, as it had been with Trahern, she began to see *more*. And that's where all similarity ended. Behind his eyes, she had discovered the man within. But behind this woman's divine exterior? Something cold, calculating, and impossibly patient, as all ancient things must be. It was like locking eyes with a dragon.

And if she wasn't very, *very* careful, she would be burned.

"There appears to be nothing of interest here at all," said the matriarch, turning her head away as she motioned for one of her cadre to come forward.

The man knelt beside the great oaken chair, staring at Lissy with a smugly superior expression that surprised her. *I thought you guys didn't do emotions. Or do you only understand the crappy ones?*

"I sought your son in Tir Hardd, as you commanded, Shining One," he said to his ruler. "He had not been there of late, and none knew where he might have gone. Then a few tongues wagged—before I silenced them—that Trahern had suddenly appeared with another Hunter, a woman. Her presence would have been of no consequence had I not also learned that your son keeps no company outside the Wild Hunt. He has never been witnessed with a companion of any kind until this day."

"This is no Hunter."

"No, Most Fair One, it is not." He paused until a faint movement of Eirianwen's finger indicated he should continue. "I followed the pair to the Green Stag's forest and witnessed for myself the woman's true form, the one you see before you now."

Anger and embarrassment washed over Lissy. She'd not only been human in that forest, she'd been naked—and definitely not sunbathing! Nevertheless, she kept her features as neutral as possible. Hadn't

Trahern once warned her to hide her feelings from the fae? That it would give her an advantage? She surely needed all the cards she could get right now. *Think about Fox*, she told herself. *My job is to* survive *by any means possible so I can get back to Fox*. She could handle a little humiliation. *Whatever they say, whatever they do, I can't afford to show anger or anything else. I can't let them get under my skin.*

Speaking of skin, she sure hoped she wasn't blushing . . .

"I find it difficult to believe that the heir to the House of Oak would dally with such a drab little creature. It is even more difficult to believe you would bring it here to me and sully my hall." Her voice softened then, yet was far more frightening than if she'd shouted. "Do you think my son such a fool that he would come all the way here to fetch a mere *toy*?"

"No, Shining One. But this one bears a mark." He appeared to hesitate then, and his smug expression disappeared. "I—I believe it may be a blood pledge."

Eirianwen's gaze again rested on Lissy, though she hadn't seen the ruler move. Certainly, no one else moved. Perhaps no one else breathed, either, because the very air seemed to have fled the room. The ruler of the House of Oak became as a statue, silent and unblinking, her taloned fingers gripping the arms of the massive chair. Time might move differently in the faery realm, but it was certainly dragging now . . .

"Mortal." The words were like a whiplash as Eirianwen addressed her directly. "Show me your hand."

Her first impulse was to say *no*, of course. Lissy wasn't in the habit of obeying commands, no matter who issued them. But neither protest nor resistance was in her best interests at the moment. She held out her hand, palm outward, knowing that the intricate blue design Trahern had placed there with his own blood was plain to see.

Among those who stood behind the ruler, there was a subtle ripple of discomfort, confusion, and even revulsion. *Yeah, yeah, humans have cooties. I get it.* As expected, the matriarch's exquisite face was still a perfect mask, revealing nothing. Within her exotic eyes, however, Lissy saw not the rage or indignation she expected, but shrewdness. The ruler was thinking, considering . . . This was someone who played a long-term chess game and was accustomed to winning.

"How did a mortal maneuver my son into pledging his life?" Eirianwen said at last.

"What? No! I didn't ask for this at all. He gave it to me. I didn't even know what it was—I still don't."

The ruler shot a look at the man still kneeling beside her. "Explain." She turned and confronted those behind her as well. "Any of you, explain how it is that one of the Fair Ones, an heir of the everlasting House of Oak, freely gifted the *addnned gwaed* to a dull human."

"Perhaps the tedium of his existence in Tir Hardd played a role," ventured the one closest to the ruler's right.

Lissy fully expected him to be magicked right out of existence, and judging by a couple of faint but audible gasps, so did his fellow fae. Instead, Eirianwen laughed outright. "Then the sooner my son returns, the sooner he can recover from his boredom."

"What do you want from me?" Lissy was going for *unafraid but respectful.* Still, a hard slap by an unseen hand nearly knocked her down.

"Humans do not address the grand matriarch of the House of Oak," pronounced another member of the retinue.

But Eirianwen held up a gold-tipped finger. "Perhaps the grand matriarch *wishes* to experience the novelty of conversing with a mortal. If indeed they even are capable of intelligent speech," she said. "Leave us, all of you." The eight vanished at once, and she turned to regard Lissy with a perfectly arched eyebrow that was a match for Trahern's own.

*Damn. I liked it better when I couldn't see him in you.*

"There is nothing I need or want from a human. Yet my son seems to have more than a passing interest in you, so we will test how much. Trahern enjoys the protection of the Hunt at present, but perhaps he can be persuaded to leave it of his own volition."

*Omigod, I'm bait.* Lissy's insides constricted, and it was once again hard to breathe, but she kept her face carefully blank. "I don't think I'm that important to him." If she wanted to survive, maybe she should have made herself sound a lot more valuable . . . but no way did she want Trahern within a thousand miles of this place.

"*Not important* when you hold the keys to his very life? I would know what vow he gave you."

"He didn't reveal it to me. He said nothing when he did it, and I wasn't happy about being marked like a possession." True enough. Best to act as if she were on trial—and in a very real way, she was—and answer questions as literally and simply as possible. If she were lucky, she could be just honest enough that any omissions would go undetected.

"What is the nature of your relationship?"

She gambled on being blunt. "Sex."

The ruler was blunt in return. "That is, no doubt, what you are to my son. But what is my son to you?"

"Temporary pleasure. Fun. Enjoyment for what little time it will last."

"Truly? You have no aspirations?" The matriarch sounded incredulous.

Lissy shrugged deliberately. "I knew from the beginning that a human has no future with a fae." And why did it have to hurt so much to say that? "I'm a realist."

"As am I. Whatever you might believe, the presence of the blood pledge on your hand signifies you are far more valuable to my son than simple gratification. Perhaps he has taken his brother's path and chosen a pairing with a creature of lesser station." Her perfect lips pursed in a little moue of distaste. "In this case, of lesser *species*."

Lissy struggled not to react to the insult, to keep her voice even. "I don't think so. I'm sure I'm more of a pastime. A hobby at best."

"Indeed. Nevertheless, we will wait together, you and I, and we will see."

*Great. I get to spend quality time with a murderer. Guess I'd better keep up the conversation.* With some extra respect, just in case . . . "Your eminence." It was the only term of address she could come up with, something she'd heard in an old movie. Speaking with dignitaries and nobility wasn't her forte. "May I please ask a question?" She braced herself to be struck again, but nothing happened. In fact, Eirianwen paused a moment as if considering.

"Speak freely, then. And I prefer not to be bored."

*No pressure there.* "I thought it was an honor to ride with the Hunt. Why would you want your son to abandon it?"

"I require his service, of course. He is of use to me. That is what children are for, is it not? Their future utility?"

"Perhaps in the faery realm," she said carefully. Even experiencing Trahern's memories didn't prepare her for how appalled she was by the ruler's attitude. "It's not the same in my world. Ideally, children are an outward sign of love, one that continues forever into the future."

"Love is nothing. But a legacy is something else again. After I had been in power for a time, I thought to secure my own legacy with an heir, and I brought forth twain to make certain of it. The very existence of Trahern and Braith sent a clear message that *we* would lead the House of Oak for millennia to come, and those who coveted my position knew they had not one but three to contend with. As I grew in strength, however, my sons did as well. And I found I did not wish for them to eclipse me."

"It's not supposed to be a competition."

Eirianwen's laugh was derisive. "Of course it is. All of existence is a contest, otherwise what would be the point? My sons were talented. I knew Trahern was gifted in sorcery, but I ensured that no one of the House of Oak would teach him beyond the basics. Too much power and he might attempt to seize my position."

"He didn't even want it." *Careful*, she told herself. *Playthings aren't supposed to know too much.*

"So he may say, and perhaps he does not. Not yet. But as one grows in power, one naturally desires more. Is it not so in your world?"

Lissy couldn't disagree with that. "What about Braith? Was he a sorcerer as well?"

"Braith was willful from the beginning, with little magic of his own. But he possessed a single gift that balanced the scale, one rare among the Tylwyth Teg. He could perceive what is to come."

"You mean he could foretell the future? For real?" Trahern hadn't mentioned that.

"Braith was a farseer, a strong one. And therefore exceedingly useful. He predicted much that I was able to turn to my benefit. But one day he dared to tell me that a *child* would bring about my downfall. That this mighty oak"—she waved her gold-tipped hand to encompass the tree that supported the vast hall—"which has been the symbol of our family for millennia, would be razed to the ground, *and the entire House with it*. What choice did I have after such a revelation but to take steps to protect both my sons?"

"But I—I heard that Trahern's brother was turned into some kind of dog."

Something in Eirianwen's pretty laugh made the hair on the back of Lissy's neck stand up. A shadow instantly appeared at the matriarch's right hand and coalesced into an enormous black grim laden with silver chain-mail. He towered beside the thronelike chair like a stone lion. Had the creature been there all along? The ruler stood and lifted the dark canine's chin with a single taloned finger, forcing it to look first at her, then at her captive. The dog made no sound and offered neither resistance nor affection.

"Permit me the pleasure of presenting to you my son and heir, Braith."

# THIRTY-ONE

The black dog automatically bowed to Lissy before returning to rigid attention. Astonishment left her wordless, but it didn't stop her heart from being wrung by the animal's dull, haunted eyes. *Does Eirianwen think that's really Braith, or is she testing me to see what* I *know?* Whatever the game was, however, she needed to play along. And she'd say *nothing* about the great gray grim that had befriended her son.

Eirianwen left the golden branch of her office on the mighty chair and strolled elegantly along the length of the dais. "It cannot be said that I do not treasure my children," she said. "But I could not permit either of them to fulfill Braith's prediction. And thus, he remains well protected in the form you see before you. As a grim, he can do nothing but obey, yet he is alive and will remain so indefinitely. And though I did not plan it so, his fate protected his brother as well. Rather than share his twin's destiny, Trahern went straightway to the Hunt and has remained safely with them ever since."

"You talk of safety and protection. Protection from what?" Lissy suspected the answer but hoped like hell she was wrong.

"From me, of course." The ruler's tone affected patience, as if she thought mortals incredibly stupid. Or just this one in particular. "I would have had to kill them both, otherwise."

*Okay. I'd like to ring up the warden now and tell him my interview with the homicidal maniac is over.* Lissy glanced over at the black dog just in time to see the creature shudder before resuming its rigid pose. *You too, huh?*

The matriarch of the House of Oak wandered casually to the wall of branches, which immediately parted to form a tall oval window that spilled sunlight into a great golden pool around her. She lingered there as if looking out upon an interesting scene, but Lissy wasn't fooled. The pose was too artful, every movement designed to take fullest advantage of the light, to enhance her appearance to the max. How many years had the woman spent rehearsing such subtleties? *Powerful people often have powerful egos.* Lissy searched her mind for any way that knowledge could be used to help her escape, but short of somehow flattering Eirianwen into letting her go, she couldn't think of a damn thing. *Yet.* For now, she'd do her best to keep the conversation going—and try not to think of every movie she'd ever seen where the villains explained themselves to the captives because the captives weren't going to live long.

But Eirianwen spoke first. "What of your own offspring?"

The question was like a snake strike, unexpected, terrifying . . . and a poison that stopped Lissy's heart. *Omigod, Fox!* Trahern had warned her from the very beginning, mincing no words: *They will take him and use him, or they will kill him.* And this woman had just talked about murdering her own children without a qualm.

"Mine?"

"You have a child, of course. My guards reported the presence of toys in your dwelling."

She set aside her indignation at the idea of strangers searching her house—and just when the hell had they done that? Instead, she focused on the problem at hand. Maybe she couldn't keep Fox's existence a secret, but the most important thing in the whole damn universe was that his *gifts* remain hidden from the faery realm—and especially from this angelic-looking horror. "I only have one child, a very young boy."

"Trahern's seed?"

Now it made sense why the toys were important enough to be reported. The power-hungry matriarch was worried about future contenders for her position! "My child is one hundred percent human. His father, Matt Lovell, was killed before his son was born, and that was nearly ten years ago. As for Trahern, I only met him within the past couple of months."

"Months. Years," repeated Eirianwen. "Breaths. Heartbeats. A mortal is a mere blade of grass, while we are as mountains. You cannot even comprehend how long I have existed."

Lissy turned slowly, suppressing a shiver and ordering herself to think about the volcanic stone that spanned the Hall, until she regained her composure. *Blue, gold, green.* Just the floor. *Labradorite, feldspar, plagioclase, anorthite, refractive, calcium sodium aluminum silicate . . .* "As a geologist in my world, I study the processes that create mountains."

"Study upon this: the fae walked the earth long before men. As men became more plentiful and began to alter the world to suit themselves, we gradually withdrew to realms of our own making, our own design. We would have a world suited to us."

"And what about your children? Do you try to make them suit you as well?" She didn't mean for that to come out, but it was almost impossible not to react. *I've got to be more careful, dammit!*

Far from being offended, Eirianwen laughed. "Of course! What good would they be if we did not? But I sense that you do not approve. Answer me this, then: Of what real use is your child to you? His father is dead and left you no kingdom, no wealth, no legacy worth securing. Your life span is appallingly short, yet you spend your limited time seeing to your offspring's needs. What does your son do but take from you, even the very food from your mouth?"

"My child, my son, takes nothing away from me," said Lissy, her hands fisted at her sides as she fought to keep indignation and anger out of her voice. "I am not made less by his existence. Because of him, I am *more* than I would otherwise have been. He is not my competitor; he is my teacher. I learn from him every day. I see my child experience life and laugh and love and grow. Sometimes I cry, too, because growing sometimes hurts both of us. And sometimes I stand in absolute wonder at his insight and perspective. My life is enhanced by my son, and I am so goddamn lucky to have him."

"A pretty speech, but naive. You speak to me of children, yet you are but a very young child yourself. And because you are mortal, you will never be more than that."

"And you will never know what a good man your own son has become, and he's done it despite all your attempts to twist him."

"*Good?* A human failing, and hardly a compliment. I wanted my sons to be strong enough to rule."

"And when they became so, you sought to use them or imprison them. Was there any possible way to please you?"

"Perhaps not," she said unexpectedly. "So, mortal, you were afforded the rare privilege of visiting Tir Hardd. Tell me, how do you find the faery realm?"

The change of subject was abrupt but welcome. Lissy felt that she'd said far too much already, and it was a wonder she was still alive. "I have no words to describe how beautiful your world is, the wonders of it," she said honestly. "This spectacular stone, for instance. I've never seen anything like it. And the workmanship—I can't see a single seam. Where is the mine that produced it?"

"It is but a single stone, and certainly not *mined*." Eirianwen had returned to her glorious chair, and the golden branch in her hand had become an elaborate fan of gilded oak leaves. "Are we coblynau, to scrabble in the dirt? We grew it ourselves, of course. What you stand upon is called *carreg o ddraig*—dragonstone. But a master sorcerer does not choose it for its pleasing appearance." Eirianwen leaned forward in the massive chair, her smile suddenly wide and feral. "In combination with an ancient spell, it bestows a highly desirable power in the magic wielder that can be used upon lesser creatures, including mortals. The more dragonstone there is, the greater the power."

Without warning, a flurry of small winged creatures swooped down from above and surrounded Lissy, buzzing, whirring, fluttering, flapping. She tried to cover her head and protect her eyes with one arm as birds jabbed at her with needle-sharp bills. White bats flashed pointed teeth. Shiny beetles the size of apples exposed enormous pincers. With her free arm, she swung at them all, trying to knock them out of the air.

The matriarch casually examined the filigree talon that sheathed one of her long, elegant fingers. "I need but a drop of your blood to fall upon the stone to complete the spell," she continued. "And then I will be able to read your simple little mind. I am certain there must be something of interest in there, something you have not yet shared with me."

Lissy connected with a beetle, sending it skittering to the floor. And noticed that the onslaught seemed to be lessening. Not only were the creatures keeping their distance from her, but not one had managed to touch her. She stopped moving and slowly, slowly lowered her arms to her sides. The whirling mass took no advantage of her vulnerability. They didn't even move closer. Why was that?

Now that she wasn't being attacked, a strange warmth just below her throat won her attention. Her fingertips identified the pendant that held the ash leaf. It had worked its way to the outside of her shirt, and she looked down to see that tiny sparks of green light leapt from it like indignant aphids.

"What is that? What do you have?" Eirianwen rose from her chair, and the creatures fled upward to the canopy of the ancient oak. She was silent for a long moment, her exquisite features a still porcelain mask, as she stared at Lissy. Understanding lit in her many-colored eyes. "A mortal with a blood pledge *and* the ash tree's favor . . . how very unusual. You are indeed more than you appear, but no matter. While the ash may shield you from some things in this world, it cannot protect you from me. And I will have all your little secrets before I'm done with you."

The golden fan in the ruler's hands transformed to a bright dagger that leapt into the air and arrowed straight at Lissy. She threw herself to the floor to avoid the gleaming blade, but it slowed in midair and changed its trajectory. It feinted at her as she dodged and rolled, coming within a hairsbreadth, then tumbling away whenever she moved in order to reposition itself and strike at her again.

Eirianwen's bright laughter rang throughout the vast room, and Lissy caught a glimpse of her lounging sideways in the great oaken chair, her head upon her arm as the fingers of her other hand flicked and danced like a puppeteer pulling strings. *Dammit, she's playing with me!* When the dagger drew back yet again, Lissy grabbed one of her own running shoes and threw it with the overhand pitcher's technique her brother had taught her as a kid. And then ran like hellhounds were after her.

The shoe slammed into the knife, impaling itself on the shining blade and sending it clattering to the stone floor. The laughter stopped while Lissy was already at the farthest point from the dais with her back pressed against the rough branches that formed the wall. She didn't need to be any closer to know that she had succeeded in infuriating the woman.

But there was nowhere else to run.

The golden dagger shook itself free like a dog shaking off water, then hovered in the air once more. Sunlight gleamed along the blade, calling up a sudden flash of colors from the iridescent floor. Lissy prepared to dodge yet again. It was completely hopeless as, sooner or later, exhaustion or error would allow Eirianwen to win. Yet she wouldn't give up; she couldn't let this murderous creature learn about Fox . . . and an idea born of desperation formed.

The knife hurtled toward her as if shot from a bow, and this time Lissy didn't try to avoid it. Instead, she made a running leap to meet it—

And was thrown backward in a brilliant flash of light.

~

Cadell was true to his promise of speed.

The long, glittering span of the Great Way was a blur as they galloped through. And when they left it behind for the sheer cliffs of Angsley Island, Cadell paused long enough to veil his stallion form and extend his invisibility to his rider. Trahern accepted the concealment. *The fewer who know we are in the old kingdom, the better*, he thought. Eirianwen had eyes and ears everywhere, but even magic could not reveal a pwca who did not wish to be seen. They resumed their headlong pace into the faery realm—

And darkness. Though Wales was enjoying a rare sunny morning, night had already fallen in the faery realm under the deep violet shadow of a new moon. Swift and silent, they raced across both Alder and Rowan territories until at last they approached the seat of Eirianwen's power. Cadell slackened his pace only when the great House itself loomed in the distance. Trahern studied the high, sprawling castle as thousands of pale-white starflowers floated up from the expansive gardens like ghosts escaping a graveyard. He had grown up here, knew every finger width of it, yet it seemed all at once unfamiliar, even sinister. Had it changed in his absence or had he?

He reached out to Lissy again. And as with all his other attempts since returning to the Nine Realms, there was no response. Not even Braith could have heard him from such a distance . . . Yet Trahern's need to hear Lissy's voice, to know that she was safe, kept him trying just the same.

As always, the ancient heavy gates stood wide-open. It was not a sign of welcome at all but rather a sign of certainty. The House of Oak's reputation was such that no one in their right mind would dare venture inside without a signed invitation. To his credit, Cadell didn't hesitate, but strode through the gates with his great hooves stepping high as if he were on parade.

Again, Trahern's mind reached out—and wild relief washed over him like an ocean wave. *Where are you? Are you well?*

*What the hell are you doing here? You shouldn't have come!*

It wasn't the response he'd expected, but he cared not. The feel of her voice in his mind again, angry or not, was purest joy. *Where else would I be? Answer me truly—have you been harmed?*

*I'm okay. Look, I need you to take care of Fox for me, to teach him and help him cope with his gifts. Don't come here. Please don't. I don't know what she's up to, but it's you she wants.*

Brave as always. But there was nothing in any world that would make him leave Lissy in Eirianwen's hands. *Does she know of Fox?*

*No. At least not about his gifts. She tried a spell but . . . well, it got interrupted. She knows all about you and me, though. Someone saw us in Tir Hardd.*

*So it would seem.* There was no other reason for his mother to have taken Lissy, unless she knew she could use her as leverage. *Whatever my mother has planned, she will not give up. Do you understand? Eirianwen* never *gives up what she wants. She will tear your mind and body to pieces until you have told her all. And then she will go after Fox with everything at her disposal.*

Lissy was quiet for a long moment, and he could feel her struggling between her fear for him and her terror for her child. *Can't you just* poof *me out of here?*

By all the stars of the Seven Sisters, he wished it were that simple. *The Hall is warded so that magic may enter freely. It cannot escape.* Eirianwen had created the elaborate spell when he was a small child, and she'd made both her sons watch. He didn't know why, save to further impress upon them how powerful she was and how pointless it was to rebel. What he remembered most, however, were the frightened eyes of the nine fae creatures whose blood she'd spilled on the colorful stone floor to seal the enchantment . . . *I have a friend with me, a pwca. He cannot be seen, but you need not fear him. Go with him, and he will take you to get Fox. And then he will carry you both to a place of safety until I send word.*

*But—*

*Do this for me or Eirianwen will use you to weaken me.*

He could feel her sigh. *Okay. There's something else, though—she has a big black grim that she introduced to me as Braith. I don't know if it's some kind of trick or if she really thinks that's him. I just played along with it as if I believed her.*

*Wise of you. And I am now forewarned. Go with the pwca.*

*You'll come when you can, right?*

It was all too possible that he would not prevail, that he would be unable to join her, that he would never send word that it was safe to leave the place where Cadell had hidden her, but Trahern dared not tell her that. Nor could he lie outright. *I have a toaster to repair, do I not? And Fox is expecting me to watch* Tiger Ninja *with him.*

She laughed a little then. *All right. Look, Trahern, in case I don't get another chance—you should know that I love you.*

Her words struck him hard, like the long-ago warth that had knocked him from his horse. For a moment, he was breathless and stunned . . . and then light and warmth seemed to flow into him, filling all the dark, empty spaces, making him whole in a way he had never been. Making him *more*, somehow. Words had power, as he had once told her, but these words, *her* words, freely given, lifted and enlivened him like strong magic.

And there was only one answer for it: *Truly, we are Pâr Enaid.*

*What does that mean?*

He came to himself then, both stronger and weaker. More determined than ever to defeat Eirianwen, yet more vulnerable at the same time. *Have Fox ask Braith to explain it. And do not be surprised if my brother laughs at me.*

Reluctantly, he walled his mind from any further connection.

"She is in the Hall of the Great Oak, upon the roof," he said aloud. He could translate himself there, but he wasn't certain if the pwca needed assistance. "Can you take us up there?"

Cadell grinned wide, with every pointed tooth showing. He shook himself hard until his equine form sprouted enormous wings.

# THIRTY-TWO

Trahern stood outside the vast living dome of enchanted oak, with Cadell now hidden as a mouse in his pocket. *There is no point in making a simple appeal*, he thought. Mercy did not exist in his mother, nor was there the slightest vestige of compassion that could be entreated. But there was Eirianwen's pride. That he could count upon, that he could work with.

Plus, of course, a little diversion.

The great tree shuddered in every limb, and a hail of leaves and acorns fell to the stone floor as Trahern translated into the Hall within a blinding flash of magenta energy.

"What need has the House of Oak for a *human*?" he demanded, his words infused with disdain as the colorful flare crackled and dissipated at the far end of the oaken dais. Drawing attention to himself permitted the invisible pwca to slip away to find Lissy. It took considerable resolve for Trahern not to turn his head to look for her himself. Instead, he kept his eyes forward, his riding boots loud upon the golden wood as he stalked toward the great thronelike *cadair*—and the woman who stood beside it idly balancing a bright dagger on the end of a gold-tipped finger.

Eirianwen laughed when he came near. He'd forgotten how much he hated that sound, how often it had heralded some new triumph that cost someone else dearly. She had laughed like that when she'd forced him to join in the transformation of his brother . . . "No need at all, now that you are here," she said lightly. Her knife became a golden fan of oak leaves. She did not sit but strolled the broad platform ahead of him. The long satin train of her embroidered gown glowed like a comet's trail.

"I have little time for games. I am charged with the mortal woman's safekeeping. What have you done with her?" Playing the role of a prince of the House of Oak, Trahern's demeanor was deliberately cold, eminently haughty. At all costs, his mother must not guess that he cared for Lissy.

"Nothing really. Though the little fool did just attempt to escape me with her death." She waved an airy hand at the far side of the great empty room where a dark-haired woman sat with her back against the interlaced branches of the wall.

Trahern's heart stuttered, but he held himself in check and refrained from looking in Lissy's direction. "I assume she is unharmed?" he asked, as if the answer meant little to him one way or the other.

"Of course the human is unharmed!" she snapped, whirling on him as if to strike him. "I had to shield her myself, or you would be dead and useless to me as well! Whatever were you *thinking* to give a blood pledge to a mortal? Not only are they ridiculously fragile, but their lives are as brief as an insect's. *How dare you* bind your very existence to such a being!"

"It was necessary to secure her safety."

"Fah!" Her gaze fastened on him as if she could will his skull to open and reveal the answers she sought. "What is this pathetic creature to you?"

"I am on my lord Lurien's mission. You will have to ask *him*." Trahern rested his hand on the light whip at his side, and a bright-blue flicker of energy traveled over the coils at his touch. Few ever saw one and got the chance to tell about it. And no one would have such a weapon on their person unless Lurien himself had given it to them.

"You act for the Hunt in this matter?" There was a carefully crafted incredulity in her voice. But then, were not all her words crafted?

"I do." The ring of veracity could be coaxed from vague and partial truths, omissions, and deflections, but an outright lie would be detected immediately, even by Eirianwen. Silently, he thanked whatever gods were listening that Lurien had thought to officially assign him the child and, by extension, his mother.

"How very fascinating," she said at last, folding her fan. "I wonder what the Lord of the Wild Hunt finds so interesting about this little mortal. Perhaps we should take her apart and examine the pieces? Who knows what secrets we may find and turn to our advantage?" Her face was suddenly animated, her fine white teeth visible.

Trahern hadn't spent eons sparring and posturing in the shallow Court for nothing. He merely lifted a disdainful eyebrow. "Lord Lurien is not of the House of Oak, nor is his blood noble. His condescending taste in pleasure is none of my concern."

She struck him then, scoring the side of his face with the heavy golden fan. "Do you think me witless? I have eyes and ears everywhere, even in Tir Hardd. You bedded her yourself, in a forest like an animal." Revulsion dripped from every word, and he was surprised she didn't spit at him as well. "You, a prince and heir of the House of Oak, lying with a *human*!"

Though he seethed on the inside, Trahern maintained his indifferent mask and invoked a brief wordless spell that not only mended the cut but sought out spilled blood and destroyed it wherever it fell. No sorcerer would risk a single drop of their life's essence falling into the hands of an enemy. And he had no illusions about what his mother was. "As a prince and heir of such a powerful house, should the Lord of the Wild Hunt possess something that I do not?" he asked, and held tight to the memory of the three fae horses gifted to Lurien by Aurddolen, using that couple's rumored relationship to color his next words with verity. "I thought perhaps my lord had discovered some new novelty, and I decided to sample it for myself. However, I failed to discern what it is that holds his interest or affords him such pleasure." He shrugged carelessly and offered her a tiny vulnerability that might distract her further. "It would, of course, be best if he did not learn of my attempt to satisfy my curiosity."

He could almost see Eirianwen's interest in Lissy dissipate like the last vestiges of a whirlwind as it returned to the clouds that spawned it. "Pleasure, is it?" she said. "Such a profound waste of time when the only true and lasting satisfaction lies in power. Of course, that is precisely why I've brought you here. I require your service."

"Your camarilla is yet loyal to you. Surely the magic of my cousins and uncles is sufficient to whatever conquest you have before you. The House of Oak is no longer my responsibility. I ride with the Hunt."

"Do you truly think that protects you from me?"

"I think only that I must return Lord Lurien's property to him." He turned away from her, but she suddenly appeared in his path.

"Which Houses are the most powerful in the Nine Realms?" she asked.

"Thorn, the Royal House," he recited, his tone bored. "Oak, and then Ash. It has ever been so."

"It has *not* ever been so." Eirianwen didn't wait for him to digest that but hurried on. "How long have I led the House of Oak?"

Forever, it seemed. Too long, most certainly. She'd been in power for eons before he was even born. "In truth, I know not. I know of no other leader before you."

"There was only one. My father, Brenin Derw, was first, when there were yet only Seven Realms. And he ruled those as well. He was king."

The revelation rocked him, but his voice was deliberately dubious. "I have studied much and never read of this. Nor have you ever spoken of it to me."

Her own practiced mask appeared to slip for an instant—or was that a calculated move? "I allow that may have been a mistake on my part. Perhaps you would have a better appreciation for your position if you knew from whence you came!" Her fan became a golden branch once more. "Under Brenin's reign, the realms were prosperous, and my father's word was law. We neither traded nor corresponded with other fae kingdoms. We had no need of them. Then, two of the Dark Fae territories appealed to form a union with our kingdom—the Draigddynion and the Pobl Dŵr. My father and the House of Oak refused, of course. There were more than enough ugly and inferior creatures in the realms already. And what could the Dragon Men and the Water People possibly offer us? They had little wealth, and their lands were undesirable.

"But the other Houses—indeed, nearly the whole of the kingdom—wished for an accord. *Stronger together* was their rallying cry." She no longer glided but stormed about the dais, pausing only to strike the great oak *cadair* repeatedly with the gilded symbol of her office to emphasize her words, applying such force that tiny chips and splinters flew from the living hardwood. Even the gilded branch bent in her hand, losing some of its leaves.

Trahern had seen his mother angry countless times. He had never once witnessed her out of control. "A mildly interesting history lesson," he said, his tone carefully noncommittal. "Should I inquire as to the outcome?"

"Brenin opposed the union, of course, and rightfully sought to suppress those who spoke in favor of it. He sent his soldiers to restore order, but the House of Thorn led a revolt that unseated my father and left him sorely wounded. The Realms united to place Rhiannon, grandmother of Gwenhidw, upon the Glass Throne in his stead. And the Seven Realms became Nine."

Eirianwen stood still then, looking off into nothingness, as if she were watching it all happen before her. Her strident voice quieted to almost a whisper. "The House of Oak was all but destroyed, and my father's will to live with it. When he died, the name of Brenin was struck from the records and never uttered again."

"I knew none of this. However, that was long ago, and I fail to see any connection to the present."

Ferocity was in her gaze when she turned again. "I inherited what was left of the House of Oak, and I alone have built it up, piece by piece, acquisition after acquisition. I have always done whatever was necessary for the good of the House and for the family. Spell by spell, and blood by blood, for millennia."

*How much blood? How many lives destroyed for your ambitions, for your pleasure?*

"Now we are wealthy and strong once more." She spread her arms wide, the sleeves of her gown like glittering wings. "Our humiliation is forgotten. Is not our name feared throughout the kingdom? Do we not stand above the others?"

He bit back what he really wanted to say. With lives weighing in the balance, better to placate and distract his mother. At the far end of the Great Hall, it appeared as if Lissy still rested on the floor against the wall. In truth, it was only a simple spell, and there was no one there at all. His woman was mounted on the winged Cadell, and the invisible pair waited in silence for him to find them a way out of the doorless Hall—or make one. "Truly, we are the envy of many, and all are aware that Eirianwen, the Shining One, has done it." He offered her a small polite bow for good measure and hated himself for doing so. Too many times in the past he'd been forced to do the same. *Only for Lissy's sake do I do this,* he thought. *Now and never again.*

Apparently pleased with his answer, his mother recovered control of her features and smiled prettily. She sat upon the oaken *cadair*, her glittering train automatically curling around her feet as if alive. The damaged wood on the arms and back of the chair healed smoothly before Trahern's eyes. The gilded branch also mended itself before becoming a fan that she again fluttered before her. "And now you understand why I have kept you in reserve and why I have now brought you back," she said. "It is long past time that the House of Oak took its rightful place."

"Which is?"

"We must take our throne from the usurpers. Gwenhidw must die."

He felt no surprise, save that his mother hadn't made an attempt on the Glass Throne long before now. But the thought of Eirianwen ruling the Nine Realms was truly horrifying. "We?"

"Don't be obtuse. Of course, you will assist me. Your sorcery is useful, but the diplomatic skills and contacts acquired while trading on behalf of our House are far more valuable. Your ability to negotiate agreements will help us raise alliances."

"Surely you do not believe that other Houses will help you overthrow the queen?"

"I do not have to believe. I *know* that there are many among the Tylwyth Teg who would be quite pleased to see Gwenhidw dead. She ignores counsel or petition from the great Houses in favor of indulging the mixed rabble that have followed her to the new territory. She has even invited them to participate in ruling it!"

"Perhaps her methods will infuse new life into an aging system."

"Listen to yourself!" Eirianwen looked at him askance over the top of the fan, as if she could not quite believe what he had just said. "One would think you had no ambition at all. The Tylwyth Teg were born to rule, and those of the House of Oak above all. Shall I now take orders from a bwbach or a coblyn? Should I submit to foolish new laws invented by the Draigddynion?"

"Truly, I fail to see the threat to you. Tir Hardd is a long way from the Nine Realms. An experiment, a colony, a crude frontier, if you will. It does not dictate policy here."

"An *idea* is the most dangerous weapon in existence," she hissed. "Gwenhidw's radical vision threatens us all. If it is not stopped, it *will* spread to the Nine Realms."

*Such a change is long overdue.* He folded his arms in front of him. "If treachery is your goal, your skills at subterfuge are far beyond mine. And surely you would not trust my help were I to give it to you. Braith once said you feared us, and that he told you one of us would be your undoing. It surprises me that you did not slay us both outright the moment he uttered the words."

"Even if I feared you, what would your deaths have gained me then?" she asked. "Have I not told you many times that the key to successful conquest is *never waste a potential asset*? Your brother's fate strengthened my grip on the Court in a way that simply killing him could not. And whenever they begin to forget what they witnessed, I have only to call him to heel before their eyes." She lifted a hand and crooked a long golden talon. An enormous black grim slunk into view, its belly close to the ground as it made its way over to lie at Eirianwen's gold-clad feet.

Trahern successfully hid his bafflement, grateful for Lissy's warning. The dog was indeed the twin of Braith save for its color—and its hopeless demeanor. Slowly, the large noble head turned toward him, the heavy silver links of its chain-mail collar clinking together. Though the form of the grim was male, for one fleeting instant, it was a *woman* who looked out from behind the great golden eyes. One he recognized.

*Saffir!*

Immediately, Trahern knelt before the immense dog and touched its broad forehead with his own, humbled in the presence of such terrible sacrifice. It was plain to him now why she had not accompanied

Braith: she had deliberately taken his place! *I knew not that you yet lived*, he spoke in his mind. There was no answer, but he continued anyway. *If you can hear me, if you can only feel my words, know that Braith is well. That he loves you truly—*

"Such a charming little reunion, but the celebration will have to wait," announced Eirianwen. "Now that both my sons are home, we have much to discuss. I have already set our plans into motion."

Her *sons*. Lissy had been right, it seemed, and Eirianwen believed the grim she commanded was indeed his twin. He tested his mother further, however. "My brother cannot discuss very much in his present condition. Surely you plan to restore him?"

She laughed. "Why ever would I do such a thing?"

Unexpected rage flooded him. *Because he is your child and deserves your love and protection! Because you should never have committed such a cruel act to begin with!* He hid his anger with the greatest difficulty, and his voice carried no hint of it when he finally spoke. "Surely you have need of a farseer in your ambitious plans?"

"Do you think I did not glean the information I required before your brother was changed? And while I have much power at my beck and call, even I am constrained by a few certainties. There is no reversal for such a spell. Braith will always be a grim." The dog vanished from Trahern's sight, undoubtedly sent to some barren stone kennel until the next time Eirianwen wanted to strike fear into someone.

*I will never stop trying to save my brother.* And now he would seek a way to help the woman Braith loved as well. Plainly, however, there were no further answers to be gained here. *Cadell waits.* "I, too, have my constraints. I must return to the Hunt."

She laughed—not the pretty chime that so charmed the Court but a dark wave-tossed slurry of ice that raised the hair on his flesh. "Ah, yes, you think you are a Hunter now. As if that would somehow shield you from me."

"The Wild Hunt will certainly shield *Gwenhidw* from you."

"Not if its leader is busy elsewhere. And I have seen to it that he will be. By the time the moon rises twice more, my mercenaries will attack the seat of power in Tir Hardd. Lurien will put down the insurrection himself and send Gwenhidw here for safety. And I will be waiting."

"Then I have a queen to defend."

"I am your queen!" shouted Eirianwen. "And I will not permit you to turn your back on who you are!"

"I know who I am, and I am not yours to command." Trahern rose and turned on his heel, but he knew his mother well. Just as he reached the end of the platform, he dropped flat to the polished wooden floor. A roaring blast of searing heat passed over him, singeing exposed skin and hair. Remaining prone, he simply spun in place, shooting out a glittering rope of energy that snared his mother's feet and yanked her from the oaken chair. With the other hand, he hurled a fiery ball, as white-hot as a miniature sun.

She swatted it away before it could touch her, sending the deadly sphere straight toward Trahern's face—just as he anticipated. Deliberately, he raised his hand a fraction too late to redirect the ball, causing it to rebound wildly. His other hand, however, had been a heartbeat faster, sending a raging wall of green water to engulf Eirianwen before she could see where the sphere was headed and intervene.

The wooden floor shook beneath his body as the fireball impacted high up the wall of the dome to his left—and soared away into the night like a meteor. Fragments of burning wood and scorched leaves fell from the gaping hole, even as Eirianwen shook off the drenching that had distracted her, evaporating it entirely without a word. Fury radiated from her, plus something else—purest frustration, he realized. Even a twisted disappointment.

"You would rather have me dead than not be able to control me," he said. "Why bring forth children at all, if only to destroy them in the end? Surely this is not the legacy you set out to create?"

"Ah, but my legacy was not uppermost in my mind, not at first. I found that I wanted there to be someone like me in our world." For a moment, she seemed almost wistful. Real or not, it didn't last. "But you were nothing like me, either of you! Nothing!" She threw her golden fan across the dais. "You grew your own way like wild grapes that would not heed the arbor I set for you. The three of us might have ruled the Nine Realms together if not for the stubbornness of your brother and you!"

"Stubbornness? To be ourselves and not mere shadows of you? Your true desire was never for sons and partners but for mirrors and puppets. You wanted only what you could use."

His mother did not respond. She still sat upon the oak wood floor like an elegant statue, but her anger radiated from her in waves he could almost see. It was like facing down a venomous serpent, waiting for the strike that would surely come.

Rising slowly to his feet, on guard for any move from her, he spared only a quick glance upward. The charred hole in the dome was more than sufficient for the pwca. Trahern couldn't see or sense him, but it was a simple matter to reach out to Lissy's mind. Saying nothing, brushing lightly against her thoughts like a caress, he peered through her eyes for an instant. Long enough to see that Cadell had wasted no time. The faithful creature flew swiftly for the borders of Eirianwen's territory, spiriting Lissy to safety, leaving her illusory image to linger motionless at the far end of the Hall. Leaving Trahern behind as well but also leaving him free to act.

Perhaps for the first time.

"No more masks," he said, his full attention falling upon Eirianwen. "No more posturing, no more games. I do not serve the House of Oak, nor do I serve you. And I will not participate in treason."

"As you wish." With her power, she drew herself upright in one fluid move—and drew something else with her. With her gold-clad feet hovering a handspan above the platform, an inky shadow steamed from the wood to envelop her like thick writhing smoke: the essence of the Great Oak itself. The massive tree was soaked in magics, from root tip to tallest twig, from rough bark to smooth leaf to rounded acorn—and as the matriarch of the House of Oak, she alone could call upon it. Every blood sacrifice, every torture, every cry of fear or pain, every dark and terrible act that had ever taken place beneath the living dome now enhanced her already formidable abilities. For a wild moment, Trahern considered attacking the tree itself, but Eirianwen would kill him long before he succeeded in destroying the oak.

With pinpoint focus, he wrapped a bright-orange blaze around her, hoping to sever her connection to the tree. But a scant heartbeat later, the fiery cocoon burst apart, forcing Trahern to leap to the stone floor below, rolling beneath the edge of the dais to evade the very flames he'd created as they rocketed through the air around him. Luckily, he *had* created them. Without his will to sustain them, the small fires fizzled into nothingness wherever they landed. Meanwhile, the roiling shadows fell away from Eirianwen, revealing something unrecognizable in her stead.

She was tall now, far taller than he, her once-perfect features distorted and crudely formed. Flawless white skin was now gray and deeply furrowed; bright almond-shaped eyes sank to expressionless hollows that glowed pale green. Gone were the fine raiments, leaving only tatters of fine gray mist and dull droplets of oozing sap clinging to her rough form. The glory of her hair was likewise the shade of corpses, matted like the hanging mosses in damp forests. And the long arm reaching toward him was a branch clad in thick runneled bark ending in massive knotted hands.

*Ysbryd pren.* A woodwight, a rare being far more dangerous than bwganod and warths combined. Trahern ducked and rolled as the long gray fingers snatched at him, and a long low hiss escaped the jagged hole of her mouth. Eirianwen had become one with the Great Oak, its dark heart fused with her own. Instead of repeating her first swipe, she clawed a gobbet of resin from her side and fashioned it into a lumpy sphere more nimbly than such rudimentary hands should have been able to. Before she could complete her spell, Trahern summoned a blade-thin disk of spinning air and threw it—

A heavy arm crashed to the floor like a chopped bough even as a high-pitched shriek stabbed his eardrums and brought down a flurry of oak leaves from the high-domed ceiling. Still, the maddened wight raised her remaining arm. Trahern flung up a shield of protection, but the creature changed her target. With the speed and power of a trebuchet, she flung the sphere overhand toward the inert form of Lissy on the other side of the Hall, where it exploded on impact and ignited into a rippling blanket of burning pitch.

The image vanished, revealing Trahern's ruse. Roaring out her rage, the wight drew one spear-size splinter of wood after another from her back, like arrows from a quiver, and threw them. Though he dodged repeatedly, each spear merely turned in midair and came at him from a new angle. He'd seen this game before. A simple spell designed to keep the quarry busy while Eirianwen watched for an opening to administer something far more lethal. *I will not be distracted!* As if to invoke a shield of energy, he threw his hands up—and a half dozen glowing blue hawks took wing. Magical constructs, their reflexes were far faster than those of living birds. As they swooped and dove, they snatched the flying spears from the air. As their claws closed on each one, the wood dissolved away into fine dust.

While the hawks did their work, Trahern had not been idle. *Teigr! Teigr mawr!* With a single powerful bound, he now clung to the trunk of the wight as a great striped tiger, a form he had borrowed from the mortal plane—but no earthly cat was ever such size. With teeth and claws, he ripped chunks of bark from the wight, roaring like a maddened basilisk as the wight sought in vain to reach him. He got one final swipe across her face before a huge gray hand seized him by the skin of his shoulders and flung him across the Hall.

The monstrosity that was Eirianwen didn't wait to see what he would do next but stepped down from the edge of the dais on tree-trunk legs far thicker at the ankle than the thigh, her feet immediately sporting long twisted roots that spread over the stone floor and tried to trip him. Still a big cat, Trahern leapt high and bounded back out of their reach. Just as quickly, he feinted to the left before running to the right, testing the wight's speed and agility—

*Fast but awkward.* Turning was difficult for her. The stiff movements would smooth out, however, as Eirianwen grew accustomed to the body she'd bound herself to. *She'll be even faster then.* Somehow, he had to bring the struggle to a decisive end before that happened. He shed the tiger form at once and gathered his focus.

*"Tân du!"* he shouted, throwing all his strength behind it. Black fire licked over the vivid colors of the dragonstone floor, racing toward the creature in a rapidly growing wall. A woodwight, even a magical one, could not draw power from rock, but Trahern could and did. The flames burned higher, lapping at the monster's extremities and searing off the twisted roots from her feet. Eirianwen swung her remaining arm, conjuring a blast of frigid air that turned back the flames with a thick wall of ice, a temporary defense against the pulsing heat. But as meltwater ran freely, enormous living branches tore themselves away from the dome high overhead and joined the battle—

Trahern ran as long limbs crashed down on either side of him like kraken tentacles.

Lissy was grateful that the night wind high over the faery realm was warm—she sure wasn't dressed for flying. Her hair streamed behind her, and the pwca's mane flowed around her like a soft river of dark silk as she crouched on his broad back between the enormous wings.

From time to time, she stole glances at the land below, illumined by strange bright stars. The stunning and surreal beauty made up for the disconcerting height in some ways, but her stomach wasn't quite convinced. At least she wasn't afraid of falling. *Cadell must know the same keep-my-butt-on-the-horse spell as Trahern does.* She kept one hand wound tightly in the pwca's long mane just the same.

While she was grateful she was no longer in Eirianwen's hands, her heart protested that she was going in the wrong direction, flying away from the man she loved while he was in grave danger. But what else could she do? He was right that his psycho mother would only use her against him, but still . . .

Something warm and gentle suddenly stirred in her mind, reminding her of when she'd shared Trahern's mind to experience his memories. And then it was gone, leaving her strangely comforted. *I have to trust him,* she thought. *I have to trust that he'll do what he needs to do and come back to us. Fox needs him.*

*I need him.*

A blinding flash of bloodred light replaced the magnificent night-scape. Dazed, she lurched to one side, scrambling to keep her balance, as the pwca banked hard. Before she could think to ask what was wrong, Cadell screamed—

And then they were falling.

# THIRTY-THREE

Not one but several gaping holes now pierced the dome of the Great Hall. Broken tree limbs littered the floor, charred black by magic. Dark flakes of ash, the remains of thousands of fallen oak leaves, eddied upward into small whirlwinds. Somewhere among the fragments were the remains of Trahern's riding leathers and even his boots. He'd burned them from his skin with a single word to reveal his *ledrith* marks to the element of air. The words of conjurations and symbols of power glowed bright enough to cast a halo of light around him as he fought, clad only in simple gray braies that barely reached his knees.

Now, however, Trahern had drawn nearly all the magical energy he could from the rock beneath his bare feet and the swirling air around him. Sweating, winded, burned, and bleeding freely from a dozen wounds large and small, he stood as far from the oaken dais as possible, carefully contemplating his next move. His muscles ached, and his *ledrith* had begun to fade, but—a small comfort—the thing that was Eirianwen looked far worse.

One rough gray leg dragged, nearly sliced through and leaking strange oily tannins onto the bright stone floor. Her matted hair was charred and missing entirely from one side, and a greenish eye had gone dark. Bark peeled back like rind from a fruit in many places and was nonexistent in others. She'd managed to replace her lost arm, but such a rapid regenerative spell must have consumed an immense amount of power from the Great Oak—it no longer sent its branches to chase him. Those that yet upheld the walls and ceiling of the dome seemed visibly shriveled in the dawn's light, and the remaining leaves had darkened and wilted.

The two of them had struggled throughout the night, until slowly, surely, Trahern had begun to prevail. Still, Eirianwen was far from defeated. Though exhaustion and rage had made her slightly careless, she was no less dangerous and was already forming up another spell. *She will not stop*, he thought. *If she succeeds here, she will move on to hunt Lissy and Fox. It will not end unless I end it.*

His leathers were gone but not the tangible weapons he carried. Imperishable, they lay somewhere among the debris. *"I fy llaw!"* His light whip flew to his open hand. Its leathern handle fit comfortably in his palm, and the tingle of electricity was familiar and welcome. As a glittering web of dark magic hurtled toward him, he snapped the whip into the air. Blue light flashed as it destroyed the grasping net, sundering it into a shower of tiny, harmless sparks.

A pity he couldn't do the same with Eirianwen. She could subvert the power to her own purpose if he struck her directly. *But perhaps there is another way . . .*

Again, he raised the whip, and this time called to the very sky itself with all that was left in him—and the sky answered. Thunder filled his ears, and static electricity, the presage and promise of unfathomable power, traveled the length of his arm into his body, enlivening and strengthening him even as it shook him like a warth with a bone. Steadying himself as best as he could, Trahern breathed deep, breathed again, and *drew down lightning*. The blinding bolt latched on to the tip of the light whip—and obeyed it as he snapped it full-length along the floor at Eirianwen's feet. The castle shook to its ancient foundations as earthen elements struggled, then finally bowed to the rule of air. Dragonstone flared and caught fire, crumbling away to create a broad crevasse that plunged through the many floors as easily as a knife through a cake, stabbing deep, *deep* into the mountain's heart beneath.

Hoarse, guttural screams issued from the wight's jagged mouth, and Eirianwen pounded the sundered rock at the edge of the gaping chasm that now separated them. Quickly, Trahern coiled the whip again. If he could just catch her good leg, jerk it from under her—

But it was Lissy who stood there, shivering as cold air blew up from the abyss, whipping through her long dark curls and plucking at her thin clothes. The sight of those sable eyes so wide and frightened scored his heart with an invisible knife.

The wight was nowhere to be seen.

*An illusion. It must be.* Raw power yet surrounded him, his snowy hair flying free from its tether as electricity gathered to his call. His arm hovered in midair, muscles trembling, ready to release the light whip one last time.

*Trahern?*

By all the stars, it was her. Though the sound of Lissy's voice might be mimicked, there was no mistaking the *feel* of her voice in his mind. Pleasure, happiness, even joy had accompanied it at other times, in other places. Here, however, every word sank his heart and his hopes like stones in a well. *Trahern, I'm sorry. They knocked us out of the sky just before we got to the Great Way. I think—I think they left Cadell where he fell.*

*Step back from the edge at once! You are far too close.*

*I can't. There's some kind of spell on my foot. It won't—*

A long, low, throaty laugh drew his attention to the charred dais at the opposite end of the battered dome, where Eirianwen was once again seated in the great chair. Having shed the woodwight form, the matriarch was radiant and smiling, every inch the Shining One, as regally clad as if she sat the Glass Throne already. *A glamour, no doubt*—he knew she was injured, and badly. In the heartbeat it took to recalculate his plan, however, eight men in claret robes coalesced behind her. His mother's camarilla had arrived—

Turning her defeat into triumph.

"So close," she mocked. "So very close. I do concede that you have become a veritable master of magicks, dear Trahern, and a potentially valuable resource. However, I cannot permit you to oppose me further. I will reclaim the throne with your help or, at the very least, *without your interference.*" A gleaming artifact appeared in the air a few feet to his left. A half mask of copper, cleverly inset with stones and symbols. "If you fight me, this mortal woman will die, and you with her. Put on the mask, and she will live. As will you."

*Don't do it!* Lissy's voice was loud in his head. *That's the thing I dreamed about. It controls your mind!*

*I know what it does.* He'd seen the mask used far too many times. The moment he pressed it to his face, he would be *gaethiwyd.* Enslaved. And worse than the prospect of allying himself with his mother in her quest to overthrow the queen was the certainty that *she would know everything that he knew.* Those who wore the mask could keep no secrets from her.

Fox would be revealed and taken. So would Braith. And Lissy would be killed outright or, worse, tortured to keep her son in line.

"Not to your taste? Perhaps I can find something that suits you better," said Eirianwen. To his right appeared a broad silver collar of many links that together were stronger than iron. Braith bore one exactly like it. "Choose, Trahern. A mindless slave in your present form or a voiceless grim like your brother? Two legs or four? The mask or the collar?"

"I will make my choice," he said. "After the woman is returned to her world, unharmed, for Lord Lurien to do with her as he pleases." A moment later he added, almost conversationally, "If you truly wish to take the throne, it would seem prudent not to spar with the Lord of the Wild Hunt who defends it."

*Don't you do this! Don't give in to her!*

He didn't answer Lissy. Trahern had no illusions about escaping, but he could sell himself as dearly as possible to secure her safety and the safety of her child.

"It is unlike you to give in so easily." His mother sounded suspicious. Apparently, he'd struck a little fear into the matriarch of the House of Oak. He would have that much satisfaction at least.

"I do not yield. I offer an *adduned gwaed*—a blood pledge," he said, "that I will make my choice peacefully. But I would have your own pledge in return. Blood for blood."

"You forget to whom you speak!"

Ignoring her, he continued. "On your life, the woman will be returned to her world, unharmed and unbound in any way. Subject to the will of Lurien only, she will otherwise be free to go where she will, unwatched and untouched by fae or by spell, and she will be left in peace, as will all her family and friends, her children and her children's children, so long as the House of Oak shall stand."

Eirianwen stood slowly—and shakily. The glamour might hide her wounds, but it couldn't completely disguise her weakness. Raw fury contorted her features, and her voice was low and dangerous, but still he detected a faint tremble beneath it. "Who do you think you are to dictate such terms to *me*?"

"I am my mother's son, and therefore not a fool. Were I to place you on the throne with my own hands, eventually you would kill me or offer me the same choice that is before me now." He felt the truth of that in his very bones. "Nor will this mortal be safe after I meet my fate unless something constrains you. I gave my word to the Lord of the Wild Hunt. I will keep it, and my honor, before I give up my freedom. Else, we will end this now."

"You would not prevail."

"Perhaps not, but you would lose considerable *assets*." He nodded at her camarilla. At full strength, he was far more powerful than he had been when the sorcerers had acted together to transform Braith. Now he was nearly spent and couldn't hope to eliminate more than half their number. Those who remained would act in concert to kill him. Or, far more likely, his mother would draw on their energy so she could destroy him *personally*.

She sank back in the great oaken chair, tapping the gilded branch on her arm as she considered. "As things stand between us, it would seem an accord cannot be reached. Therefore, *things* will simply have to change."

The sudden blast of power from the dais could barely be seen, save as an odd rippling of air that skimmed along the stone even as it stretched to twice Trahern's height. It could surely be felt, however, its rumbling dynamism shaking the entire Hall, plowing aside heavy branches and rubble in an arrow-straight line as it surged toward Lissy. Instinctively, Trahern flicked out his light whip, trying to snatch her from the magic's path, but it was much too far and far too late—

But Lissy wasn't swept over the edge. In fact, the invisible torrent of magic had somehow vanished before it even reached her. Had the spell failed? Had someone called it back? Trahern sensed no backlash of residual energy. It was simply *gone*.

"What have you done!" Eirianwen screamed, then threw the golden branch at one of her camarilla. "What has happened?" she demanded of them all.

Trahern didn't care. He was already focused on one of his last *ledrith*. A string of words that ran diagonally across his right thigh, it wasn't a weapon but a tool—and not precisely the right tool for this situation. Still, it was all he had to work with, and he placed his hand over it. "*Taith ddiogel*," he said, looking down into the chasm that separated him from Lissy. *Safe passage*. Save for a fleeting shimmer, as if a dust mote had caught the light for a scant instant, the yawning crevasse appeared exactly the same. Had it worked?

Without waiting to find out, Trahern leapt.

~

When the floor stopped shaking—and she did, too—Lissy rose from her crouch and gingerly tested her foot yet again, leaning as far from the frightening chasm as she could. As before, the only thing she managed to dislodge was a handful of shattered stones and gravel, which tumbled over the edge into silence. Whatever spell was tethering her wasn't budging. She looked over, expecting to see Trahern on the other side, when a sudden hand on her back made her jump.

*Are you well?*

"Thought I told you not to come here," she managed.

"You are not the boss of me."

The silly quip—no doubt learned from Fox—helped her steer clear of the tsunami of emotions threatening to swamp her. She'd been ready to throw her arms around his neck, burst into tears, yell at him for offering his life in her place, and kiss him into next week. And thankfully succeeded in doing *none of it*. Revealing their relationship to Eirianwen would likely be an immediate death sentence. In fact, Lissy had been certain she *was* dead when that huge and powerful force had shoved through the debris like an invisible train bent on running her down. *Thanks for saving me. I think that one would have hurt.*

*I am not the one who stopped it.* He was already examining her foot, and suddenly she was free. Trahern grabbed her hand, yanked her away from the crumbling edge—and paused to stare at the floor.

*What's wrong? Why aren't we running?* Following his gaze, she both saw and felt a strange current of air hugging the broken stone, flowing around her ankles. Arctic cold and desert hot, almost tangible like water, yet only partially visible like smoke . . . Like a ghostly mountain stream, it swirled into small vortices of dust and ash, then hurried on around and beneath their feet. More currents appeared from all directions, each one tumbling and rolling to a single point, the spot where the onrushing spell had vanished.

*Someone draws power*, said Trahern, turning to study the strange phenomenon.

So maybe Eirianwen and her psychos were sucking up energy for another terrifying display. Even her inner scientist, who normally would be fascinated, knew that *getting away* was paramount right now. "Come on, we don't have time for—"

*There.*

Something strummed along her senses as if a tripwire had been triggered, and Lissy found herself listening with her entire being. Amid all that was going on, she shouldn't have heard a single thing. But she did. A voice. A small voice . . .

Her mind exploded into a cacophony of frantic prayers, curses, and denials, but a shadow wavered in front of them nonetheless. Faint and formless at first, then rapidly gaining substance until fully tangible.

*Fox!*

In the space of a breath she couldn't manage to take, her brain processed the sight of her son standing motionless, dressed in Scooby-Doo pajamas that had seen better days. His slight figure faced away from her, toward the dais where Eirianwen continued to rail at her sorcerers. Soft blond hair that he still would never let her comb waved upward from his head as if drawn by static. One small hand was knotted tight in Braith's blue-gray fur. The other hand pulled frantically, rhythmically, at the hem of his shirt. *Stimming*, she realized. How Fox got here or why wasn't important right now—what mattered was getting him out of sight before Eirianwen reacted to his presence. And Fox was obviously overwhelmed and heading for a major meltdown.

Lissy charged toward her child, but Trahern intercepted her. "Let me go, dammit! What's the matter with you? Can't you see he's in trouble? *Lemme go!*" He was holding her so tightly that she couldn't get her arms free to hit him. Frantic now, she kicked with everything she had and even bit him, but the tall fae didn't release her.

*LISTEN TO ME!* His voice was suddenly not just loud in her head but forceful enough to push everything else out. *It was Fox who stopped the spell that would have killed you. He absorbed all its energy. And Fox is the one who is now drawing power from earth and air and everything in Oaken territory.*

"And you can give him a fucking gold star later! Look at him! He's just a little boy, and he can't do it! It's hurting him! *Let me go, damn you!*"

*If he stops now, we will die, and he will be in Eirianwen's hands. Do you understand? Eirianwen will do whatever she pleases to Fox, make him into whatever she wants him to be. And there will be no one to save him.*

Trahern's words were a hard, cold slap to her senses, and she ceased to struggle. The horror of such a future for her son nearly made her throw up. A quick glance confirmed that the cruel matriarch was already wildly gesticulating at Fox and Braith as she raged at her followers. Dear God, what had gone through Eirianwen's mind when they'd appeared out of nowhere? Had she already guessed what Fox could do, the abilities he had? "We can't let her, Trahern. We can't let her have him." She squeezed her eyes tight for a moment, willing back the tears. "But how are we going to stop her?"

*Perhaps Fox himself has an idea,* he continued in a gentler tone as he released her. *Let me try to help him. Please.*

She let him go, watching as he approached her son and knelt beside him, careful to leave enough space between them so her sensitive child wouldn't feel crowded or confronted. Fox looked small, almost frail, between the powerful fae and the giant grim. Strangely, she couldn't hear Trahern's thoughts—perhaps he was concentrating. And it was impossible to hear whatever he said to her son. She could only make out that he spoke slowly and carefully. Maybe he'd put up that *sensory-deprivation bubble thingy* that proved so helpful to Fox before, but she couldn't tell.

Instead, Lissy kept a wary eye on Eirianwen. The matriarch appeared calmer—no doubt because one of her accomplices now lay deathly still on the stone floor below the platform. And she wasn't staring at Fox anymore, either. Had she dismissed him or simply realized she had all the time in the world to make her next move? *She's already got us trapped here. The miserable bitch can decide what to do with us at her leisure.* Lissy expected the other sorcerers to fan out, circle around Eirianwen's prey, and get into position for some final showdown. Instead, they bowed in a tight circle before their ruler. *Like a damn huddle for the opposing team.*

Her own little team was woefully outmatched yet doing better than expected. Fox miraculously hadn't gone into a meltdown, at least not yet. Instead of pulling frantically at his shirt, he was now focused on his arm—probably looking at the little dragon tattoo. Trahern had somehow managed to coax a few hiccupped words from him, and she knew that the kindhearted Braith would be lending as much help and comfort as possible.

Finally, Trahern held out a hand behind him, beckoning for Lissy to come, then drew her down next to him. From this new angle, the sight of her son's stark white face was a punch to her heart. Those serious blue eyes were wide and scared, and he'd bitten his lip repeatedly until it bled. His small body jerked and shook as if electrified.

Lissy swallowed hard, gripping Trahern's hand with both of hers as hard as she could to keep herself from reaching out to touch Fox. Even Braith's great wrinkled face looked more worried than usual. The enormous dog leaned close against his young charge, physically propping him up, but even that didn't seem like enough. Surely, her son was going to collapse any moment now, and Lissy ached to scoop him up into her arms. *Not possible, goddammit.* Human touch at this moment, even from her, could trigger the very meltdown they wanted to avoid.

"Your mother is safe now. You saved her life," said Trahern, and though Fox didn't turn his head, he glanced at her for a moment as if to see for himself.

She smiled up at him. "That makes you a hero, dude, just like Tiger Ninja."

"Yes, it does," agreed Trahern, seizing on the analogy. "And like Tiger Ninja, now you have to stop the *bad guys* from winning. You did well to draw so much energy from around you, and you even pulled power away from the spell the bad guys sent."

The irony of a card-carrying member of the Wild Hunt using a term like *bad guys* wasn't lost on Lissy. She'd have to tease him about it later. If there ever was a later . . .

Fox sniffled and hiccupped, but he bravely tried to hold himself together. "Do I get a—get a—get a crystal?"

"Most certainly. I have a new collection of stones, and you may pick *three*. But before we can go home, there is one more thing to do," he continued. "You have—"

Another, stronger tremor made Lissy glad she was already on the floor . . . but this one didn't stop. As the vibrations continued, rocks tumbled into the abyss, and leaves and acorns rained thickly from the canopy overhead. She reached out to Trahern. *What's wrong?*

*Eirianwen has changed tactics. She seeks to bring the Hall down on top of us. The camarilla is directing their spells at the trunk of the oak behind her.* Aloud, he spoke to her son as calmly and easily as if they were discussing the ants in the garden: "You have all the power you need, Master Fox. Now is the time to push it out and away from you, just like you do with our *deadly mega-force bombs* in the backyard. Push it all away *now.*"

Fox gave a quick nod, looking a little less scared. As he had done countless times at home, he drew both hands and one foot up into a comically exaggerated fighting stance . . . And Trahern suddenly threw himself on top of Lissy, knocking her flat to the hard stone floor. For a long moment, there was no sound, and since she could barely breathe, she was about to tell him to *get the hell off—*

Then all hell broke loose.

# THIRTY-FOUR

A loud *crack* deafened Lissy, as if a lightning bolt had struck only yards away, but far worse was the enormous weight that suddenly rolled over her and Trahern. A scream fought for release, but she didn't have enough air. Just as she was certain they would both be crushed or smothered, the terrible pressure moved past them, and they were free of it. Trahern shifted, and she gulped in several breaths until the dots in her vision cleared, but he refused to let her up.

*It is not yet safe. Look*, he whispered in her mind.

Fox stood above them, still in ninja mode, unmoved and unharmed. Beyond them, an invisible force radiated outward in a great ring, picking up speed and driving everything it touched ahead of it—rocks, branches, leaves, and debris—leaving only the scoured stone floor behind. *It's some weird kind of pressure wave.* Her inner scientist considered. *But it's so slow—*

Then Fox threw a punch at the air.

A deep, monstrous *thud* assaulted her senses anew, vibrating through every cell in her body, and she squeezed her eyes shut as even the floor undulated beneath her. Sudden vicious wind filled her ears with its roaring and pulled at her, yanking her hair and clothes. If Trahern hadn't been on top of her, it would have dragged her away, perhaps even over the edge of the chasm. She couldn't see, and she fought to reach out for Fox, but she was powerless to control her body in any way. The suction of the wind—the shaking, the roaring—went on and on until she felt she would fly apart.

Abruptly, everything stilled. The floor seemed solid again, nothing moved, and she heard no sound. *Maybe I'm deaf.*

*You are not deaf. It is simply finished.* Trahern moved off her, and she quickly raised herself to her elbows to look for Fox.

Standing, simply standing, her little boy rested one hand on the ever-faithful Braith. His small face was calm, but his eyes had that bruised look they sometimes got when he was tired. Lissy sat up to ask if he was okay—

And realized that Fox was the tallest thing in every direction for as far as the eye could see. There was nothing left of the domed Hall. No walls remained, and the Great Oak itself had vanished, dais and all, leaving only a massive hole behind, as if the tree had been plucked up by the roots. There was nothing left standing on the castle roof, either, and its surrounding towers were gone, sheared off cleanly. Beyond, the entire forest that had surrounded the House of Oak was completely flattened, its trees stripped of branches and lying in concentric rings. *Dear God, it looks like Tunguska after the meteor blast.*

And that meant that the earthshaking *thud* had been some sort of sonic boom. Stunned, she looked back at Fox, searching for words. She had a million and one questions, but that wasn't what he needed right now. *What do you say to a kid who's pretty much a superhero?* "You did good, dude!" she managed, and held her hand out, knuckles first.

"Dude," he said with great seriousness. He bumped her fist with his—and held it there for several seconds while she did her level best not to start bawling like crazy. "Can we go home now? I don't like this place, and Jake says he's hungry."

It took her a moment to realize who he meant. *I'm going to get confused between Jake the Dragon and Jake the Dachshund. But I can hardly wait to tell Tina.* "Well, let Jake know that I'll make him a grilled-cheese sandwich as soon as we get home. And you can both watch TV together."

"In four triangles. With *two* pickles."

"I know it, dude. And I won't let the pickles touch the bread, either."

Fox nodded, his eyes half-closed, and plunked down between her and Braith. A moment later, he snuggled into the dog's furry side. She wished he would snuggle with her instead, but she couldn't have everything. Her son was safe, and that was enough. Besides, she'd finally gotten a fist bump, hadn't she? The sheer enormity of the small gesture made her tear up all over again. Before she lost all composure, Lissy leaned over to look at Fox's arm, curious to see what the dragon image was doing—

It wasn't there.

"Where did Jake go?" she asked.

"He was scared," Fox mumbled through a yawn. "So I said he could hide under my shirt, and I'd protect him."

"That was very kind—oh!" A large lump wriggled its way up his back beneath the fabric of his pajamas. Before she could react, a tiny glittering head—bright blue—emerged from the neckline and regarded her with enormous yellow eyes the size of nickels, fringed with delicate lashes. A slender, sinuous neck followed, until a dragon barely bigger than a coffee cup climbed out onto her son's shoulder and curled there, where it promptly fell asleep. It was then that she realized Fox had fallen asleep as well.

Mouth open, Lissy was unable to decide what she should do or even *think* about this strange new development. Then gave herself a mental shake and pushed her jaw firmly closed with her finger. She didn't need to do anything—except make a grilled-cheese sandwich or maybe *two*—and all things considered, was this new situation really all that strange?

*My son is a sorcerer. Of course he has a dragon.*

A strong arm slid around her shoulders, and she leaned back against a familiar hard body as a welcome voice caressed her mind. *Fox has done extraordinary things this day.*

*You've done some amazing things yourself. Is Eirianwen gone? Is she dead?* And if so, how would Fox react? How would she explain to him that he'd killed someone, even someone who wished them all harm?

*I do not think that she perished, but wherever she is, I am certain she is too weak to harm us at present. Your son drew away all her magic, and that of her camarilla as well. They are powerless, thanks to Fox. And thanks also to Braith and his farsight.*

*What do you mean?*

*Braith predicted that a child would destroy Eirianwen's power and raze the great oak to the ground. I thought—and Eirianwen did, too—that it was one of us, her sons. But it was Fox all along, and that is why my brother brought him here.*

She sat up. "*Braith* brought him? He endangered my son to fulfill some crazy prophecy?"

"He says he saw the outcome. Fox would prevail."

"I thought you couldn't talk to him?"

"I can now." There was an unmistakable smile in his voice. "Another side effect of Fox's magic this day, I think."

Later, she would have a few choice words with Braith herself, whether he could respond or not. For now, Lissy relaxed back against Trahern with a long sigh and was surprised that every muscle in her body hurt. She hadn't realized just how tightly, and for how long, she had held herself alert and ready. *You're the one who helped him keep it together, Trahern. Fox may have power*—and wasn't that an understatement now?—*but he's a little boy and he was really scared.*

*I was also afraid.* The arm around her tightened. *I have known little fear in my life, but I feared for you, and for Fox.*

*You got through to him. He listened to you, and that's what saved us.* Then she remembered: *but not all of us.* "Cadell! I don't even know where he is or if he's okay. We have to go find him."

*We will look for him, I promise. I need but a few moments' rest . . .*

Maybe it was something in his voice or perhaps she was just finally paying enough attention to sense it. Lissy wriggled out from under his arm and turned to study him. The man beside her looked exhausted and drawn. His marble skin was grayish, and she suspected it wasn't just dirt and smoke. The beautiful *ledrith* were pale, as if some inner light had faded. Blue blood was caked in several places, trickling in others.

*Omigod.* "How badly are you hurt?"

He didn't answer, but he also didn't resist when she helped ease him down to the floor, where his unbound hair lay tangled upon the cold stone. *I wish I had a pillow and a blanket for you. Let's put your head in my lap.*

*Not yet. It is good simply to rest.* As Trahern closed his eyes on a sigh, it hit her hard that he shouldn't have been bleeding at all, that he should have been able to heal himself. Had Fox absorbed his magic as well? Or had he used it all up in the struggle with Eirianwen?

"I would speak with my brother," he said aloud.

The great dog raised his massive head at once but didn't move from beneath his sleeping charge. Lissy immediately leaned over and gathered up Fox, dragon and all, hoping he wouldn't wake up. She needn't have worried—he was as limp as spaghetti in her arms, and she shifted him so his head rested on her shoulder. Thankfully, his dragon seemed glued in place, and both emitted small snoring sounds.

Freed of mattress duty, Braith rose to stand over Trahern, his enormous wrinkled muzzle close to his twin's pallid face. Chuffing, he nosed Trahern into opening his eyes slightly.

"Brother." He raised a hand long enough to stroke an ear. "You must find Saffir. I know not how, but she took your place as a grim to ensure your safety, to keep our mother from searching for you. She is somewhere in this castle—"

The enormous dog was gone. Just gone. A moment later, Lissy could hear wild baying from somewhere far below them, and there was no mistaking the note of desperation in the heartbreaking sound as Braith searched for the woman he loved. *The black grim chained to the chair.* No wonder the sad creature had looked so haunted. Balancing Fox, Lissy reached for Trahern's hand. *What'll your brother do if he can't find her? What if she's dead? What if the blast killed her?*

*We will hope for better. I could not have kept this from him, whatever the outcome. He loves her and deserves to know her fate.*

*You're right.* She bent and skimmed her lips gently over his forehead. *And I deserve to know how to help* you. *You still haven't told me how badly you're hurt. What can I do?*

*This.* With an effort, he placed something small but heavy in the palm of her hand, and she brought it close to her face to examine it. A tiny silver horn, intricately made, coiled like a French horn with a large bell, yet it was both simpler and more elegant.

*You must sound this, as I cannot.*

*You mean blow it?* She eyed it dubiously. *It's awfully small.*

*Trust me. And do not stop until you know it has been heard.* His voice faded.

"Trahern?" Her hand sought his pulse, his forehead. "Trahern, are you okay?" She hoped he was just sleeping, but how would she know? Quickly but gently, she laid Fox on the stone floor with a murmured apology, tucking one of his small hands beneath his cheek. She checked Trahern over to make sure he was breathing, that his heart beat normally—at least, normally for *him.* From nights spent in his arms, she knew it should be faster than a human heart. Now, however, it seemed slow, even sluggish. And she couldn't rouse him. *Dammit,*

*I need to take a course on fae physiology!* Trahern's wounds weren't bleeding profusely—well, nothing that required a tourniquet anyway. She even rolled him to his side for a moment so she could see if she'd missed a gaping wound on his back. Though there were many injuries there as well, they looked more like burns than cuts. Most likely they were magically induced, and she wasn't sure how to treat them. *Not that there's a first-aid kit handy around here.*

Whatever it did, the horn was her only hope. Lissy scooped up Fox and sat as close to Trahern as possible, hoping that he might gain a little of her warmth, and drew the tiny silver instrument from her pocket. It still looked like a Christmas ornament, but she pressed the miniature mouthpiece to her lips—

And the horn delivered a long, low tone that sent shivers up her spine.

Tentatively, she blew into it again, and the horn began to grow in her hand! Encouraged, Lissy put everything she had into coaxing the rich, deep sounds from the instrument, and as she did so, it continued to expand until its concentric coils rested in her lap alongside Fox. Whether it was the magic or a measure of just how exhausted he was, Fox didn't wake up, and neither did the little dragon on his shoulder. With one arm, she hugged her child tightly to her. Her other arm vibrated as it supported the horn. Even so, she couldn't stop her fingers from running lightly over the raised figures that decorated the silver spiral, and energy ran up her hand as she caressed the great gleaming bell. She'd never played a musical instrument in her life, but the ancient horn seemed to draw the notes from *her* instead of the other way around, discovering something wild within her and urging it to the surface, to expression. Her mind filled with images, sounds, scents . . . night winds strumming dark trees, clouds billowing over the moon like waves swamping a ship, pale dogs baying and quarry crashing through rain-silvered grasses, the tang of ozone and petrichor—

"You may stop now if you wish," said a man's voice, as deep and melodic as the notes of the horn.

Lissy blinked, and for a moment it seemed that all the things she'd heard and felt in the music had come together into a single being. Tall and lithe like Trahern—and there the resemblance ended. The stranger's hair fell to his waist in hundreds of braids, each as black as the riding leathers he wore, as onyx as his cloak stirred by a breeze she couldn't feel. Blacker still were his commanding eyes, and she sensed there were secrets in their depths beyond imagining. Eirianwen had been strong, but this dark fae's power was tangible, like the charged air before a lightning strike.

And he was not alone. Behind him, the empty expanse of sheered rooftop now bore an enormous cavalcade of night-clothed men and women astride strange horses whose hooves didn't touch the ground. A hundred riders or more, and all as still as death itself . . .

The horn had called the Wild Hunt.

Adrift in the green-black depths, Trahern's thoughts were scattered and confused. The entire world had narrowed to this dark place, as if he had been dragged underwater to a kelpie's lair, yet he could not remember how he'd gotten here. Where he had come from eluded him as well. Suddenly, a tiny pinprick of light appeared high above him, bright as a star at the new moon. Another joined it, and another. Five in all, a constellation, beckoning him, guiding him. He tried to swim upward, but his limbs were leaden and clumsy, and exhaustion dragged at him as if undines clutched his feet. As he faltered, the array of lights ceased to coax him. Instead, they *summoned* him, and he could not disobey. Slowly, painfully, he struggled toward their glimmering imperative. The harder he fought, the more intensely they shone, their glowing rays seeming to tug and pull at him. Upward. Slowly, haltingly, but surely upward—

As he broke through the surface of awareness, the constellation of lights resolved into strong fingertips pressed to five points on his forehead, his face. They drew away, and he found himself blinking up at Lord Lurien's furrowed brow.

"You are in worse shape than when I found you the first time," Lurien chided him. "I hope the cause was as noble."

Thoughts, impressions, memories flooded his mind then, and he battled to form words. Still, his voice was little better than a croak. "Lissy. Fox."

"I'm here. We're okay. We're both okay." Lissy's voice was close, very close, and her hand squeezed his. The simple act filled him with warmth. Women of the Tylwyth Teg prized their long slender hands with narrow fingers, often adorning their nails with thin slivers of gemstones or artful claws. Lissy's hands were small and plain by Court standards, yet they were hardworking, strong, and, above all, kind. And when he was skin to skin with her, Lissy's touch, both gentle and eager, was more powerful than all his sorcerer's skills . . .

Someone cleared his throat, and Trahern opened his eyes in surprise. Had he drifted off? "Forgive me, my lord."

"There is no need. You require much healing, and this is a poor place for it. Save for the child's own gifts, there seems to be no magic, no energy, no power here at all to draw upon. Tell me why that is."

"Treason," he rasped. "There is treason. Eirianwen plans to take the throne. In two moons' time, her forces attack Tir Hardd." He gripped Lissy's hand and raised it with an effort. "This woman . . . *Pâr Enaid* . . . this woman is my word." Exhausted, he abandoned speech and continued in Lissy's mind. *Tell him all. He will believe you and will protect you both. Tell him about Cadell. And Saffir. And . . .*

Darkness rose as a wave and pulled him down into a dark sea.

# THIRTY-FIVE

Trahern gazed up at the once-great castle, the seat of power of the House of Oak for untold millennia. The towers had all fallen, and a third of the enormous building was split off from the rest by a yawning rift, leagues long and cut so deeply into the bedrock that the bottom could not be seen—the rock-splitting result of the lightning he'd called down during the battle with Eirianwen. Even as he watched, several stones crumbled from a wall and fell soundlessly into the chasm.

Beside him, Ranyon whistled. "I'm thinkin' ya shoulda *started* with the light whip in the first place. Ya mighta cut the castle out from under Eirianwen and finished the fight a mite sooner."

"I will try to remember that for next time," said Trahern. But there wouldn't be a next time. Eirianwen would never regain her magic or position, and certainly not the life she was accustomed to. Injured and powerless, she'd been quickly found and cornered by Lord Lurien's relentless white hounds. For her many crimes, the former matriarch had been condemned to follow after the Hunt forever *as a true grim*, among the dead and the damned, the betrayers and the murderers. The members of the camarilla—even the ones who'd been killed—were likewise sentenced.

For Ranyon, however, much more was due. With so many of his family and his people to avenge, the little ellyll had been utterly devastated that he'd been unable to participate in the battle. Trahern hoped that today's task might provide a measure of what Lissy would call *closure*. "I find that my magic has not yet fully returned to me. I asked you to come here in hopes that you might take the lead," he said, and motioned to the castle.

Ranyon reached beneath his ubiquitous baseball shirt and produced numerous strange charms. Pinecones, crystals, silver spoons, even a coffee cup, each wrapped with copper wire in a complex pattern of knots and spirals. From under his strange blue hat, he produced an exceptionally large charm made from a scallop shell, then proceeded to arrange them all into five groups of five. Trahern recognized the number of power, a catalyst for change.

*There will be mighty change here this day.*

Before the ellyll enacted his spells, he drew a deep breath that shuddered his little frame. "I thought chance alone saved me, dontcha know. Just cruel and foolish chance. I was at an Undine wedding on the seashore near the dragon territories, far from the slaughter. I knew nothing of it save feeling more and more ill till I fainted dead away. My friends cared for me for days. And when I woke up, they told me my family was gone. My clan was gone. My people were no more. I wished I had died myself then." Sniffling, he wiped his face on his sleeve. "But maybe there was method. Maybe I'm still here so I can do this much fer them." Ranyon looked up at Trahern. "Yer sure o' this? 'Tis a foul enough symbol to the Ellyllon and more, but it's yer own family's home."

"It was never a home to anyone," said Trahern. "And there was no family in anything but name. I did not know that when I lived here, but seeing Lissy and Fox together has taught me a great deal." *And by all the stars of the Seven Sisters, I miss them both.* It was a constant physical ache far worse than any of his injuries. Though he'd sent Lissy many notes and small gifts for her son, he hadn't yet left the Nine Realms. There were things to be done.

As the heir to the House of Oak, all authority and all holdings were now in Trahern's hands. He'd dictated seemingly endless missives even from his bed during his long convalescence. And when he was stronger, he set about enacting many of those directives in person, parceling out the wealth and land of the vast domain until the House of Oak no longer existed as a power in the Nine Realms. Few were left with familial ties to it, and Trahern judged that they possessed sufficient properties and wealth of their own. The rest of the territory's inhabitants had been more slave than subject, however, with no love for their bloodthirsty matriarch. To each of them he gave the land they had once managed for her, with ample resources to improve upon it as they saw fit. Only one final task, *this task*, remained before he crossed the Great Way to Tir Hardd and the human world that lay above it. *And then I will not return to this land again.* "One night we saw shooting stars together, and Lissy told me to make wishes. I wished for my mother's countless cruel acts to be undone."

"Ya cannot change what was."

"I know. But I can ensure that neither I nor anyone else will have any reminders of this place or of those who ruled here. Work your magic, Ranyon, and may your people rest easier because of it."

The task they had set themselves took the better part of a mortal week, though the fickle faerie sun crossed the sky only twice. When they finished, a rich orange-gold sunset cast long, soft shadows across a new landscape. The castle was completely gone, razed to the ground, and every stone of it pushed into the chasm. Trahern had insisted that even the massive blocks of the foundations be torn from the bedrock like rotted teeth and cast into the rift with the rest. The earth itself had heaved and settled until the castle site was level with the surrounding land.

All that remained was the immense crevasse. The great quantity of material from the castle had done little to fill it. Trahern utilized a spell to *call water*, and a distant river answered. Serpentlike, it reassembled its shimmering coils, carving out a new bed that led to the narrow end of the rift—and plunged over the rocky edge. For a time, the torrent resembled Palouse Falls swollen with spring meltwater. But while the earthly river would never fill its basin, this one was enchanted. The chasm filled completely to create a long, deep lake, drained only by small streams that watered the land.

"It is a great pity that it will take time to regrow the forest," he said, deliberately injecting notes of sadness and resignation into his words.

"Ha! I've a charm fer that!" Ranyon set to work immediately, and Trahern hid his smile.

The dense forest of oak that had surrounded the castle had been utterly destroyed by Fox's defensive magic. Now, under the little elemental's skilled direction, a green blush overtook the blasted land. Ash trees supplanted the former oaks, rapidly rising to great heights. Bright, blooming bushes, star-shaped wildflowers, and soft, striped grasses sprang up around the new trees. Even the former castle site became indistinguishable from the rest of the forest, and the lush greenery clustered close to the banks of the lake.

"Truly, it looks better than it ever has," said Trahern, and the admiration in his voice was genuine. "I find there is but one thing left to be done." He knelt and presented Ranyon with a very large bound book, thick with many pages of leather parchment.

The ellyll groaned and staggered a little as he repositioned its awkward weight. The book was nearly half his height. "'Tis kind and all, but if this is a story, I'd be happy to wait fer the movie, dontcha know."

"It is not a story. This contains the deeds to all the territories of the Ellyllon that were stolen by my mother, and full title to this portion of land as well. I believe you will make a good and honest steward on behalf of the remnants of your people scattered throughout the Nine Realms and beyond."

Ranyon sat down so abruptly that it was a good thing he wasn't far from the ground to begin with. He stared at the enormous book in his lap, running his twiggy fingers over it in a kind of stunned wonder.

"I spoke with Cadell," continued Trahern. "He is looking forward to learning more about the Ellyllon and says he will be *most pleased* to assist you in searching them out."

"I—I can't put two words together fer such a gift. There's not a thanks worthy of it."

"None are necessary. It is precious little reparation for a dark and foul deed." The sun disappeared below the horizon, but there was light enough to reveal the soft dappled gold of a horse's hide as it trotted out of the trees. *Cyflym.* "I cannot linger more. I have not seen Lissy since I was taken to the den of the Hunt to heal. You are welcome to travel with me this night."

Ranyon shook his head. "I'll just be sittin' here awhile. Maybe a *long* while. Seems I've a lot of thinkin' to do." He waved Trahern off with a long spindly hand. "Off ya go, then. I'll be along after you two get all yer snoggin' out of the way."

~

It was a birthday party . . . of sorts. Other kids liked lots of guests, rowdy games, presents, surprises, and decorations galore. Fox preferred his immediate circle and everything as low-key as possible. Which meant it was practically indistinguishable from a normal day, except for the groaning table of food in the backyard. Brooke said that Ranyon had spelled the table before he left. Lissy suspected the magic steadily added to the feast, too. That pirate ship made of chocolate toffee éclairs certainly hadn't been there a few minutes ago.

And today's unseasonably warm and sunny weather—imagine shirtsleeves in mid-November!—had nothing to do with global warming and everything to do with the ellyll's desire to please Fox. *I hope he makes it back in time for the party. But I'm glad he went to visit Trahern.*

For the hundredth time today, as every day, Lissy wondered about the man she loved. The top drawer of her bedroom dresser bulged with notes and letters from him, through which she could follow the course of his recovery. The first few were brief and dictated; the next flurry was in his own hand. It was plain that as he felt better, he wrote longer, as the notes were followed by letters. Still, she wished she could see for herself how he was doing. *Maybe I shouldn't have left.* But Fox, for all his newfound earth-shaking powers, was still a little boy who needed his own familiar environment, and so a band of Hunters had escorted them home with great deference.

She hadn't realized just how long it would take Trahern to heal.

Summer ended. Lissy returned to her classroom, and Fox returned to school—not without taking a toll on her nerves, of course. She worried every day that she'd get a call that Fox's desk had exploded or the playground equipment had mysteriously melted. Or, just as bad, she'd get a note asking for a parent-teacher meeting because Fox was telling fantastic stories about the faery realm and what he'd done there. But so far, nothing more than a minor disagreement over homework had occurred. And he hadn't said a single word about his adventure to anyone—not even to his grandmamma when she came home from her trip at the end of August.

*Sheesh, I haven't told Mama yet, either. And I don't even know where to start* . . . At least Olivia had been amply distracted by the welcome news that her daughter was finally in a relationship, even accepting the fact that Trahern was fae without turning a hair.

Over by the fire pit, Brooke passed tiny Griffin to his father. Griff was practically lost in Aidan's big hands, but the man had proved a natural when it came to babies. Fox was unexpectedly fascinated with his new "cousin" and spent time lying on the floor with him, usually surrounded by the trio of cats. Lissy couldn't prove it—and Fox didn't say—but she was sure they *all* talked to each other, Griff included.

Right now, however, Fox and the cats were camped under the food table with Jake the Dragon, studying a new geology book and sorting a fresh box of crystals and stone specimens. She'd half expected Jake to once again become just a pretty picture on Fox's wrist after they returned to the mortal world, but that didn't happen. At least the little dragon was as friendly as he was cute. And he'd only burned a hole in the rug once.

It had been harder to get used to Braith not being around as much. After all, for a while he'd been Fox's shadow every minute of every day. Fox appeared to take it in stride, though. He seemed to understand that his large friend was happy, and certainly the presence of Jake helped smooth the transition. The great gray grim still spent plenty of time with her son—they unquestionably adored each other—but Braith now had another love in his life to pay attention to.

*Speaking of which* . . . Lissy looked around until she spotted the pair sitting together in the ivy in the far end of the yard: a beautiful fae woman, impossibly long white hair tumbling to mingle with the silver-green leaves, had her arms around Braith's great gray neck. With their heads gently touching, they were the picture of bliss. Braith had found Saffir not far from the Oaken castle—or what was left of it—and the spell that produced her canine disguise had been completely undone. With Eirianwen's power dissolved, Saffir was confident that a cure would eventually be found to restore Braith to his true form as well. In the meantime, she was now able to talk with him, mind to mind, as easily as Lissy could with Trahern. They weren't exactly a typical couple, but after being apart for so long, they were content with whatever connection they could have.

It was Saffir who had told Lissy of Eirianwen's sentence at the hands of the Wild Hunt. *Poetic justice for certain, but kinda creepy just the same.*

Lissy welcomed the distraction when Cadell bounced over the fence as a huge black rabbit. The powerful spell that had knocked the pwca from the sky had left him *stuck* in the form of a winged horse until very recently. Whatever his shape, he'd inexplicably taken to sitting in on her science classes at the college—though thankfully her students were unaware of their otherworldly classmate. The pwca devoured morsels of information like Ranyon devoured pickles, and human knowledge was a great novelty to him. In return, Cadell helped her better understand some of the physics of fae magic.

His best friend was clearly Fox, however. The pair had bonded instantly, and the pwca joined her son's little circle of four-footed friends as often as possible. *Like right now*, she thought. Just as expected, he thumped his big hind foot on the ground in greeting and dashed under the table.

As she turned to gather a couple of Tiger Ninja paper plates—the only nod to birthday decorations Fox had agreed to—a familiar voice caressed her mind, warm and intimate as sin, causing her insides to heat up even as her heart leapt.

*I am confused. Is the party in the yard or beneath the table?*

*Trahern! Where are you?*

*Watching from your bedroom window. I would see you first before I greet the others.*

Ever so casually, not wanting to arouse attention from her friends, Lissy picked up the used plates and walked slowly into the house . . . then threw them in the general direction of the kitchen and took the stairs two at a time. She stopped in the doorway, though, to look. Just look. To drink in the sight of him as he turned from the window. A dark cloak was thrown back over one shoulder, and his riding leathers seemed black with the bright daylight behind him. Sun haloed his snowy hair and threw fascinating shadows over the ethereal planes of his face. *An angel of darkness and light*, she thought. His eyes—still not a color she could define—lacked the predatory gleam they'd had the night she met him, however. Instead, there was warmth. Hope. Yearning. And as she looked deeper, she saw the one thing she wanted most.

It was impossible to tell who moved first, but suddenly they were in each other's arms in the middle of the room. The world was a blur of hands and lips and—

"Gross, dude!" Fox stood in the doorway, rolling his eyes. "Do ya *have* to kiss her?"

They pulled apart, though Trahern kept his arm firmly around Lissy's shoulders. "Yes, I do have to kiss her. But since you find it distasteful, I *might* promise to kiss her only when you're not watching." *Which I believed I was*, he said in Lissy's mind.

*Welcome to dating while parenting.*

*We are not dating. We are* Pâr Enaid.

*You know, I think it's about time you explained—*

Without warning, Fox launched himself from the doorway and threw his arms around Trahern's waist! "You were gone, dude. I don't want you to be gone."

Both hands pressed tightly over her mouth, Lissy hardly dared to breathe. But Trahern wisely did not attempt to hug him back. Instead, he accepted the gesture, and when Fox let go, he knelt in front of him. "I will not be gone again," he said gently. "Would it be acceptable if I remained here with you and your mother?"

"Are you going to kiss her a lot?"

"It is very probable."

Fox heaved an exaggerated sigh. "I guess that's okay. She probably likes it. Are you coming to my party?"

"I would not miss it."

Satisfied, her son raced from the room and down the stairs. *Omigod, what just happened here? What just happened?* Shock gave way to reaction. As hard as Lissy tried to keep herself together, the tears would not be denied. "He—he hugged you!" she managed between sobs.

Trahern brushed her hair from her eyes and kissed her forehead. "I am deeply sorry. It is you he should have embraced."

"No, no, you d-don't understand." The words came out as a series of hiccups, and she gave up and turned to mind speech instead. *I'm not sad! I'm not sad at all! He hugged you. You're the first person he's ever done that with. It's a huge accomplishment, Trahern. Bigger than what he did at the castle—*way *bigger!* She slid her arms around him and held on, just held on as sheer elation rocked her to her very foundation. *I don't care that Fox didn't hug me—okay, I care a little bit, but I finally got my own fist bump, so I'll be fine. I'm just happy he hugged* anyone, *and I'm glad it was you.*

"So was Fox correct when he said that you *probably* like my kisses?"

*You know I do.*

Tenderly, he kissed every tear from her face. By the time he finished, comfort had become something else entirely. He cupped her face in his hands and brushed her lips lightly with his before kissing her long and deep and slow until every nerve ending was at attention. Arousal rippled through her until she nearly moaned aloud.

*You told me that you loved me, but I did not get the opportunity to respond. Melissa Santiago-Callahan, you are the very heart of me.*

*Does that mean you're finally going to explain what* Pâr Enaid *means?*

He drew back with a confused expression. "Did I not instruct you to have Fox obtain the information from Braith?"

"Are you kidding me? A woman doesn't want to hear tender words relayed through a series of messengers." She laughed. "I waited for you to tell me yourself!"

"What makes you think *Pâr Enaid* has anything to do with tenderness? Perhaps it means we are *efficient hunting companions* or perhaps even *awesome ninjas*," he teased, then grinned when she punched his shoulder.

Damn, she loved that pirate grin. She'd have to see what she could do to coax it out of him more often. Meanwhile, his expression sobered, and she saw her own heart in his eyes.

"Twinned souls," he said softly. "It is very rare among the fae, rarer than love itself, but those who are *Pâr Enaid* are so close as to be twinned souls. That is what you are to me."

"Then it's true what you said to Fox? You're really going to stay here with us in our drab little human world?"

It was his turn to laugh. "I like your world very much. And all that I need is here with you. Of course, should you tire of me, I do have a place with the Hunt."

"I don't think I'm going to tire of you anytime soon. But I have no magic—at least, nothing to speak of." It was an issue she'd been thinking a lot about lately, and she might as well confront it head-on. "I'm mortal, Trahern, and you aren't. I'm going to age, and you won't. And then—well, it's going to be hard to deal with for both of us."

"I will hold precious every moment I have with you . . ."

She looked at him sharply. "I hear a *but*."

"*But* your years cannot be known. The presence of magic bears much influence on the body. The greater the magic, the greater the influence. Eirianwen lived far longer than most Tylwyth Teg, and it was due to her power alone. With mortals, the effect is even stronger."

"I just told you I don't have much magic."

He smiled at that. "I find your touch to be quite magical."

"Come on, you know what I mean!"

"Let me begin by telling you that your Fox will live a very long life. The magic he possesses is like that of Merlin himself. And Merlin yet lives. Lurien called upon him to aid in my healing."

She could feel her own eyes widen until her lids hurt. "I—I thought he was a storybook character. Even if he's real, how is that even possible? Merlin was—*is* human, right?"

Trahern nodded. "His powers, his magic, have extended his lifetime far beyond that of most."

"And you think that Fox is going to—" It was so fantastical, she couldn't even say it.

"There is no doubt. You witnessed his ability for yourself, and he has only begun to learn. However, you forget that *you* have been in Fox's presence, and therefore surrounded by extremely powerful magic, from his very conception. It cannot help but have a potent effect. And then, of course, there is my own magic as well." He kissed the top of her head just as she felt it would explode. "So we may have a little longer together than you anticipate."

"You have a real knack for dropping bombshells on people, you know that?"

Brooke's voice rang out from the kitchen below. "Lissy? Lissy, are you okay?"

"I'll be down in a minute!" she called back, and sighed as she leaned against Trahern. *What I really want is to dive into that perfectly good bed with you and not leave it until next Tuesday. But I think we'd better go down to the party.*

"I did promise Fox I would attend." *You and I will come together tonight, in the garden. And I will make it last a* very *long time.*

Instantly, her entire body lit up like a Christmas tree—and he hadn't even touched her yet. *Dammit!* She had to force herself to leave the room before she couldn't. As they headed down the stairs, she tried to change the subject. "By the way, you have a living, breathing, *flame-producing* little blue dragon to explain."

"Merlin has a red one."

*Of course he does.*

# ACKNOWLEDGMENTS

Behind every published writer stands an entire team! I'm tremendously fortunate to have a great one in the form of family, friends, and professionals who help me make my stories the best they can be—and keep me sane with coffee, kind words, and unbelievable patience.

To my publisher, Montlake Romance; my wonderful editors, copy editors, and proofreaders; and my intrepid Author Team. You guys seriously rock! I could not ask for more positive people to work with.

To artist Jason Blackburn for another amazing cover. You captured the hero on the first try! And to narrator Justine Eyre for bringing my Grim Series to vibrant life as audiobooks—my readers adore your voice work and I do, too. To my agent, Stephany Evans of Ayesha Pande Literary. Your encouragement helped more than you know during an especially challenging year.

To Melody Guy for once again helping me sharpen my focus and tighten my prose. And to Sharon Stogner of Devil in the Details Editing for her fearless red-pen work on the very first draft. Thanks to both of you, my story isn't walking around with spinach in its teeth!

To all of Dani's Darklings for cheering me on through thick and thin. What began as a street team has become one lucky writer's online support group, filled with truly amazing friends. And to Melissa Toews, Tina Clare, Sharon Stogner, Katie Dalton, and

Honorary Darkling Jake S. Black, for permitting some of my characters to borrow your names.

To cosplayer Heidi Taylor (aka Triniti's Ghost) for once again loaning me her irrepressible cats. Bouncer, Jade, and Rory first appeared in *Storm Bound* and insisted on returning! And to Gay Bamburg McDonald and Mike McDonald for sharing their handsome Neapolitan mastiff and Honorary Grim, Vincent de BluHouse. Calm, steady, and dignified, Vincent has been the perfect inspiration for the unique grim in this story.

To my mountain-man husband, Ron Silvester. For reading and rereading every page of every version of this book, usually in frustratingly unconnected bits and chunks. For courage under fire (otherwise known as living with an introverted, obsessive, and frequently discouraged writer). For giving me the time and space to write in peace but occasionally staging an intervention to get me out of the house (and also for not taking the kicking and screaming personally). I love you.

# AUTHOR'S NOTE

Let me say up front that I do not speak the Welsh language. My beloved grandmother did so fluently, but I didn't think to ask her to teach me. (I was too young and too interested in other things. Like her faery stories!) So the Welsh words that I use, while carefully and lovingly researched, are not guaranteed to be accurate. And the fae languages in my books are only very *loosely* based on Welsh.

In response to reader requests for meanings and interpretations of some of the terms used in the Grim Series books, a glossary is being put together for my website. Watch for it at www.daniharper.com.

# ABOUT THE AUTHOR

*Legend, lore, love, and magic*. These are the hallmarks of Dani Harper's transformational tales of faeries, shapeshifters, ghosts, and more—for a mature audience.

A former newspaper editor, Dani's passion for all things supernatural led her to a second career writing fiction. A longtime resident of the Canadian north and southeastern Alaska, she now lives in rural Washington with her retired mountain-man husband. Together they do battle with runaway garden gnomes, rampant fruit trees, and a roving herd of predatory chickens.

Dani Harper is the author of *Storm Crossed*, *Storm Warned*, *Storm Bound*, and *Storm Warrior* (the Grim Series), as well as *First Bite* (a Dark Wolf novel) for Montlake Romance. She is also the author of a yuletide ghost story, *The Holiday Spirit*, plus a popular shapeshifter series that includes *Changeling Moon*, *Changeling Dream*, and *Changeling Dawn*.

Visit her website at www.daniharper.com.